Scruffy Chicken

A Mystery set in Derbyshire 1965

by

Narvel S Annable

British Library Cataloguing in Publication Data
A catalogue record for this book is available
from the British Library

ISBN 0 9530419 4 8

Published by
Narvel S Annable
44 Dovedale Crescent
Belper
Derbyshire
DE56 1HJ

narvel@narvelannable.co.uk
www.narvelannable.co.uk
Tel: 01 773 82 44 83

To

Ted Barlow and David Betts

Living Legends of the Nottingham Scene

With gratitude for friendship and kindness over the last forty years

"A rare pleasure I never thought I'd see: a gay thriller set in Derbyshire."

Matthew Parris of *The Times*

Pronunciation

In the speaking voice of some characters, I have attempted to capture the Derbyshire accent. A principal feature is the 'closed U', which is sounded 'oo' as in 'took', *not* the sound as in 'boot'. The native Derbyshire tongue makes no distinction between the past tense of take - 'took' and 'tuck' - something to eat. To the Derbyshire ear, the 'open U' or standard pronunciation of 'tuck' sounds rather like 'tack', a short nail. Accordingly, when local Derbyshire folk say 'duck' (which they often say) I have indicated it as 'dook'.

Relatives are often referred to as 'our' pronounced as 'arr', such as 'Arr Fred'.

In an attempt to maintain the flavour and accuracy of the 1960's, I have referred to African-Americans as Negroes.

CONTENTS

Introduction to *Scruffy Chicken*
A Mystery set in Derbyshire 1965.

Nineteen hundred and sixty five was the most eventful year of my life. The hilarious adventures, anecdotes and laughter still echo around my head. They now cry out to be preserved in these pages, hopefully for others to enjoy.

The following is a novel inspired by a summer cycling holiday I enjoyed in one of England's most beautiful counties. As a 19-year-old I encountered an interesting selection of some curious and colourful characters which constituted a rich experience. Sadly, most of them are no longer with us. These events took place in real places, in this book peopled by a fictitious cast. Allow me to introduce you to these caricatured composites who are inspired by a selection of the types I met forty years ago. However real flesh and blood the original model, who actually ends up on these pages (after being processed through my brain) is very far from being any real person - alive or dead. The Peak District is the main setting, but my adventures also took me into Nottinghamshire and occasionally further afield.

Here follows a secret subterranean world which could have been penned by Jakob and Wilhelm Grimm. Do you remember when you were very small? You were told that if you had enough faith, if you could feel at one with nature, believe in the magic of trees and peer into dark cavities formed by dense hedgerows, look into the caves of tangled root systems - you might just catch a glimpse of the fairies. Well, I *did* look; not under hedgerows, but in those special Derbyshire places where 'fairies' can be seen - if you know how to make contact. Those strange types were invisible to the majority in that they were un-noticed. You had to believe in them, be aware of them and want to meet them. I did. I met a goblin, a gnome, a talking toad, a talking ball, a cartoon character, a pantomime dame and a whole circus of confused gender. Here follows my painting. This was the world as I saw it, as I found it, to the best of my knowledge - hitherto unwritten.

This secret history of Derbyshire and Nottinghamshire, to be unfolded in the following pages, is largely oral and unwritten. For example, when I am dead, Edna will be dead. In other words, I may be one of the few who can recall any hearsay regarding Edna. Edna, an old Derby eccentric, spoken of in the 1960's, was notorious back in the 1920's. No one has ever written about Edna. When the last person who can remember Edna is gone, Edna will be gone forever - and that is sad.

This is not intended to be a bawdy book. It will gain strength from *between* the lines, from the unspoken and the subtle. It will be bitchy, happy and sad, snooty and snobby, pretentious and unpretentious but, most of all, it should be funny.

These people lived on the edge of a disapproving society. They took shelter in their twilight private world. They varied from the old, decrepit and grotesque, to the young, beautiful, fit and full of fun; from the pompous, punctilious pedant to the common, crude peasant; from the professional to the plebeian. These people dealt with the prejudices of mid-twentieth century Britain and coped with homophobic intolerance in their different ways. Cruelty and bigotry shaped these individuals into their interesting forms which, in turn, influenced a teenager on a bicycle, who was coming to terms with a fundamental new self-awareness.

Four decades have now passed, old laws have been repealed, education is more enlightened, clubs have been opened, support services are available and society is a little kinder. The odd, craggy, quirky characters of yesteryear seem to have disappeared. We will not see their like again.

Scruffy Chicken is the book I have always wanted to write. I wanted to write it before I wrote *Miss Calder's Children.* This is another autobiographical book, another chance to examine and explore the characters who have shaped my life. The monsters, the freaks and the clowns - I met them all in 1965. *Scruffy Chicken* is a social history of Detroit and Derbyshire, a comparison and contrast of the gay scenes of the US and the UK as they were in the mid 20th century.

Come with me. Meander with me on my cycling trip through the leafy sun mottled lanes during the summer of 1965 and let me introduce you to the secret world of a scruffy chicken as he discovers the curious characters of Derbyshire.

Chapter 1

Five Days with an Old Queen

It had been a dreadful mistake. On that cold morning of Thursday, November 21st in 1963, Simeon Hogg, sitting on a large trunk, guarding his luggage, was thinking that he had made a big mistake. He was surrounded by crowds of strangers. He was surrounded by an alien cacophony of confusion and disorder - and he hated it. Even at the age of 18, he did not take kindly to change. He never would take kindly to change and this was the biggest change of all: this was emigration to a new country. For the Derbyshire working-classes back in 1963, emigration was final. It was forever. Simeon Hogg had been uprooted from everything which was warm, kind and familiar. He had been torn away from everything which was British, English and Derbyshire. This, single, stressful experience had made a powerful impression on the teenage Simeon. Even at the age of 60, he would still suffer the same recurring nightmare. A suicidal scenario - arrival in the cold, hostile environment of the USA with very little money, no friends, no job, no qualifications, no prospects and the dread realisation that all the security, comfort and familiarity of Derbyshire, an ocean away, was out of reach - for ever.

This was not Ellis Island. The notorious Ellis Island, just off New York, had been closed down twenty years before. This massive, impersonal building, which now dwarfed and depressed Simeon, was just as bad. It was the major immigration station of the United States. A customs officer, under stress, too busy, overworked and underpaid, was barking orders at him in a thick New York accent. His rough rudeness and contempt completely lacked the oil and balm of a polite British official, who would have been more sensitive to the obvious distress and disorientation before him. The trunk was summarily opened and the unfeeling foreigner rummaged through the young Englishman's personal effects, destroying hours of neat, painstaking packing and leaving a sad, sorry jumble on the cold concrete floor. In future years Simeon would note the sharp contrast between -

"Good afternoon, sir. Do you have anything to declare? Would you mind opening this one, sir? Thank you, sir." and -

"Wot ya got? Open it."

The New York customs officer unzipped a slim leather briefcase and removed an ornate certificate: 'City and Guilds, Technicians Intermediate, second class'.

"What's this?"

"A qualification. I 'ope ta be an engineer one day."

"One day!" he laughed. "Why not *two* days, why not a week?"

It had been a bad start. He should be happy here in the 'Promised Land', but he was not happy. He was utterly miserable. This was the land he had dreamed of for many years, but now ... now he was thinking of a pot of steaming tea in a quaint cafe at Matlock Bath, mossy walls, lush green Derbyshire dales, Tony Hancock and Billy Fury. Later, it came as a shock to discover that the Americans had never even heard of those men.

An hour before he had, effectively, still been in England. An hour before he was on board the Queen Elizabeth. Not the QE2, but the first (and at 80,000 tons much larger) original, White Star Cunard Liner of that name, which was launched 25 years before in September 1938. It had been an exciting and stormy five days, the roughest crossing she had endured in 14 years. Simeon was often outside on the deck, loving every minute, battling the wind, tasting the salt, holding tight to the rail, marvelling at the gigantic waves crashing about him, bigger than houses, pitching and rolling that great British ship.

On dry land he clung on to the hope that things would get better. They got worse. The cab driver charged $5 for a journey of several blocks, (less than a third of a mile) to the Greyhound Bus Station. At that time $5 was 35 shillings, a little more than half his previous weekly wage at Spondon Power Station near Derby. Even with all his luggage, the going rate for one mile should not have exceed $2. Perhaps the charge included the good advice he was given when deposited at the dazzling, fluorescent-lit, gleaming white, cold, stainless steel bus station.

"Hey, listen a here - don't ya take ya eyes off this here!"

"Pardon?"

"Ya luggage! There are monkeys here. Ya know, monkeys? Listen, buster, they'll take one. They're looking for you. They'll just walk away with it. Look, I gotta go."

His trunk went on to Detroit by freight. The bus driver was belligerent. He challenged the amount of luggage, saying that the number of separate items exceeded the company limit.

"What am I supposed to do wid ya? Rules are rules! Right? Hello!", knocking with hard knuckles on the boy's head, "Anybody home?"

Simeon stood mute. Seeing the lad's wounded, worried expression, the irritated driver testily threw the suitcases into the wide gaping luggage compartment.

"Jesus Christ! Get on the bus, dummy."

Sick with misery and fearing a further reprimand, he made absolutely sure he was in the right seat. A soldier about his own age confirmed that the ticket indicated a window-seat next to himself. They sat in silence. He could not see much. The window was dirty. After the bumpy boneshakers of Derbyshire, the great bus felt like a giant sponge with its squishy-squashy suspension as it lumbered out of the station. Years later, Simeon recognised his bus in the film *Midnight Cowboy*. Simeon's bus was very similar to Joe Buck's bus; a similar collection of scroungy, rough-looking people. The only character missing was the tasteless gum chewing nun. Ever in low gear, a roaring engine powered the vehicle through the alien streets of lower Manhattan and on and on through a vast, flat, urban jungle of hideous, never-ending sameness.

The journey went on and on. It never occurred to the young man to check on how long the trip would take. The bus departed at noon and would not arrive in downtown Detroit until 3.00am the following day. This he had not considered.

So much he had not considered. Why was he here? Mr Hogg, the mature schoolmaster, asked the same question of himself four decades later. He saw the boy sitting on that bus like a child, obediently under the influence of his parents and relatives. Not that Mr and Mrs Hogg were strict. It was more of a family culture of 'the land of plenty', the only sensible place to go, the need to get out of Britain - old-fashioned, decaying, rotting Britain. Fifteen years before, his sister had married Hank Kurtz, a GI. She escaped from a world which was collectively perceived as a dowdy, coal mining community, scarred by slag tips under endless grey skies and always dampened by constant drizzle. Lauren Hogg escaped into a world of beautiful large cars, warm-air centrally heated, detached houses with ultra modern kitchens and large gardens bathed by endless hot sunshine. Throughout the 1950's, in the drab, tiny living rooms of Bog Hole in Horsley Woodhouse, relatives would scrutinise long letters from America describing an exotic life-style, sharply contrasted to their own humdrum reality. At a time when occasional small black and white photographs were regarded as a luxury, the Hoggs studied large colour prints proudly displaying a dark beauty. Lauren was a poser, smiling or frowning, voluptuously leaning against an impossibly long, low car. Sometimes she was seductively sunbathing, displaying physical splendour. It was always -

"Arr [our] Lauren! Look at 'er, Gertie, owe's [she's] skiin' in this one. Skiin'! Arr Lauren! Oo'd a thought it! Look at t' snow. In tit nice."

"Ooo a say, arr Nelly, int 'er loovly in 't sunshine."

"Arr Vivienne's got a dress like that."

"Ay oop, it sez 'ere ... err ... a man said she looks like Ava Gardner."

"Ava Gardner! Nay lass!"

"It's right, arr Gertie, owe does, owe's joost like 'er in this snap."

"Let's 'ave a look, arr Dorothy ... ooo int she nice. Look at this, arr Fred."

So it came to pass that Simeon Hogg was swept along by a powerful tide of parental and family pressure to 'Go west, young man' and improve his prospects for the future. According to Lauren's endless stream of glossy and glitzy propaganda, America was the most wonderful place in the whole wide world. Accordingly, in the summer of 1963 a decision was taken to emigrate the following year and Simeon was sent on in advance to 'get settled'. He had mixed feelings about this 'wonderful new life', but it never once occurred to him to fly the family nest. He had no money, neither did he have any courage to assert his independence to leave home.

And why should he? During the dark miserable days of Mundy Street Boys School - a culture of cruelty - America was the golden hope for the future. It was during the daily tortures of vicious bullying that skyscrapers, satellites, Studebakers, DeSotos and Cadillacs lifted him just above the level of complete despair. But after the wonderful years of 1959 and 1960 at the leafy green, William Howitt Secondary Modern School - a culture of kindness - America became less important and the sheer magnificence of Derbyshire was already starting to make an impact.

The bus droned along an endless expanse of concrete freeway. It droned on for several hours, into darkness, before pulling into a service area. At the self-service counter, a Negress said -

"Ya?"

"Tea please."

"Cheese?"

"No. A pot o' tea ... well, a coop [cup] 'll do."

"Tea?"

She scratched her head. Several things confused her. The foreign accent was difficult to understand. She was thrown by the unusual and unnecessary word 'please' and had never made tea in her life. The girl said something to another girl, who pointed to an un-opened packet of tea bags. Eventually, Simeon was presented with a thick saucer supporting a thick cup from which dangled a piece of string attached to a tea bag - the first one he had ever seen. The warm water was clear and only reluctantly changed to dark red when agitated for several minutes. After adding milk, Simeon sipped the worst tea he had ever tasted. It was foul. It was an insult. It was undrinkable because the water was not boiling and the milk was not milk, it was cream for coffee. The insult had cost him 15 cents. He struggled with the calculations of conversion. If a dollar was worth about seven shillings, then this vile liquid left in his cup had cost him the unbelievable price of just over one shilling - more than three times the price of a cup of tea served in the Heanor Milk Bar! He was hungry and saw a sign for doughnuts. Another disappointment. It was old and cold. It was nothing like the delicious, freshly-made hot doughnuts he had enjoyed with his mates on the Central Pier at Blackpool.

Blackpool. Would he ever see Blackpool again?

Chapter 2

The Soldier's Shoulder

The soldier was still silent. Simeon looked down at his leg. Nice leg. A few passengers nearby had switched on their overhead seat lights, which lifted the general darkness into a half gloom for the two teenagers who had nothing to read anyway. Simeon snatched a few crafty looks at his near-neighbour, who was assessed as a dark, clean-shaven, handsome, all-American boy, with a square jaw, probably younger than 20. The smart uniform perfectly fitted the sensuous contours of a hard, fit body. The pleasing and tempting profile at his side caused the Englishman to, very carefully, steal further stealthy glances. Bitter experience had taught him to be quick. The occasional shufti had to be pre-planned, so that, in the fearful event of eye contact, Simeon, with a flash movement of pupil, could appear to be innocent. He could appear to be observing something of interest on the other side of the bus.

These subtle skills had been long practised and honed at a level which could almost be described as subconscious and automatic. At this stage of his life, Simeon Hogg could not yet bring himself to admit, even to himself, that he desired this young man who was almost touching his body. A few weeks before at the Eastwood fair, his mouth went completely dry when he was suddenly threatened by an aggressive rough youth brandishing his fist. He wanted to know -

"Wot ya lookin' at me fa? Ya want trouble, do ya? Aye! An trouble ya'll fookin' get! Nar fook off!"

In the hard, macho, homophobic world of Eastwood, Heanor and Horsley Woodhouse, boys like Simeon Hogg quickly learned to avert their gaze from the fascination of a comely working-class face connected to a strapping body, round protruding bottom and interesting bulges packed inside sexy, tight jeans. Deep down, he knew why he had been looking at that particular youth yet, even after that appalling trauma witnessed by a group of his pals, Simeon was not prepared to be honest with himself. He was not prepared to face the clear and self evident implications of that embarrassing and wounding experience. It was just too awful.

Simeon was not queer! Queers were dirty old men who haunted public lavatories. Simeon was not like that. He was not like that softly-spoken, polite and gentle man who ran the village shop, the man who had suddenly disappeared one day because -

" ... 'e'd bin caught doin' summat rude we another man! Dotty [dirty] owd [old] bogga ... Good riddance a say. Yo keep away from that sort, arr Simeon."

"Are ya listenin', lad? Owe's right. Listen ta ya Aunty Gertie. 'e'll get it in prison. 'e'll get 'is bloody teeth knocked down 'is bloody filthy throat! An serve 'im right an all!"

"Ooo a don't know, Nelly. That's not right. 'e 'ad nice manners in t' shop dint 'e? 'e were allus [always] nice to us, an 'elpful like, wont 'e, arr Gertie?"

"Nay, arr Dorothy, 'is a filthy bogga, we don't want 'im back 'ere. Is no better than that dotty owd sod, t' owd man Steptoe. 'e were doin t' same. Thee all want lockin' oop."

Simeon was intrigued by the scandal of Wilfrid Brambell, who, after being entrapped, was arrested in November 1962 for importuning in a public toilet. He was fascinated by the idea of one man wishing to have sex with another man, but wisely kept that fascination closely to himself. This incident was splashed over the front pages of the popular Press. It reinforced the generally-held prejudice that a 'homosexual' looked and acted just like the shambling, dirty, decrepit, toothless, unshaven old man, who was better known to the nation as Albert Steptoe.

Simeon Hogg could not conceive of a beautiful young man who was 'queer'. There was simply no precedent for such a thing in his experience. Images of the butch and the attractive, the well-known icons of male beauty such as Marty Wilde, Adam Faith, Billy Fury and the ultra masculine Rock Hudson; all these were very firmly heterosexual. Wilfrid Brambell might well be 'queer', but never, ever in a thousand years could Rock Hudson be 'queer'.

Consequently, the young immigrant now travelling west at 70 mph in winter darkness, seeking a new life and a new start, had resigned himself to celibacy with regard to his true sexuality. He took his hope from the ever active brainwashing, heterosexual propaganda machine and took his lead from the examples of those around him who had demonstrated success with girlfriends. He took his hope from books which spoke of a 'homosexual phase' which would pass. In the deepest recesses of his mind, if Simeon did briefly flirt with such an alarming thought, it would be -

"I'll grow out of it."

If there was ever a showdown with his conscience which forced him to articulate a deeply suppressed thought, that little tiny part of his mind would cower and say -

"I know what I like, but I don't *want* to like it."

However, the human spirit is not easily broken. The sexual soul, with its ever-seeking servomechanism, is always on automatic pilot. The mind of Simeon Hogg may well have been consciously thinking of sleep in that nice warm bus, but the carnal desires below - those naughty desires - were burning bright and that force of lust conceived a plan.

The serviceman had removed his jacket and was now sitting in a blue, short sleeved shirt which exposed tempting tanned arms, nice arms. Simeon closed his eyes and ... gently, very gently, began to nod off. His head began to loll. His head began to loll very slowly to the left, nearer and nearer to the soldier's right arm. Eventually, the boy's cheek almost touched that much-desired arm. Moments later, cheek and arm actually made contact. A delicious moment which lasted barely a second - but, for this hopeful youth, it was a very pleasant second and one which would be remembered for the rest of his life. Sadly, that sensuous second was abruptly terminated by a sharp nudge from the military shoulder. Simeon woke up, looked dozy and innocent. He looked surprised and a touch hurt. He turned an enquiring look at his neighbour. The soldier responded tersely in a deep macho voice -

"You were falling asleep on me."

"Oh? Was I? Sorry."

At long last, somewhere in the depths of that long dark night, Simeon was standing in front of a telephone in the Detroit Greyhound Bus Station, struggling with small American change, looking for a dime. It was only the second phone-call he had ever made in his life but, more simple, in this more advanced country. This time he was not confused by 'Button A' or 'Button B'. Slowly and carefully he dialled the many digits of the long number written at the top of Lauren's letter -

"Ya! That you, Simeon?"

"'ello! Is that you, 'ank?"

Hank Kurtz cheerfully set out on the 20 mile drive from Allen Park to Downtown Detroit at that ungodly hour to collect his unknown brother-in-law. He was both a gentleman and a gentle man. During the half-hour wait, Simeon sat guarding his many pieces of luggage under a blitz of cold fluorescent light, idly observing occasional Greyhound staff and a Negro cleaning the floor. It was not a comfortable wait. At one point, an elderly Negro, obviously drunk, staggered across the concourse. Later, another Negro showed interest in the young foreigner by walking near several times, going in and out of the 'Rest Room'. The significance of this puzzling episode was totally lost upon a lad fresh out of Derbyshire.

Hank Kurtz arrived in his large, lime green Oldsmobile Ninety Eight. At last! This was the America Simeon Hogg had come to see. He had never been close to his parents but, in later years, was grateful for the good manners they had taught. Accordingly, he made the appropriate polite comments, profusely thanking this generous man, a stranger, who had left his warm bed in the middle of that icy night to retrieve him from the centre of a dangerous and crime-ridden city. Hank was cheerful, with a cheeky, boyish grin. Sporting his neat and clean GI flat-top crew cut, he looked many years younger than his 33 years. In truth, Hank and Simeon had little in common, but communication was always easy and comfortable and never more enthusiastic than now, inside this magnificent metal sculpture which was effortlessly gliding along the drab and dreary black streets of Detroit, en route westwards to the all Anglo Saxon suburbs, en route to 291812 Coolidge Boulevard, Allen Park, Michigan.

"Aint she just! This baby has the new 'panoramic windshield' and the 'three, (yes I did say three) three, two barrel carburettor Rocket Engine'. Move! Baby just watch her go! Zero to 60 in eight seconds and peaks at 125 mph."

"It's fantastic, 'ank! It's just gorgeous! Look at these controls, just like a space ship."

"See the back? Did ya look at that back? She looks just like the rear of a jet engine in flight. I'll tell ya, since '59, Olds takes the cake."

"Like floating on air ..."

"Listen, pal, at this moment no less than 394 cubic inches are pushing us along this Edsel Ford Freeway. Eight - Big - Cylinders, baby!

No sweat, no effort, I'm hardly touching the gas ... and smoooth ... Hydra-Matic transmission. You will never, ever know that a gear has ever changed. Did ya see the grill with four, yes, I said *four* headlights and did you notice ... "

Simeon, very groggy after eight hours of sleep, woke up in a small, white, warm bedroom. It was not the refreshing sleep to which he had been accustomed; not the sleep which comes from being snuggled under lots of heavy blankets in a room cooled by a window open to the elements. This was Michigan in late November. The overnight temperature had dipped to several degrees below zero and soon December would certainly bring snow. The house had been 'winterised' several weeks before by installing a second pane of glass in each window, which made opening impossible. In this land where fuel was cheap, it was the accepted custom and practice that warm-air central heating was generally maintained by a thermostat, set at 70 degrees, day and night. This explained the odd experience of waking up under a sheet and the lightness of one single thin blanket.

Gradually coming to his senses, Simeon could hear a steady thrum of a fast talking man combined with great crowds of cheering men. In pyjamas he stumbled out into an unknown corridor, thick with expensive carpet, and found Hank in a large open-plan living room, watching a ball game on the television set. He greeted his brother-in-law -

"Hey, hey, hey! Rip Van Winkle awakes! How ya doin', Buddy? Breakfast? Or should we say lunch?"

It was past noon and the long-sleeping teenager was especially grateful for his first decent cup of tea since leaving the Queen Elizabeth. Having been married to Lauren for 12 years, Hank was well trained in the making of good tea. With his tongue lubricated by the all important nectar of 'first tea', more talk followed, consisting of many questions and more admiration. This was 'future shock'. After the draughty, drab, late nineteenth century kitchens of Bog Hole in Horsley Woodhouse, he was now enjoying an excellent grill, sitting on a high stool at a breakfast bar in a spacious, ultra-modern, high-tech, ergonomically custom-designed kitchen. All the flush matching integral units fascinated him. The refrigerator, the separate freezer, the electric range and the electric waste disposal unit were equally as mind-boggling as the twin power antennae on Hank's Oldsmobile.

Simeon Hogg had been catapulted into the future. Things were definitely looking up. He was hopeful.

Chapter 3

Empty, Inane, Asinine and Idiotic

Hank had taken the day off work to welcome and ease Simeon Hogg into his first day in the United States. It was Friday, November 22nd, 1963. An offer to wash the dishes was firmly refused and the guest was invited to be entertained in front of a large and tubby television screen surrounded by a hideous antique effect. The ball game had finished and some sort of soap drama was being played out by poor quality, droning actors moving in front of cheap, tacky sets. One, with a green face, was obviously reading from an 'idiot board'. This clumsy splash of exotic and garish hues was Simeon's first experience of colour TV, which had been available, albeit unrefined, in the United States since the mid 1950's. In contrast to the accustomed 14" Bog Hole standard, which offered a choice between the BBC and ITV, this foreign viewer had more choices. In fact, he had four choices including Channel 9, which came from over the river in Canada. Hank had placed in Simeon's hand something which he found very exciting -

"Hey hey hey, Englishman! What do ya think of that then?"

It was a device called a 'remote control'. In those first few minutes of commercial American television, Simeon quickly realised that he had four choices of pure rubbish. The soap on Channel 2 was soon interrupted by a commercial. 'Mr Belvedere' was saying "We do good work." Channel 4 was showing a cartoon. Bugs Bunny looked good in the garish colour. Simeon was just getting interested, but minutes later the rabbit was interrupted by 'Friendly Bob Adams', who was encouraging Simeon to borrow anything from -

"Twenty five to a thousand dollars! That's right folks, 'Loan by Phone'. Just ask for me, Friendly Bob Adams."

This was followed by an irritating jingle which screamed out 'Save a week's pay at Gene Morola Chevrolet'. To escape such inane salesmanship, the control was pressed to Channel 7. A Negro was shouting something in fast, staccato sentences; so fast and so guttural that the Derbyshire ear could make little sense of it - clearly another commercial. On to Canadian TV, which looked more promising. An old black and white film was showing. Simeon liked old films, but just two minutes later 'Friendly Bob

Adams' was back with his familiar message. Simeon went round the dial once more, but again, he found that all the channels were interrupted every few minutes by a loud sales pitch and all the channels specialised in pure entertainment which was geared and tailored to low taste. Years later he said to a friend -

"I suppose I should be grateful to American television. It forced me out of the house! I escaped to the library and discovered books."

By general standards, he had received a reasonable education and possessed average intelligence, but Simeon Hogg missed the high quality of British television and British radio; quality he had come to expect, quality he had always taken for granted. As well as light entertainment, he enjoyed current affairs, documentaries, educational programmes and radio plays.

Sitting in front of that television watching the endless stream of trivia, he felt a deep sense of despair but did not understand why. This sad 18-year-old was not yet equipped with the intellectual ability to analyse and rationalise his present circumstances. The older and wiser Simeon Hogg could have explained to the younger Simeon why he was so profoundly depressed by those first 20 minutes of American television -

"You are utterly miserable because you are looking at the true face of America. Into this trashy goggle box you are seeing deep into the soul of America. This is how it's going to be. This is your future. This is a taste of the tasteless, a taste of the mindless stupidity you have come to. It is empty, it is asinine, it is idiotic - and it won't get any better."

Suddenly the room was filled by an attractive and harmonic peal of electric door chimes.

"Come right on in guys," said Hank, welcoming the two boys who lived next door. Ben was 18 and Ricky was 16. Ben was stocky and average looking. Ricky was a touch small but perfectly shaped. Ricky was a doll and Simeon had to make a great effort to control his drooling lust. They had come directly from school to welcome the new arrival and obtained 'time out' to give him a personal tour of the Dwight D Eisenhower High School.

"Hi ya doin', buddy! We heard a lot about ya. Welcome to the good ole US of A", said Ben heartily with enthusiasm, offering his hand.

"Thank you," said Simeon.

"Hi," said Ricky.

"Hello," said Simeon, repressing emotion and trying not to sound too much like the famous Leslie Phillips's lecherous *'Hel-lo!'*. At the same time, he held on to that sweet little hand just as long as social acceptability would permit. Brief pleasantries were exchanged at a level of sophistication which surprised and impressed the working class lad from Horsley Woodhouse. These boys behaved like gentlemen. A social interaction between three Heanor lads of similar age would have been quite different; no hand shake, little eye contact, a rough and brief acknowledgement of the meeting with a quick nod of head or, if you were lucky, perhaps a gruff -

"Yor rate then, youth?"

Simeon was even more impressed when he saw Ben's car in the driveway. Catching the Englishman's quick intake of breath, Ben enthusiastically described his 1959, pillarless, DeSoto Firedome Sportsman which featured 'rocket launcher' tail lights. That rear was almost as desirable as Ricky's cute little rear. Nicely filling out close fitting trousers, Simeon had been trying very hard not to leer ... well, that is, not to leer *all* the time. And at least it was socially acceptable for the admirer to rave about, compliment, enthuse, touch, caress, fondle and generally show great appreciation of the backside of Ben's fabulous automobile.

This was culture shock and future shock combined. Back home, most of the Heanor lads envied Scott North's brand new BSA ten-speed racing bicycle. As an object of desire, it stood out proudly against the other dirty old, third and fourth-hand bikes which had been passed down from brother to brother. Within the circles in which Simeon moved, no working-class boy possessed any motorised transport. A motorcycle might be a distant aspiration, but even a small, drab, used, cheap motorcar was beyond the reach of most coal-mining fathers - let alone their sons. Yet, here was 18-year-old Ben, the boy next door, still at school, proudly drawing attention to the aggressive orgy of chrome; his 18 foot, two ton metal monster with beautifully sculptured fins.

Simeon was given the seat of honour in front with Ben, who was still boasting, this time about his finger-tip controlled, translucent, power-assisted steering wheel. The question -

"'as this car got a 'eater?" caused an avalanche of laughter. Ricky began to explain the purpose of a modern 'air-conditioning' system, an explanation which immediately aroused in Simeon a profound interest. Sitting sideways, twisting his neck through 90 degrees, he avidly followed the twists and turns of a spirited technical exposition from the beautiful boy who reposed in the spaciousness of that large, long, luxurious back seat, sadly sitting on, and now hiding his best asset. Ricky spoke of the hot, dusty summers and the necessity of turning the inside of an automobile into a mobile refrigerator. He spoke of the great power needed for such refrigeration, which could be provided by a large V8 engine only, and Simeon, nodding, agreeing, taking it all in, delighted in those lovely dark, dancing eyes. Ricky stopped, he had finished! Ben had jumped into the breach saying something about his friend's Fairlane Skyliner with a retractable hardtop.

"Sounds good. I'll 'ave ta see it, Ben. Ricky," said Simeon, craning around and leaning over, even closer - "you were on about that 're-circulation control'. A don't quite see ... "

But high tech air systems, big engines and impressive fins did not make up for the flat, featureless landscape which lay beyond the windows of that large, silent car floating along upon a cushion of air. Like all the other suburbs of Detroit, Allen Park was called a city, but in reality, it was a vast sea of houses dotted along the sides of dead straight concrete roads, fixed in a monotonous grid, running north to south and east to west. All the homes shared a dull, if pleasant, sameness. They were all spaciously separated, all single storey, all neat, all middle-class and all rabidly white, Anglo-Saxon Protestant. Here was a mind-blowing contrast to the familiar gritty and shabby terraced cottages crowded into the crooked back streets of Heanor and Horsley Woodhouse. All these nice houses were fronted by large, flat, brown lawns. Not green - brown. The predictable hot scorching sun of regular arid summer had burnt the grass. It would soon become a blanket of white at Christmas, before returning to brown again in March. For a few weeks in May the grass would turn bright green before being scorched back to brown in June, staying brown until the following Christmas. Simeon had been used to weather, now he had climate. And with that harsh climate of extreme heat and extreme cold, he could say goodbye to the luxuriant green moss, green ferns, green meadows and the kind green woods of his gentle Derbyshire.

Monotonously, Ben's big car had to keep stopping at junctions where the sign said 'STOP'. Every junction looked the same. Every road looked the same. They were all sun drenched, salted, bleached, dazzling white hard concrete under that clear blue sky. Simeon noted that he had not seen a single pedestrian. This was a land where nobody walked. There was nowhere to walk to. There was no contrast, everything looked the same. Everybody had a car - no point in walking. After about five miles, Ben proudly announced that they were now in the city of Lincoln Gardens. Allen Park - Lincoln Gardens? They looked exactly the same to Simeon and they were certainly not 'parks' or 'gardens' as he understood the terms. But these misgivings and dreads he kept firmly to himself. He masked his true feelings with suitable comments and was very polite to his two new friends. Back in Southampton, on the quay, he was cheered off with a chorus of 'Bon Voyage' and many urgings to embrace the new culture and give his new life every chance to succeed.

"Nar dunna ya be tellin' 'em 'we do this' an 'we do that', lad. Are ya listin', lad? It's not goin' ta be t' same. Don't expect it ta be. It's goin' ta be better!"

"That's right, lad. Listen ta ya Aunty Gertie. Owe knows best."

Finally, the long car turned a corner and was floating due east. They had left the endless residential area and entered an ugly commercial zone. It was littered with myriad poles supporting a hideous hotchpotch and profusion of power lines and telephone wires. This was a three-lane highway, but, as it seemed in such a large car, they crawled from red light to red light. It was explained that the speed limit of 45 meant just that. The police were very keen. About a mile passed, a mile which was cluttered with scruffy hamburger joints and shabby gas stations. The former screamed out cheap food in garish flashing neon signs and the latter yelled out low, low prices, as low as 19 cents a gallon, on tacky boards. No grass, no trees, not even weeds would grow from the roadside which had been poisoned by years of winter salt.

They turned south into a wide, main entrance of a very large high school of gleaming white stone, a handsome work of modern architecture, which rose powerfully out of a vast, brown, perfect horizontal plane. This neat smoothness was a relief after the offensive confusion of the main road and this boy, fresh from his green hills of Derbyshire, had never experienced a sky which was so vast. He was also relieved that Ben had turned off the radio. For the last fifteen minutes his ears had been bombarded by a group of unremitting women shrieking inane jingles about -

"WKNR - Keener 13 on your dial!"

This would be followed by an immature DJ, so loud he hardly needed a radio station. He was yelling out endless trivia, so vacuous it was forgotten in seconds. Then there were more jingles, more commercials, more of 'Friendly Bob Adams', more of 'Mr Belvedere' followed by more mindless frivolity. At one point, squeezed between this nonsense, was a form of weather forecast and quick news bulletin [... at 15 and 45 ...] practically useless, as it was shot at the listener like a machine gun. Simeon was trying to recapture a comforting memory; the slow, gentle, cultured voice of the BBC, the voice of civilisation -

"This is the BBC Home Service. Here is the news ..."

But within that quarter hour of complete trash, there were inserted two shining jewels of sublime quality which was music, and very sweet music, to the ears of the newcomer. Just two records were played - *Be My Baby* by the Ronettes and *One Fine Day* by The Chiffons. It was yet to be discovered, but the best part of the United States for Simeon Hogg would be the Black United States. The sheer joy of Motown with its exciting 'wall of sound' would be a major part of this new culture.

As the great DeSoto sailed down the long drive, Simeon looked up at the brilliant sun which was comfortably viewed through the deepening blue tint near the top of that massive windshield. At eye level, in the distance, he noted little specks of humanity moving towards the white building to attend classes for the afternoon session.

The time was exactly 1.30pm. All three boys were blissfully ignorant of an assassination which took place at that moment under that same golden sun. More than a thousand miles to the south in Dallas, Texas, John F Kennedy, the President of the United States, had just been shot in the head. Jackie Kennedy, covered in his blood, was cradling him in her arms.

Chapter 4

Death of the American Dream

Ben and Ricky were quite excited to have an Englishman to parade around and to show off. It made a nice change from the regular routine at Dwight D Eisenhower High School. By pre-arrangement, the first port of call was room 489, the home-room of a popular teacher, who gave the trio a warm welcome. The 12th graders were only too delighted to receive this exotic interruption. A group of exuberant girls at the back acknowledged Mr Hackett's formal introduction by frantic waving, followed by a chorus of -

"Hi, Simeon!" "Hi ya doin'?" "Hello, Simeon!" "Hey there!" "How d ya like America?" "Wot ya think of us?" "Hello!"

The guest received this extraordinary reception with mixed feelings. Part of him was amused and part of him was pleased to have suddenly gained the apparent adoration of this impromptu fan club, largely because Simeon had never experienced success with girls. However, the bigger part was listening to a voice inside his head, the commonsense voice of his Heanor mate Danny Forrester who was saying -

"Tek na notice on 'em, Dobba. Thee tekin' t' piss!"

Simeon's eyes wandered over the hunky boys in that group, many of whom were lounging casually on their seats. One in particular, on the front row, leaning back with legs wide apart, was assessing the foreigner with concentrated curiosity. These clean-cut, all-American boys chimed in with a more low-key response of head nods and an occasional -

"Greetings England!" "Welcome to the USA." "Hi, buddy." "Welcome!" "Hi ya, Englishman." "Hey, when is he gonna talk?" "Yeah! Talk, England!"

"If you gave him a chance, if you could manage to ask a sensible question, he may well talk to you," responded Mr Hackett.

Sensible questions were asked. All went well until Simeon started to describe his house which, he explained, was joined up to all the other houses. This produced a sea of shocked faces and a deafening silence. Half a second later the silence was smashed by a cascade of loud guffaws from the more raucous males in the room. What Simeon actually said was -

"We don't 'av asses [houses] like yours. Arr ass's touchin' t' next ass. Ya know, like ... sort a - all asses in a row, like. Nar me Aunty Lizabeth, she's got a nice ass, she as, an thee all like ta look at it ... "

Mr Hackett came to the rescue with an important clarification.

"Perhaps, Simeon, you'll run us through that one again. I think you're referring to the *building* in which you live, if I'm not mistaken. No sweat. Nothing wrong with the way you speak. If these kids were better educated they would know that the French don't sound the H either."

The rest of it went very well but for one blip when Simeon was asked to comment on English rates of pay -

"Nar me ooncle Terry, 'e were a coal adler, an 'e got a regular good screw ... "

Another blip caused uproar when a girl wanted to know if it was true that every British house was full of pets.

"We 'ad a dog, an me Aunty Gertie, two doors down, she's got a loovely pussy ... "

The proceedings amounted to a cultural exchange and were valuable for both parties. Simeon learned a great deal about the custom and practice of his new country and a great deal about his old country. It became apparent that he had never really connected with the other half of British society, never far away, which he knew vaguely as the 'middle-class'. This was the English society with which the Americans were more familiar from books, film and television - the posh English with posh accents. Simeon had attended school and met his teachers. Occasionally, he consulted the doctor or was spoken to by a vicar, but, beyond these few formal meetings, he never socialised outside of his class - the 'working-class'.

At one point, the discussion became very personal and embarrassing. Simeon answered questions honestly. He was surprised at their appalled reaction. The girls were horrified to discover that he actually bathed in a bath - only once a week! They made noises of disgust when he calmly admitted to changing his socks - once a week! He was surprised that Americans took a shower and shampooed their hair every single morning, in the same casual way in which Simeon would wash his face.

In general, the discussion was sincere and good natured. He spoke of pop music and was incredulous that they had never even heard of The Beatles! Three months later they would speak of nothing else when 'Beatlemania' gripped the whole country.

Suddenly, the whole class became still and quiet. Mr Hackett and all the students stood to attention. A strikingly handsome, distinguished-looking man in his early 50's had walked into the room and was reverently received in silence. He was smiling a sad, weary smile. Briefly, Mr Hackett made necessary introductions.

"Dr DeLoach! Welcome. This is the Englishman, Simeon Hogg, the one I was telling you about. He's fresh off the Queen Elizabeth. Simeon, this Dr DeLoach, our Principal."

"Glad to know you, Simeon. I hope you'll be very happy here in the United States." His eyes swept over the class before returning to meet the newcomer. He continued in a deep, rich voice. "I'm sure we're all going to pull together to make you feel at home."

Simeon accepted the large hand which had been graciously extended and replied with a barely audible -

"Thank you, sir."

During that moment, the moment of the firm warm grip, he felt honoured and took an immediate liking to this charming and cordial gentleman. The time was exactly ten minutes past two.

"Please be seated, Mr Hackett, Simeon, ladies and gentlemen. As you know, I normally use the public address system to make announcements, but this one needs the personal touch. It is rather different. My three Vice-Principals are gradually getting around the school with the same news, tragic news, I'm afraid. A few minutes ago it was confirmed that our President, Jack Kennedy, is dead. He died 25 minutes after being shot several times by an unknown assassin ... "

He said a few more words to his hushed and shocked audience. Little by little, they slowly absorbed this doleful intelligence. Each individual interpreted the news in a slightly different way, but Simeon's private feelings were fairly typical of the general view. John Fitzgerald Kennedy, with his attractive boyish smile, came across as sincere and had come to symbolise all the fresh green hopes of young America. His auspicious inauguration speech included -

"The torch has been passed to a new generation of Americans."

At the age of 43, he was the youngest ever President of the United States. He had been in office barely three years since his election on November 9th, 1960. The 15-year-old Simeon Hogg, at school in Heanor, welcomed his appearance as a good omen for his personal future. The desirable, dashing, eloquent and calm Kennedy contrasted strongly with his opposite number who ruled the Communist world. Nikita Khrushchev was old and repulsive, a little, bald rotundity who was given to tantrums. He once took off his shoe and banged it against the podium at the United Nations. Often ominous, he threatened to 'bury' the west. His wife, plump, dowdy and grey, looked more like a Russian road sweeper. She looked like a cleaner at Simeon's school; hardly the 'First Lady of the Soviet Union'. Seeing her walk alongside the beautiful and glamorous Jacqueline Kennedy reinforced the deepening fear and prejudice.

Very soon Simeon would be seeing television images of a tragic blood-splattered Jackie, desperately clambering on the back of an accelerating open top Lincoln Continental, in a panic-stricken, pathetic attempt to rescue bits of her husband's brain, the handsome husband who was as good as dead. For Simeon Hogg, John F Kennedy had come to be the essence of all the promise, all that was best, all that was good in the United States. For Simeon, the 35th American President had come to symbolise the American Dream ... and, at that moment, Simeon's American Dream died with that young President.

Hank had driven to the local grade school to collect Chuckie, his eight year old boy. They, their new guest and a shocked nation were in sombre mood, silently sitting in front of the television screen, eager to devour fresh details which were given out minute by minute. Friendly Bob Adams and Mr Belvedere had been banished from all the television channels. All channels were now covering the world-shattering tragedy.

A Ford Thunderbird bounced up the driveway. Chuckie bounded through the door like an excited dog.

"Mom! Dad said some kook shot the President!"

"I know, honey. Help me with these, please," she replied in soft languid tones.

Chuckie took the heavy shopping bag off Lauren Kurtz as she slued sideways her space age steering wheel for an easy and graceful exit from her beautiful new car. An important symbol which personified power and prosperity. A shapely figure with oodles of sex appeal sauntered to the door, both doors (the main door and additional storm door) struggled open by the child clutching a bag nearly as big as himself. The sleek and elegant woman of 28 was preceded by a waft of expensive scent before she made a polished and professional entrance. An observer, casting an eye over the carefully-crafted coiffeur with its attractive lustre, might well have guessed 'beautician' - and the guess would have been correct. This girl from Bog Hole in Horsley Woodhouse had come about as far away from Bog Hole as it was possible to get. Everything about her said 'chic' 'expensive cuts' 'tasteful' and 'discerning'.

Simeon had not seen his famous sister since he was a little boy of six, younger than Chuckie. Consequently they were strangers to each other and they met formally - as strangers. Hank turned off the TV whilst Lauren Kurtz flowed her sensuous body onto a breakfast stool. Casually, with royal hand motions, she lit a cigarette. With total indifference, she inhaled, puffed out a smoke ring which ascended and was followed in total silence by three admiring males who might well have been three dogs. She purred a well-rehearsed greeting to her husband and, eventually, languidly, her beautiful, blasé eyes rested on the newcomer, opening wide.

"Well, hello, big brother," she purred, insouciantly. "Welcome to the US of one big drama. How was your trip?"

Simeon was pleased, at long last, to be addressed and poured out excited details of the stormy voyage, even though his innate intelligence told him she clearly did not give a damn. His initial warmth and enthusiasm during these first few minutes of reunion was returned by a cool courtesy. Here was chemistry Simeon did not understand. It was entirely possible that Lauren did not fully understand the chemistry either.

That puzzling chemistry was never fully de-coded until years later when Simeon discussed his sister with a group of relatives at Bog Hole during one of his annual vacations. They related their memories of 1945. An envious and resentful 10-year-old, having been the centre of attention, was now helplessly standing by, watching the endless doting and constant fussing - all heaped upon a new baby boy by hordes of excited Hoggs. This might well be true, but cute little Simeon, gurgling and wriggling with pleasure as Aunty Gertie tickled his tummy, was hardly in a position to fully appreciate the enthusiastic reception. In mature reflection, he saw the situation rather differently and brought his own childhood memories to bear on that revealing conference.

From Simeon's earliest memories, Lauren had always seemed an adult, an adult detached and completely disinterested in him, except, when he got in her way - which was often. He had no memory of how or why he was naughty, no memory of the ways in which he was a nuisance, but he was never to forget the response from his sister. He remembered the intensity of her anger and hostility. Once, she did something which infuriated him. He could not recall what it was, but clearly recalled his childish act of vengeance in the small second bedroom which they shared. He disarranged the items of make-up which reposed on her dressing table. She came home late one night, found them, untidy, knocked over and pushed into a corner. Lauren flew into a rage and bitterly complained to her father. As a result, Mr Hogg acted immediately. He clomped up the wooden stairs, up into the bedroom in which his little son was fast asleep. Simeon was dragged out of his bed and soundly thrashed. By the usual custom and practice of post-war Bog Hole standards, this beating was not unduly savage. Notwithstanding, the child's screams in that dark night did not avail him any mercy from the big man who made sure that the punishment took its full course. In working-class culture, kids were not reasoned with. They were not spoken to calmly and 'nicely' as in the case of the siblings of a barrister or an architect. No. Discipline at Bog Hole was rough and ready.

The pain was not the issue. The pain might well have been forgotten in the fullness of time. The issue was one of injustice, a bitter injustice branded into the mind of a small child. A five-year-old may well be inarticulate and have difficulty explaining a sequence of events, but this five-year-old was never given the slightest chance to explain his behaviour. He was not invited to put his case before the parental jury, result - outrage. Outrage which would be subsumed deep into the subconscious and there slowly smoulder, burning for the rest of his life.

Mr and Mrs Hogg were proud of the daughter who had escaped from the dingy and drab world of Bog Hole and had achieved high status with glamour and riches, but they were ashamed of the son who was bullied at Mundy Street Boys School and hated football. In Heanor and Horsley Woodhouse, football was important. It was very important for the prestige of Jack Hogg that his son could defend himself and play the game. Fortunately, the Hoggs were spared the ultimate humiliation suffered by the fictitious and celluloid 'Mr Elliot'. Unlike 'Billy', Simeon had no desire to become a ballet dancer. He was compliant. He avoided going 'down the pit', but generally went with the cultural flow and became a craft apprentice at Spondon Power Station. Jack Hogg took some small satisfaction seeing his son in a dark blue boiler suit, getting his hands dirty by assisting the fitters, welders and riggers.

The stresses and strains of an Atlantic crossing, emigration, uprooting and the culture shock of an alien environment can expose the body to an alien virus. The voices around Simeon became diffuse, faces started to blur, his concentration melted into sleepiness and his body seemed to withdraw into itself, seemed to shut down, craving silence and bed. Simeon was ill.

Chapter 5

A Rude Awakening

It would be sometime in the late afternoon of Saturday, November 23rd, that a very sick and weak boy emerged, only briefly, from the depths of a heavy comatose sleep. He was hot, very hot, in a hot, unfamiliar, airless bedroom and totally unable to move. A dry mouth and an all-consuming, desperate thirst urged him to call out, but, in his prostrate and debilitated body, he could find no voice and there was no energy available to make that voice. The best thing in the world would have been a cup of tea, but no tea was ever offered and nobody, except the child, had come near the stricken teenager during the previous 24 hours. As the mind struggled to reach a conscious state, far away he heard the excited sound of a little boy who had just come into the house with his father. Both boy and father spoke the name 'Simeon' to a third person and he caught a few words.

"Gee Mom! He could be dead! You should look in there ... "

He would never forget those kind words of concern, uttered by an anxious child, but, at that point, the few moments of consciousness ended. The patient slipped back into pain, darkness and the miserable miasma of a raging cruel virus.

The nation was also hurting and miserable. It, too, had shut down. It was in mourning. As a mark of respect the beauty parlour was closed and, like millions of other Americans, Lauren Kurtz was home with her family, watching the television. She was not sure how to deal with the sudden and unwelcome illness of her brother but took full advantage of her husband's comment the evening before.

"Chuckie said he's asleep. I guess that's the best thing for flu. Better leave him be."

He was 'left be' for several more hours until Hank put a glass of water on the side table of the sickroom before retiring. Ten hours later, once again, Simeon 'came to' on a brilliant, sunny, Sunday morning. Enervated and fragile, he slowly struggled to reach the water, which tasted like nectar. Minutes later he dropped back on the bed and dozed. Later still, he felt strong enough to reach out for his watch, a generous bon voyage present from Aunty Joyce, which displayed the time and date: November 24th,

4.17pm. Very slowly, he dragged his body over to the closet and managed to don a dressing gown. Swaying for a moment, he staggered out of that little room, nearly 48 hours since he had first entered it on the day of the assassination. The television was off and the depth of silence told of just one quiet person in the house. Lauren, in a seemingly 'painted on skin' white garment, had lounged her voluptuous body across a massive 'Early American' couch, idly perusing a magazine. A smoking cigarette was artistically arranged between her long fine fingers. The invalid made painstaking progress across that spacious room and carefully lowered his delicate self into one of the matching, equally ugly, but comfortable easy chairs.

She did not look up. She did not look at him. It appeared that she was unaware of his presence during that strange, strained long minute which passed. A fit Simeon would have become impatient and spoken, but this was a defeated Simeon, an enervated Simeon, desperate for a drink of tea, but also entranced by the ballet of twisting, curling, blue smoke, ever upwards, en route to the modern ceiling finished in pine. Eyes still sweeping across glossy pages, she speaks in slow sighs -

"So now we have another screwball who shoots the first screwball right on television. How about that!" Eventually, she raised her head to observe her missing brother of two days and two nights. "What happened to you?"

In the following exchange Simeon learned that Lee Harvey Oswald was the alleged murderer of President Kennedy. He also learned that, just a few hours before, Oswald was shot dead by a man called Jack Ruby who owned a striptease club in Dallas. He also learned that Lauren had no intention of making him a cup of tea. Flashing him an expressionless look with big, cool, unfeeling eyes -

"Time to grow up, brother! Sister is *not* Mummy."

With admirable choreography, she pointed a long sardonic finger in the direction of the open plan kitchen. A cruel finger made longer and accentuated by a long, immaculately manicured, sharp nail. She murmured and purred a request to return all items to their original and correct location. Although Simeon was making slow progress in the kitchen and slow progress with the devastating virus, he mentioned the possibility of a visit from the doctor. This precipitated a short, formal lecture about his new circumstances and new responsibilities. In an accent which was still strange and fascinating, she drawled out -

"Doctor! You have to be joking! Wave 'bye bye' to the 'something for nothing' society, little brother. It is gone. Do you have any idea of what it would cost to get a doctor to visit you? You have a virus. People recover from a virus. And I strongly advise you to recover real quick because, little brother, you need to get a job!"

She managed to say 'jjaaaarrrbb' as though it was composed of ten letters. The following day, Monday, November 25th, she was silent. They were all silent, sitting in front of that large television of antique design. The image of a little boy of three, saluting the coffin of his slain father, a fallen warrior, was heartbreaking. Six grey horses pulled the gun carriage past a heavily-veiled Jacqueline Kennedy to the sound of muffled drums and the tolling of a single bell.

A few days later America had returned to normality and Simeon was feeling able to study the newspaper for jobs. Having taken a crash course from Chuckie on how to use the telephone, he dialled up a few numbers. Lauren made it perfectly clear that he was in no position to be choosy.

"Oh yes! I know all about it, at the 'Employment Exchange'. English kids are mollycoddled. It's an allowance for this and a special benefit for that. This is America ... and it's real simple, brother - no work, no dough! Understand? So you can't cook. So what? Watch the others. Ben made pizza - *you* can make pizza. Get down there now and make pizza. You can walk, it's less than a mile. Go."

Although it was the most monotonous, totally flat walk he had ever walked, Simeon enjoyed the fresh air and the change. He arrived at the pizza joint, a featureless white cube, littered with neon, cheap and tacky.

"Sorry, kid, we got somebody already."

Back at the house he made several more phone-calls. Lauren became irritated. This was nothing to do with the cost. Picking up the phone in Allen Park was like turning on the tap in Bog Hole. Calls were cheap in the USA, just like gasoline at 19 cents a gallon, contrasted to four shillings [60 cents] for an English gallon of petrol. And, anyway, the cost of petrol was irrelevant to the relatives of Simeon Hogg, who could as near afford a motorcar as a holiday in Bermuda.

No, Lauren Kurtz had other reasons to be irritated. She had been plunged into the 'do or die' jungle of hard American capitalism at an early age. Lauren had had it tough and felt that Simeon had always had it too soft. By the standards and deeply-ingrained philosophy of the United States, she was quite right. Back in gentle and kind Derbyshire, her brother would be offered numerous sources of help and support. He would be persuaded to try a job. If he did not like that job, the civil servants would be sympathetic. Something different would be suggested. If that was college, the taxpayer would pay, not only the tuition and cost of all books, but also give Simeon a fairly generous maintenance grant upon which to live. If he did not feel like college, he could pretend to look for work, could go on 'The Assistance' - and that could go on for years!

Simeon Hogg was about to get a rude awakening! He had arrived in the US with £20, which would soon be used up on food. If not exactly 'flowing with the milk of human kindness', Lauren Kurtz, was, by nature, disposed to be generous. But Lauren Kurtz was definitely not 'The Assistance'!

"You won't get hired over the phone! Get out there, find work and get working," she snapped.

More kindly, Hank suggested that Downtown Detroit would be the most productive place for a person with no car to seek employment. In the Metropolitan area of Detroit, 'no car' was almost equivalent to having 'no legs'. It was entirely reasonable that Chuckie would be without private means of transport or someone like Hank's great-grandmother, who was nearly ninety, but, apart from a handful of poor Negroes, everybody else had a car - except Simeon. But how does the job seeker get to Downtown Detroit which is more than 10 miles away? In Derbyshire buses went everywhere and they went frequently. Chuckie had never seen a bus. No one had ever seen a bus in Allen Park. However, buses obviously did exist. After all, Simeon had proved it by arriving on one in Detroit.

Michigan Avenue was a dead straight, east-west, three lane, main artery into the centre of Detroit from another suburban city called Dearborn. Rumour had it that a public bus service existed on Michigan Avenue. Hank suggested driving Simeon the four miles to Dearborn, where he could catch the bus.

Simeon had great faith in the ability of his City and Guilds Mechanical Engineering Technicians Certificate to get him a desirable appointment. He had worked long and hard to achieve that qualification. Unfortunately, his sister demeaned this achievement with remarks similar to the insulting sneers made by the New York customs official. Unfortunately, as it turned out, she was entirely correct. With devastating accuracy, she argued that a Michigan employer would want to know 'what he could do'. Simeon could do nothing - and he knew it. In the total absence of academic achievement, Derbyshire working-class ethos had channelled him along the path of the practical and the technical. His much prized certificate (unknown and of no value in the USA) was acquired by success in the examination room from the embryonic skills of creative writing. He could not spell, but was able to convince the marker that he was proficient in mechanics, physics, simple maths and the basic principles of workshop technology - theory and practice. He hated the workshop. He hated the dirt and the grease. He hated the crude and rude conduct of his working-class work-mates. He hated their boasting, their obscene obsession with 'birds'; the endless fart jokes and snot jokes. He hated engineering but could not admit this to himself any more than he could admit that he hated kissing girls.

And all this came sharply into focus in Downtown Detroit on that Monday of December 2nd in 1963.

Chapter 6

Frozen Chicken

Simeon was blue with cold when the bus arrived. At below freezing temperatures, he was frozen to the marrow simply because he was not properly dressed for a Michigan winter. He would not be seen dead wearing a hat, but he *was* prepared to be seen blue in a state of uncontrollable shivering. As an old man, he would look back to his most miserable moments; being bullied at Mundy Street Boys School, suffering the acid tongue of his sister Lauren, enduring dismal years of progressive education - and public bus travel in the Motor City.

It was standing room only in that public vehicle filled with the dross of Detroit society, the people without cars, a mixture of miserable and curious faces. Ten miles is a long way with frequent stops for passengers and numerous traffic lights. Ten miles is a long way when one block, blighted by unplanned and uncontrolled commercial paraphernalia, looks exactly the same as another block. Ten miles is a long way when everything looks a mess.

The city centre was an improvement. An impressive skyline announced the hub of a major industrial complex providing homes and work for one and a half million people. The 47-storey Penobscot Building dominated a small group of handsome skyscrapers which looked across the international boundary to Windsor, Ontario. An invisible line in the centre of the Detroit River separated the United States from Canada. The French connection was everywhere to be seen; The Lafayette Building, Gratiot Avenue, Orleans and La Salle. As a Francophobe, it came as an unpleasant surprise to Simeon to discover that a golden name which had always thrilled and excited him, a name which he had come to know as the very pinnacle of futuristic automotive excellence was, in fact, the name of a Frenchman! A fur trader called Antonine de la Mothe Cadillac founded Detroit in 1701. Detroit being the French word for strait, a narrow passage of water which linked Lake St Clair to the much larger Lake Erie.

Africa was the other main influence. Everywhere black faces, many living in nearby crumbling ghettos. Depressing ghettos which were slowly smouldering a civic malaise of racial tensions, at this point, only four years away from the forthcoming explosion of the burning war-torn riots of 1967. Simeon Hogg, a member of an oppressed minority himself, was destined for a better and much closer relationship with the Negro race. The Negro was a novelty. Heanor had been 100% white but, on occasional visits to Derby, he may have glimpsed a person of colour which was unusual. Black men interested this teenager. He was intrigued by the neat, short, frizzy hair, big eyes, wide nose and thick lips.

The naive enthusiasm which kick-started that cold morning soon cooled to despondency as secretary after secretary, on various floors of tall buildings, slowly shook their heads on the conclusion of his short spiel spoken in an alien accent. Sometimes he was invited to fill out a job application form which, on completion, disappeared into a mysterious repository underneath her desk.

"We'll let you know."

Sometimes the girl would save his time, ask a few questions and give an honest reply.

"I'm so sorry. We do have vacancies but you don't even have a high school diploma! Your engineering certificate ... well ... it looks real nice. It may well be good in England, but ... well ... England is England! Isn't it?"

Unfortunately, Simeon Hogg was not able to hear the authorial voice of experience from forty years into the future speaking over his head in this book. It would tell him to take any clean job - such as the job he eventually took in Downtown Detroit, a nice, easy job requiring no qualifications and rewarded with reasonable pay - a bank messenger. If it could be heard, the authorial voice would remind the boy that he was a desirable 18-year-old. It would tell him to walk several blocks westwards to Trumbull and Vernor, just behind Tiger Stadium, where he would find the old and filthy Vernor Baths. The $5 entry fee would be a good investment, since he could probably leave with $100 - no problem. But Simeon would be horrified and refuse such lascivious mercenary advice. Weeks later, at his first visit to that den of iniquity, he was affronted by a frustrated nuisance who offered him a ten dollar bill - half the going rate. Simeon could not believe his eyes. Quite sincerely, he said -

"You can't buy it!"

But you could. Simeon was shocked. He was trapped inside the guidelines of an internalised moral code and did not understand the concept of buying sex. He thought that a 'prostitute' was a woman who liked lots of sex with lots of different men. This youth had something to sell. After a few years he had come to terms with the principle of a 'fair exchange' but, at that point - it was already too late. He had passed his 'sell by date'. *C'est la vie.*

After a long, tiring day of form filling and shaking heads in various personnel offices of the leading automotive giants and subsidiary industries, he passed a door marked 'Excellent Engineering', walked in and, for the first time, received a genuinely enthusiastic reception.

"Why sure! We could certainly use a smart young guy like ya self. Just fill out this application form for our records."

Simeon was immediately offered the position of 'lathe hand' in a small machine shop on Michigan Avenue in Dearborn at forty dollars a week. Checking the paper work later, Lauren explained his sudden turn of luck.

"Lesson one brother: learn to read the *large* print. Excellent Engineering is an employment agency. They don't pay you, *you* pay them, and, according to this, you'll be paying them half your first month's salary! Clever boy. Lesson two: forty dollars is about fourteen pounds a week. That may be reasonable in Heanor, but it's starvation pay in Dearborn. You'd make twice that sweeping the streets."

But Simeon did not fancy sweeping the streets. He could operate a lathe and 'turn between centres' and, as such, was of some small use to Mr Patrick, who owned the small factory at Telegraph Road and Michigan Avenue. At a brisk rate, the dull, flat, four mile walk took him just over an hour and a quarter on his first morning of Tuesday, December 3rd. That was the day he learned the meaning of hard work. The nationalised Spondon Power station had been a leisurely affair in contrast to this private sweat shop where each man had to work hard, had to work fast and earned every dime.

Organising himself to get up and off in time for an 8.00am start had precluded any thought about sandwiches. Simeon Hogg had never made a sandwich in his life. A loud character called 'Al' felt sorry for the young guy who simply sat watching others eat during the half hour lunch break.

Al offered Simeon a sandwich. It was received with enthusiasm and found to be delicious. Not so the thick black coffee which was graciously accepted but found to be foul. The new guy knew nothing about boxing. Al was disappointed. In a highly charged racial polemic, he held forth, at length, on the iniquity of having 'dumb' Negroes in the ring.

"Niggers have ruined the fight game. You bet! Ya have Niggers back in England?"

Simeon became very depressed at that moment. From a greasy stained old radio, a male group were singing a beautiful, if melancholic composition called *Look Homeward Angel*. On the line - 'Do the folks I use to know remember me?', he thought of his former pals back home in Heanor with a frisson of nostalgia. It was like looking back into a different dimension, looking back to a previous existence; so far back and so different, he wondered if it ever really existed. Michigan had become a hell-hole and he recalled a comment made to him on the ship -

"Detroit! You're kidding? Detroit. God! No brains, all beer and hamburger. You're heading for the *toilet* of the United States, buster."

Four hours later, any observer with an ounce of sensitivity could have read the body language of the solitary youngster dragging his sad, weary body southwards along the right side of Telegraph Road. He was going home. At the end of a hard day he should be pleased. But what was home? Home was a house of strangers. He tried to make sense of these strangers. There was the hostile woman with cruel lips, who hated him. A woman as cold as the freezing and biting air of that dark December evening alongside that flat, dreary, straight road. She reminded him of the evil but beautiful queen who asked a question of a magic mirror in the film *Snow White*. But Simeon had a different question -

"How did this happen? Why had she allowed me to come? She is very much the boss and what she says goes. Why did she not prevent it?"

As that thought dissolved into the ether, he already knew the answer. Like her brother, Lauren was also complying with family pressure to allow -

" ... arr Simeon ta get 'im sen nice an settled before ya Mam an Dad get there."

A dramatic confrontation later that evening threw more light on the subject. It was precipitated when Simeon was writing a letter to his Aunty Gertie, outlining his many grievances. He was just warming to the particular complaint of having to make his own sandwiches every morning when Chuckie ran past, knocked the table and spilt a bottle of ink on his paper, which obliterated the previous 14 points of extreme dissatisfaction. This provoked a sharp response from the writer - which, in turn, inflamed a protective mother who was already all too keen to attack an unwanted lodger. In the ensuing exchange, Lauren spat out the hard truth that she had never said to any relative 'come to America' and made it clear that her brother was barely tolerated and certainly not welcome.

Returning to Allen Park after work, alongside Telegraph Road, he discovered that it was fairly easy to hitch a ride. Frigid grey days went by, one very much like another, until a decisive day arrived, a day which would change his life. It was the following Tuesday, December 10th.

A large, white, Chevrolet Impala smoothly floated to his side. He was invited to enter and sink into the warm, lush interior. A plain, ordinary face began conversation. It was a grey face, as grey as the cold iron-grey weather. It was a face easily forgotten, a face of about 35 which claimed to be 25.

"Gees! You are one frozen chicken! You need a winter coat. I'll warm ya." He turned up the heat and rubbed Simeon's leg, the wrong part: he was colder below. "Let me introduce myself. My name is Leehegeegee - Lee is fine."

He gave an unpronounceable Eastern European surname consisting of many syllables. He said it was Russian. He was lying - it was Polish. He said he was a doctor. Simeon was impressed meeting a doctor. A doctor was a prestigious job, commanding respect and a high salary. Again, Lee was lying. Here is a paradox. If he had told the simple truth that he was a teacher of English at a local High School, it would have attracted even more esteem and kudos from this young passenger, who apportioned great value to the position of schoolmaster.

"How's that go again? Simeon! Like out of the Bible. Ya, 'Simeon'. Sounds nice. Cute kid. Working! You don't look old enough to work. You should be in school. Ha? Run that past me again? Gees, that accent! I could cut it with a knife. What's that? Tups, Tups? Oh! You mean that department store we just passed."

The boy read the name and spoke it. To Lee it sounded strange, clipped and short. When Lee said 'Tops' to Simeon, it sounded long and drawn out like 'Taaarrrps'. They pulled up to a drive-in and ate a hamburger. Further conversation established the sad situation with Lauren, the fact that her brother was not keen to return to Allen Park and not expected at any special time. In this last, Simeon was quite wrong. It was 5.00pm and dinner, usually prepared by Hank, was served at 7.30pm prompt. It was a matter of considerable concern when, eventually, the family started the meal half an hour late without the thoughtless lodger. A phone-call had crossed his mind but, unfortunately, the boy was not sufficiently organised to have memorised the long number or have it written down. The simple expedient of consulting the phone book did, in fact, cross Lee's mind, but - he was consumed with a combination of lust and fear. He was all to aware of his precarious position.

Michigan was an old-fashioned and strait-laced state. At the capital city in Lansing there was a conservative legislature which even prohibited heterosexual intercourse in any position, save for the acceptable 'Missionary Position' of face-to-face. So-called from the brainwashing sex education imposed by puritanical Christian missionaries of the previous century. They were appalled after witnessing the candid and imaginative eroticism of 'savage' Africans. Deviant heterosexual sex in Michigan was tightly proscribed and, even more so, was the deeply-ingrained and rabid homophobia, which attracted barbarously long prison sentences for a 'degenerate' man who would dare to touch a boy.

Lee was not sufficiently responsible to insist that his young friend, at least, do the right thing, make the necessary phone call to allay the worries of his sister and brother-in-law. Lauren had little love for her brother, but these considerations were important in a metropolitan area which averaged three murders a day. When he finally returned at 10.45pm, an enraged sister laid into him mercilessly about his selfish irresponsibility. She slashed him with the sword of truth. She had right on her side and Simeon knew it. Her public reprimand was vicious, but he was more hurt by Hank's dark silence. He felt ashamed when Hank graciously accepted his apology and the assurance that it would never happen again. Hank had worked hard to produce an excellent meal. His forgiveness and lack of reproach was painful. Hank was disappointed in his brother-in-law, and rightly so. Simeon was devastated to hear little Chuckie express relief that the absent uncle was OK. He had stayed up late to hear any news and, as ever, gave his uncle full details of the day at school.

So what, in fact, did Simeon do all that evening with his new friend?

Chapter 7

When Them Lips Close Up

Excited by the proximity of his desirable new acquisition, together with a mouth full of half masticated cheeseburger, Lee struggled to articulate his well polished grooming technique -

"So what else ya like Simeon? How about niggers, big black niggers? Ya like niggers? A know a good nigger. Ya wanna go there, meet him? Yeah?"

The word 'him' was a crucial moment for Simeon Hogg. Since having a crush on a handsome teacher from the age of ten, he had been denying and suppressing inappropriate sexual feelings. Queers were dirty old men who haunted toilets - or so he had been told, never having seen a queer. Which was not surprising, since, for the most part, gay activity in public places is carried out with a polished skill in very subtle ways and, consequently, invisible to the general public. Being entertained by his work mates doing a stereotypical impression of a 'bum boy' was the nearest he had ever come to meeting an effeminate man. Such types were occasionally heard on the radio but never encountered in Simeon's working class, ultra butch world. And therefore, it followed that Simeon could not possibly be queer, since he was not a dirty old man and did not behave like a girl. He was not seeing a 'Nancy boy' in Lee. Lee was a big normal man. Lee was masculine, but was clearly 'straining at the bit'.

At that defining moment, it became perfectly clear this man had shown the frustrated and repressed youth, for the first time, the hidden door to the secret garden of homosexuality. His words were somewhat jocular and ambiguous, yet the invitation was clear. A small part of Simeon, the respectable part, was prepared to say no, thank Lee for the hamburger and ask to be returned to 291812 Coolidge Boulevard, Allen Park. But the larger part ... that was curious. And the larger part was more than ready to break free from the sickening chains of heterosexual repression and brainwashing. The larger part craved an end to what he was supposed to seek out and enjoy. Nay, *urged* to seek out and enjoy; dubious pleasures such as the repulsive touch of the small female hand, the smell and nauseating softness of the female body. Thank God that every female within the compass of Simeon's limited experience had resisted his half-hearted advances!

During that conversation in that hamburger joint, for the first time ever Simeon Hogg came to terms with his homosexuality. He had 'come out', if only to himself and that one other, the stranger with the unpronounceable last name. Hours later, alone in bed, he would have his usual 'wank'. But this would be a wayward wank, a wank with a difference. This would be the very first one in which he would fantasise about boys. Heretofore, such thoughts had been strictly banished by a puritanical effort of self discipline. Macho he may have been, but Lee was too old. Simeon did not desire him, yet he represented an opportunity and his chosen carrot, although expressed in offensive racist terms was, for this boy - a 'turn on'.

This experienced predator had found Telegraph Road fertile ground and this particular line often succeeded with horny boys. The persuasive groomer lowered his voice and leaned closer -

"How about it, kid? Look-a-here ... it's like this ... Guys like us, we can't always land the chicks. OK? How long is it since you were laid, Simeon? Too long huh." He forced a short cynical laugh. "Sure. Well, I'll tell ya, kid, there aint nothing, nothing like those *big* juicy lips - big - black - lips, an a slimy tongue that'll keep ya hangin' on, make ya cry with pleasure. You'll beg, baby! Oh yeah. You'll beg Tod for release. Better than any pussy you've ever dipped! Man, ya gonna hit the roof! When - them - lips - close up - mmmm mmmm!!"

Simeon, a cat lover, was puzzled and somewhat disturbed by that odd reference to his furry friends, but gathered from his new friend that a visit to a black man called 'Tod', somewhere in the Detroit ghetto, was going to be a ground-breaking and enjoyable experience. En route they laughed over the same joke of pronunciation as with the department store. When Lee said 'Tod', it sounded like a long word. When Simeon said 'Tod', it sounded like three, very short letters.

Half an hour later they were driving slowly down a tree-lined street which, just a few decades before, had once been all white and home to professional, middle class Detroiters. Former handsome detached houses with distinctive verandas, over the years, had become slightly shabby. To

Simeon's eye they looked unusual, but at least they had some character. He liked this area.

The door was opened by a quintessential Negroid man, an unsmiling, intimidating man with a powerful build. That warm house and warm man were well matched; they were both very dark and exuded a strange tropical scent. Everywhere, artificial foliage and exotic flowers whose colours were enhanced by small tinted spot-lights.

"Hey! Look what I got! Nice - sweet - chicken!" said Lee.

Just for a second the big dark eyes of the big silent man appraised and rested on Simeon. A slight nod was an indication to enter and ascend the stairs. Lee stood back and let his 'chicken' follow. He was riveted by those two large, but perfectly formed black globes, beautiful globes, side by side, filling out sexy blue jeans, poetry in motion, climbing up to the bedroom.

After following such a glowing trailer of impending oral ecstasy, the novice was now staring at that compelling, but formidable, unfriendly face. Trying to read the dark orbital eyes was difficult. They seemed to speak of something between contempt and curiosity. Perhaps they spoke of lust; yes, definitely lust. Which was mutual, because Simeon, having been primed by his groomer, was now bewitched by those dark thick lips and the deeper succulent promise from the orifice within.

The first time is special. You never forget the first time. Simeon had heard that many times before. He had heard it in the film *A Taste of Honey* and was fully aware of the significance of this moment. It would, however, take longer to appreciate the *cultural* significance of the moment; the fact that he was going to be 'Americanised'. Years later, during debates with friends, he would argue that he was already pre-disposed to enjoying American sex as opposed to British or European sex. Unusually for an English boy, Simeon had been circumcised. If that were not the case, the evening would have turned out differently and been very disappointing. 'Coliseum curtains' and concomitant hygiene problems were the stuff of jokes in Detroit gay circles.

Those same circles included an obligatory sprinkling of outrageous queens, but most men were manlike, behaving as men, able to move invisibly and pass off as 'straight' in straight circles. One word, 'butch', meant a manly man, a man who conducted himself as a man. In England, Simeon would discover that butch indicated something quite different. Butch meant you 'gave it' in anal intercourse and 'bitch' was the term for the passive partner. Simeon was neither butch nor bitch. In England, Simeon the ardent Englishman who would spend most of his life pining for the green hills and beautiful dales of Derbyshire, was a sexual disaster! A misfit in his own land, because his initiation had taken place in America - or so his English friends argued. Gay Britain was long infused with an anal culture. Gay America was predominately an oral culture, long-wedded to the practice of fellatio; the quickie, the convenient and anonymous 'blow job' by the simple expedient of a brief, deep knee bend. The Derbyshire equivalent of 'gamming' was less common and less skilled. It was a happy coincidence that Simeon Hogg, now 'coming out' in Michigan, had an in-built predisposition to be repelled by the practice of buggery, a practice which was often derided in the United States as 'hitting the dirt road'. Fifteen years later, with the advent of Aids, that same predisposition, probably saved his life.

And, another point: tonight Simeon will learn a new language. In the fullness of time, two new languages, British and American gay terms. On that evening he heard the word 'gay' several times and came to understand that a gay guy was a guy like himself. During his 1965 vacation, discovering the hidden gay culture of Derbyshire, he was appalled to hear local gay men describing each other as queer! They used the same insulting term to describe each other as was used by the straight world. A bloke who was not queer was quite simply referred to as 'normal'. In the homosexual underworld of Detroit, it was rare and novel to come across an effeminate man. In the Derbyshire homosexual underworld, it was rare and novel to find a homosexual man who was masculine, the majority being 'camp' and a number of those quite quirky to boot.

Watching Lee undress, carelessly throwing his clothes on the floor, created a mixture of conflicting emotions for this boy who was, at this stage, a genuine innocent. It was outrageous! It was unknown and unacceptable for a grown man, an adult, to behave in such a lewd manner in front of a boy. Simeon considered himself to be a boy in these strange circumstances. He was embarrassed. He wanted to run down the stairs and run out of the house into the security of Lee's big car. He was shy, especially on Lee's impatient order -

"Get 'em off! The man's got work to do. Don't keep him waiting. He's hungry. He's thirsty."

He was afraid of the big silent Negro whose body scent had now become more powerful, the glaring unfriendly African with a taste for white meat. This covetous carnivore was also disrobing, exposing a powerful, magnificent, black body. But yes, in spite of his fear, Simeon was definitely excited - very excited. He was not about to run anywhere.

"Come over here, by me. Relax, kid," said Lee, man and boy, side by side, now both lying naked on the bed. It was all new to the lad from Derbyshire, whose previous sexual experience had been limited to a few quick gropes and an occasional fondle at school some years before. It was new for him to see a big man, all hard, raring to go. For the first time he was able to assess his rating in the scale of size. Contrasted with the massive Lee, he was definitely in the middle range until ... He drew breath on first sight of the black man! Make that lower middle range - very low. So all the stories and rumours he had heard about Negroes turned out to be true. At least, this was the case with Tod, who was not yet fully pumped up. Not that it mattered much to Tod. He was there to serve, to provide a service. This would be another surprise to Simeon who assumed that sex would always be a mutual activity. He assumed he would be required to do something in return. Indeed, he was eager to do something to Tod but - that was not required. Tod was too busy. He started on Lee, who groaned something about -

"Arr yeah! It's been a long time, baby - too long ... "

Lee became inarticulate as his thick, long manhood slowly disappeared down the deep throat of this amazing sword-swallowing Negro, who was kneeling before him like a slave. During the four short minutes to climax, the boy was mesmerised by this extraordinary event; then it was his turn, a turn which lasted two minutes ...

Chapter 8

The Empress of England

Christmas was a sad affair. It made Simeon feel isolated. He was more homesick than ever trying to be a part of the family, trying to fit in, trying to be merry amid the tinsel and glitter of the ultra-heterosexual Kurtz home. He failed to communicate in any meaningful way with boys his own age, in spite of the good-intentioned efforts of Ben and Ricky next door.

The nearest thing to a 'friend' was the mysterious Lee who, quite naturally, never telephoned. The rule was simple; no letters, nothing in writing. Simeon had to phone Lee and hope he would be at home, which was rare. The meeting place was always on Telegraph Road. Simeon would put out his thumb at the sight of Lee's white Chevrolet and appear to be an innocent lad begging a ride. Through Lee, he met several casual acquaintances who were visited for sex, always the same type of sex. Lee took his new chicken to the Vernor Baths to show him off. He was also taken to a similar bath house over the river in Windsor, Canada. Little by little, Simeon gained more confidence and met more people in this new, mysterious, twilight world. A world in which you never asked a man what he did for a living, where he lived or whether or not he was married. A world in which meetings often took place without any conversation and sometimes in total darkness. The American experience was secretive, skilful, masculine, strong and silent. Simeon would find the English experience *very* different.

The iron grey of January, 1964, passed into an equally cold and miserable February when the United States became seized by 'Beatlemania'. Every radio was alive with the 'Fab Four' joyfully singing out *I Want to Hold Your Hand* and thick Liverpudlian accents made Simeon even more nostalgic, ever more pining for his homeland. It became an obsession. He had to get back home. He had to escape from an ugly, commercial, functional world which was flat, cheap and plastic.

Winter was followed by a quick Spring, which in turn was quickly followed by unbearable humidity when sleepless nights could see an ungodly 4.00am dip to a stifling seventy degrees, the coolest time of day. During one of those hot nights, ever filled with the chorus of a thousand crickets, a young man in a convertible was driving his recently acquired English friend around the plush millionaire neighbourhood of Grosse Pointe, proving that -

" ... some parts of America are really nice. You just haven't seen them yet. You should get around more."

"These people are rich!" replied Simeon.

"You bet."

"Which means ... " The passenger pondered the implications and possibilities of personal wealth. "They can live where they want! Why do they stay here? They could move. They don't have to be here. They could sell up, escape, go and live in Derbyshire!"

This last infuriated the American driver, who had already heard too much about England during that evening. Effectively, this remark brought a swift end to (what had been) a pleasant nocturnal tour.

That summer brought two good things. Firstly, Simeon escaped from Lauren when his parents arrived and bought a house nearby. Secondly, he managed to get a more suitable job with better pay as a camera salesman in a department store. Most important, he was able to save money. In the spring of 1965 he had saved enough money to fund an extended vacation in England. On May 24th, a Diesel Electric train smoothly speeded him along a straight, flat 'railroad' to Montreal, where he embarked on the Empress of England. She sailed through the St Lawrence Seaway, past Quebec, out into the North Atlantic Ocean and arrived in Liverpool on Tuesday, June 1st.

Everything looked small. The cars were tiny. The people were slightly smaller and slightly more scruffy. The streets seemed narrow, crooked and pleasantly complicated. Buildings were old, interesting, worth looking at. Everything had acquired a flavour. The Victorian pollutants of coal, coke and smut at Lime Street Station held a nostalgic flavour. Simeon, glued to the window, was now enjoying a multiplicity of changing vistas, rhythmically steaming along in an old train, on the 'railway' to Derby - to home.

Horsley Woodhouse appeared to be deserted in the late afternoon of that cool, windy day in early summer. With just two suitcases, Simeon had been able to avoid the expense of a taxi and lugged his burden the short distance from the bus stop to a quaint row of terraced houses known locally as Bog Hole. It was the last of several rows with attractive views to the north over the valley created by Bottle Brook, which ran through the village of Denby. The six humble dwellings of Bog Hole had been home to the coal-mining Hogg family for more than a hundred years and convention decreed that 'Our Simeon' would not knock, but simply walk through any door of Bog Hole. It had just started to rain when he entered number four, which had once been the home of his grandparents, who had both died a few years before. In years past the two bedrooms provided accommodation for 'Mam' and 'Dad', one girl and three boys, one of whom would become Simeon's father. The boys were now men and the girl had become maiden 'Aunty Joyce', the last remaining inhabitant of that once crowded and busy household. After an exchange of letters, cautiously, she had agreed to allow her nephew to lodge in the spare room for the duration of his holiday and was expecting him on this day.

Simeon passed through the 'best', front room and the darkened middle living room which provided a shrine to the precious 14" Pye television. This 67 guinea set, loving polished over the previous ten years, not only dominated the room but also dominated the rather small and restricted world of this shy spinster. Aunty Joyce was, as usual, sitting at the kitchen table, which was pushed hard up against the wall of that drab, narrow room on the north side of the house. She had been staring through the window which gave a restricted view on to the neighbour's wall and, up above, to a grey sky made more interesting by dark, fast-moving clouds. At that moment Simeon felt great comfort. He was comforted by the profound silence, broken only by the familiar faint sound of wind passing through the branches of a large ash tree in the garden. But comfort was mixed with a deep sadness at the reality laid before him. Here was a woman alone, so very much alone in that dingy primitive kitchen with its depressing stone sink and disused Victorian water pump. Even the bird in the cage on the table was downcast and doleful. A captive creature, like its mistress, doing nothing, going nowhere, existing from one dismal day to the next.

At the soft sound of his footfall she slowly turned her old, grey head and gradually focused suspicious eyes on the strange man framed in the kitchen door. Joyce Hogg had led a sheltered life and was very nervous of men but brief alarm gradually softened to pleasurable surprise recognising the son of her brother.

"Well, well, well!" she whined in a measured, weak, light voice. "Yav coom 'ave ya! A didn't know when yad coom. A was joost thinkin' about a bit a tea. Shall ya 'ave a bit a tea?"

To Simeon, Aunty Joyce had always been old. She looked old, moved slowly, dressed and acted old. An observer would have suggested a woman past 60 and be very surprised to be told that this quaint rustic was only a few weeks short of her 40th birthday.

After a degree of gentle fluttering and fussing, a cold light meal was prepared and presented just inches from the budgerigar, which had now become active. Aunty Joyce twittered out her pleasure to her constant companion at the return of the wanderer -

"Look ooes coom back, Joey! Look ooes coom ta see us. Now then! Ave ya forgotten arr Simeon? Arn't ya goin' ta say 'ello?"

Joey put his head on one side, hopped to another perch and inserted his head underneath a small silver bell.

"That's it! Put ya 'at on, Joey! Joey Joey Joey! Clever Joey!"

After tea, Simeon made a progress around other relatives of Bog Hole. He was fussed and celebrated as a world traveller before he could escape to the solitude and tranquillity of a lonely bench on the recreation ground with its magnificent views to the north-west hills. These were the long days. It was still light past 9.30pm. The sky had been wind swept from blanket grey to broken and shredded cloud, now revealing a flaming progression of pink, orange and red. It was good to be home. It was good to identify the familiar landmark of Crich Stand. This high point, a distant, historic stone tower, was now silhouetted against a thrilling sunburst of bright golden light. Perhaps an omen? Yes, definitely a sign, an indication of a good holiday to follow.

Chapter 9

The Derby Turkish Baths

Somewhat unwillingly, with cold face and warm body, he travelled the long journey to consciousness from a deep sleep, the sleep of the gods. A distant cockerel had called him back from dreams to reality. Joyfully he became aware of the wide-open window and breathed in the cool breeze from the far hills of Derbyshire. After stifling nights in America, the fresh air of Horsley Woodhouse underneath a glittering blue sky was like nectar. Busy blackbirds, squabbling starlings and cheery voices of early neighbours filled the room with nostalgic memories. Slow creaks ascending the stairs heralded a soft tap on the bedroom door. Cautiously it opened -

"Shall ya 'ave a bita breakfast?"

Also offered were bits of village gossip mixed with inane chatter to the bird and a weather proverb which, today, Wednesday, June 2nd, proved entirely correct when she whined -

"Sun before seven, rain before eleven."

The summer of 1965 was by no means brilliant. On this cool wet afternoon he announced to Aunty Joyce his intention of catching the bus to the nearest large town about seven miles to the south.

"Ya goin' ta Derby?" said she, slowly and thoughtfully; a woman of severely limited horizons. Every Saturday morning, Aunty Joyce shopped in the small mining town of Heanor, three miles to the east. She had not visited Derby for many years. Apart from a memorable day trip to Skegness on the east coast, more than a decade before, she had hardly been out of Horsley Woodhouse.

Her nephew intended to seek out a place he had heard of before. A place where he might find friendship among his own kind; the Turkish Baths on Reginald Street. An hour later he was standing in front of a nicely-proportioned, ornate, Edwardian green tiled frontage to the old baths. This consisted of the self-contained turkish bath suite and a separate area of individual slipper baths. These enormous Victorian versions of the domestic bath were still much in demand in 1965 for many British citizens who were without access to a private bathroom. In the weeks to follow,

Simeon often immersed himself into a wonderful sea of hot water. At one shilling and sixpence (7.5p) it was an affordable luxury for the itinerant chicken. In addition, on a number of lucky occasions, it offered much more than just a chance to get wet, warm and clean.

Entertaining such hopes on this first visit, he entered the musty, comfortable-smelling foyer and paid the expensive five shillings entrance fee to the kiosk lady of the Derby Turkish Baths. This price kept out many scruffy youths of his ilk. Consequently, the exotic halls within were occupied by older, well-spoken, flabby professionals and those who were older still; the soft, the shapeless and the retired. Through an ancient and expensively crafted oaken door, the carpet became thicker and so did the atmosphere. Here was the silence and restfulness consistent with a gentleman's club in London. This was a scene of deep maroon. Lush curtained cubicles, gently decaying, had seen better days earlier in the century.

At the end of this plush hall sat two elderly and slightly shabby attendants, lazily sipping tea. The cantankerous, ever-complaining Charlie was bald and plump. Fred, whose mission in life was to do as little work as possible, was tall and gaunt. Since Simeon was assessed as a 'too young to tip' bather, his ticket was received with little interest. He was vaguely directed to strip in one of the individual curtained cubicles. Taking in the air, warm and scented with damp towels and cleanly scrubbed white flesh, he became aware of pale shapes silently moving around, with interested eyes measuring his progress. Like most young first time visitors, he was a touch shy, carefully covering nether regions with a towel.

Leaving the dry hall of curtains and beds, he went through a Turkish arched door and into a 'Cecil B DeMille' set. Suddenly all was wet and warm, an area of hissing steam, fountains and echoing running water. It was like an ancient Eastern temple dedicated to the god of pleasure and sensuality. In sharp contrast to the cool wet public street, with its fully dressed conventions of just minutes before, here was a delicious eroticism, born of naked freedom in this tropical, special, secret world just yards from the gloom and rain of Derby outside. A sudden great splash echoed around the tiled central area. It announced a large gentleman who had taken the 'cold plunge', a small pool barely large enough to allow for a very short swim. He emerged from the depths, dripping from his bald head, smiling encouragement to the newcomer in the hope that he might discard the towel and follow the example. But a warmer experience beckoned. Simeon decided to investigate the bijou, cosy steam room.

An angry, gurgling, hissing seemed to emanate from the deep subterranean depths of Derby as he walked into an opaque blinding fog of hot steam. Through the grey haze, just for a moment, he thought that he had seen a quick movement. Fleshy parts appeared to quickly disentangle somewhere just beyond the dim, limited visibility in the light of a dull, amber, low-powered bulb. A few moments after groping for a spare seat, his eyes gradually became accustomed to the nebulous atmosphere. Peering into the vapours, he could hazily discern the vague outline of these naked lords of lard who, in British tradition, exchanged no words at all. Ostensibly they were indifferent to his presence and each other, but an instinct told him that the arrival of a young, unknown face had been noted - and noted well. On such a cool day the heat felt good, penetrated his bones and caused him to sink into a lethargic reverie. The daydream was interrupted by a toe!

Out of the mist at the end of a leg, was a foot with a toe which was touching one of his own toes. If it was an accident it would have been quickly withdrawn. But this toe was persistent in its search to meet other toes. Toe to toe, he had to consider his position and decide a plan of action. Should Simeon see this development as an outrage - or an opportunity? From a brief survey of the males within, few appeared to be under 50 years of age. Consequently, the chances of this particular digit connecting to a young Adonis were somewhere between slim and non-existent. As the toe continued in its naughty communication, he affected an expression of wide eyed innocence, at variance with the fact that his own foot had not moved an inch!

Simeon's mind went back to earlier in the year, when he was socialising with the boys in the S & C Coffee Bar in Uptown Detroit. This was the main venue for those under 21, who were not allowed to enter the main bars. He once mentioned to these young companions that he had visited the steam baths over the river in Windsor. They were horrified.

"The Vesuvio! OH NO! You go *there*!

"That place!" said another. "Old men! You have to be kidding. You *like* old men?"

He retreated into an offended sulky silence. Like most boys his age, Simeon certainly did not desire to get his hands on pot bellies or cuddle up to sagging breasts or allow a wrinkly old face anywhere near his own face. God forbid! But - he had already discovered that where beauty is absent, compensatory talent often came in abundance. The more hideous the server, the more exquisite the service. He soon learned that, in this particular culture of age intolerance to 'go with' anyone much over 25 was frowned upon. Thirty was definitely the top limit. To be seen with anyone approaching 40 would have meant social isolation and permanent exclusion from the S & C Coffee Bar. He was pushing his luck being seen with Lee.

Back in the Derby steam room, someone had opened the door to go out, which had slightly improved the visibility. With difficulty, he was able to glean a better outline of the mystery leg, which appeared to be connected to a soft, white, smiling ball.

Ten minutes later, Simeon Hogg was being treated to tea and toast in one of the several larger curtained cubicles which resided in the musty, fusty hall of faded maroon drapes. Each cubicle, a virtual room of limited privacy, consisted of two beds and a small bedside table between. All was quiet and calm, save for the gentle sound of munching delicious toast and the occasional clink of tea pot and cups. The boy was assessing his new-found friend, the soft, white, smiling ball reposing on the opposite bed, happily munching, after the style of an obese Roman Senator. He said his name was John, he had signed in as John, he was lying. Simeon liked John; most people did. The little fat man of so very soft skin - skin which had never seen the sunshine - spoke nicely through thick, feminine lips, carefully enunciating beautifully-rounded vowels. His ball-like head cocked from one side to the other as he listened intently to the candid boy giving full and frank details of his history to a comfortable stranger. Simeon was mesmerised by his large orbicular eyes and kindly style of rapport. Kindly or not, this teenager was also grateful that physical contact had never advanced beyond the touching of toes with this repulsive little fat man. The talking ball was now giving information about his secret world and was keen, very keen to show Simeon - 'the ropes'.

Chapter 10

Goblins, Gnomes and Fairies

Later that afternoon, it had stopped raining and they were motoring along the A6, heading north. With measured sentences, the fat driver continued to groom, to purr out his sage advice to the novice, the interested passenger who was reminded of a similar ride with Lee. But there the similarity ended. This was no gleaming 1963 Chevrolet Impala, this was a tiny, dark green, 1956 Morris 1000 and the plump driver (with his frequent soft, sibilant pronunciation of 'Simeon') was, effectively, almost a different gender to the all butch American Lee. If Simeon entertained any hopes that he would be delivered to a large talented Negro, he was in for a profound disappointment.

Becksitch Lane was tucked away in a craggy old part of Belper underneath Cow Hill. The ancient terraced houses were precipitously perched on a westerly-facing hillside in the Derwent Valley. At the northerly top end, the front gardens were narrow, steep and long. At the bottom end, the cottages became smaller, more humble with shorter gardens. Eventually, there were no gardens at all at a point where front doors opened directly onto the pavement.

The little car lifted several inches as Simeon and his recently-found rotundity alighted and walked straight through the door of one such humble cottage.

"'Allo, Dolly!" was the delighted, effeminate, falsetto response from the ugliest man Simcon had ever seen. "Ooo's this then? Ooo a say, Dolly, yav bin robbin' t' cradle!"

'Dolly'. It was perfect. Of course! It was the only name for this 'dolly tub'-like creature. The ugly inhabitant was introduced in a miasma of chuckles as 'Betty', the famous (or infamous) Becksitch Betty of Belper. His features and extraordinary colouring had the boy utterly transfixed. Discoloured skin was tightly pulled across a hideously sharp bone structure which would have made Betty's head an effective weapon. In the poor light of that tiny room, it was difficult to describe such a repulsive facial tint which, at times, seemed to be livid, at other times to be pallid, occasionally to blend into a most unhealthy grey.

They all sat down in a comfortable old-fashioned front (best) living room, which had seen little change since the previous century. The guests sank into a well-worn, two seater sofa, which dominated the small area. Man and boy were in close proximity, but the latter did not feel at all threatened. Thankfully, the leering host used the single seater.

It had been a separation of a few weeks and the two old friends had much news to exchange. In full spate of outpouring chatter, that horrible face was mesmerising to the young observer. In a lowly, common accent, the mouth contorted and distorted as it painfully heaved forth its words. In sympathy, the jaw deformed from side to side causing the full countenance to twist and writhe. The effect on the boy was curiously mixed. He was amused and yet repelled. Here was a quirky individual displaying a highly-mobile face of twisting, intertwining, constantly-changing expressions which Simeon was trying to read. He read kindness and understanding in the full, fat lips of Dolly, but detected a viciousness in the moving flesh, the kinks and warps of the unpleasant countenance of Becksitch Betty. It reminded Simeon of an anecdote he had read recently about Abraham Lincoln, who once refused to be introduced to a certain stranger who was nearby.

"How can you be so prejudiced! You don't know this man. You've never met him before," protested his political advisor. Lincoln was relying on his instincts.

"I don't like his face," responded the President.

"He can't help his face," said the other.

"Yes he can," insisted the President of the United States. "He's well over 40. Every man over 40 is responsible for his face."

Becksitch Betty was well over 40. To Simeon he seemed well past 60 but Dolly, more experienced in these matters, had judged that this drag queen had probably not quite reached the big six. Both visitors were in for a big surprise when the truth was revealed in the ongoing animated conversation.

"Ya know, Dolly, a shall be 50 next year! In tit awful? *Fifty!* Ooos goin' ta want a bloody owd 'ag like me? It's bad enough now. On Blackpool front, ya know, just top side at t' tower, ya know, were we go at night? Well, young ones can be nasty. One said ta me - 'Bugger off ya camp owd cow! Wot you come 'ere for? Is it pensioners night then? Ya'll get nowt 'ere. Sod off ya ugly bastard.' Well, it's not nice is it, Dolly? An me on me 'olidays as well. Wot's 'e laughin' at?"

Simeon was shaking, practically in tears of mirth.

"It's not bloody funny," continued the effeminate whine of Betty. "It's all right for you laughin' now, an only 16, but just you wait 'till *you're* pushin' 50 like me, an tryin' ta pull a bloke. Ay oop, Dolly, is 'e queer?"

Dolly replied with impressive subtlety, using the oily phrase Francis Urquart would coin some 20 years later -

"I couldn't possibly comment, Betty. But I think he's a bit safer than 16."

More was said about the Blackpool vacation. 'Blaack-poouuwll', as Betty seemed to drag it out of a twisting contorted mouth. He had 'boarded' on the Albert Road at an establishment owned by one Dolly Clacket. This name alone made both visitors laugh out loud.

"Oh yes, a know it's like t' Music 'all," continued Betty, also enjoying the joke. "Albert Road in't like t' owd days, ya know - 'Saturday to Saturday - ten in a bed'. No. Dolly Clacket does me three or four days if she's got room. Nice place, good snap. [food] That's all ya want intit? Ya only want a bit a comfort an a bit a nice snap."

Dolly Clacket? Simeon had heard the name before somewhere but, couldn't quite recall where. Having been out of Derbyshire for nearly two years and having become attuned to American speech, he was continuing to be enthralled and entertained by the roughly-spoken tones and curious accent of his host. It featured a total absence of the 'H', and 'the' was diminished to a faint hint of t'. A thick, strong, closed 'U' turned a word like funny into 'foonny' and bugger became 'booger'. This was the familiar language of his boyhood, the language of Horsley Woodhouse but, as spoken by this quaint pantomime dame, it came over as much more exaggerated and sounded somewhat antique, as if echoing a much earlier period of local history which would be, sadly, lost with the eventual death of Becksitch Betty.

The small room, very Derbyshire, had a comfortable, quaint simplicity. Darkened by small heavily-curtained windows, a blazing fire shot out a cheerful warm orange illumination.

"Nice fire," complimented Simeon."

"Could be better," replied their host. "Woodside 'ards!" (a cheap type of local coal) "Like tryin' ta burn bloody slate! Grey as me granny's 'air. That loose bitch next door gets Derby Brights .. " (the best local coal) " .. for nowt." [nothing]

This last precipitated a tirade against Betty's neighbours and his personal assessment of the social scene of lower Becksitch Lane.

"She stands need ta go on about *my* morals. She's 'ad bloody coalman, dustman ... nowt but a tart - dirty cow! She's 'ad more prick than a second 'and dart-board. *Criticisin' me!* A cut off all 'eads of 'ere daffodils. That's what a bloody did. That'll learn 'er .. callin' me ta that dotty bugga other side, ya know, 'im as keeps piddlin' 'is bloody dotty toes. An 'er filthy kids! They run round with their knickers droppin' down. And that fat lass that stinks, one tooth black, one wobblin'. What's up we 'im?"

Once again, Simeon was trembling with laughter. Even his much-loved Aunty Gerty, a leading character in Horsley Woodhouse, could not have equalled such a splendid performance. Both guests, however, took note. Becksitch Betty, when crossed, was capable of a spiteful act; vandalising the garden of a neighbour. The old queen ranted on -

"Can't keep 'er bloody legs closed." Dolly looked suitably shocked. "Big family .. yes. All ignorant as pigs. She feeds 'em boiled bones ya know .. oo are, an little 'n in t' chair, like a bloody monkey. 'Eee is enjoyin' them bones,' she sez. An grandma sitin' there, all bloody day, daft old bogga, three sheets ta wind, red face, piddlin' scabs on 'er legs, veins stickin' out, six bloody chins ... "

The show cantered on apace, continuing to hold the boy's attention. Eventually, Dolly steered the subject away from neighbours. With some difficulty, he was trying to persuade Betty to visit a certain Mr Toad.

"Ooo a don't know, Dolly. 'e never speaks ta me. 'e looks grotesque. 'e does!" This hilarious spectacle of the hideous passing judgement on the hideous caused Simeon to eject an involuntarily shriek. "It's right! 'e looks just like a toad: ugly as bloody sin. 'av ya seen 'im, Dolly, in that 'orrible car?"

"Oh yes, I've told him to get a different car, if only to change the number plate - for cottaging you understand."

"Lives in them smelly lavatories," said Betty, addressing the remark to Simeon.

"That ugly little car doesn't help," continued Dolly. "It's the pugnacious way he's huddled over the wheel. It rather suits him actually. It looks like a slug."

"Toot toot! Toot toot!" added Betty by way of sound effects. "You've ta get out t' way before 'e knocks ya out."

"Oh yes, he *does* like his tooter. All part of his pushy personality you know."

Eventually, Simeon gathered that it was the pupils of the Herbert Strutt Grammar School who had, many years before, christened their odd little Music Master 'Mr Toad'. His real name was Aubrey Pod. According to Dolly, Mr Pod was not only a very talented musician but he had other delightful talents to offer.

"But you should let me introduce you to him, Betty." Dolly's voice dropped an octave and became conspiratorial. "It's not what he looks like, it's what he can *do* for *you*, Betty. Now then!" This last, was uttered in a deep purr of strong significance as the fat man, with wide, orbicular eyes, head cocked to one side, advised his friend after the style of a parent giving sage advice to a child. To emphasise this wisdom, Dolly raised up his index finger.

"How many times have I've told you? What do they say about Mr Toad? I've told him myself: 'You were on the front row when they were given out'. He's especially good at what *you* like, Betty."

Becksitch Betty was getting interested. His body writhed in anticipation. His face twisted. His crooked mouth became gymnastic.

"Ooo a say! A sometimes think, Dolly, eee, if somebody 'd just give me one - ooo it 'd be *grand* it would."

Simeon was appalled. At this point Dolly asked if he might visit the toilet.

"Ya know where it is in t' back yard."

As his ample form ponderously moved through a primitive creaking door, the ugly old queen stood up, came over and sat down, very close to Simeon. In fact, too close, *much* too close to Simeon on that sofa; so close, that he felt his flesh crawl with utter revulsion. And then it happened.

"Ooo, a bet you're a big lad!" This, as his hand dropped on the boy's thigh and groped further in and further up. Simeon quickly disengaged, jumped up and took shelter behind the sofa.

"Ooo, don't be like that. Let's 'av a feel," said the queen in a manoeuvring, scheming tone, now prowling to the back of the settee, hand outstretched, all ready for his intended rude grope. At the point where the predator, stalking clockwise, had reached the back of the obstacle, the prey had retreated back to the front. For a moment there was a stand-off. The chicken stood his ground, eyeing the harpy, for a harpy it was. The dame had become a loathsome, voracious monster with a harridan's head. Outstretched hands were threatening like talons.

"Don't be shy. Come on, come 'ere, let's 'av a feel. Let's see wot yav got."

He continued clockwise - so did Simeon. Becksitch Betty increased his speed - so did Simeon. The scene became ludicrous, rather like the Keystone Kops. The pursued chicken could almost hear the urgent tinkling of a piano, allegro, after the style of an old silent film with increasing tempo, when the evil villain is chasing a distressed maid; round and round, faster and faster - until it stopped. Dolly was back in the room.

"Now, now boys! Dignity."

Original places were resumed. Once again the conversation took off and went into a gallop. References to a selection of strange people became mind-blowing. Something was said about 'Nobby the Gnome' warning 'Jasper the Goblin' that the cast iron urinal at Bridgefoot was being watched by the police.

"Must tell the Toad," said Dolly.

Toads, goblins, gnomes and this bizarre pantomime dame. What sort of a weird world had this boy stumbled into? It made America seem so normal, and yet ... less interesting? Had Detroit been black and white? Has the movie now changed to colour - like Dorothy who stumbled into the Land of Oz? As Simeon struggled to focus and make sense of his new environment, he had to consider the comparisons as well as the contrasts. The two gay worlds of Detroit and Derbyshire were different, but they also shared similarities. Homosexual men needed to hide their homosexuality on both sides of the Atlantic. It was relatively easy for butch American types such as Lee. Lee's sexual orientation was invisible to everybody; everybody except the occasional chicken during the occasional hunt. At all other times, he was invisible. He would be careful to mention girlfriends in the staff-room and exchange lewd jokes with 'the guys'. His true self was seen when he wanted it to be seen. In the same way, the ghost of Billy Bigalow became visible when he wanted to be seen by his daughter.

"Who is 'the goblin'?" asked Simeon.

"Oh definitely not suitable for a young lad such as yourself, *much* too frightening," said Dolly, in warm sexy tones, waving a podgy finger of warning. "Tinker Bell's never been the same you know! No. It was since that dark, foggy night last November. You might recall it, Betty, when I took him to see Jasper in his old cottage."

"Shire Oakes?" said Betty.

"No. One of his public lavatories. I'm not telling you which one, but it was his favourite. It's very old with several loose bricks which can be removed - conveniently. It was a peace offering, really. I needed to get Jasper back into the freak show, my tour of ugly old queens, you know. But it all went wrong."

"Who is Tinker Bell?" asked Simeon.

"A little fairy," answered Dolly with a twinkle.

Dolly went on, tongue in cheek, to narrate a short horror story about a pretty little queen with golden curls and a hideously deformed old man called Jasper Wormall who sat, for hours, in a crumbling old cottage. He was like a ghastly spider, humped and bent, patiently waiting for its prey. The young lad was being initiated on one of Dolly's famous tours of Victorian toilets. It was a little after eight when man and boy left the main shopping area and turned into an ill-lit alley. The cold fog seemed to thicken as they turned again into some sort of narrow, dark jitty. High walls, blackened by decades of industrial dirt were barely visible in the impenetrable murkiness and strange, dank quiet amplified their footsteps. Due to a sense of menace, the boy slowed, but Dolly urged him on with promises of exquisite pleasure, pleasure which was now very near, unseen pleasure, pleasure a plenty, lurking somewhere within the spectral vapour.

And there it was. Out of the cold, silent mist, there appeared the warmth of an ornate weak lamp which was more than a hundred years old. It announced the entrance of a primordial gentleman's lavatory. Dolly guided the novice past the ghostly outline of several dark, silent figures lined up at the urinal. There were three WC cubicles. The first two were closed and occupied but, in the faint dirty amber light available, it could just be seen that the door of the last one was ajar several inches. Gently, Dolly urged his young friend forward, placing him in front of that partly open door and gave it a soft push. The eyes of little Tinker Bell strained to adjust to the darker gloom of that cave-like entrance, to penetrate the night fog, to pierce the dismal depths, to discern, to make sense of that strange crooked shape within. In that silent moment, a silence which seemed profound, there came, from inside that cave to the boy's ear, a short sound, a sort of 'click'.

"Did you hear that?" whispered Dolly. "Lucky boy!" The click of a crone. It's the prelude to pleasure," sighed the little fat man in soft, round vowels. "Advance! Yield! Offer yourself to this master of the extended orgasm, give yourself - and know *true* bliss," he lisped rather theatrically into the youthful ear.

But an instinct told Tinker Bell to stand his ground. He felt grateful for the protection of his strong, form-hugging blue jeans and had different values with regard to the choice of a sexual partner. Having barely turned 15, this alluring child had a romantic inclination and dreamed of meeting strong, masculine boys who had a full set of beautiful white natural teeth. On this tour, he was hoping that Dolly would push him into the arms of a strapping young footballer of firm straight body, a footballer with no hump. Or, alternatively, a virile coal miner of rough manners who would not be too gentle and would 'bend him over t' bog'.

Alas, as gradually became clear, this particular bog was not inhabited by a footballer, a miner or even a young minor such as Tinker Bell of the dainty golden curls. There *was* a man in that bog, but not the man this little queen would have chosen. It started with two points of reflected lecherous amber light, gleaming with lewd intent which, as the boy's eyes continued to adjust, eventually revealed two grizzled leering eyes - horrible to behold. These deep, salacious sockets were set behind a rough-hewn beak of a nose, thrust forward, bent forward in eager anticipation of the juicy morsel at hand. Out of a drooling slash of toothless mouth emerged a snake of oscillating tongue, inviting, beckoning, urging its prey to enter, to be caressed, stroked, slurped and finally drained with oodles of Jurassic slobber.

But it was all too much; too much for a pretty little fairy! The dark, the fog, the sudden horror of being confronted by that grotesque goblin who dwelt within his murky cavern. It caused a sudden panic. Tinker Bell let out a shriek of terror and fled that toilet as if the very devil were at his heels. Such a cry gave great alarm to other loiterers who quickly departed.

"Spoilt it for everybody else," concluded Dolly, sadly.

"Silly queen!" snapped Becksitch Betty.

"Spoilt it for himself," added Dolly. "He could have had a marvellous time. I would have taken him to be serviced by others, lots of others - the toad, the gnome, Toby Jug, the dalek on York Wall and Stan in his shed.

"Don't waste ya petrol on the stupid bitch. Ad 'ave slapped 'er bloody chops!"

"Jasper Wormall was furious," said Dolly. "Naturally, the cottage emptied instantly. It was as if a policeman had walked in."

It was like a tennis match. Simeon looked from the fat face to the ugly face, back to the fat face, back to the ugly face - as the gossip continued to bounce about.

Toads, goblins, gnomes and fairies. Detroit had offered nothing like this. Toads were difficult to see and it was impossible to see goblins or gnomes since they did not exist any more than fairies existed. Fairies. Simeon recalled Duck. Duck often took him to the Belper River Gardens some fifteen years before. To a small boy it was a magical experience, made all the more magical as interpreted by a caring and imaginative adult. Plump, cosy Duck, he was always kind and considerate. Duck was so named because he always called the child 'dook' and that name seemed to blend with the cushy, downy personality of this odd, ductile chap who always made him feel safe, secure and loved. Man and boy would explore the old osier bed alongside the slow, green River Derwent which had, in 1905, been transformed into a beautiful garden. It was a delight of glades, rock formations, alcoves, islets, avenues and terraces. Simeon enjoyed the contrasts between the open promenade, lovers' walk, the fish pond, the fountain and those special nooks and crannies, apparently known only to Duck. Here the imagination could run riot. There were rocks picturesque and rocks grotesque. The child was guided into hidden glades. Here he would see deep, spongy moss growing on damp boulders. Here he was entertained with stories about the 'little people', the fairies. Bright sunlight became dazzling bright green when reflected off the ubiquitous fern. Such unusual illuminations complemented various dank corners and black caves. Duck explained to little Simeon that if he had enough faith, if he tried hard enough, if he believed in the spirits of nature, if he was lucky enough, he might just get a glimpse of elementals in human form. The small boy was very happy. He recalled the warmth of the sun, the cool of the shade, the light and the dark, the scent of ramsons, the music of birdsong and the gentle coaxing voice of nice, cushy Duck, gentle Duck, but - he never did see the fairies.

Perhaps now, in 1965, at long last - he had found them.

Chapter 11

The Secret Life of Mr Toad

It was good to be outside that tiny cottage, enjoying fresh air, sunshine and exercise. Simeon had successfully dissuaded Dolly from motoring the short distance which was only a short walk up Becksitch Lane. In an effort to pay Aubrey Pod an impromptu visit, they made slow progress ascending the hill. Minutes later, a strange parked car, shaped like a slug, announced their arrival. It was at the foot of a long, steep and overgrown garden which, to scale, was definitely going to be quite a trudge. Looking up through gaps in the foliage, Simeon could just about discern the house of Mr Toad. It was an interesting trudge, slowly climbing the long flight of steps. The visiting trio were soon out of breath. They took a moment to rest and survey the impressive perspective.

At the age of 19, months are like years. It did seem to Simeon that he had been away from Derbyshire for 19 years rather than 19 months. He had been brutalised by the endless, cruel, unrelenting flat landscape of Michigan. Casting his eyes over the panorama before him was like balm, soothing, slowly seeping into and healing the soul. Distant green fields of the high Chevin surmounted the deeper green quarried woodland of Firestone Hill. Down below, numerous waterside alders sporting new light green foliage, tantalisingly obscured the River Derwent, but for a few short, shimmering stretches. It was all magnificent. The boy was happy to be back home. The river put him in mind of Kenneth Graham's funny little character Mr Toad and he wondered about the quirky music master he was about to meet. When they finally arrived at the very top, puffing and panting, Simeon Hogg was not disappointed.

The first sight of Aubrey Pod was never to be forgotten. Yes, certainly a toad. The pupils of the last ten years had christened him well. He looked like a toad. His exuberant bulging eyes, full of ardour, were set wide over a tight mouth which seemed more like a long crack. He inspired something of the repulsion, the aversion felt at the nearness of a reptile. Like Graham's Mr Toad, he was comical, eager, impatient and entirely puffed up with his own importance. Catching sight of the three visitors, the little creature ran, actually ran, to the already open door. He registered a childlike delight in that someone had come to call. Dolly, he recognised immediately, Becksitch Betty he ignored and Simeon (being forced to retreat several steps) was all but physically consumed on the spot.

"Oh! Hello! Hel-lo! And what's *your* name, young man?"

Simeon's retreat was of no avail. An avid toad face was pushed up hard against his own, causing him to suffer an assault of foul breath. The interrogation rapidly continued, so rapidly indeed, the boy could not find a gap in which to make a response. Dolly came to the rescue, calming the atmosphere with soft sibilance.

"He's my new friend. His name is Simeon. And this is Betty, the entertainer, the one I was telling you about."

Aubrey Pod's enthusiasm collapsed as quickly as it had originally exploded. He slunk back slightly, being forced by common civility to note the presence of an ugly old queen, an ugly old queen he knew well. The term is 'familiar stranger'. Mr Pod was slightly embarrassed during this moment, the moment of having to meet formally, acknowledge and speak to Arthur Bestwick - the real name of Becksitch Betty. As familiar strangers, they had met many times before, often as rivals at the Derby Turkish Baths and at some notorious public toilets. They had met even more frequently in Belper's King Street, but the respectable schoolmaster had studiously avoided eye contact and conscientiously avoided any social situation which, God forbid, might risk an exchange of words with a well-known homosexual. Aubrey did not want anyone to think *he* was like that.

It has always been in the nature of many gay men that they think 'nobody knows'. Everybody knew about Aubrey Pod. The staff of the Derby Turkish Baths, they all knew. Toilet attendants knew. The congregation of Christ Church, where he had been the organist since 1937, they knew. The shopkeepers on King Street, they knew. The staff and the more perceptive pupils of the Herbert Strutt Grammar School, they all knew. Aubrey was not only effeminate, he was also odd. He was a funny little man with goggling toad eyes who, unable to maintain discipline in the classroom, suffered the chronic pain of a daily assault on his dignity. Girls were especially cruel.

Aubrey Pod was a good teacher for those who were disposed to avail themselves of his ability, to those few pupils who would sit still, listen and accord him due respect. Alas, such pupils were in the minority. In the 21st century, when society became more enlightened, more interested in hearing the secrets of the twilight homosexual world of the mid-20th century, Simeon Hogg penned several biographies, histories about gay men in Derbyshire. He used his personal experiences. He used his memories. He interviewed contemporary eye witnesses and compiled all this data to explore the details of the quirky characters he had discovered in 1965 - Becksitch Betty, Jasper Wormall, Simon Tonks, Guzzly Granddad, Dolly, Nobby the Gnome, Claud Hoadley, Hilary Raymond Hawley, Clarence Soames and especially Aubrey Pod. For the most part, these sexual eccentrics were treated in the text with empathy and sympathy. A common aim of the author's work was to show the reader what happened to fearful, secretive men who became warped by the unforgiving attitudes of an oppressive and bigoted heterosexual majority. Hogg posed the question -

'What does it do to a man when he spends his whole life denying himself? What happens to a man who has spent a lifetime repressing his sexuality? Is this similar to the African-American who tries to deny his true colour?'

The Secret Life of Mr Toad, published in 2020, was highly entertaining and a huge success. Women in their 60's, 70's and 80's related hilarious anecdotes about poor Mr Pod, who was often made to play the fool; poor Mr Pod, struggling to keep order at the Herbert Strutt Grammar School.

"I can see it now, on the school stage in the hall - Mr Toad conducting. There he was, knees bent, arms wide in exaggerated sweeping motions, beating time high on the platform ... "

"That's right, all puffed up, full of self importance ... "

"Do you remember when he sent us out for mucking about?"

"I do! You, me and Sheila."

"We went to the back of the stage, we did, found the curtain winding mechanism and ... "

At this point they collapsed in a heap of giggles, recalling how they closed the stage curtains, obscuring the music master from his class amid an uproar of laughter. A ridiculous spectacle - a silly little man extinguished by eclipsing drapes. The girls of the Herbert Strutt Grammar School certainly knew how to wind up Mr Toad. Aubrey Pod made matters worse by chasing the culprits along the corridor. They escaped into the girls' lavatory where he banged on the door, demanding that they should come out - at once. Another Belper woman described his temper.

"D' you know, he was just like one of those puffer fishes! He'd turn bright red, blow up like a balloon and let loose a squeal like a little girl." This witness suddenly lost her smile and looked troubled. "Of course ... we were young. It was great fun at the time - I suppose. Poor Mr Pod. We were too cruel. We must have made him very unhappy."

Chapter 12

Shell Bay, Bournemouth

But on this day, Wednesday, June 2nd, 1965, Mr Pod *was* happy. Mr Pod was full of hope. He had been buying new clothes in an attempt to improve his image and his guests were treated to a fashion parade featuring various ensembles. Like an over-wound toy, Aubrey scuttled into his study and donned a creation which would, according to his own assessment, make him look much younger and transform his prospects in the gay pubs, trolling areas and cottages. After a few minutes, he emerged wearing tight blue jeans and a black leather jacket. Unfortunately, it was a *toad* wearing tight blue jeans and a black leather jacket. Simeon Hogg would look back on this afternoon as being one of the most amusing of his whole life; more amusing even than his favourite Tony Hancock or Kenneth Williams - but, this was real! Aubrey Pod - excited, gesticulating, mincing up and down before his small audience - actually believed that this investment would enhance his chances of landing the man of his choice. The jeans (as jeans are supposed to) faithfully followed the contours of his repulsive belly and revolting bottom. If not actually fat, this soft and flabby 32-year-old was hideously formless after a lifetime of despising exercise, attacking large, greasy breakfasts, wolfing down unwholesome sugary cakes and sweet tarts for tea. The scene before them was both hilarious and pathetic when the optimistic Aubrey said -

"What do you think? Does it help? Of course," he looked straight at Betty, "I realise there comes a time when *nothing* helps."

Dolly whispered to Simeon -

"I think that time has come!" Aloud, tapping his fleshy cheek, he addressed his host in meditative tone, "I think, perhaps, dark glasses to complete the picture; yes, dark glasses, the mysterious look, you know."

Thus encouraged, the little man scampered back into the study, urging his guests to be patient and prepare for a second ensemble, another impressive display. This was the signal for Dolly to become mischievous. He urged Becksitch Betty to follow Aubrey into his study.

"Go on, he's got his clothes off now, get in there, quick!"

"Ooo. Should a? D' ya think so?"

"Yes! Now! Quick!

Simeon was staggered that anyone (even the revolting Becksitch Betty) might wish to have sexual contact with someone quite as repulsive as Mr Toad. Indeed, if the boy's true values and inclinations were clarified, he found it difficult to imagine any two males beyond teenage years genuinely desiring each other. To Simeon Hogg, late forties was much the same as death warmed over, but, ever the rascal, he saw comic potential and exploited this playful scene. He supported Dolly and urged Betty to seize the moment.

"Go on, Betty. He's dying for it. Get in there quick!

Seconds later, the drag queen was out of sight and they heard his camp and common enunciations drifting from Aubrey's study -

"Do ya want any 'elp, Aubrey?"

"No I do not!" came the sharp and rather annoyed response from Mr Pod, suddenly finding his privacy invaded by such an appalling creature.

"Are ya sure?"

"I am certain!" snapped the irate toad. "Go back into the living room."

Betty returned. He was downcast and rejected, only to be assailed by more urgent urgings.

"Don't give up," encouraged a smooth, optimistic Dolly. "He's still undressed, get in there and get busy - go on - quick!"

"That's right," chimed in Simeon and, recalling advice once given by school chums, "'No' really means 'yes'. Get stuck in. Take him by surprise. Hurry up!"

Emboldened by this strong vote of confidence, Becksitch Betty returned to the front line for yet another assault.

"Let me 'elp ya, Aubrey. Ya seem ta be strugglin' we them underpants. Let me joost put me 'and .... "

"LOOK! Stop it! Just stop it will you. I've told you once. Keep your paws to yourself ... no .. no," exclaimed the outraged and struggling toad.

Back in the living room, the other guests were hugely entertained, falling about laughing. This ceased abruptly when an embarrassed, battle-scarred

Betty emerged and retreated to the safety of the sofa. But the show must go on and it did, when Aubrey Pod made his second appearance, donning the very latest trendy beachwear for attractive young men. There was just one problem: a shapeless toad-like form had been shoe-horned into the small sexy shorts and the snappy shirt of exotic blooms was putting intolerable stress on the front buttons. The whole effect amounted to a joke: a joke after the style of an old fashioned sea-side post card.

"They'll go wild when they see you in that get-up at Shell Bay," said Dolly, with twinkling eyes barely concealing the sardonic gleam. This was a reference to the English equivalent of New York's Fire Island. A short distance from Bournemouth, Shell Bay was an ecstasy of sand dunes located behind the broad, sun-drenched beaches of (the appropriately-named) Studland Bay. Naughty men, often naked, predators and prey, would lurk in these hollows, behind small hills, trying to avoid being cut to pieces by the razor-sharp marram grass. Aubrey, a sun-blotched blob, constantly scuttling from dune to dune, was a familiar sight in that sandy scene. He was the butt of jokes. He was constantly being 'sent up' by annual regulars, such as the Nottingham crowd, Tommy and Martin and their extensive entourage. He was conscientiously ignored by the insouciant young, the indifferent beautiful, whose desirable skin would gently bronze under a kind, cloudless sky. But, the hot south coast sun warming the Atlantic Ocean was never kind to the milky, repulsive, slug-like sensitivity of Aubrey's skin.

"I have to keep well covered up," he was saying to his guests. "I don't go brown, I burn and go all blotchy. Anyway, I've learned the secret of success at Shell Bay!"

"What's that?" asked Dolly.

"Keep your clothes *on*," replied Aubrey.

"Oh *very* wise," purred Dolly in an octave lower with suggestive irony and a quick wink for Simeon. "I suppose you managed to actually arrive there last week?"

This last was a reference to Mr Pod's half-term spring holiday in which he always visited Bournemouth and stayed at the sumptuous Norfolk Hotel, a central location which conveniently incorporated 'a pub for queers'. During the previous year it was a great mystery, the talk of gay circles - the toad had failed to arrive at his hotel! What had happened to him? Arrested at a notorious toilet en route? Beaten up by 'queer bashers'? All was revealed when he returned to home territory, as ever, circulating with frenetic energy around the usual run of cottages in Derby and Nottingham.

He told Dolly about this eventful journey down to Bournemouth. He was feeling the call of a large, greasy fry-up and had discovered a seedy old transport cafe, near Ringwood, some ten miles short of his destination. The ugly little car gave several urgent toots and raced into a bumpy, unmetalled lorry park. The funny little man shot out, but was pulled up short by a shabby sign - 'MEN' - and promptly shot in.

"I can always tell if a cottage is ticking. The atmosphere was perfect - dirty, dingy and just two sit-downs - no problem with any competition. There was a hole between as big as a dinner plate! It was three o'clock and I sat there until nine when starvation *forced* me out."

He was so candid. It was this childlike honesty which always impressed Simeon down the years. A total contrast to the pretentious types he would be meeting in the next few days. Aubrey Pod reminisced to his guests about that wonderful week, in which he sat, every day, next to that wonderful hole, in that wonderful lavatory. As usual, when telling of triumphs in excitement, the little arms would come up to shoulder level and podgy hands gesticulate with waggling fingers -

"I was never refused once! Lorry driver after lorry driver, van driver after van driver ... "

"Cock after cock," interrupted Becksitch Betty with tortuous mobile mouth, dragging the subject down to its lowest level. "I'll 'ave ta buy ya a bib for ya birthday."

"There was no point in me going on to Bournemouth," snapped the toad. "Why should I suffer annual abuse from those nasty young queens in the dunes when I can get *real* men in a toilet? There was a cheap bed and breakfast in Ringwood - quite adequate for my needs. I'm not ashamed to admit that I was back in that smelly cottage the next morning with sandwiches and two flasks of tea. You've to get there *early* before an old queen gets in. They won't budge once they get established - so I beat them to it!" he giggled and gloated.

"Holes can be very useful to some people," explained Dolly, using smooth round vowels.

"Too right!" replied Aubrey. "It wasn't a beauty contest in that toilet. Nobody wanted to see me. Nobody *could* see me."

"That were lucky," said Betty, with a touch of acid.

"They only wanted my mouth," retorted an irritated toad.

"You must understand," purred Dolly to Simeon, "Mr Pod supplies a much needed and valuable service to these butch lorry drivers ..." He broke off to respond to a sarcastic chuckle from Becksitch Betty. "Well, it's true. Some of them can get very frustrated - violent at times!" He looked at Simeon, coyly, with huge, serious eyes. "A young innocent like me ... well, I have to be very careful in a lavatory. My precious virginity could be at risk! They won't wait." Dolly's sensuous voice trailed off into a breathy whisper "Those men need urgent relief!"

"They got it!" responded a triumphant Pod, jutting his ugly head forward - with great glee.

"Wouldn't some of those men ... well, what I mean is ... wouldn't at least a few be there for the proper purpose?" inquired Simeon.

"Certainly," said Aubrey Pod. "That's when I had a tea break, or lunch, or afternoon tea, or high tea, or dinner. If you want to achieve anything in this world, you've to put in the time."

The young man was fascinated by Aubrey's highly individual and expressive body language. On the last - 'you've to put in the time', his arms came up to face level and, to give added emphasis to those words, he pushed out, to the listener, his open palms with all the art, all the grace, all the beautiful movement worthy of a minor ballet - albeit a comic ballet.

Simeon pressed on with further concerns regarding these highly-specialised and erotic techniques.

"How did those men ... how did they *know* what you wanted to do?"

At this moment Aubrey Pod went into his hunting mode and a silence descended on the small gathering, who were now giving full attention. The toady countenance re-shaped into a look of pure mischief. It reclaimed something of its younger form. It expressed an anticipatory cheeky grin of a spoiled brat; the brat which had been little Aubrey, many years before, the brat who used to kick the maid. Slightly, very slightly, he bent his head down to the level of an imaginary hole. Eager bayonet eyes fixed on something very exciting in the gloom, something rough and manly; a succulent tumescence located at a point beyond the hole. Slowly, crooked lips parted to reveal a slimy orifice. From the orifice emerged a stealthy tongue making crooked lips viscous in an unspoken lewd invitation. Dolly was amused. Becksitch Betty, with his very British anal orientation, was disgusted. To the Americanised boy, the whole effect was at once utterly repulsive and yet, utterly compelling. If his fussy friends back in the S & C Coffee Bar could have seen into his mind at that moment, indeed, into his trousers at that moment, he would have felt deeply ashamed. The S & C set would have seen Aubrey Pod as a piece of vile slime creeping across the ground - but to Simeon, oh no, Aubrey Pod was more than that - much more.

In the next few weeks Simeon Hogg found Aubrey Pod to be, quintessentially, the very essence of old-fashioned Englishness in its purest form. Aubrey was as salty and as vulgar as a seaside postcard. The best times in Simeon's life would not be sitting in the S & C Coffee Bar in Uptown Detroit in the company of intolerant chickens. No. The best times would be spent with his dear old friend Aubrey Pod, being tossed and blown about on the North Sea on board the Bridlington Belle. Aubrey was quaint. Aubrey was funny. Aubrey was a bundle of fun. Aubrey was a barrel of laughs. He represented an amusing character in caricature - perhaps one of the last of the type. He did not know it at the time, but for Simeon Hogg, these precious hilarious moments were the beginning of a lifelong friendship with Mr Toad, nay, a love affair; a love affair which would last for the whole of the remaining 20th century and into part of the 21st century.

Chapter 13

The Consultant Surgeon

Thursday was fine and dry. Simeon went to Belper and paid £20 for a brand new Hercules bicycle. Friday was wet, so he took the bus to Derby and paid a second visit to the Turkish Baths, where he met James Mason. Well, David Bond *looked* like James Mason.

On that busy afternoon, the cantankerous attendant Charlie was more irritated and irritating than usual, and, as usual, being extremely rude to Mr Pod. Yes, Aubrey Pod, feeling the call of fleshly pleasures, had feigned illness to be able to attend the steam baths. The headmaster of the Herbert Strutt Grammar School was beginning to notice that Mr Pod's migraine attacks usually occurred on the cool wet afternoons of Monday, Wednesday and Friday. Tuesdays and Thursdays were ladies days at the Derby Turkish Baths.

"I'm sorry, sir," Charlie growled at the insistent toad, sinking deeper into his chair. "You'll just have to wait for your tea and toast. It's *our* tea break at the moment - as you can see."

A few minutes before, Mr Bond had requested egg on toast for two and tea for two.

"Certainly, Mr Bond," said the fawning bald rotundity with a quick salute of forefinger raised to eye level. Even the indolent and taciturn Fred would stir himself to oblige Mr Bond, the eminent consultant surgeon, one of their regulars, a generous-tipping regular. So very different to Mr Pod, who would only tip under extreme duress, such as occurred during the end of his last visit, when he was attempting to creep out.

"Excuse me, sir," said Charlie in an arresting knife-edged tone which held more reprimand than civility.

"Yes?"

"Have you enjoyed your Turkish bath?" The tone had become sardonic.

"Err ... yes."

"Everything's been satisfactory?"

"I suppose so ... "

"Well, *do* the usual, sir!" pointing to a tin containing an assortment of silver coins. "It *is* customary."

Aubrey Pod fumbled through his small change, selected the smallest silver coin and reluctantly tossed a sixpence into the tin. The lascivious toad was in no position to complain about Charlie and Fred, who were as permanent and as immovable as the Arabic decor. They had been in the service of the Derby Turkish Baths since they had left school nearly half a century before. A few naive men would wonder - 'Do they know?' Of course they knew! And they took full advantage of that knowledge. They were fully aware that the vast majority of bathers, the 'regulars', were homosexual. These attendants, working class boys from the Edwardian age, were old-fashioned and took the view that a 'gentleman' was entitled to his privacy, to his secrets. During many moments over the previous fifty years they had occasion to turn a blind eye. Over those years, there were some unfortunate and embarrassing moments when mutual pleasure had been rudely disturbed in the course of their duties; appearing with tea and toast at the wrong moment, or walking into the steam room to adjust the heat at a crucial moment - on one shattering occasion - an orgasmic moment. Gratuities were very effective in keeping this grumpy, shabby old couple content and quiescent.

Of course, over the decades, the 'regulars' did *their* bit to help the attendants and the occasional Turkish bather who had paid his five shillings to luxuriate in a Turkish bath - and no more than a Turkish bath. On his first two visits, Simeon Hogg rapidly learned the skills and techniques of enjoying sex without embarrassing Charlie, Fred or any innocent heterosexual customers. Teamwork was helpful, such as a look-out who might suddenly develop a cough. Also important was knowledge of the visual geography. Anyone in the cool central fountain area, looking down the line of Moorish arches of the three hot rooms, could see right into the very end of the hottest section. Recumbent bodies of the two occupants in that last part were hidden. An observer saw two heads only, just the heads, keeping vigil. If the bather's lips were slightly parted, if he appeared to pant, if his face appeared to register subtle signals such as gratification, pure pleasure, perhaps contorting to ecstasy, *if* any of this were noticed by an outsider, an innocent - it would be put down to the heat. The observer would not be aware that other men, possibly busy men, ministering men, naughty men *also* occupied that end room. The opaque steam room was safer still. On crowded days the floor could become slippery and naked bodies acquired convenient lubrication from other bodies. Sometimes it was an orgy of hot steamy eroticism with some sitting, others standing - according to taste.

For the most part, all was well save for the occasional maverick whose excessive enthusiasm might put others in danger. Aubrey Pod, often described by Dolly as an over-sexed, over-wound toy, was such a maverick. He rushed around, as Jasper Wormall often complained, 'not meaning to miss anything'. He grabbed and groped, pushed and shoved, irritated and annoyed in a frenzy of energy expended on getting as much as he could in the shortest possible time. Aubrey was still the spoilt over-indulged child who insisted on instant gratification, never quite learning the rules of the game.

Later in the afternoon he finally came to rest, sharing a curtained cubicle with Sid, one of the few regulars who was prepared to be sociable with the toad. Sid was typical of his type; masculine, good-natured, indeterminate age and unremarkable appearance. In fact, Sid was invisible, a valuable attribute for a gay man in 1965.

"There's some nasty folk here today!" complained Aubrey.

"Why? What do you mean?"

"I've been pushed, slapped and punched."

"Oh dear! All in one day?" Since he rather liked Aubrey and wouldn't have hurt him, Sid tried to keep a straight face. "Monks and Muckles?"

"God, no! I don't go anywhere near those hooligans. No. I was pushed away by that rough thing with the tattoo. I think you said he was a plumber."

"Oh yes. He wouldn't want you. Chickens for that one. Did the spotty chicken slap you?"

"No! He did not. I nearly got him but for an unfortunate incident."

Aubrey Pod had been chasing the 'spotty chicken' around the baths all afternoon. Worn down by pursuit and taking into consideration yesterday's promise of oral delights, Simeon agreed to follow the instructions of Mr Toad.

"When I've gone, count to 30, go to the cold plunge, turn right along a narrow passage. You'll see a door marked 'Sun Lamp'. Just before you reach the door, look to your right and you'll see a small dark alcove - just big enough for *me* to fit in! I'll be on my knees," whispered Aubrey, with ardent anticipation and a gloating leer spreading across his frog-like face.

Dark alcove was the most appealing part of this indecent proposal. If the ugly amphibian could not be seen, reasoned the youth, he might be better enjoyed. Accordingly, Simeon started to count. Unfortunately, as he approached the cold plunge, Charlie forged ahead, en route to the sun room, which was also used as a store for clean towels. From the shadows, a kneeling, over-excited toad very nearly performed an act of gross indecency upon a cantankerous attendant, who was startled to see his most irritating customer in such an undignified and inexplicable position. Well, perhaps not quite 'inexplicable'. The music master's first thought was to elucidate. He would insist that, as a church organist, he was deeply religious and in need of occasional prayer in a quiet spot. But, since his toadal mouth was wide open at the time, that desperate thought died almost as quickly as it was conceived.

Sid laughed so loud he had to be shushed in that quiet curtained hall by a fellow bather. Aubrey continued the conversation in a whisper.

"Anyway, that chicken has expressed a desire to visit Bridlington. I *seized* the moment. I'm taking him there tomorrow." He became conspiratorial, leaning closer to Sid. Sid leaned further away. "I could have had him yesterday in my own home. Dolly brought him. And he brought that horrible Becksitch Betty. I had to fight him off!"

"Ooo, be careful of Mr Bestwick. Never cross *him*. He's dangerous, very dangerous. I once saw him take a knife to an expensive suit. Oh yes! It was just over there in that changing cubicle. Some poor sod who'd made a comment he didn't like. Vicious. A nasty piece of work. Keep away from that one."

"I've told Dolly to bring me chickens, but fancy turning up at the same time with such a hideous old queen."

"Arthur's only 49," said Sid with a smile.

"Becksitch Betty is 70 - and that's being kind," insisted the toad.

"Hey, make sure that spotty chicken isn't too young before you whip him away to the seaside with a bucket and spade. You know what happened to Mr Toad in the book don't you? They put him in prison!"

"He told me he's 19."

"Mmm. Could be. Could be 16. Could be less. Just be careful."

Two cubicles away, the spotty chicken was telling David Bond that, in spite of consuming a delicious egg on toast, he was still very hungry.

"We'd better do something about that," said the deeply-tanned gentleman of splendid body, in his soft cultured accent. Simeon was flattered by his interest and accepted an invitation to dine with the suave surgeon. It was clear to all that this urbane bather held himself aloof from the others. An extreme opposite to the Pod, Simeon had seen no evidence at all of his new friend showing even the slightest interest in any other man. David Bond had lazily glided from area to area with supreme indifference to the stressful plotting, stalking and hunting going on all around him. He had spoken to nobody, indeed seemed to notice nobody until, in the fountain area, Simeon heard a comment apparently addressed to the marble centrepiece.

"A rather pretentious display, don't you think? Definitely owing more to Hollywood than to anything genuinely Arabian. Quite incongruous in this failed effort to re-create the royal palace of Saladin."

At this point, the gentleman with the cut-glass accent turned a dark, handsome face to Simeon. "Perhaps we should start a jihad against bad taste."

He understood hardly one word. Notwithstanding, this uneducated working-class youth was mesmerised by the culture, erudition and pedantry which flowed over him. A pleasant interview followed in which man and boy introduced themselves and exchanged information. Feeling privileged, the lad politely addressed the gentleman as Dr Bond. The latter smiled and explained that, in his case, 'Mr' was correct.

"Anyway, formality is hardly appropriate in this place. My friends call me David."

David summed up Simeon's character and, on balance, felt that he was, perhaps, too candid, too naive, but at least appeared wholesome and trustworthy. As with Aubrey, this was the inception of a friendship which would span two centuries. Simeon would continue to be the link between the two very different men. During that long time, David continued to ignore Aubrey and Aubrey continued to be irritated by David's indifference.

Dressing was a leisurely affair in that soft, padded, rich atmosphere - the luxurious hall of curtains. Fellow bathers were discussed in hushed tones, for this boy, a steep learning curve.

"The toad? Oh yes, I saw somebody thump him. That pushy fool will get us all thrown out one day. I hope you managed to manoeuvre around him? You *did* repel his advances, didn't you?"

Obeying an ill-formed instinct, Simeon Hogg lied. He was ashamed of the lie and ashamed of his freakish desire to be touched and fondled by a toad. He claimed that he had not spoken to Aubrey Pod. A slight pause followed. Vaguely, Simeon observed that there was a greater mix of ages today than on his first visit. The new friend fixed him with a stern eye and warned of danger in this new, secret world.

"You'll recall the two rough youths who hardly left the steam room? They are known as 'Monks and Muckles'. God knows why! I don't think they have Christian names. From Chesterfield, it's said. Keep well clear! *If* you don't want to get involved with the police, that is." David became thoughtful. "Odd really. Nobody ever says Muckles and Monks, always Monks and Muckles. Oh well, keep well away. They're trouble, big trouble. Rent and worse."

He explained the meaning of 'rent'. Simeon found the word quaint. He understood prostitution under the American term 'hustler' but asked what David meant by 'worse'. The following discourse was quite shocking, even by Detroit standards. This amoral couple lived on their wits, occasional blackmail, occasional rent and the occasional proceeds of petty crime. He outlined a painful occasion when they tried extortion.

"They're both desirable, but, for my taste, Muckles has the edge. Rough and common, oh yes, a real honey trap that one. I never could resist freckles and red hair. It wasn't much, a fiddle in the steam room, that's all. They approached me when I was about to leave and suggested that the short interlude of pleasure, witnessed by Monks, was worth £5.

"Did you give it to them," asked a horrified Simeon.

"Do you know, I very nearly did - but for a welling up of instant outrage. I ignored the request and made for the exit. Menacingly, Monks blocked my path and, in a slightly louder voice, suggested that the police might be interested in the aforementioned incident, 'a lewd act with a young teenager'. Madness came over me. I heard myself agreeing with him. OK, I said, get dressed and I'll drive you both to the main Derby police station and we'll have a chat with the Chief Constable. As you wish, we'll discuss the alleged 'lewd act', together with a number of other incidents which I've observed. Such as an expensive leather jacket I saw you remove last week.

Oh yes, and what about that elderly gentleman, the one who regularly gives you money - for services rendered? No doubt. Go on then, get dressed. What are you waiting for?"

"And ... "

"And ... they slunk away", he sighed, "The whole thing left me depressed."

He looked it. At that moment he recalled his lifelong *bete noire,* the ugly reality of a homophobic society which gave power to such scum as Monks and Muckles; it had dogged him all his life. Just at that moment David Bond appeared sad, sagged slightly and looked all of his 47 years. Simeon felt empathy and outrage.

The moment passed and they were now both dressed. After a quick groom, David Bond looked taller and confident in his Savile Row suit. The dapper gentleman smartly padded over thick carpet and approached the two attendants, who were very comfortable, still sinking deep into ancient armchairs, enjoying their extended afternoon tea break. Charlie did his usual quick bit of flannel and arithmetic.

"Ready for the off, sir? I think it's stopped raining now. Amm, let's see ... egg on toast, twice 1/6 plus two teas which is twice 1/-, that's .. ah .. three and two ... amm ... five shillings in total, sir, if you please." His eyes eagerly followed David's hand which, from his pocket, scooped out a load of large, heavy silver coins. He tendered two half-crowns and then a third half-crown for the tip. Charlie's face lit up like a Christmas tree. "Thank *you*, sir. Thank you very much. Most kind."

Simeon was very impressed. These pleasantries were addressed directly to the affluent-looking professional. It was quietly understood by the attendants why this gentleman had taken an interest in the casual youth at his side, a youth young enough to be his son and, giving heed to a long-standing tradition of diplomacy, the youth was completely ignored. As the two bathers walked out of the plush hall of curtains, Charlie was heard to say to Fred -

"Lovely gentleman, Mr Bond."

"They seem to like you, David."

"A half-crown is very effective," replied the cynical surgeon as they left the building. "A good example of the current 'British Disease', those two; *appearing* to be busy some of the time, in reality, bone idle *all* of the time.

Chapter 14

Lea Gardens

Outside on Reginald Street, Simeon was thrilled to be led over to a large, stately motorcar, opposite the baths entrance. It was a Bentley. After a minute of expressing admiration for the coachwork, wood and leather interior, he offered David two shillings and a sixpence to cover his share of the bill, an offer which was firmly rejected. Two cars in front, two fellow bathers were getting into another motorcar which Simeon admired. It was the smaller version of the Vanden Plas 'R' with the Rolls Royce engine. This was the Vanden Plas 1300 made by the British Motor Corporation. David responded to Simeon's curiosity.

"Bob and Clarence, the Nottingham Camp, the enemy! We don't speak to them." He commented with a smile and a touch of self mockery: "A predatory couple."

"They didn't prey on me," replied Simeon, feeling pleased with himself that he had demonstrated the connection between prey and predation.

"Of course not. None of us could get near you for that confounded toad. Anyway, enough of the competition. Let's see." He looked at his watch. "Four thirty. Can you manage for a couple of hours before I feed you? You'll not pass out or anything like that? We'll consider the recent snack a late lunch. I hope you ate breakfast?"

Simeon explained that Aunty Joyce had provided a sparse fry up of bacon and egg, but, having mooched around Derby until entering the baths at 2.00pm, he had simply neglected to eat. Pulling out, they could see that the Vanden Plas had now departed and revealed the next car along, a hideous vehicle, patiently waiting for its frantic owner who would be staying in the baths until closing time. David noticed that Simeon was amused by such an unusual contraption.

"The man who designed that car should be shot. Ghastly! It looks like him. We call it the 'toadmobile'; quite well known. Sometimes it's here - but more often, parked outside public toilets. Take warning, young man! Leave that sort of dangerous activity to the rubbish of this world - such as these two fools."

The graceful Bentley was, at that moment, floating past Monks and Muckles walking along the pavement. They appeared to be having fun at the expense of a hapless old man making a slow, painful progress with a walking cane - '*Show* me what you can do with that stick!'

"Harum-scarum!" commented David, as the cruel remark drifted into the car.

"'arum ... what?"

"Harum-scarum; lacking a sense of responsibility - rash, reckless."

Once again Simeon was motoring north along the A6, this time first class. Again, it started to rain on a road still wet from the previous shower. David had declared his intention of showing the boy one of the little-known treasures of Derbyshire, a mystery destination which turned out to be located several miles north of Belper. The luxurious excursion, sailing along at a stately 30mph, gave an opportunity for the man to introduce his young friend to his new world, the covert society as it functioned at the professional level. He explained the terms 'Derby Camp', 'Nottingham Camp' and outlined the rivalry and animosity between the two social groups.

"All very sad really. So much back-biting, bitchiness and tittle-tattle. We've been daggers drawn for years. We should pull together and help each other. Living in Detroit, you'll know all about the Negro and his on-going struggle for equality. I admire Dr King. I wish him well. You and I, Simeon, are rather like Negroes. We're despised, feared, hated, loathed and mocked. Somewhere in the Bible it says we're an 'abomination'! Last week a Muslim cleric said we should be burned alive. We suffer. We suffer discrimination. We suffer prejudice and bigotry. We suffer all these things *if* they can see us. So therefore we hide - and they *don't* see us. Do you understand me, Simeon?"

"I think so, David." This line of thought reminded him of the conversation he had heard between Dolly and Becksitch Betty. References to a goblin and a gnome had stirred childhood memories of the fairies who were difficult to see.

"The Negro," continued David, "has no choice. His black face is there for all the world to see. He must deal with the problem. We can *avoid* the problem and most of us, the majority of us who are not effeminate, not too eccentric, not on public display - *do* avoid the problem. We hide."

"How?"

"My hobby is a garden pond; quite a large one. I'm proud of it. Very soon, on a fine day, a rather repulsive dragonfly larva will crawl out of the deep, dark slime and up the stalks of a reed into the sunshine. It'll dry out in the sun, discard its dull grey body and emerge as a bright, beautiful new dragonfly, a large, impressive insect. If I'm able to get away from the hospital on a warm bright afternoon, I go home and look into the reeds in an effort to see the new dragonflies and you know what? I see - nothing! I can't see them, but I know they are there. Do you know how I find them?"

Simeon was fascinated by this cryptic line of argument and very eager for David to bring his analogy to a, hopefully, credible conclusion. The driver's attention was consumed as the car turned right at Whatstandwell just before the road crosses the River Derwent. Immediately, under great pressure, the automatic transmission selected the lowest gear as the car laboured up a steep hill to a small bridge which crossed over the Cromford Canal. A sharp turn to the left took Simeon into a pleasant green darkness, one of his beloved leafy glades, all the more effective as the sun made a sudden appearance above the canopy. This was the very pretty and narrow Robin Hood Road which leads to the steeply wooded Leashaw Road.

"How do you find the dragonflies?"

"Very simple. I relax onto my garden *chaise longue*, which is placed next to the pond, and slowly wind down, sipping a large gin and tonic. The pond is well-matured now and I stare into the tangle of reeds. They're soothing, hypnotic, especially when they sway in a breeze; so quiet, so peaceful. It's my little piece of heaven. And ... and then it happens. My eyes drift across the jungle and, eventually, penetrate the camouflage. I learn to read the reeds. I begin to see the dragonflies."

Simeon was silent for a few moments as the car climbed ever higher to the top of the world. Emerging out of Bracken Lane, they came into Holloway, a lovely village sheltering under the crest of a wooded ridge. With care, David executed a sharp right up a precipitous narrow road called The Hollow. It was a feast of quaint, ancient stone cottages adorned with roses, possibly one of the prettiest sights Simeon had ever seen. The great car continued to climb still further, as it seemed, right up to the sky which at this moment, between showers, was deep blue and beautiful. Leaning over, the passenger began to savour magnificent views to the south, over the

Derwent valley, all rocks and trees. Nearer, his eyes travelled over the shaded gritstone walls, luxurious with deep moss.

"Like the fairies!" said Simeon.

"Pardon?"

"Dragonflies are like fairies. You need to be in a certain frame of mind to be able to see them. You need to be relaxed. You need to believe in them. Is that your point?"

"Something like that, I suppose. Go to Markeaton Park on a sunny afternoon, sit under a tree, get comfortable and watch people drift by. Eventually you'll see a pattern; some men glancing at other men, sometimes one will follow ... that sort of thing. Of course, the general public, the vast majority, see nothing at all. In that way we are ... invisible. We are safe."

An acute left turn took them northwards on to Long Lane, giving distant westerly views over Lea Bridge, along the river valley, up over the wooded Cromford Moor and on to Black Rocks beyond.

"Can we stop ... please!" pleaded the boy, desperate to get his fill of this sublime view and to taste the magic of Derbyshire here at the top of the world. The car pulled over, edging on purple bell heather, cowberry and bilberry, now sparkling from the raindrops of a recent shower under clean, clear sunshine. They left the car and hopped on to a large boulder of gritstone to take full advantage of the glorious panorama, all the more effective in these crystal-clear conditions of cool low pressure. This happy place was in dramatic contrast to an angry black rainstorm, on the horizon, drenching the far off town of Matlock. A profound peace was broken only by a single skylark. David smiled at his new friend.

"Come to think of it, you're rather like a dragonfly yourself."

"How'd make that out?"

"Well ... you were telling me about, as you put it, 'working-class' humiliations? You spoke of having no success with girls, how sexually frustrated you've been, about not fitting into the macho heterosexual scene and not being liked and how miserable you were in America. Time to put that behind you. Time to move on. You've discovered a new world. You've cast off the old body of the skinny adolescent. You've crawled out of the slime, out of the bottom of your heterosexual working-class pond and into the sunshine. You're about to spread your wings, Simeon. Just look at you! Everybody will want you now. Everybody will like you. This afternoon should have convinced you of that. They *all* wanted you."

"Even with these pimples?"

"Those pimples didn't seem to deter Mr Toad!" he laughed, "Don't worry about acne. Bathe your face in sunshine for about 30 minutes a day. Watch them disappear."

This was the best medical advice Simeon Hogg had ever received. Over the next few weeks he followed David's instructions. The sun, when it showed its face, dried up greasy skin and all those nasty spots ... they melted away.

"But a word of warning, Simeon. Dragonflies live for a few weeks only. It won't last. You'll not be 19 for very long. It passes very quickly, more quickly than you realise. Make the best of it."

Five minutes later, the car was rolling again, descending into what seemed like a tunnel, a dense woodland of beech, oak and birch. Soon the darkness gave way to sunlit brilliance on the left, a riot of colour in this beautiful woodland glade. They had arrived at the mystery destination, the promised, little known treasure of Derbyshire. David pulled up near the entrance of Lea Rhododendron Gardens which, at this time of day, were deserted. Clearly he was well acquainted with the lady who was just about to close up. It was all very friendly and informal as pleasantries were exchanged. A 'poor season' was drawing to its close, 'too much rain, too little sun', but today, it was 'looking quite good'. Simeon thought it was looking absolutely magnificent. This was the complete opposite of Detroit. It was the Garden of Eden and in this enchanted place, he could hear the heartbeat of Derbyshire.

David followed his usual route, first to the north and then west, down through a labyrinth of pathways weaving this way and that through Scots pine, yew, chestnut, oak and silver birch; a personal tour conducted with enthusiasm. He explained that they were, in fact, exploring the site of an old quarry, long since healed over by a rainbow of lovely rhododendron trees growing inside a sheltered micro-climate - an ideal position.

"Put your nose in that one. Sweet, isn't it." They moved on. "Here we are, my favourite - Loderi Pink Diamond. All this is the work of a local woollen manufacturer. John Marsden Smedley *started* creating this garden when he was 68 years old! An inspiration for us all, don't you think?"

"Is 'e still around?"

"God, no! But he had a good innings, over 90 when he died. Not so long ago. Five or six years? No more than that."

"Perhaps in a place like this ... you could live for ever," mused Simeon.

They reached an area where David selected a comfortable rock for a sit-down. Simeon wandered over to an old drystone wall beyond which, to the south, lay a wood of beech trees. He mounted a boulder to stare into this intriguing green paradise, broken up by bright spots of sunlight illuminating a carpet of fallen leaves. The sun seemed to be playing with him, playing tricks, creating interesting effects. Smooth grey trunks supported a canopy of gleaming, lime green leaves and, beyond, in a distant glade, a miniature forest of new bracken, wet and glistening with fresh rain, looked inviting. Loderi called him to look back into the garden. He caught the scent, one of a multitude of sweet scents, enhanced by the damp carried on gentle cool zephyrs. That same fragrant air was also full of the song of blackbirds. Some seemed to have rhythmic motifs. One in particular could be pictured as saucer shaped - up, down and up again - and so on. Another seemed to vocalise - 'Billy Fury' 'Billy Fury'. To change his views, Simeon changed his position by jumping around from boulder to boulder - all different; some upholstered with thick moss, some hairy, some bald and some decorated with flyaway fine grass. He took in splashes of colour, lavender, magenta, peach, tangerine and lots of whites - soft whites, creamy whites and those delicious whites which show a hint of lemon ...

"What do you want, Simeon?"

He had not noticed David, who had stealthily come up to his side, shattering this private reverie. The voice had startled him and, since he was not aware that his behaviour and countenance were so revealing, the question was slightly embarrassing. Notwithstanding, he attempted an answer, an honest answer.

"A want this. A want to stay in Derbyshire. A don't want to go back to Detroit."

The sun went in. It looked very much like another shower. They walked back to the car in silence.

Chapter 15

The Elite Derby Camp

Simeon Hogg had never fully realised that he was a scruffy chicken until he was standing in the plush reception area of the New Bath Hotel. In 1965, this rather posh and hushed foyer had that special British quality of making him feel inferior. No place or part of America, no matter how impressive or expensive, quite achieved the same effect. He often pondered the point. Perhaps it was because, in the United States, he was never 'working-class'. As long as you were white in Detroit, the population was covered by an invisible blanket of social equality. He was unable to rank a person's class by the way they spoke. The dustman spoke with much the same accent as the doctor. Both had a car, both lived in a nice detached house, both had a colour TV, both had a radiogram and both enjoyed all the conveniences of modern gadgets.

Simeon was uncomfortable. He looked uncomfortable, standing there in his jeans and favourite 'palm beach' shirt waiting for David Bond, who seemed to be taking an eternity in the gentleman's toilet. A smart-looking duty manager eyed the boy with suspicion as he descended an impressive staircase and made a silent, stately progress across the luxurious carpet and into the exclusive restaurant. A similar unwelcoming expression was worn by a elegant waiter who came out of that same restaurant and entered the bar. To Simeon's horror, the waiter returned and addressed him directly in a discreet and cultured whisper.

"Excuse me, sir. Are you intending to dine?"

"Well ... yes, but ... I'm waitin' for me friend an ... "

"Please don't think I'm being rude but, we do maintain a dress code here, and ... well, you see ... this *is* a rather expensive establishment. I don't wish to offend, but might I suggest ... "

"Hello! Problems?"

David Bond had appeared to find a furious friend and an embarrassed waiter who, in the seconds which followed, had a opportunity to take in, and assess, the cut of a Savile Row suit, highly-polished handmade shoes and a cut-glass accent.

"I must apologise," explained David, with firm confidence, "we haven't booked but we are both very hungry. As it's rather early in the evening, well, I did think ... "

"Of course, sir. No problem at all. Please follow me."

During the next ten minutes a humiliated and smarting Simeon grudgingly admitted that the soup was delicious, the service excellent and his surroundings were magnificent. Most impressive was a window seat giving views over the Derwent Valley which, in Matlock Bath, was more of a wooded ravine. The sun had returned with dazzling brilliance and was picking out interesting features on the face of a limestone cliff.

"You're to be presented at Court. I've just decided," said David, suddenly determined to rid himself of the ongoing sulk and simmering grudge still being nursed before him.

"Pardon?"

"The Court of Claud Hoadley - no less."

"Who is Claud Hoadley?"

"A product of his own imagination. Forgive me, I'm being very disloyal. In fact, I'm quoting Nottingham's arch-bitch Tommy Sperry - the best thing he's ever said, and, for that matter - the truth. We all dread the acid tongue of Tommy. His barbs usually hit home. He's both arch-bitch and arch-enemy. He and Martin run the Nottingham Camp. They are just as snobbish, just as exclusive, but ... well, perhaps not *quite* as pompous, pretentious or as downright cruel as Claud and his claque."

"What's a 'claque'?

"You must understand, Simeon, that I'm being very sarcastic and bitter this evening. I'm using you. I'm behaving rather badly; feeling sorry for myself."

At this point, the main course arrived. It was a visual as well as a gastronomic treat and definitely outside the experience of the ravenous boy who enthusiastically repeated 'yes please' over and over to the silver service waiter who was saying -

"Parsnips, sir? Courgettes? Croquette potatoes? Mangetout? Carrots? ... "

"A claque," explained David, "is a group of people hired to applaud. I'm doing 'a Tommy', I'm trying to paint Hoadley as being surrounded by an admiring group of fawning followers, the hangers-on - which is the simple truth. 'Claque' is not *entirely* fair, not accurate. In the case of Claud Hoadley, I regret to admit, the adoration is genuine. You'll see that for yourself when he kindly deigns to 'receive' you this evening at the Friary. Friday at the Friary - it's an institution, Hoadley disciples are 'commanded' to attend."

Simeon, mulling over the recent problem presented by his casual dress, was looking troubled and concerned. If he was to meet such a venerable figure as Mr Hoadley and his posh friends ...

"Is this ... Friary ... what *is* the Friary?"

"Now you must not worry. It's my bit of mischief. I'll look after you and I'll take the responsibility. It's much like this place, an expensive hotel with a very comfortable bar, finished in dark leather and dark panelling. Very dimly-lit; I doubt that anyone will be able to see you very well. Err ... I don't suppose you have a ... a suit? Perhaps a pair of nice shoes, that is, clean shoes?"

Somewhat unwillingly, Simeon gave David a brief inventory of his meagre wardrobe back at Horsley Woodhouse. He had another pair of blue jeans, another shirt, a bright red anorak and sexy short shorts for walking and cycling. He had no wish to own anything as drab and baggy as a suit. He made sure that all his clothes, as far as possible, revealed the contours of his body. Hence the importance of his 'palm beach' shirt, first acquired at the age of 14, now too small, too old and tatty - but greatly valued on the grounds that it fitted his slim frame. He took the advice of the S&C Coffee Bar set - 'Always wear pants with a tight fit, never, ever cover the ass. Ass is ace, ass pulls the chickens and ass drives the old guys crazy!'

It was just after 8.30pm when Simeon, with difficulty, reluctantly lifted himself out of a comfortable and commodious armchair in the corner of the opulent Georgian hotel lounge. It was also difficult to leave his large, now empty, second pot of tea surrounded by litter, evidence of consumed bonbons, the last traces of a meal to remember. Once again, the great car was sailing along the verdant Derwent Valley, now widening into meadow and distant woodland lit by a sinking north westerly sun.

"Hoadley will want to know all about the meal. Do *not* mention the two pots of tea and numerous bonbons! It'll incur his acute displeasure and we'll both be reprimanded publicly - you for being an ignoramus and me for allowing you to indulge in gluttony. He's a stickler for dining etiquette and correct procedure."

"What did I do wrong?" replied the youth, bristling with irritation even before he had entered the august 'presence' of Claud Hoadley.

"Nothing," breathed out the surgeon, with a heavy heart, "You did nothing wrong at all, but that pompous prat will point out .. " here David's voice became artificial and effected - "'A gentleman concludes a meal with coffee - never tea. The choice of tea betrays a taste of the lower orders.' *And* I'll get a right old rollicking for taking a youth like you to the New Bath Hotel. I can just hear it, he'll be spitting feathers - 'You have put us *all* in danger, David! It's well known that you move in *our* circles. Think of your own position if you will not consider us. You should have known better than to permit a rough common boy, dressed like that, to enter a high-class hotel. It doesn't bear thinking about; an embarrassment to the management as well as yourself.'"

By anticipating the wrath of the great Claud Hoadley, David had worked himself into a state of agitation. Simeon was going to ask if he really was such a 'rough common boy'. If, indeed, he was an 'embarrassment' to David, it might be better if the fledging friendship ended here and now. There was, however, some quality of tragedy, an element of melancholia about this distressed man which turned the boy's anger into concern. So, instead, he asked another question.

"Why don't you defect?"

"Defect! What on earth do you mean?"

"You obviously hate this Hoadley. Every time you mention him ... well, it's with loathing. You practically spit out his name. He sounds like a monster! Why don't you go over to (as you put it) the enemy, the Nottingham Camp?"

David laughed. For the moment he was cheered by innocence, by the boy's naiveté.

"Many reasons, Simeon. And those reasons go back a long way over many years. First of all, the Nottingham Camp, ruled by Tommy and Martin, wouldn't have me. I 'signed up' with Hoadley long before you were born, before the war. You must remember that we're homosexuals ... " He observed Simeon's wince of disapproval. "Oh yes, I know you Americans don't like that term. Homosexual. It does rather sound like a disease. I agree that your new word ... 'gay' did you say? is a better term, albeit inaccurate for most of us. I digress. How can I put it? We are under a constant state of siege, young man. An ongoing siege from a disapproving majority. In such conditions we form ourselves into tight social knots, a sort of platoon. We swear allegiance to a self-appointed lieutenant and obey orders. Hoadley has been 'running' Derby since the 1920's! He'll not brook any disloyalty or any disobedience."

"I still don't understand. It wasn't like this in Detroit. Why can't you just tell him to get stuffed? Go it alone? Surely you must have your own friends? What do you get for this ... loyalty and obedience?"

"Protection," he sighed, "Social protection within a group of respected professional gentlemen - I suppose. My friends, such as they are, are all part of the Derby set and they are all under Hoadley's mighty thumb. We give dinner parties in our homes. We flock together in certain approved pubs, dine in approved restaurants, approved, that is, by the Great Leader. I'm sorely tempted to take your advice. I'd love to tell our Fuhrer of the Friary to 'get stuffed', but, if I did that, I'd end up like the toad and be cut adrift."

"He's not so bad! Aubrey Pod's an entertaining chap. He's a grammar school master. You told me Hoadley was a teacher before retirement. Doesn't that make them equals? Isn't Aubrey Pod a professional?"

"That vulgar little man! 'Toad of the toilets'! He's not a cat in hell's chance of getting anywhere near to our group. Horrible! Under *no* circumstances breathe his name within the hearing of Mr Hoadley or we may both be thrown out of The Friary. Incidentally, it will be *Mr* Hoadley to you. After thirty years of suffering his censure, his corrections, his suggestions, his frequent advice and endless humiliations then - you *might* be invited to address him by his Christian name."

At Duffield, David turned into a country lane which mounted Cumber Hill. Several complicated twists and turns brought them into a pretty little village called Quarndon, to Simeon's surprise, only a few miles short of the centre of Derby. Just minutes later they were entering an elegant tree lined street.

"Impressive isn't it? Friar Gate with its Georgian splendour. The best part of Derby. Two hundred years ago only the best people lived here. Where else would Claud Hoadley have his headquarters?"

The car silently entered a cobbled car park ennobled by very old lime trees. It came to rest in front of two classical columns supporting a tall porch, the grand entrance to this dignified 18th century mansion which was the Friary Hotel; all very intimidating for a scruffy chicken.

Chapter 16

Friday Night at The Friary

As David had indicated, the Friary Hotel public bar was dark and fusty. The very fabric of ancient drapes, worn carpets and leather chairs seemed to have absorbed a century of snobbery emanating from snooty, stuffy old men in dingy suits. Notwithstanding, Simeon Hogg would come to look back at The Friary with some small affection. He was, in fact, privileged to be a witness to the end of a long era of gay history. In just a few short years, before the end of that decade, dramatic changes would herald the new gay era. 'The scene' would be born. The advent of 'the disco', new openly gay pubs and clubs would appear. But here and now in the face of this soft silence, this fading grandeur, this power structure of sneering disciples, here and now in this temple of theatrical affectation; here in 1965, in The Friary - such base innovations were unthinkable.

At first, there was, indeed, soft silence and darkness. The darkness receded as the eyes adjusted to dim lighting revealing a large Georgian emptiness, empty except for a group of shadowy, dark brown / grey gentlemen standing near the bar. The silence receded when Simeon gradually discerned a low murmur of ornate voices in conversation. David and Simeon approached the gathering, apparently without being noticed, but, every single person in that gathering noticed the newcomers, especially the sexy, inappropriately dressed teenager.

All eyes were inclined to a big man, a slightly stocky man wearing an aristocratic sneer on his aquiline profile. It was a classically handsome face yet, Simeon was utterly repelled by an artificial slimy drawl in which words were exhaled in a breathy whisper. Instinctively, the boy knew that the sibilance of voice was matched by a sickening softness of body, the touch of which he would (if it ever came to the test) find utterly revolting. Here was a big, soft, pappy queen. The queen was entertaining his audience with one of his many anecdotes about Queen Mary.

"Hilary Raymond Hawley," whispered David, sardonically in the style of a grand announcement. "He's HRH to the bitchy Nottingham Camp. Has an encyclopaedic knowledge of royal families, past and present, English and European. He knows all the royal highnesses and all the serene highnesses. It fascinates him."

"Shush! It's interesting," whispered Simeon, who was always intrigued by this disapproving lady, the cool, stern and remote wife of George V, who died when Simeon was only seven years old. This was an account of a motor accident, an occasion when her limousine overturned, forcing the Queen to attempt an escape, to struggle out of a window, clutching the ever-present toque in an effort to maintain her dignity. Hilary Raymond Hawley seemed to punctuate his narrative with a frequent, forced laugh, a nauseating wheeze which accentuated the aristocratic sneer.

"He's the number two," whispered David. "Watch out! He's powerful. Not one to be crossed or it could mean social death. Have you identified the boss?"

At the moment of entry Simeon had indeed identified the Top Man. About a dozen pairs of eyes were on him ever looking for approval. And yet he was surprised. He had vaguely imagined Claud Hoadley to be an older man, a tall man with no smile, but here was an man of average size, of average, indeterminate age, wearing a slight smile - if not a warm smile, perhaps not quite as repellent as the sneer of his deputy. The most striking aspect of Claud Hoadley was his posture. Possibly this gave him that indefinable air of authority. Hoadley was bolt upright, straight as a pole - always. To the stern schoolmaster, slouching was a sin and, in that room, every person appeared to be affected, appeared to be standing at attention, in dread of imminent reprimand which might shoot out like a whiplash. Simeon could feel it, could imagine it, could fear it.

"Straighten up there boy! How *dare* you loll in front of me! Such disrespectful drooping is indicative of an indolent and disorderly mind."

An independent observer would have assessed his age at mid-fifties, more than a decade short of his 67 years. The same observer would have described sharp, handsome, clear-cut features but a more perceptive observer might notice shrewd, cold, grey eyes and cruel lips. Even in a group of quality suits in poor light, Hoadley's suit was distinguished by its superb cut. He was the very quintessence of good taste and excellent grooming, from the top of his perfectly combed hair down to his highly polished, expensive shoes. Everything about Claud Hoadley was correct and those around him seemed to be anxious to approach the high standards which he had set. Like so many before, Simeon Hogg was very impressed and even more impressed when the paragon broke into speech. The conversation had turned to an absentee who had just obtained his Ph.D.

"I suppose we shall have to call him *Dr* Fisher now," laughed a man with a sickly grin.

"It's unlikely we need be quite so formal," replied Hoadley, nonchalantly, as he carefully removed a tiny speck from his immaculate sleeve. "After all, it *is* a degree in engineering and from a university which can hardly command our full esteem."

This resulted in an eager row of nodding heads, each wearing a simpering smile, each uttering disparaging, sardonic murmurs. Dr Fisher was an infrequent attender at The Friary and could only be considered an 'associate' member of this elite group. If he had read the classics from Oxford University instead of Sheffield University, and if he had not dared to challenge Claud Hoadley (albeit ever so mildly) after his rant which followed the recent dedication of the historic meadow of Runnymede to the late President Kennedy, the good name of Dr Fisher might have been treated with more respect. Claud Hoadley hated America and anything American.

Nevertheless, Britain's rapid decline as a major industrial power and the significance of a comment which belittled the practical subject of engineering at a northern university, entirely escaped the lowly Derbyshire teenager, who was in awe of an extraordinary accent. If David's 'cut-glass' diction had been impressive, this orgy of enunciation, such high art of lavish articulation - hit the boy's Derbyshire ear like a thunderbolt. Two words in particular were drawn out with striking embellishment: 'after' became very southern, sounding like arrrrfter and 'command' was elongated to commarrrrnd.

Simeon Hogg began to absorb the subtle middle-class values which were being communicated to him from that group of professional homosexuals on that first evening. Members of the club were encouraged to appear to be, at all times, inwardly assured, stable, smug - even arrogant. Simeon was experiencing a culture shock. Unlike in the United States, here in Derby discussion of money was considered vulgar, unearned privilege was admired and American pushiness deplored. Steered by Hoadley and Hawley, the conversation meandered around various subjects but the correct code of conduct came out loud and clear; manual work, technical skills, people in trade, self-made types and all manner of 'doers' were to be despised by these nodding heads. Years later, Simeon would reflect upon that sad 'elite' Derby Camp of oppressed people who (to make their own position safer) felt the need to denigrate other human beings regarded as inferior in the mid-20th century British class structure.

Claud Hoadley was now in full flow, holding full attention, denouncing The Beatles who had just been awarded the MBE.

"It *was* an honour we should all aspire to. But I ask you, what can we expect from a Labour Prime Minister? Outrageous! Utterly, utterly outrageous. That Canadian Member of Parliament ... what was his name?"

"Hector Dupuis," said Hilary Raymond Hawley helpfully.

"Oh yes. That man is quite right. They *are* 'vulgar nincompoops'. Mr Dupuis has been cheapened, a gentleman of his position!" He spat out the next sentence with gathering fury. "That poor gentleman has been debased down to the humble level of common, caterwauling, working-class ruffians. I applaud his action. I would certainly have returned *my* insignia of the Order back to the Palace." All heads nodded with approval.

Simeon Hogg listened to this polemic with mixed feelings. On the one hand, he resented the attack on popular music but, he could not help being impressed by the majesty of the open 'u' which, in Hoadley's Royal diction, had been opened out to breaking point. Simeon had been forced to improve his speech to make it intelligible to the Americans. He was now sounding the 'h', but his Derbyshire 'utterly' would have sounded like 'ooterly'. Hoadley's utterly mesmerised his audience, it was stretched out to sound like 'atterly'. Simeon's 'humble' would have been 'hoomble' and his 'ruffian' would have been 'rooffian'. To the delight of his admiring disciples, the ostentatious efforts of Hoadley came out as 'hamble' and 'raffian'. Simeon noticed something else. Other members of that ever-nodding group tended to sound more affected in their *own* speech within the hearing of Claud Hoadley. Even David Bond enunciated more carefully, more formally, in the regal presence of Claud Hoadley.

At long last the lofty shrewd eyes came to rest upon the scruffy youth who stood at the side of the consultant surgeon. The tone was sharp, clearly cool and censorial.

"Good evening, David. A soupcon late, perhaps, this evening. I see you appear to have acquired ... a young person. May we know the name of this ... new acquisition?"

"Good evening, Claud. Good evening all. Well now, this is Simeon Hogg. He's on holiday from Detroit but ..." he added quickly, noting the disapproving thin lips of Hoadley pressing closer together, "he is as English as the rest of us."

"Indeed," replied the pedant. "What part of England, may one ask?"

"Horsley Woodhouse," said the boy, awestruck by all the Rs inserted into the short word 'ask'. Simeon had carefully and slowly pronounced both H's in Horsley Woodhouse, so carefully and so slowly that it sounded like a foreign place to his own ears. That gathering (with their critical ears) noted with smug satisfaction that Simeon was not accustomed to enunciate the name of his family village in that posh manner. That critical gathering knew, only too well, that the rough lad before them was much more accustomed to saying 'Ossly Wuddus'. Simeon winced under the slimy sneer of Hilary Raymond Hawley, who emitted one of his numerous breathy 'ha ha ha ha's'. Also noticed, with acute discomfort, was a macabre grin gradually breaking out on one of the nodding heads. This head was like a deaths head. The ghastly skin seemed to be stretched tight across the facial bones. Simeon found difficulty understanding what this man said on the rare occasions when he did speak.

"Who's the skull?" he whispered to David.

"I'll get into terrible trouble if I start to answer those sort of questions," came the amused reply. "I'll tell you this much, he's a professor and, in this circle, he's referred to as 'Aggie'.

"God! He's hideous!

"I agree. I've seen better looking cadavers at the hospital."

"He talks like he's got a mouth full of stones."

"Yes. I've noticed that. It could be to blur his diction so that 'the boss' can't be quite sure what's been said. Aggie's terrified of being corrected by Hoadley."

"Terrified! A professor terrified of a teacher? Look, David, I know it's against the rules but just give me ... can you at least give me an *idea* of the jobs of this lot. No names, no jobs to faces, just give me a list of professions. Can you do that?"

David led the boy to the end of the bar in order to buy him a drink.

"Better this way," he whispered. "It's seen as 'bad form' to have a private conversation when Hawley has the floor. Anyway, I'm getting bored with his tirades against the new progressive Canon at Derby Cathedral."

"They go to church?"

"My dear boy! You have *so* much to learn - they practically *own* Derby Cathedral! I kid you not. Smells and bells; they *invented* it. I'm surprised the whole congregation don't rise when Hoadley and Hawley make the grand entrance. It's the same each Sunday, the great and good of Derby sit near the front, always in the same order. First Miss Bulstrode, the headmistress of the prestigious Derby High School for Girls. She chats with Hoadley in Latin and Greek. Then we have Hawley, who sits next to the tweedy Miss Penelope DeHaviland, the editor of *Derbyshire Life and Countryside Magazine*. They exchange bits of gossip about the Lord High Sheriff and the Lord Lieutenant. Last, but not least, is the bolt-upright form of Hoadley himself, keeping trunk and legs at a precise 90 degrees. *Woe* to the cleric who dares to depart from traditional form. After the service, he must face the wrath of Miss Hoadley!"

"*Miss* Hoadley!"

"Sorry about that. The title of 'Miss' is fairly common in our catty world. You'll learn. I grant you that those two are not as ladylike as some ... but Hawley in particular, well he's so bloody slimy! And then, don't you think there's something of an 'old maid' about them?"

David ended his flow abruptly. They noticed the bartender standing before them. Simeon gave his usual apology for not wanting anything alcoholic and asked for his usual orange juice. David asked for a 'gin and it', paid for both drinks, received very little change out of a ten shilling note and tipped. When the man was out of earshot, well out of earshot, the conversation resumed.

"Can't be too careful. Our leader has spies everywhere. No joke! This place is like the Kremlin. And Hoadley is more Stalin than Brezhnev. If one of his subjects is found to transgress they disappear."

"What!"

"I mean socially of course. Like poor old Bill last year." David lowered his voice still further and leaned closer. "Horrible, really. He was arrested by the police in a public loo. It's called 'cottaging'. You need to know this, Simeon. The CID occasionally go in toilets and pretend to be like us, they pretend to be interested but, as soon as you make *your* move ... Well, that's the end. It's usually young officers who tempt you into suggesting a sexual act which, of course, they consider to be a crime. They're known as 'agents provocateurs'.

"We never mention Bill anymore. It's as if he never existed. The one time Bill really needed his friends they - we, I should say - were not there. We all fled; Hoadley's orders and Hoadley has expunged his memory as though Bill never existed. I was sick with guilt. Quite a nice chap, really. It was all over the front page of *The Derby Evening Telegraph.* Naturally he had to leave the area."

"Why?"

"Because, my lad, he was a professional man - like us. He was one of Derby's leading architects. It ruined him. God knows where he is now."

David glanced over to the fawning group with disdain. Claud Hoadley was fulminating against *The Sound of Music*, condemning it as 'yet another exa-rrr-mple of American trash polluting British Cinema-rrr-s'. A small number of the nodding heads, including Bond, had enjoyed that excellent film and knew that this particular diatribe said more about the bigotry of Claud Hoadley than it said about *The Sound of Music*, but such private thoughts remained private - always.

"Just look at them! Do you know, Simeon. At least half of that lot of kowtowing hypocrites dabble in the cottages now and again."

"I asked you about jobs. I promise to be discreet."

"Well now, professor Aggie you know about. In addition, I see two local politicians, err, two vicars, one curate, one headmaster, one accountant, one shop assistant and ... oh yes, there he is - one solicitor. I honestly don't know about the other one. Satisfied?"

"How did the shop assistant get in?"

"Because Claud likes him and because he's very well-connected. We'd better get back."

"Must we. The skull keeps looking at me."

"He's ogling your bottom. Bottoms are his speciality."

"No chance! Who could go with that?"

"Does very well, according to all accounts."

Back in the group, the conversation continued to follow the theme of entertainment. Derby Playhouse was mentioned, together with some tittle-tattle about an indiscreet promiscuous actor. Feeling the need to make a contribution, Simeon plucked up the courage to address the gathering.

Proudly he announced that he had had the pleasure of meeting a famous local entertainer.

"I've not actually seen a performance meself, but they say he's very good. He's a sort of impressionist, you know, takes people off. He does Norman Evans - 'over the garden wall' and Old Mother Riley. He's got all the right gear, wigs and costume. Oh, yes. And he can sing! He sings 'Sally'. Dresses up like Gracie Fields. And then ... "

Simeon came to a sudden stop; an embarrassed stop. A profound silence had descended upon The Friary. Even the bartender was looking over to see what had happened. It was a silence of censure, originating from the cold grey countenance of Hoadley. Stern and disapproving, his anaemic thin lips, cruel, crooked lips, were pressed tightly together, white with reproof. Others had taken their cue, had taken on a mask of remonstration. David looked miserable. The skull's lusting leer had changed slightly to a sadistic gloat and Hawley's snobbish sneer now seemed to relish the painful reprimand which they all knew would follow.

Chapter 17

The Corporation at the Cattle Market

"Well how was I supposed to know that Becksitch Betty was never to be mentioned to that prissy prat?" wailed an irritated Simeon after his public dressing down. The car was turning right at Coxbench into a quiet lane which would climb through Horsley into Lady Lea Road.

"If only you had told me that you'd met all the dross on Wednesday. I could have warned you! I could have saved you from committing such an appalling faux pas."

"What's a fo par?"

"It's French, literally, 'false step' - putting your foot in it! I'm very much afraid, Simeon, that this evening was probably your first and last appearance in The Friary."

"Oh dear! I'm really cut up about that - I *don't* think."

"Of course, there's always the Corporation Hotel at the Cattle Market which, unfortunately, is very *down* market."

"Another gay bar in Derby? Does it have *real* people?"

"It doesn't have me. Strictly forbidden by order. And in all conscience, Simeon, I have to say to you that I can't recommend it. There are some rough types in that place. Claud is not always wrong and he's not all bad. He was quite right to warn you about those awful men. It was for your own good. I agree with him, they *are* 'the trash of society'. Becksitch Betty is a hideous old hag, as low and as common as dirt. And that little fat Dolly! He has an atrocious reputation. For God's sake, keep well away from him and his car. Both are well-known to the police. He actually charges a fee for taking people on a tour of old Victorian toilets, sexually active toilets that is. He has an antique collection of strange old men, a sort of freak show, dotted around Derbyshire. There are dark rumours of a 'dancing gnome' somewhere in the wilds. Then there's that unspeakable mediaeval horror who, I'm informed, does massage! It's like a story from the Brothers Grimm, an ancient crone in the woods known as The Goblin. I know it's a cliché, but if you want to mix with nice people and have nice friends you must not associate with the dregs of society.

At this point, entering into Horsley Woodhouse, David turned his head to look directly at his passenger.

"Look here, we've only met today but I'm seriously concerned about you. You are definitely meeting the wrong people and it won't help matters going to the Corporation. To start with, homosexuals are tolerated in the passageway only. They're discouraged from entering any of the other rooms. And those rooms are pretty seedy anyway. It's standing room only for the likes of us. Rent boys hang around. Young lads who ask for money in return for sex - male prostitutes."

In fact, David was deeply regretting having mentioned The Corporation Hotel at all. He knew that Simeon would eventually find out about it from less responsible types such as Dolly, Becksitch Betty and the toad. He was particularly disturbed by the possible attraction of the two notorious toilets, one belonging to the hotel in the pub yard and another just outside on the street. Simeon admitted that he enjoyed casual sex. He said he liked -

" ... orgies in the dark, I get a kick out of being touched by men I don't know, Negroes I can't see. It was heaving inside the truck rigs on the Hoboken piers in New York ... oh yes, the New York docks! Those rigs ... they'd just sway with the rhythm, they'd drain me. I was in them until daylight sometimes."

David was shocked, but the imagery was exciting. He saw a jaunty, swaggering Marlon Brando dressed in a greasy plaid jacket and old work pants; Brando in conflict with corrupt union bosses, dealing with the mob in the film *On the Waterfront*. But this was the Cattle Market and Derby had its own perils to match its own delights. This boy was naive, inexperienced. He did not appreciate the risk, the dangers. During the next 20 minutes a serious conversation took place at Bog Hole, outside the dowdy residence of Aunty Joyce. In that time the older man tried to acquaint the boy with the sordid facts of 'queer life'. He was told about 'queer bashers' and the 'Burton Basher' in particular; a cruel character whose very appearance was enough to cause panic. He was cautioned about Becksitch Betty.

"You found him amusing, fine, but I can assure you he's much more than a funny old queen. Arthur Bestwick is an evil man, a man to be avoided. He's threatened a number of people and we hear rumours of blackmail. I know that Hoadley's lot act like a bunch of affected buffoons, but understand this, Simeon, *that* is their defence against a hostile heterosexual majority. They cling to Hoadley. They ape his manner and behaviour in a desperate attempt to acquire respectability. He's seen as the very essence of an erudite, virtuous, upright citizen, so, they try to be like him and win the good opinion of their neighbours. The problem is, they try too hard and come out like a load of pedantic ponces."

Simeon smiled.

"Too right. Hawley's smarmy 'ha ha ha'. Yuck!"

"It's just a nervous laugh. I suppose it has a sort of social function," replied David meditatively. "Probably to give Hilary time to gauge how he's doing, to see if Claud is approving or not approving. If not, he has an opportunity to shift his ground. You seem to have developed a horror of HRH, but he's only a fool, not a villain."

"*You* seem to have developed a horror of Aubrey Pod. At least he's honest. Surely he's no worse than a fool?"

"Touché. He makes my flesh creep. I suppose we all have our personal horrors."

There followed a few moments of silence as they unconsciously admired the deepening pinks, reds and purples of the north western sky. At long last, at the end of this long day, darkness had triumphed over the waning daylight. Simeon had promised Aunty Joyce that he would try to be in the house before the hour of eleven, which was approaching. David had been feeling a heavy sense of responsibility. He made a decision to break one of the cardinal rules of the Derby Camp. For his own good, he decided that Simeon should be given some privileged information.

"I was intrigued by your choice of the word 'honest' in describing the toad. Tell me, Simeon, how would you appraise the social background of the people you met at The Friary?"

"Pardon?"

"I'm afraid some of Claud's pedantry has rubbed off on me. I'm asking you to judge their class. For example, what sort of education did Hawley receive? What about his parents? What sort of job did his father do? What about Hoadley's father? Did Hoadley's family live in a big posh house? That kind of thing. I'm asking you for a guess, an impression of their past."

"Well it's not like *my* past. That's for sure. Most of my relatives are coal miners. They live here on this scruffy row. Well, let's see. Hawley's dad was a doctor like you - or something as good. And I suppose he went to one of those posh private schools where they learn them to talk posh. Hoadley the same. I'm surprised he's not a lord. How am I doing?"

"Exactly as I expected you to do. Prepare for a shock. Hilary Raymond Hawley is a shop assistant. Oh, of course, as you'd expect, a very high class gents outfitter, the best in Derby. He went to an ordinary Derby school, much the same as your own school. He taught himself to 'talk posh'. Claud Hoadley's father was a ordinary mill hand in Belper. All those people you met this evening in The Friary are self-made. They all have a working class background - including myself. My dad was a charge-hand at a Sheffield steel mill. We have all dragged ourselves out of the working class gutter. The difference between us and the next man is this; because of our homosexuality we've had to work harder at making ourselves *better* than the next man. Eventually you'll be meeting the Nottingham Camp. They're just the same. When you're sitting in the elegant drawing room of Tommy and Martin, admiring the tasteful decor, the Georgian silver, the Sickert over the fireplace and being impressed by their refined dulcet tones, remember this: Tommy's dad was a chimney sweep from Ilkeston and Martin's mum was a cleaner at the Strutt Arms in Milford."

David went on to explain why Claud Hoadley had good reason to fear Becksitch Betty.

"I shouldn't be telling you this, but ... here we go. Some weeks back your entertainer friend made advances to a young man in a Belper lavatory, quite popular with some of our lot, an old cast-iron urinal near the river. Nobody is sure what happened, but the old queen was hit in the mouth and sustained a thick lip. The youth, the attacker, complained to the law, which resulted in a charge of gross indecency against his victim. That is the way it is in our world. Bestwick was fined £10 in open court and this whole sorry story was reported in the *Belper News*. Hoadley made a tasteless comment about it."

Once again, David raised his voice an octave higher and produced the exaggerated and pretentious silken tones of Claud Hoadley.

"'I see that Becksitch Betty is in the 'society column' again! It should be valuable publicity for his next appearance as Old Mother Riley at the Matlock Lido.' They all loved it. Roars of laughter in The Friary. Take heed, Simeon, whatever is said in a public place to an audience of a dozen or more people can easily get around. Ever heard of the expression 'what goes around comes around'? Well, somehow or other, it came around to the ears of that old hag and, as I gather, he became incandescent with rage.

"Until 1951, Claud Hoadley lived in Belper. For nearly thirty years he'd always conscientiously avoided and snubbed the lowly Arthur Bestwick. Of course, Bestwick knew all about Hoadley. Belper is a small town. He knew they shared similar illegal urges and, I suppose, he felt that since both of them were queer (sorry, gay) ... Well, I suppose that Bestwick thought that they had something in common, some equality ... Anyway, he nursed his grudge, hated Claud with a passion. This unfortunate remark precipitated the most appalling incident. One morning there was a belligerent knock on Claud's door. On opening, there he was - large as life - Becksitch Betty. The last person Claud Hoadley wanted to see."

Their attention was diverted by a chink of light behind a moved curtain. Aunty Joyce was having a peep at the posh car at her front door.

"It's gone eleven. You'd better go in."

"Finish your story. What happens next?"

"It was an ugly scene. Bestwick was standing there, menacing, spitting fire, gesticulating and yelling threats. Poor Claud. In those situations he almost freezes up, but he managed to remain composed and polite.

'I'm dreadfully sorry to see your distress. Please do try to calm down. In all honesty, I have no recollection at all of making such a comment ... I never see the local papers, being a reader of the Daily Teleg-rrr-aph ...'

"It didn't help. Bestwick said he was going to pay a couple of thugs to give 'a snotty stuck-up bastard like you what you deserve, a fookin' good 'idin'.' Eventually, he stormed off. The faithful housekeeper, Miss Minchin, had to pick up the pieces. She poured out a strong drink. Claud could hardly hold it! He was in such a state of acute agitation. Miss Minchin had to steady his trembling hands all the way up to his lips. She insisted on calling the police but, quite rightly, Claud refused."

"Why?"

"He reasoned that men of that class, when enraged, often used intimidation as a weapon. Claud hoped the rage would pass. If the threatened attack actually happened, Bestwick would know he'd be in serious trouble and, anyway, hired thugs of that type are likely to be expensive."

For a moment, reviewing the intelligence he had just imparted, David Bond became pensive.

"I'm afraid I've been rather indiscreet today, Simeon. Please don't quote me. It's just that I want you to know what you're getting involved with. I get extremely irritated with Claud Hoadley. I've said things ... I've been very critical ... let off steam. It's like that with old friends and ... Claud *is* a friend. Deep down I'm rather fond of the pompous old fool. He didn't deserve that."

"The Becksitch Betty incident?"

"Quite. He hasn't got over it. It's really shook him up. He's frightened. He used to walk to The Friary, now takes a taxi."

"From Belper!"

"No. He moved nearer to his power base. He's lived in a rather nice Victorian house on the north side, the best part of town ... oh, for about 14 years now. Lovely big garden, backs on to Derwent Park, an ideal residence for a gentleman of his station," said David with a smile and a twinkle.

Chapter 18

Sweet Revenge

It was two minutes past eight on the following morning, Saturday, June 5th, at Darley Towers. The prim form of Miss Minchin had just drawn expensive drapes and deposited a tray of tea next to Claud Hoadley's bed. She had also been instructed to be silent about tea being served first thing in the morning.

"Of course, Miss Minchin, one should only take tea in the a-rrr-fternoon. To consume tea at this hour, I'm afraid, betrays one's lowly origins! Dear Miss Minchin, I know that I can depend on your loyal discretion."

"Absolutely, Mr Hoadley! Heaven forbid. It is not *my* place to discuss your private affairs with anybody. And I would never question your good judgement. I should think it would be utterly impossible for *you* to be accused of low taste."

Miss Minchin was proud to serve such a scholarly gentleman as Mr Hoadley, who was determined to keep television out of that house. She boasted to her friends that Mr Hoadley had never even heard of Ena Sharples, but he often quoted Shakespeare, Milton and Horace. An adoring smile suddenly spread across her acetous features.

"Will there be anything further, Mr Hoadley?"

"No thank you, Miss Minchin, you're too kind. I'll ring when I'm ready for breakfast. You may go."

A similar smile had softened the severe, sharp features of her master but vanished the instant Miss Minchin left the room. Over a steaming teacup, his cold countenance stared out through the large bay window which framed a stately old beech tree, partially obscuring a north-easterly view of Darley Park. But those icy eyes were not seeing a pleasant view of foliage, park and river valley, no, they were seeing the beginnings, the vague conception of a plan to destroy an enemy, to eliminate the threat of Becksitch Betty. He accepted that the boy had not intended to distress him but, nonetheless, had focused his mind on the need for a plan of action.

In the precarious minefield of the homosexual social network, Claud Hoadley had always appreciated the importance of spies, the need to gather intelligence. Naturally, a man of his position could never be seen at the Derby Turkish Baths. It was unthinkable for Mr Hoadley to be seen naked anywhere. To obtain an overview of the wider social scene, he often debriefed David Bond and Hilary Hawley, who were regular bathers at that, unofficial, club for homosexuals. Up to the present, any tittle-tattle regarding the lower orders was purely for entertainment value and had never been considered of any practical use. Unfortunately, his snooty disciples were far too aloof to hear any serious, damaging data, or any detailed information which could provide ammunition against a common drag act. Furthermore, it might be necessary to see the bigger picture of the old hag's world, to know something of his friends, his habits and his routine. As the thought process continued, as if in a flash, he suddenly saw a way forward! Hoadley's spirits rose and his thin lips gradually curled up into a grim smile. The construction of a sweet revenge was now taking shape.

The goblin! During his many years worshipping at Christ Church in Belper, Hoadley had been aware of a grotesque creature who sat at the back, in a dusty, dark corner of the old building. Few people spoke to Jasper Wormall, the hideous hunchback with a large hooked nose, far forward of deep-set, grizzled, leering eyes. The exalted classics master would shun any plebeian, even more so this deformed peasant, the gnarled, craggy collection of old rags who concealed himself in the shadows of Christ Church. For nearly half a century, this highly selective, respected schoolmaster avoided the goblin as one would avoid the plague.

Ten years before, Hoadley was intrigued to hear certain rumours which eventually reached The Friary; stories of an ugly old man in Belper who was advertising massage in various post offices and newsagents around Derbyshire. It was left to his sneering number two to clarify the situation.

"There can be no doubt about it, Claud, Aggie saw an advert in Derby. Robert, you'll recall Robert and Trevor whom you kindly received last year, well, Robert said that Roger saw a postcard in Ashbourne and Malcolm mentioned a neat little card in Matlock. Ha ha ha. They're all the same, written in tiny neat writing. It's the same man. A Mr J Wormall of Shire Oaks in Belper is offering body massage for *men* only ... ha ha ha. They all claim ... ha ha ha ... 'satisfaction guaranteed'. The mind boggles!"

"Interesting," murmured the boss. "I've often walked by his cottage. Quite a howling wilderness at the top of that rough track, quite isolated. Most picturesque really, an ancient heap of stones barely supporting a sunken roof. It's been there since the early 19th century. I wonder it doesn't fall down. No electricity, no gas and no running water. He uses a well and an earth closet lavatory. Amazing creature, he's a living link with the past! His family have been in that cottage since the reign of George IV. They were footmen, coachmen, grooms and gardeners to George Benson Strutt, who was Lord Belper at Bridge Hill House, an imposing mansion, sadly demolished in 1932 in spite of my objections."

During these historical orations, the Derby Camp were in awe, hanging on to every erudite word uttered by their cultured leader, who had been an excellent teacher at the Herbert Strutt Grammar School to several grateful generations.

"An ideal aspect for a painting; a crumbling old cottage under a copse inhabited by swirling, screaming rooks. They quite blacken the sky at times. Most quaint." He concluded in some abstraction, having noticed a slight smear on his glass.

"That rings a bell," replied Hawley, keen to make a connection. "Do you remember me telling you about that little fat Dolly, the one who does the tour of ugly old queens? Well, according to Trevor, his menagerie of freaks included something called 'the crone under the crows."

"So the goblin has found his true vocation ... and so late in life," said Hoadley to himself, softly. At normal volume to the Friary assembly - "Full marks for enterprise! Good for Mr Wormall! This shows initiative." His lordship raised his glass. "Let us all wish him well." A dozen nodding heads followed suit and echoed - "The goblin!"

Claud Hoadley rarely made a generous proclamation, but he was totally sincere in this one. He reasoned that Jasper Wormall, a typical, simple peasant, had always been severely restricted in his sexuality. He also reasoned that the old man had been isolated by that same sexuality in an oppressive, virulent, heterosexual working class culture. In 1965, the word 'racism' was available, but it would be another 40 years before the new term 'homophobia' could articulate a unjust prejudice against gay men. In the late autumn of his life, this curious old man of repellent aspect had somehow managed to make contact with the homosexual underworld and was, by 1955, giving sexual pleasure to dozens of men on a weekly basis.

Enterprise and initiative aside, the leader of the Derby Camp fixed his members with a steely eye and made it clear that it would be totally unacceptable for any them to ...

" ... attend the primitive cottage of this lowly creature. These activities, *disgusting* activities, are for the lower orders, they are not for us. After all, it is only a matter of time before the police will descend and close this mediaeval massage parlour for the desperate - assuming, of course, that the old man does not die first."

Ten years later, however, the old man had not died and the parlour had not been raided by the police. On the contrary, Jasper's business had increased in popularity and prospered. It is true that some visitors fled in panic at first sight of the leering, contorted old crone who opened the creaking old door. For many, the shock was too much. This unfortunate old deformity was now 90 years old. For as long as Hoadley could remember, a memory which went back to the Great War, the goblin had always appeared to be quite ancient. Notwithstanding, it had to be acknowledged that this human monstrosity, after a healthy lifetime of scaling the hills of Belper, was fitter than most people who were less than half his age.

Jasper needed all his fitness and energy. He could afford to be choosy and choosy he was. After weeding out the old and the effeminate, he selected the butch and the best - such as footballers, rugby players and rough labourers. They all appreciated the exquisite tactile talents of the old crone who had become highly skilled in locating all those delicious, naughty little nooks and crannies of a man's body. The goblin became adept with the application of baby oil, adept at exploring the erogenous pleasure zones. In a rough candlelit bedroom, a drooling slash of toothless mouth, with gloating goggle eyes leered over a recumbent torso. A falsetto effeminate squeak -

"Dat all right? Shall ya 'ave any extras? Ooo, what's comin' oop? Does dat want a massage?"

He teased, he prolonged the ecstasy and maddened his prostrate victim by delaying the climax as long as possible. They all paid up, were glad to pay, were offered tea and cakes and they talked - and Jasper Wormall listened. If the imposing Friary Hotel was the social centre of the higher orders, so that old, ivy-clad, tumbling down cottage under a blackness of cawing crows was the social centre of the lower orders. The goblin was visited by Dolly, Nobby the Gnome, Aubrey Pod and a number of men from the Nottingham Camp, who were not as tightly controlled as Claud's exclusive club. He reflected on these facts.

"Data," said the schoolmaster to himself, still admiring the view of Darley Park. "I wonder how often Mr Bestwick visits Mr Wormall?"

Claud Hoadley made a decision to break the habit of a lifetime. He would, for the very first time, stoop and condescend to cultivate a friendship with a lowly common man. He put on his dressing gown, descended to the ground floor, entered a book-lined study and sat down at a handsome antique desk.

Dear Mr Wormall,

As we hardly know each other, not having been introduced, please forgive me for writing to you out of the blue. Since retirement, I have developed an interest in the history of Belper and have been informed that your factual knowledge of the past is without equal in this town. You will be aware that the Convent of St Lawrence is holding an open day next Saturday. I am woefully ignorant of this fine building and would like to be shown around by a really competent guide, a guide such as your good self. If I can trespass on your valuable time next Saturday afternoon at about, shall we say, 2.00pm? I will be most grateful to find you at the convent.

Yours sincerely,
Claud Hoadley

Hoadley's hand was neat. Although clearly influenced by the Victorian school of 'copperplate', the bold flow and occasional flourish indicated confidence. A certain spikiness matched the sharpness of his facial features, suggesting power and a hardness of heart. The reply he received three days later was equally as neat and was also influenced by the old school of 'copperplate'. But, in contrast, this was a tiny, painstaking hand, suggesting a crabbed, narrow, small-minded and isolated personality.

Dear Mr Hoadley,

I was honoured to receive a letter from a gentleman such as your good self and will be very pleased to show you around the convent this Saturday afternoon at two of the clock in accordance with your good wishes. I have got a good memory and will tell you all that I know of the convent and anything else you want to know about the history of Belper. In the meantime I look forward to Saturday to be in your illustrious presence. Thanking you very much,

I remain yours very respectfully,
Mr J. Wormall.

A reptilian smile creased Hoadley's features as he filed away this letter. He reflected on the likely reaction of one of his pupils reading such a missive and knew they would see sarcasm in those carefully, slowly-written lines where, in fact, Hoadley had seen only sincerity, obedience and genuine deference. Essentially, Wormall and Hoadley were both Victorians and both had a strong sense of their place in society.

Chapter 19

Canning Circus Cottage

It was 8.25 on that same Saturday morning of June 5th. Joyce Hogg, Simeon's shy maiden aunt, suffered an unexpected rude invasion into her quiet, tranquil world at number four, Bog Hole in Horsley Woodhouse. It started with an urgent 'toot toot', rapidly followed by an equally urgent banging at her front door. The tooting, slamming of a car door and loud knocks had alerted the other relatives on that humble row. Several bewildered Hoggs were now craning their necks and ogling the excited toad. As the door opened, with arms up to shoulder level, he pushed past the ponderous, bovine spinster in an effort to locate his new chicken. Words escaped Aubrey Pod, cascading nineteen to the dozen without benefit of a single breath.

"Hello. I'm Mr Pod!" Pushing his toad face up to the other - "I've come to collect Simeon to take him to Bridlington because it's nearly half past eight and we should be ... Where is he?"

"Well ... am not sure ... "

"You'll be Aunty Joyce. Where is he? Is he in there?"

Aubrey, a bundle of energy, spinning around like a top in the centre of the front (best) room, scanning for any sign of his recent prize acquisition. A second later, an alarmed Aunty Joyce chased after him into the central living room where he was still spinning and scanning for his prey.

"He's not in the kitchen is he? We should be getting off ... "

"Hello?" said Simeon, who just come down the stairs. He was very groggy, still in his pyjamas, wondering if the house was on fire. A pained and bemused expression on the old-fashioned face of Joyce was concerning her nephew. In her narrow world she knew very few people outside of the village. She was especially nervous of strange men and they seldom came stranger than Aubrey Pod, who had just forced his way into her home. Simeon could see she was disorientated, unnerved and disapproving of this intrusion. Quickly, he apologised, made a belated introduction and explained that, rising so late, it had not been possible to warn her about the Bridlington excursion.

Twenty minutes later, Joyce was still uneasy but now slightly mollified. She waved off the two friends in a frenzy of haste and loud tooting.

Motorcars were rare visitors to Bog Hole and several other relatives were at their front doors. Uncle Wilfred, baffled and grumpy, stood at number three. He grunted at the receding, ugly little car and the ruckled old hag next to him, Aunty Nelly, stared at it with hard bullet eyes still listening to its distant toots.

It was a bright day. Simeon was suitably clad for the sunshine in his close fitting white shorts and equally close-fitting palm-beach shirt, but he slightly resented being stuck inside Aubrey's car, a car which could not have been more different from the luxurious Bentley of the previous day. Basic, plain and noisy. The podgy driver was hunched over the steering wheel of the toadmobile, aggressively jutting out his chin, forcing progress northwards, ever twittering away to his passenger.

This twittering interested Simeon because, eccentricity aside, Aubrey Pod came over as intelligent, perceptive and honest. He castigated most members of the gay community with an accurate assessment of his unpopular position. He complained that he was never invited to the big posh Nottingham parties and was frozen out of the Derby Camp when he once ventured into The Friary.

"I *tried* to be friendly but nobody spoke to me. They treated me like dirt. The hypocrisy of it! Call themselves Christians; that Claud Hoadley has done more damage to the Christian Church than the Spanish Inquisition. And that affected Hawley! He reminded me of one of those wealthy aristocrats of the 1920s, the type Evelyn Waugh despised in his novels."

Unconsciously, Simeon was picking up the subtle nuances of speech from his friend. He was judging Pod's social level. He was continually assessing the wide social divide between Pod and the Hoadley set, the nodding heads with their 1920's upper-class accent which had so impressed him the evening before. Pod could hardly be described as 'commonly spoken', but the Derbyshire twang was unmistakable. Aside from his appalling reputation in public lavatories, the flat A and closed U were unacceptable and unforgivable. Alone, the flat A and closed U were enough to exclude Aubrey Pod from the elite Derby Camp.

Notwithstanding, Simeon Hogg, a poorly-educated youth, was fascinated by Aubrey's extensive literary knowledge and his appraisal of the local gay social scene.

"I'm surprised *you* managed to get into The Friary with your dress and speech. It's a wonder they don't have a commissionaire guarding the door, giving some sort of elocution test for admittance. 'Read the words on this card.' One word wrong, like 'bootter' instead of 'batter' and out you go! Derby and Nottingham, they're much the same, they're all living in a time warp. Don't get stuck in Derbyshire, Simeon. Go further afield. Let me show you Brighton. I always say, if you can't get it at Brighton, you can't get it anywhere! The under-25s cave - fantastic!

"Pardon?"

"It's a nice dark cave at Telscombe Cliffs. The entrance is so high, you need to be young and fit to climb up there. The likes of Tommy and Martin wouldn't cope. They must be pushing 60. None of Claud Hoadley's gang could possibly scramble up; much too old, all of them. *Your* toffee-nosed doctor wouldn't manage it for a start! But - *I* get up there *and* I get my fill! Then, when exhausted, I sit down on a big stone guarding the entrance ... just like Circe."

"Who?"

"Circe, the enchantress of Greek mythology. She was the witch who lured sailors into her cave - and then ate them!"

Aubrey licked his lips with an unpleasant smile. He concluded with gesticulating arms which, in excitement, precariously left the steering wheel as he uttered a high-pitched giggle fired by recalled triumphs.

Simeon studied the gloating face of Aubrey Pod. Surely the toad had to be more than 25, a lot more. But then, he reasoned, perhaps this was the sort of face which could be almost any age? Perhaps this was the sort of face which would be little affected by the passage of time. It was an ugly face. The unpleasant gloat gradually disappeared and, looking at the profile in repose, Simeon suddenly felt a surge of compassion for a man who had probably suffered a great deal of abuse in his life. He recalled a feeling of horror when told that, occasionally, a baby bird was thrown out of the nest by others because it was - different. Aubrey Pod was different. In the same way, Simeon Hogg was different at Mundy Street Boys School in 1957. But the punishment for Aubrey was even greater. Not only was he rejected by the heterosexual majority, he had also been rejected by his own kind. And that kind were not kind at all, reasoned the boy, still trying to make sense of the gay world as it existed in Derbyshire and Nottinghamshire. In this year of 1965, Simeon learned that there were three camps, not just two. Derby and Nottingham were essentially two groups at war, two feuding groups of middle class professionals. But then there was a *third* group of homosexuals to which Aubrey Pod belonged. This third group was a dustbin for all the rejects. It contained the roughly-spoken, the common working-class, the poor, the ugly, the freaks, the deformed, the cottage queens and the over-sexed who were unfortunate enough to be caught by the police.

Nearly three hours later, the little car was merrily bouncing over the Yorkshire Wolds and Aubrey Pod was still in full flow, denouncing his enemies in the most amusing and entertaining diatribe Simeon had ever heard.

"I'd like to see them now! All those choosy chickens who pushed me away in the Derby Bus Station cottage during the war, during the blackout. I'd just like to see them lined up in front of me. Some will be grey, some bald, some with false teeth, hearing aids, beer bellies, love handles ... they won't be so snooty now, will they? Like that young Bruce in the Brighton cave. He's there all the time, lies on his tummy and they queue up to screw him. He'll have *anybody* - except me! And I'm good at that! Fancy refusing *me*, as well-endowed as I am. He'd love it. What will *he* look like in 20 years? Will he be so fussy then?"

"Look on the bright side, Aubrey. You need a break now and again after working so hard in that naughty cave."

"Well, that's true. I need to rest."

Aware of the American predisposition, Aubrey leered over at his passenger and lowered his voice -

"And, I'll have you know, young man, that I'm very good at what *you* like. Anyway, a hideous thing they call 'Lanky Liz' caught gonorrhoea from Bruce. Looks like something out of Belsen. Dolly said he's 'the ugliest thing that ever broke bread'. I advise you to stick to Dolly, he can be very useful for meeting people. Go on one of his 'cottaging tours' or one of his 'tours of old queens'."

"I'm not sure about meeting old queens. Aren't there any chickens in Derbyshire?"

"Not many, and most of them charge. A few chickens drift to Nottingham, Sheffield or Manchester, but most go to London. You'll be able to earn good money there. I expect the doctor paid well."

"I beg your pardon! David gave me nothing, nor did he lay a finger on me. The very idea!"

"Simmer down. There's no shame in selling your body. Sell while you've got something to sell is what I always say. You've already left it rather late, Simeon - perhaps *too* late. Sixteen-year-olds command the highest fees for 'services rendered' and past 20 is already half price and dropping rapidly ... *rapidly*."

He concluded this triumphant statement by briefly turning his head, jutting out an unpleasant smiling face, redolent of relish - so typical of Aubrey Pod. The Germans have a word for it - Schadenfreude. "Die reinste Freude ist die Schadenfreude", which means - "The purest joy is the malicious joy we take in the misfortunes of others."

However, the gloating toad reserved his greatest hatred for Claud Hoadley. The Herbert Strutt Grammar School classics master had diligently ignored Pod for the 15 years since he had been appointed music master in 1948, up to Hoadley's retirement in 1963. Aubrey was deeply hurt and offended when it became clear that Hoadley would not even look at him and communicated only when it was professionally unavoidable. Aubrey took spiteful pleasure on the rare occasions when Hoadley suffered any misfortune. A vindictive pupil once seized an opportunity to lock the excessively strict master into a tiny stockroom by the simple expedient of turning a tempting key left in the lock. Hoadley endured further humiliation when, horror of horrors, it was Pod himself who heard the frantic banging and enjoyed the pleasure of releasing the prisoner within.

"Mr Hoadley! Oh dear! I am *so* sorry. How very unfortunate. Of course you can rely on me not to breath a *word* of this incident to any of the others. Are you going to be all right? You do seem shaken ... oh dear ... "

Aubrey milked it for all it was worth. He related that embarrassing, but popular morsel year after year, entertaining the staff who had been bullied by an overbearing classics master, whose dominant personality and long tenure (a career lasting 44 years) had given him considerable power over several young headmasters. Aubrey's colleagues loved his nasty narrations, seeing the evil toad reach the punchline, hearing his squeaky laugh, jigging about, performing his evil 'dance of delight' at the conclusion.

The little car was racing along and Mr Pod was still defending the 'oldest profession'.

"I often think that hiring a rent boy is more honest and cheaper than wining and dining. Take that camp little thing they call 'Miss Mold' who's always in The Corporation. No money changes hands directly, but after I've treated him to dinner and the Theatre Royal, it's a fiver at least. And *then* he doesn't always feel like it afterwards! Better to go to the Canning Circus cottage where it's cheaper, quicker and guaranteed. There's usually a good selection. That fat chicken's cheap, but I usually go for the Chinese Chicken."

"Chinese?"

"Well he looks a bit Chinese. We go through the same ritual. He wants 15 shillings and I offer five. We settle at ten, a lot less than an evening's expenditure on Miss Mold. My Chinese Chicken's more masculine and I don't have to listen to Miss Mold's endless prattling about Godfrey Wynn."

"And you drag him all the way back to Belper?"

"Oh, no. There wouldn't be time to find another chicken. In a good night I'll have at least three chickens. Mostly we do it in the cottage, or up an alley, or by the canal, anywhere there's a dark corner."

"It all sounds rather seedy," said Simeon sadly.

This caused Aubrey Pod to become rather angry.

"I do much better in the cottages than standing in that uppity Flying Horse. Hoity-toity arrogant bastards! All airs and graces, they look at me like something the cat's brought in. And it's all run by those supercilious snobs, that acid-tongued Tommy and smarmy Martin. I hate their guts. They stop people speaking to me and see to it that I get nothing."

The long journey finally ended in a frenzied dodgem-like dash through the lively seaside resort of Bridlington. They scooted through the old town, tooting away agitated pedestrians before coming to a thankful rest near the busy harbour, which was quaintly decorated by fishing boats.

Chapter 20

Mischievous Postcards from Bridlington

It was thrilling to escape from that claustrophobic little tin box and plough into the bracing sea breeze and bright sunshine of a perfect June day. This was one of the many occasions on this extraordinary holiday when Simeon's pure English soul rejoiced at his blessed escape from American imprisonment. Aubrey Pod, the child, had known and loved Bridlington. Aubrey Pod, the impatient adult, ran like a child along the stone pier to where the Bridlington Belle was about to depart on one of its regular coastal tours around the chalk cliffs of Flamborough Head.

Embarkation was refused! A shocked toad could hardly take it in when told, firmly (and then told again) that tickets could be purchased only at the booking box at the head of the pier. Another run. He attacked the woman in her kiosk with a torrent of fussing, whittering, whittling, worrying, mythering and fretting before she gratefully released the tickets, to see chicken and toad make a frantic dash along the pier back to the boat.

Like two eager boys, they pushed and shoved their way to the front for the best view, standing on the tip of the bow. A man with an accordion appeared on the deck and played popular pre-war seaside songs. A few fat, common women - raucous ladies with fat sunburned legs - performed a jolly knees-up, encouraged by squeals of merriment. Aubrey joked that the Bridlington Belle would be highly unsuitable for Claud Hoadley and the Derby Camp's day out. On the voyage, Simeon fell into a happy reverie leaning over the prow, watching it crash, splash and cut through the sparkling blue of the cold North Sea. At his side stood Aubrey, silent, also enjoying a rare moment of pure happiness with a new friend who actually liked him, genuinely liked him for what he was - warts and all.

Back on the promenade, struggling to make himself heard above the noisy funfair, Aubrey was making suggestions regarding suitable contacts for his inexperienced young friend.

"You must let me introduce you to the goblin. He has to be seen to be believed. He really should be here in a freak show. Jasper deserves to wear the crown as the world's ugliest old queen. They do say," continued the lascivious toad, edging closer, "that he's very good with his hands *and* his mouth." At this point he stopped and looked Simeon directly in the face. "Not that *I've* ever been tempted. Dolly tells me that Jasper has had two telegrams from The Queen already."

"He's over 100!"

"Well, Dolly can be very bitchy. It was foolish of him to fall out with Jasper. The 'goblin' was the jewel of his 'tour of ugly old queens'. He's down to about five old queens now. Guzzly Granddad lives in a slummy part of Chesterfield and specialises in what you Americans like. A repulsive lump of lard! Sits in that old chair all day long waiting for it. You just walk in off the street and watch his mouth open. Just like Jasper, not a tooth in his head. I make sure I keep on the right side of 'the goblin' as they call him."

Simeon wondered if Aubrey Pod was aware that he was referred to as 'the toad'.

"Shire Oakes is a useful place to meet people, make contacts. There's no point in fighting over territory and so I have an arrangement with Jasper Wormall. He's agreed that I can do his cottages on massage days, which are Monday to Thursday - keeps him sweet. He can be quite cantankerous in his old age." Noting Simeon's puzzled expression, Aubrey explained a few basic facts of queer life. "You see, Simeon, old queens are very territorial when it comes to cottaging. Some of them can become violent! Now, there's a funny little chap called Simon Tonks, well known, pretty little fairy, thin, young ... although he must be older now? Anyway, he haunts the toilets all over Derbyshire. He was once physically thrown out of a public lavatory in Buxton because, inadvertently, he sat in the cubicle next to 'Toby Jug', one of Dolly's old queens who had sat in that cottage, known as Toby's cottage, for over forty years."

"Why?"

"Competition. Toby Jug is a filthy old tramp who is probably homeless. His sort can only tolerate rough, manly types. He'd look through his hole and weigh up Simon at first glance."

"What's wrong with Simon?"

"I don't know where to start! Young and pretty, but hideously camp and most peculiar with it. Outrageous, really. I saw him last week at the Whore's Wall cottage in Chesterfield. He is never the same; sometimes blond, sometimes brunette and sometimes jet black. This time it was a sort of blue-grey. And there was something new about Simon, something utterly repulsive - he looked like a *doll*."

"A doll!"

"A child's doll. It was the eyelashes. He'd had them curled up or something. It was most unnatural. He looked like a freak! Anyway, at Buxton, Toby Jug chucked him out of the loo into a busy street. Poor Simon. In front of bemused shoppers, there he was, suffering loud abuse, hopping around trying to pull up his trousers."

"That's terrible!" said Simeon, trying not to laugh. "What did the old man shout at him?"

"Something like - '... and dunna come back, ya dotty little bitch.' He was threatening him with his fist. 'Yol get this down ya gob. Find ya own bloody cottage, ya camp little slut.'"

"My God! America was never like this."

"Anyway, Jasper's cottage days are Friday and Saturday, he rests on Sunday attending Christ Church - where I play the organ."

"So Jasper has his own cottage?"

"Jasper Wormall has *four* cottages. Ugly old queens sitting in public toilets is an old Derbyshire tradition. Every Friday morning, he packs up his picnic of cracker biscuits, makes a flask of tea, puts it all in that beaten up old bag and scuttles to catch the bus to Heanor market place. He'll sit there all morning. In the afternoon, he goes to a very busy lavatory in Ilkeston's Victoria Park. On Saturday, it's Ripley in the morning and Matlock in the afternoon. It used to be Chesterfield in the afternoon, but that vicious couple, Monks and Muckles, started to plague him."

"What do you mean?"

"Well, for devilment they bombed him with flour to get him out. You see, it's a very active cottage and folks used to come from miles away to sample Jasper's special touch and, after all, Jasper had spent many hours making that useful hole with his little hammer and chisel."

At this point, Aubrey Pod stopped. He became hunched, one eye closed and the other wide and leering at some invisible object inches from his face. He mimed the action of a small imaginary hammer and chisel with quick little knocks, as he explained, creating a hole between one WC cubicle and another ending with: "Meh! Gettin' bigger," an impression of the old man's cackly voice.

"So from Monday to Thursday you do a 'cottage crawl' and get the benefit of Jasper's hard work?"

"After school, on holidays when I'm not at the baths - yes. Look, it's Saturday," exclaimed the toad with sudden rising enthusiasm, "Jasper will be massaging at Shire Oakes, let's go and visit him today."

"Perhaps another time," replied the boy, feeling a moment of panic.

"I understand. Neutral ground would be better ... I know! It's the Field Lane Convent annual open day next Saturday. Jasper is always there. He sits at the entrance, looking just like a gargoyle. There'll be folks all over the place. You'll be perfectly safe."

"It's a date," said Simeon, curious to meet the extraordinary phenomenon, known as 'the goblin'.

They stopped at an old fashioned, slightly shabby, sea-front cafe with a few tables and chairs outside on the promenade. Aubrey invited his chicken to be seated, dashed inside, shouted something to a startled and somewhat affronted elderly lady and darted back to his chicken. For Aubrey Pod life was all urgency, life was lived at top speed and it was all about what was going to happen next. He rarely lived in the present moment, rarely enjoyed the present moment and, at this moment, was feverishly working out how he could continue to lay claim to this desirable new possession - a genuinely young chicken who actually appeared to *like* him; him, Aubrey Pod, the despised toad, the butt of jokes.

He had to think quick. It was important to book Simeon, to engage him for as many 'dates' as possible. Simeon was, at this early stage in England, an innocent. At this stage he was malleable, could still be moulded and would be useful. A chicken was a status symbol. Consciously or unconsciously, David Bond had used the young man to 'show off' on the previous evening at The Friary - 'look what I've got!' Aubrey's thoughts were travelling along similar paths. He had used chickens before. They were not only good for sex but could be used as bait to catch more sex. Unfortunately, there was not a single chicken in Derby or Nottingham who would be seen with Aubrey Pod in the principal public gathering places of the Corporation or the Flying Horse - not even for ready cash. No self-respecting chicken could be seen with the toad ... but, perhaps the unsuspecting Simeon Hogg ... ?

"Do you know, Simeon," said Aubrey, eagerly jutting out his face close, too close, "You need guidance! Oh yes, you do. You need an older advisor to introduce you to these pubs in Derby and Nottingham. Why don't I take you around tonight?" purred the gesticulating luster, with waggling fingers.

A grim elderly lady interrupted with tea and toasted teacakes. With a slam, she dropped the tray on the table, causing Simeon to look up. Having heard part of the conversation, she took in the situation at a glance. A boy of no more than 16 years being groomed by an ogling, older man, who was certainly not a relative.

"Two shillings and ninepence," barked she of frosty features in a hard voice as sharp as a knife edge. Indifferent to this cool atmosphere, Aubrey fumbled, avoided eye contact and tendered the exact amount. He was delighted that his Saturday night suggestion had been accepted and wanted to leave for Derby straight away. Simeon protested. They had been in Bridlington a short time only. The day was still young and he had no desire to be incarcerated in that claustrophobic little car for yet another three hours, notwithstanding Aubrey's constant entertaining patter, which would accompany the long trek back.

Bravely, the toad returned within to face the disapproving old woman and purchased a number of postcards. She placed them into a small paper bag and, with a grunt, thrust them at her customer. Back at the table, he plunged into furious writing. Aubrey's hand was childlike, neat and clear, but betrayed no trace of the mischief, malice and spite aimed at the addressee. On the face of it, a postcard from Aubrey Pod was friendly and polite. Behind that face, and between the lines, were cleverly woven sardonic messages calculated to irritate and needle the recipient. He invited Simeon to read his naughty cards.

To Jasper Wormall - "Enjoying a sunny day with an American teenage friend you may meet next Saturday afternoon - but must <u>not</u> touch. Hope this finds you well, as it leaves me highly satisfied and smug. Glad you're not here. Aubrey".

To Claud Hoadley - "The chicken you drooled over last night is sitting by my side here in sunny Bridlington. I expect to know him better before the end of the day. Isn't life funny! Sorry to hear about your recent trouble with Betty, who you described as "low and common". Yes, I'm afraid <u>everybody</u> knows. I only wish I could offer you some words of comfort for the distress you have endured. Hello, Miss Minchin! Greetings to you, too. Aubrey Pod."

To Hilary Hawley - "Weather here, wish you were beautiful. Aubrey Pod."

He wrote a card to David Bond and one to Tommy and Martin in similar gloating vein, with a face of pure evil.

"My cards are legendary!" was proudly stated with hunched shoulders, pushing out his arms in emphasis. "They are not intended to greet these folks, no, they're intended to torment them. It's a good way of telling them that I know where they live; a sort of subtle threat. It'll make them feel very uncomfortable." Again his ugly puffed face screwed up into a dastardly, unpleasant smile. "A postcard says - 'I am here and you are there'. Claud Hoadley will be *furious* when Miss Minchin hands him that card. He'll know full well that both she and the postman have read every word!" He dissolved into a deluge of spiteful giggles.

"Aubrey Pod! You are one *wicked* little man!" said Simeon in mock censure.

"I know. It's terrible, isn't it? But I *do* so enjoy it," replied the toad with a further cascade of rising, shrieking giggles. In his sinful excitement, he jumped up and, for a few seconds, skipped his impish dance of delight; a cruel caper, a perverted prance which horrified, mesmerised and yet amused the audience of one. Make that two, the old woman was also watching.

"You're surely not going to send *this* one to ... who is it ... Tommy and Martin? Why, it's criminal! And you tell me he's a lawyer! It's too awful. It's plain nasty."

"That's my favourite. It'll hit the mark beautifully. I've found their weak point. They'll be more careful what they say about me in future. They deserve what I've put."

"Why?"

"I'll tell you why. For starters, umpteen vicious comments at my expense from that acid tongued Tommy over the last 20 years. *Odious* queen. Last week, in the Flying Horse, he told Sid that I had a mouth like a crack in a pie."

"I'm not sure it was so kind of Sid to repeat a comment like that," replied the other, glancing at the toadal features, taking note that Tommy had made a rather accurate observation.

"I'd rather know what folks are saying about me."

Abruptly, he put the cards in his jacket pocket and announced his intention of giving his friend a real treat.

"We'll go to Flamborough Head. A beautiful spot, very quiet, with lots of caves, well away from the bucket and spade brigade."

The mighty headland was brilliant white in the sunshine, a striking example of coastal scenery. In great excitement, Aubrey hurried out of the car, leaving Simeon struggling to keep up with him. A rough path zigzagged them down some 300 feet into a small cove, which echoed to the cries of gulls, gannets, puffins and cormorants. In contrast to the cool sea breeze, the warm afternoon sun felt good on Simeon's legs - but not for long.

He knew it would come to this. He knew it when he followed the toad into the hole, one of the many caves in those cliffs. The repulsive, shapeless form scrambled over various boulders, progressing high enough to escape the splashes of sea water which crashed and resounded around the roof of that ever-darkening cavern. Eventually, he selected a rock, lecherously crouched down, slowly turned his head, leered at his prey, salivated from that 'crack in the pie' and stuck out his crafty tongue in anticipation of the chicken who was about to stand before him.

Simeon had always had difficulty in rationalising his choice of partner in casual sex. Perhaps the handsome, older David Bond had sensed that his touch would be utterly repellent to the boy. David disliked being declined and his instinct had served him well. The old, the soft, the sophisticated, the well-spoken, the polite and the charming were all repulsive to this scruffy chicken, who, if he had any choice at all, would select a similar chicken from a similar social background; rough, ready, common, crude and rude. The ugly toad was rude but not his first choice. In this cave, choice was limited.

However, nobody was looking. This cave, facing the North Sea, was well away from the critical eyes of the S&C Coffee Bar set. They would never know. His reputation in Detroit was safe. And, yes, it had to be acknowledged, there was, deep in his sexual psyche, a perverse desire to be touched by this vile, mouth-watering little man, crouching, wanting and willing to work. And work he did. He worked well with tongue and clever, crafty hands. Naughty little fingers, naughty fingers sticky with drool, searched and slid around the nooks and crannies of bliss, as the boy's half focused eyes idly explored the dark recesses of that cave, now reverberating with crashing ecstasy. All these sensations were enjoyed, greatly enjoyed, safe in the knowledge that the worker with his hideous head would remain low, far away, far below navel level. After a few precious minutes of pleasure, Simeon finally succumbed. He succumbed to the succulent sounds of toadal slurps and slobber. He succumbed to overwhelming toadal touches, tickles, titillations and the soothing sounds of the North Sea. It all ended in that last familiar sound, that finality, the escaping sigh, the last, long, low murmur.

Chapter 21

Black Witch / White Witch

The toad shot out of that cave in triumph. He could now tell the world that he had *had* the spotty chicken, at minimal cost, during a very pleasant day out. The latter was feeling pleasantly drained and, at the same time, pleasantly replete. He was grateful that the former had not asked for reciprocation. In those days, a familiar sign in small shops said, 'Please do not ask for credit as refusal often offends'. In this instance, Mr Toad would certainly have been refused, since this particular chicken was a drone for all, except - other teenage boys. Accordingly, all was well because this particular toad happened to be a worker, a very effective worker.

Having caught a whiff of tomato and bacon sandwich from a quaint, if somewhat ramshackle cafe, the worker was now salivating with hunger. A few minutes later, hot sandwiches, thick, large and luscious, were eagerly consumed on a bench outside, under a cacophony of swirling gannets. It was a peaceful view. Bempton Cliffs, stretching out to Filey Brigg, were turning slightly tangerine in the late afternoon sun, which began to weaken and move further down to the north-west. After his busy munching, Aubrey became silent. Once again, Simeon noted the profile. Somehow, in this more gentle light, in complete repose, it was less repulsive and appeared more boyish. It was a peaceful moment. Like the day before, Simeon experienced that dread of returning to the USA, having to leave behind England, everything English - and Aubrey Pod.

The return journey was quiet and less urgent. Simeon was thinking about the postcards and noticed two omissions.

"Why didn't you send cards to Dolly and Becksitch Betty?"

"You may as well ask why I didn't send a card to Nobby the Gnome. I'd love to aggravate that silly, stupid little queen if he lived anywhere, but he lives nowhere at all. He wanders all over Derbyshire." He became thoughtful and tapped his crack of a mouth with the back of his thumb. "I suppose I could address a card to one of his favourite homes - Nobby the Gnome, Second Cubicle, Chester Green Public Convenience, Chester Green, Derby. That might get him into trouble!" Aubrey giggled and gloated.

"It's just the same with Dolly," he continued, "Nobody knows anything at all about Dolly, where he lives or works. At least he *does* work. He won't write or sign anything and will never be photographed. Dolly is a mystery. Becksitch Betty is *not* a mystery. Becksitch Betty is dangerous. Now, listen to me, Simeon, and listen well."

For emphasis, Aubrey Pod slowed the car, pulled over into a lay-by and faced his passenger to ensure maximum attention. It was one of the occasions when this childish, sometimes foolish, often funny little man showed a serious side and revealed a shrewd intelligence.

"This is good advice. Take heed. We, you and I, inhabit a world of backbiting catty queers, Derby, Nottingham - they are both as bad - but it rarely gets worse than insults. Now Becksitch Betty - he is something else, something more than just a bitchy drag queen. You won't catch me sending *him* a postcard! Don't be taken in by his entertaining patter. That one is deep and dark. Have *nothing* at all to do with him and, whatever you do, don't pass any comment about him. It can get back. The consequences could be perilous, because he's vengeful and vindictive. Becksitch Betty will never forgive. He's an evil man who may try to do you real harm. Last year, we had a regular at the Derby Turkish Baths called George who said something to Betty, some sort of tease or insult. Nobody seems to know the details. It doesn't matter. But listen here; the next day he was found in the Cattle Market cottage, badly beaten: a hospital job! I don't think for a minute that Arthur Bestwick did it himself, but he does have links with some very undesirable types. George has never been seen since - anywhere."

"I suppose Claud Hoadley ought to be very careful."

"Claud Hoadley will be *most* careful. And there is worse. Betty has had a sinister conversation with Dolly. He discussed killing a boy in the steam room of the Derby Turkish Baths! Dolly was horrified. You see, there was this cute chicken called Mickey, a rent boy, wouldn't look at me at any price. There'd been some dispute, something had gone wrong. Anyway, Betty was following through a plan he'd hatched, sort of thinking aloud, and suggested a situation in which he would be alone in the steam with Mickey. Betty mentioned all the noise, all the hissing and gurgling and said it would be a simple matter to grab at Mickey's face and crash his head back on those hard tiles. 'One good bang would be enough', Betty said. He'd casually walk out, have a shower, order his tea and than be as appalled as the rest of them when the awful news came. 'Poor Mickey. Who'd do a dirty trick like that? I was only talking to him 20 minutes ago.' I can just see that horrible twisting mouth moving all round that ugly face. Now then! See what I mean?"

"Well, what *did* happen to Mickey?"

"You tell me! Nobody seems to know. Nobby the Gnome used to see him a lot on his travels; various canals, various woods, parks, toilets - but that was last year. You hear bits of gossip. He was an orphan living in a council home in Derby. They've not seen him since winter. Sid heard somebody say that he'd gone to London. God knows."

It was approaching 8.00pm when they pulled up outside the Corporation Hotel in Derby's Cattle Market. Simeon eagerly escaped from the confines of the tin box, bounced out and stretched himself to the full. They made for the entrance, Aubrey keeping very close to his 'property' so that all within should be in no doubt that they were together, had arrived together and would leave together. The Corporation (strictly off limits to the Derby Camp) was not nearly so bad as previously painted by David Bond. Simeon had expected a dimly-lit Dickensian den of vice. Friendly faces, young and old, lined a crowded passageway humming with jolly banter. His heart leaped for joy when, near the door, he beheld the friendliest face of all. It was a nice face, a familiar pappy face of soft roundness, with big, orbicular, mischievous twinkling eyes. Once more, Simeon savoured those distinctive, beautiful round vowels softly spoken by the famous Dolly of Derby.

"Aren't you rather young to be in this tawdry tavern, Simeon? Naughty child! Look at this lot, leering at you, undressing you with their eyes. It's disgraceful." Several people nearby were highly entertained and laughed heartily. "And I shouldn't want you to be led astray by any of these saucy men," said he, waving an admonishing finger. Beckoning Simeon closer, he lowered his voice and, at the same time, made sure they could all hear the mock performance. "They don't come here just to play tiddly-winks you know. No. Some of these men are *naughty* men. Look at them. Some of them tiddle when they should be winking! Some of this lot are *rude*!"

"Who are you on about?" said a man with prominent fleshy jowls, in mock complaint.

"Well ... *you* for a start," said Dolly, softly, head slightly tilted with contrasting full face. "How many times have I told you to keep out of the Normanton Road cottage? And there you were again, yesterday, in and out like a yo-yo! It's dangerous. The police are watching it. I keep warning you, don't I? You'll not be told."

"You were there!" responded Jowls, with smug satisfaction, now looking rather like a hamster.

"I know the ropes," purred Dolly.

"Anyway," said Jowls, "I've got my excuses all ready." He raised his voice as if addressing a court of law. "May it please, Your Worship, I have - bladder trouble. So there!"

"Oh yes?" replied Dolly, not at all impressed. "And do you know what? They'll take you *straight* down to your doctor. And if you've not been in there for 'bladder trouble', you'll have trouble, and it won't be bladder trouble! You'll be in the 'Society Column'! I can see it now on the front page of the *Derby Evening Telegraph* - 'Lecherous Lecturer'."

Aubrey interrupted this trivia with an impatient declaration of buying them a drink. This signalled the end of the show and the audience returned to their private conversations.

"And how is your holiday progressing?" whispered Dolly in his characteristic purr.

Simeon liked Dolly. So did many others. He caressed the boy with soothing banter, gentle understanding, subtle counselling and suggestive undertones which encouraged a copious flow of useful information for Dolly's already pregnant data bank. It was a one-way flow. Dolly took in much - and gave out little. Five minutes later, he was still busy debriefing the chicken, mixing deep murmurs with occasional nods. Aubrey struggled back through the crush, precariously holding two glasses of orange. He presented the first to Dolly and the second to Simeon.

"This my new friend from America. We've had a lovely day out at Flamborough, exploring caves," shouted Aubrey, addressing the total assembly to make absolutely sure that they had all heard him. "We've been getting to know each other better," he added, licking his lips in a effort to hammer the point home. Half of this assembly ignored Mr Toad, exhibiting his catch, well known for his boasting. The other half looked, but looked as though they were looking at vermin, regarding the unsightly little man with utter contempt. Aubrey was not prepared to waste his time in the Corporation passageway. "I'll see you two later," he said defiantly, before zigzagging, pushing and manoeuvring his shapeless body out of the building.

"He didn't get himself a drink."

"Of course not. He's not interested in a drink," replied Dolly, "He's gone to find excitement elsewhere, outside, in the public lavatory," he added in a deepening, vibrant tone. "Aubrey needs a dark, dirty, disreputable place. Just as Bela Lugosi once said, our toad is 'a child of the night'. Long summer days are not exactly the best time of year for Aubrey. He finds it difficult to score in any light, even in this dim light."

Seizing on the subject of darkness, Simeon guided it towards Becksitch Betty. Was he really as evil as everybody seemed to think? Dolly gave him a typical 'Dolly answer' - clever, but cryptic.

"Do you know Simeon, Derbyshire has many interesting old queens, but I would say that only two are witches. One is a black witch and the other is a white witch. Becksitch Betty is the black witch. Aubrey has given you good advice. At all costs don't offend Betty with any casual comment. Mr Bestwick will fly into a rage and put a curse on you. He'll then take practical steps to make sure it's effective. You *might* just get away with calling Betty an unsightly old hag, but you'll not escape the consequences of belittling or making snide remarks about his work. He's proud of his impressions. Strictly speaking, from a legal point of view, it has to be an impression rather than an impersonation. Anyway, it's a laugh, all very droll. He does an entertaining turn."

"He's good then?"

"He's very good indeed. He might have become quite famous, but he's never wanted to be anything but a 'one man show'. He won't be managed and won't travel far. One or two appearances at Blackpool, perhaps. He's not as old as he looks, but not as active as he used to be. Still does a bit, but nothing like his shows before the war. That was Betty's golden age. He was actually quite pretty as a young lad." Dolly stared down at the floor, a wistful look in his big eyes. "Ah yes: the Alfreton Odeon, the Ripley Hippodrome and the Matlock Picture Palace."

"Somebody mentioned his shows at the Matlock Lido."

"Yes. I've taken carloads to those. Good value at 25 shillings, which includes a four-course meal. A sort of cabaret. His Carmen Miranda was effective, fruit and all, but most folks preferred his Old Mother Riley take-off."

For a moment, Simeon recalled a childhood image of Arthur Lucan's feisty old washerwoman, who was very popular in the 1930's. The squawking harridan of trademark flailing limbs would leap around the silver screen, precipitating shrieks of laughter within the darkness of the Heanor Empire.

"Who is the white witch?"

"Now there is someone you *must* meet - a real legend that one! And he'd love to meet you."

"Likes chicken?"

Giving consideration to this, gently Dolly patted his fat, fleshy lips with four white, carefully-manicured fingers.

"Not *too* young ... no ... early twenties I should say. Simon Tonks likes his lads to be rough and tough; coal miners, labourers etc. Quite a lady but doesn't want to be treated like one. Prefers them on the rugged side, likes them to be a bit ... shall we say ... wild?" Dolly was now subtly moving closer, descending into his characteristic seductive purr in a deeper register. "Yes, that's it." Going deeper still: "He likes them ... forceful, coarse and crude - if you know what I mean."

"You're turning me on!"

"Oh! I'm such a naughty Dolly."

"Where does the witchcraft come in with this old queen?"

"No, no, no. You've got it all wrong; not old at all! Simon Tonks has been young for years, many years: a real live fairy who has discovered the elixir of eternal youth. Youth is his trade mark. Peter Pan, that one, the very opposite of Jasper Wormall. In living memory, no one can recall a time when Jasper hasn't looked like a rotting old crone. Same sort of thing with this little fairy. He's been around for ever, but *never* seems to get any older than 19! Of course," continued Dolly, tongue firmly in cheek, "Simon works hard at it: various creams, make-up and the rest."

"Amazing," mused the boy, softly. "Fairies, witches, gnomes, crones, goblins, toads, hags ... "

"Yes, I see what you mean," replied Dolly, coquettishly and thoughtfully with his ball-like head on one side. "It's a strange, secret world you've stumbled into, isn't it? It would be different in London or in any big city. It's different in Nottingham, but this is Derbyshire. Derbyshire is special. Our roots go back a long way, right back to pagan days. Our towns and villages have always had a Jasper, a Toby Jug, a Guzzly Granddad, a Becksitch Betty. We've always had our gnomes, toads and fairies. I've capitalised on it. I do trips, you know.

"I've heard."

"Now what about this cycling trip you were telling me about? Where did you say, the 'far north'? When does it take place?"

"Tomorrow, if this nice weather holds."

"Would you like to meet Peter Pan?"

"Very much so - and the whole freak show."

"You're in luck. It so happens that Simon Tonks is staying in Chesterfield with friends. Go into Queen's Park and sit on a bench at about tea-time."

"What bench? And how will I know him?"

"Any bench. He'll find *you*. And when you see him - you'll know it's Peter Pan. He might have Tinker Bell with him."

"Tinker Bell!"

At this point, Aubrey Pod, wiping his mouth, burst into the passageway and, at top volume for all to hear, announced that it was time to move on. He was taking his chicken to Nottingham, to the Flying Horse.

Chapter 22

The Flying Horse

Simeon had always found Derby an interesting place. He enjoyed its character, grit, corners and cobbles. Compared to Horsley Woodhouse it was a big city, but, in 1965, Derby was just a town and more than a decade away from becoming a city. Racing along the A52 with determined jutting jaw and frequent toots, the toadmobile was entering a city which was totally confident in its city status. It had been a city since medieval days. The light was failing, but the wide road into Nottingham was green, broad and impressive. Simeon and Aubrey darted along a verdant boulevard, flashing under the attractive foliage of mature trees and unconsciously tasting a soup of late spring scents; Wollaton Park to the north and the equally sylvan University of Nottingham to the south. It was beautiful.

The Flying Horse Hotel, on Cheapside, just off the Old Market Square, had a Tudor appearance, a fairytale fantasy of steep gables overhanging the pavement. To eyes which had seen so many utilitarian box buildings in Detroit, this old travellers' inn of Elizabethan origins was a joy to behold. Pegasus, the winged steed, soared above them on the inn sign. This magical horse with the power of flight had always been interpreted as an allegory of the soul's immortality - but Simeon knew nothing of Greek mythology. Such an image should have lifted his spirits, because, in his innocence, Simeon was hoping he might find a pure white stallion within. Perhaps he might find a beautiful youth to fly him away in ecstasy; something young, hard and butch, something natural and unaffected. The total appearance, however, suggested otherwise.

It seemed forbidding. It looked posh and exclusive, threatening to exclude all scruffy chickens. Simeon was reluctant to enter. He had felt that same dread outside The Corporation and, worse, outside The Friary. So much was opposed to entry. He did not drink alcohol, he hated its taste and hated the smell. He did not want to suffer the hard stares of unknown, homosexual men standing around in (apparent) hostile groups. Had The Flying Horse been a steam bath, Simeon would have rushed in, eager to disrobe, eager to make contact with those same unknown men in a dark orgy room and eager to refresh himself with pots of tea afterwards. Entry was made easier by Aubrey leading the way. It was Aubrey's triumph (even more than The Corporation) to enter The Flying Horse with a desirable chicken.

Yet again, it became clear that Simeon was inappropriately dressed. The Flying Horse was plush, palatial and definitely a bar for smart suits. Mr Toad, who always wore a tie, barely passed muster with his slightly shabby, ill-fitting Harris Tweed jacket and trousers. Treading the York stone flags of the old carriage entrance, they turned into the reception area which had an unnerving bear's head staring down at the boy. He winced when about two dozen pairs of snooty eyes scrutinised the ill-matched, rather odd duo. After a few minutes, he was able to make observations and comparisons with the previous venues. The crush of The Corporation passageway of more 'down-to-earth' folk had forced a certain ease of communication and camaraderie. It was difficult to be stand-offish in such a small space. The Nottingham Camp, in contrast, was characterised by reserve, a dignified solemnity and the low hum of la-di-da speech, but, as David had said, perhaps not *quite* as formal, pompous or pretentious as the Derby Camp. There was more confidence in The Flying Horse, more freedom, less intimidation, more laughter and more fun. Feeling a little better-relaxed and mindful of Aubrey's generosity, Simeon braved the bar and bought the drinks. Nursing an orange juice he did not particularly want, he scanned the room, trying to identify the top two - Tommy and Martin. He failed.

"They're not here," said Aubrey. "Which means they're throwing a big party tonight. That explains why it's not so crowded. It's usually chock-a-block on Saturday night. Good riddance, I say. Better without them. I'll not miss Tommy's vicious comments. Nasty couple! Insist on the best; they'll touch nothing less than perfection. Woe to those with a bit of extra weight. They call Dolly 'Lard Arse'! Won't be a minute, I'm off to the cottage."

Simeon's heart sank. He stood there, alone, awkwardly cradling his glass. He feared that Aubrey would be gone many minutes, depending on his level of success. However, a distinguished tall gentleman with white hair broke away from one of the de-luxe groups standing by a large fireplace. He approached and addressed the uncomfortable chicken in a genteel but unaffected and comfortable accent. It was a memorable voice, a deep, brown voice, rich in sonorous tones.

"It's usual to offer a drink, but on this occasion, I don't appear to have that particular excuse." He looked down at the glass and flashed the boy a disarming, attractive smile. "I'll go away if you tell me, but I hope you don't. My name is Edward."

He offered a large, warm, well-manicured hand. The quiet assurance of his bearing spoke of breeding, a quality education and high position. After a few minutes of pleasant exchange, Simeon was hoping that Mr Toad was having a great time and would take all the time he needed. The attraction was not sexual. Edward was old enough to be Simeon's grandfather. Even so, the lad was totally charmed by this gentle gentleman and freely gave him a full account of his holiday to date. Still trying to make sense of his new world, he asked many questions and received information.

"What are they like? Well now, let me see. I would say that they are exactly what the homosexual community needs: generous, responsible, caring and very kind." Edward spoke thoughtfully, his eyes resting on the gentle amber glow of a heavy wrought-iron standard lamp. He roused himself. "You're quite right about Tommy's dreaded tongue. He can be very nasty indeed, but, you know, Simeon, his barbs are carefully aimed at those who *deserve* it. There's a lot of pretentiousness in our society and Tommy is highly skilled in pricking the bubble of pomposity. That's why he's hated in Derby. And the fact is, these verbal barbs are extremely entertaining. I don't suppose you've come across Bob and Clarence yet?"

"Not yet. Nottingham Camp?"

"Very much Nottingham. Nice chaps, not exactly top drawer. Social climbers, of course, desperately climbing during the last few years - struggling like mad, grasping, scraping, trying to ascend up to that elusive top drawer." He took a deep breath and changed key. "Seek improvement by all means, young man, but don't try *too* hard, don't become a laughing stock like Bob and Clarence. Stay true to yourself and don't try to be something which you are not."

"I think you were going to give me an example of a 'Tommy barb'.

"Indeed I was. You've probably heard of the new Vanden Plas 'R'. Beautiful job, not a Roller, but almost as big and it does have a Rolls Royce engine. It doesn't ride, it floats. Tommy and Martin took delivery of a new one last January. You've heard of 'keeping up with the Jones', well, here in Nottingham, we all try to keep up with Tommy and Martin. One day a certain comment was overheard."

Edward affected the careful, slow, artificial speech and deprecating soft laugh of Clarence -

"Vanden Plas! Somewhat *ostentatious*, don't you think? Rather a liability, one would have though."

"It is never a good idea voicing such criticisms in Nottingham," continued Edward, "They go round and round until they get back to Tommy and Martin. Nothing happened until last month, when Bob and Clarence proudly displayed *their* new car for all to admire. I must admit it was a little jewel; beautiful finish with a tasteful leather and wood interior reeking of quality. We all lavished approval and compliments on this luxury motorcar which, in fact, was the smaller version of the Vanden Plas with an Austin 1300 engine. Parked next to the real thing - it was tiny and, naturally, we all avoided obvious unkind comparisons. You see, Simeon, the Vanden Plas 1300 was somewhat like Bob and Clarence - it was trying hard to be something it was not and that gave Tommy his ammunition."

"Oh, dear. What did he say?"

"Mostly he made appropriate comments, said nice things like the rest of us. Bob talked us through the impressive polished dashboard of buttons and switches. It was when Clarence demonstrated the cocktail cabinets attached on the back seat, little trays really, that's when the verbal blow was delivered -

'Yes ... ' said Tommy, in his lazy, menacing drawl, just prior to the pounce. 'Quite a nice little touch that. How sweet. You'll be able to put your plastic cups on it won't you? You know, the ones you bought in Woolworths.'"

"I think I'll keep away from Tommy and Martin."

"You'd be making a colossal mistake if you did. They *run* Nottingham and have enormous influence in other places. Just mention them in Brighton, Bournemouth or London. Tommy and Martin - it's the gold standard, it opens doors."

"I expect it's closed the door to Bob and Clarence going to the big party tonight."

"On the contrary! They'll be there all right. Tommy's rule - 'never put an acid queen beyond swiping distance.'"

"Pardon?"

"He means that it's better to have your prey within the hearing of a caustic comment. Clarence made a mistake, but he and Bob still need to stay within the Nottingham Camp, eat humble pie and be seen at court."

Noting a puzzled look, he explained. "'The Court' is the name of Tommy and Martin's rather grand house in The Park, a rather select area here in central Nottingham. I think it's derived from Martin's surname 'Harcourt' and, possibly his job, since he works in a court of law."

Encouraged by this flow of privileged information, Simeon made bold to ask about the profession of Tommy.

"Wouldn't we all like to know! Not at all clear. According to the whispers, he's a senior executive in some big organisation. I'm told they never buy petrol for their cars - all paid for by the company."

"Cars? They have *another* car!"

"I understand the Vanden Plas is the main car. Martin runs an MGB. Oh yes, they're very well off ... and then there is Butch; hardly his real name, but very apt."

"Butch?"

"Butch is the much lusted-after Negro 'house boy' they fished out of Manhattan about five years ago. A magnificent specimen, a delight to the eye, and that superior posterior ... oh *yes*, a bum to die for!"

"Really!" replied Simeon, the Detroit white boy who had acquired a taste for black bottoms. He was quite moved by Edward's enthusiasm and entertained thoughts of gatecrashing The Court.

"Of course, he has to work very hard with all those dinner parties they give, but his presentation is impeccable. An excellent cook. I've enjoyed some of his more exotic dishes, his speciality."

"How do you get an invitation to a Tommy and Martin party?"

"In your case," laughed Edward, "just get yourself seen."

All eyes turned to the door to behold a majestic entourage making a regal entrance. Simeon was astounded to recognise the principals of the Derby Camp. Anomalous, small camp steps of the large, soft Hilary Raymond Hawley contrasted with the unremarkable gait of the skull, who was in conversation with David Bond, who was followed by about six nodding heads. After the fashion of a stately galleon, Claud Hoadley, no less, nose in the air, led the pompous procession up to the bar. Hoadley's cool eye rested on the boy for a mere fraction of a second. In that tiny space of time, Simeon attempted to smile a greeting to this man who had graciously 'received' him just 24 hours before. That fraction of time was too small. The shrewd eyes quickly reconnoitred other members in this camp, the camp of the enemy, before their attention was taken by David Bond, who was offering drinks to the inner circle. Simeon was hurt to be ignored by Hoadley, but quite wounded by David's unsmiling, unenthusiastic, very slight nod of acknowledgement.

"Forget it, my boy," broke in Edward. "Bond is firmly affiliated to Hoadley. 'Bonded' to him, if you'll forgive me. By now he's been read the Riot Act and is back in line. He'll not dare to come over here, you see."

"But coming *here*, to the Flying Horse, in enemy territory!"

"A Saturday night ritual. It's a public place. They've probably come down from The George, up the road. We go to the Derby Turkish Baths and they come here. Of course, it's not without its perils. They have to run the gauntlet of Tommy's cruel quips - a different backbite every time. Wicked as they are, those snide remarks are actually very clever. I ought to be taking notes and write a book - *Acid Drops from Tommy Sperry*. Could be a bestseller. Now what was it last Saturday? Oh, yes, as the Hoadley gang minced in, Tommy looked over, beamed his big sardonic smile and said - 'Oh, I see the Royal Family have arrived!'"

"What did Mr Hoadley say?"

"Absolutely nothing, dear boy. Nose in the air with a dignified silence. Very wise. He can't compete with Tommy Sperry and he knows it. Hoadley may be many things, but he's no fool."

A much younger and rather handsome fellow left Edward's group and joined them.

"Are you going to hog this delightful urchin all evening, Edward? Now I call that *jolly* unfair, what what."

"We're discussing Tommy's style of abuse, Alfred. You know, the quick-witted insults aimed at the Derby Camp when they make an entrance."

"Oh, I look forward to them!" beamed the ebullient Alfred. "Poor old Hawley doesn't have a chance with initials of HRH. Do you remember when Tommy said - 'Here they come, lions led by a donkey: Claud Hoadley, no less, a legend in her own lunch hour'. It's brilliant! Oscar Wilde couldn't have done better. What's your favourite, Edward?"

"Oh, I don't know. Perhaps that evening about a month ago. Do you remember when they trooped in rather late? 'Oh! Look everybody! At last! Miss Hoadley in person, complete with loyal claque, the only queen I know who is a figment of her own imagination."

"How about that for perception! Spot on," said Alfred.

"What do you mean?" said the 'urchin', looking from one face to the other, seeking enlightenment.

"Alfred is referring to Hoadley being a rather impressive self-made job," explained Edward. "Claud Hoadley has spent his whole life working very hard to be Claud Hoadley."

"Indubitably," said Alfred in keen support. "He's polished up an accent which is something close to a 1925 Nancy Mitford; an amazing assault on the ears. You could cut it with a knife. Hardly the accent of a schoolmaster in a regular state grammar school."

"No," replied Edward in a sigh, catching the occasional highly-polished vowel floating over from the bar. "No, indeed. Anyone would take him to be the Lord Chancellor."

A sudden thought flashed into the mind of Alfred.

'A Freudian slip? Now I wonder ... is it possible?'

Edward's profession had never been disclosed to anybody. Alfred suddenly saw his friend in robes and that noble head was now crowned with a wig. It all fitted, the ever-present stately seniority, the dignified demeanour, that air of authority ... is Edward a judge?

A silence descended as they looked to the bar and tuned into Mr Hoadley as he addressed his admiring audience of nodding heads. In refined tones of Royalty, he had just finished denouncing the new floating 'pirate' radio stations as an 'affront to good taste' and was now bemoaning the annual summer mayhem caused by beach battles between Mods and Rockers.

Simeon became mesmerised by the ornate body language of this pretentious troop of elegant Derby queens, moving about, parading and vaunting, reinforcing their social superiority with every sickening gesture; hands on hips: small dainty steps. All the nodding heads appeared to be smiling, sneering, progressing slowly, in an etiquette-laden mince across that floor, accentuating their social position.

In Hilary Raymond Hawley alone, he had never seen a more affected, effeminate man. This scruffy chicken - a one-time fully paid up member of macho youth, a one-time mate of solid, working-class lads who marched across Heanor Market Place with gritty gait - was utterly repelled when the big, soft Hawley emitted an aristocratic giggle, flourished his silk handkerchief and seemed to make an elaborate bow to his Lord and Master, the Great Hoadley. It was all so artificial, all so formal, so well-arranged, so well-choreographed ... What did it remind him of? The scruffy chicken had seen all this somewhere ... recently? Where? What?

And then it came to him. Marie Antoinette! He had recently seen the 1938 film, *Marie Antoinette*, starring Norma Shearer, a film full of toffs and fops, full of the exaggerated, stylised elegance of 18th century France. Of course! It was the minuet! It was the one scene which really revolted Simeon. One scene was set against the backdrop of obscene opulence, the gilded splendour of Versailles, when all these pampered ponces began to move in the most affected manner, in a slow, stately dance. Here and now, the Derby Camp appeared to be doing a minuet. They seemed to move in a co-ordinated pattern dance, in three quarter time, to the dignified strains of Bach, around Claud Hoadley. Perhaps a bow here, a curtsy there, in this impromptu ballroom in front of the Flying Horse bar. A nauseating display after the style of the worst excesses of affected 18th century French dancing.

Chapter 23

Jealousy, Envy and a Rattle Snake

Still hungry for information, looking for links, Simeon tested his companions by recycling the gossip about Becksitch Betty. Was it true? Alfred gave way to Edward.

"We'll put that question to our official historian here. Don't look surprised, old boy, you were on the scene long before I was born."

Edward smiled and decided to give a brief history lesson.

"Some of us here in Nottingham have had problems with that unpleasant 'black witch', as you call him, Becksitch Betty. Simeon, let me tell you this. A more dangerous evil is the handsome man who is subtle, the man who, over the years, puts in the poison, the man who appears to be your friend and keeps you off guard. How can I put it? Back in the early thirties, we were all scared stiff at the Pictures by a horrible monster who filled the big screen. It had been assembled from body parts by a mad scientist."

"Frankenstein," said Alfred.

"The original. We were all rather innocent in those days and that creature was seen as an image of pure evil. It really packed a punch. At about the same time, I read an article about a young man who was doing rather well in politics. A compelling photograph showed a beautifully-sculptured face, sharp chiselled features, stunning looks. He was a dream. I pasted that picture in the scrapbook and drooled over it for years."

"I say!" interrupted Alfred. "Are we speaking of His Majesty over there?"

"It could easily have been Hoadley," chuckled Edward. "Indeed," he added wistfully, "the Claud of 40 years ago was certainly a head turner. Oh yes, fine, fair and quite comely. And in those far off days, as I recall, a much nicer person." He took a deep breath and slowly shook his head. "No. My young man of the much-admired photograph died young. He was assassinated in 1942 and the Czech village of Lidice was destroyed in retaliation." In the brief silence which followed, the other two waited for more. "Reinhard Heydrich was gorgeous. He was also a German Nazi official, without mercy, deputy to Himmler, who organised the mass extermination of the Jews."

"Your point being ... " attempted Alfred slowly.

"I suppose I'm trying to say something about the nature of evil. Take that man over there." They all looked at Hoadley, the centre of attention, still holding the floor. "Yes, I knew him as a young man, but I can't honestly impugn him as evil, although he has done evil."

"Good heavens! Details, please."

"No details, no real evidence. Hoadley's far too subtle, far too careful, but I can tell you that he is the architect of this dreadful war which has been raging since the 1920's between our two camps."

Edward went on to explain that Hoadley was appointed as a classics / history master to the Herbert Strutt Grammar School at Belper in the September of 1921, when he was fresh out of university at the age of 23.

"Like many of our young chaps, he had a terrible experience in the Great War; indeed, lucky to have come home at all. All the same, I'm not at all convinced it was the war alone which warped young Hoadley. No. He was deeply ashamed of his working-class background. His father was some sort of machinist at the Belper Cotton Mill, eventually becoming a foreman ... and then there was a traumatic love affair with a local youth, a labourer. Bad business that, made him very bitter. However, Claud was clever and made his parents proud. If excessively strict, he became a good teacher. Not exactly a popular teacher, but very effective and often entertaining. Latin was not a favourite subject, but the pupils did enjoy Hoadley's history lessons. One boy in particular, who was a 'first year' in September 1921, hung on to the master's every word. He was a lad of average ability - perhaps a touch below - considering his weak spelling, poor writing in general and lack of confidence. But this boy had been blessed with reasonable intelligence, had a flair for being articulate and needed encouragement."

"Did he get it from Hoadley?" said Alfred.

"Yes ... and no," replied Edward, slowly and enigmatically, looking directly at Alfred. "Have you heard of the legend of how Mozart died?"

"Mozart! How did we get on to Mozart?"

"There's a theory that he was murdered by another composer, a mediocrity called Salieri, who was hateful and envious."

"Hate and envy! Yes, I've heard that said of Hoadley."

"Hoadley and Salieri have something else in common, my friend. They were able to disguise their hate and envy. Oh, yes. They were able to subsume those poisonous emotions and *appear* to be helpful. That child at the grammar school worshipped his teacher. That powerful personality dominated his pupil, boy and man, for a quarter of a century with a kindly smiling face of good advice; advice which was, in reality, poisonous."

"Come on Edward. Let's be knowing. Surely this 'abused boy' can't possibly be yourself! We've always assumed you were older than Hoadley, if you'll forgive me. You've worn better, of course."

"Thank you, kind sir. It's true. I can give Claud a few years and couldn't possibly have been that trusting youth who idolised and exalted that pretentious ponce." Edward spat out those words. His attractive features were temporarily marred by acrid memories and emotions. More thoughtfully, he went on. "I wonder if we are ever really conscious of our envy? It's the most toxic emotion and does the most damage."

"Why would Mr Hoadley be so envious of a pupil?" inquired Simeon.

"Probably wasn't at first. But this lad, Jack Gormley, eventually became the teacher's friend. Jack's homosexuality would soon become apparent. It's easy to spot, if you're tuned in. We look at boys. We don't look at girls. People notice. Hoadley noticed."

"Perhaps Jack was a bit camp," suggested Alfred.

"He was not the least bit effeminate. He came from a rough working-class background. He had to survive and was forced to fit in. I suppose it would be in the sixth form when Jack started to spread his wings. He found the right cottages, discovered the Turkish Baths and the Corporation passageway. Hoadley kept an eye on things and became all-powerful. He became a sort of Dutch uncle and mentor to the boy, warning him of dangers and guiding him through his academic and social development. I've no doubt that such wise counsel was beneficial to a raw recruit from humble origins, especially in those dark days when being queer was treated with even more contempt than it is today."

"Illegal is illegal. Then, as now. I can't see there's been much improvement in the last half century," moaned Alfred.

"Is it against the law to be gay?" asked Simeon.

"Not actually to *be* queer, but they'll put you in prison if you're caught having sex with a man," clarified Alfred.

"I'm a tad more hopeful," said Edward. "At least we hear the occasional voice in Parliament calling for change. Back to Hoadley. I was choosing my words carefully when I said 'mentor'."

"Teacher, advisor, counsellor?" suggested Alfred.

"More than that, a mentor is *trusted.* That is the key to the Hoadley technique. He could undermine confidence without being detected.

If ever challenged, he could deploy formidable arguments of justification, heaping onto his victim further humiliation, and the challenger always backed down in abject failure. Eaten up with envy, this power of eloquence turned Hoadley into a monster."

"But *why* and *how*?" pleaded Simeon, putting his question for the second time.

Edward fell silent for a moment in an effort to martial his thoughts to give the matter an accurate assessment and make a reasonable presentation.

"There is no easy answer and any answer must contain the biases and prejudices of the speaker. I used the word 'envy', which is often confused with 'jealousy'. Hoadley was, and is, both. He was envious of the boy's youth, his charm, his good looks, his easy-going personality and his growing popularity. He was jealous when he feared losing this boy, when he perceived that his influence and power were coming under threat. In this he was completely wrong. My friend loved Claud Hoadley, tried to be like him, trusted him and was totally obedient. It was inconceivable to this boy that his friend and teacher would try to harm him."

"How *did* he harm him?" asked Alfred.

"The Derby lot think that Hoadley is a saint, but we know better. Hoadley is a sadist. He seeks out the sensitive, the vulnerable. He operates at a low level which is barely detectable. He specialises in humiliation, making people feel uncomfortable in front of a crowd."

"For example?" said Alfred.

"Well, you've heard of his obsession with table manners. Jack was mortified during several dinner parties."

Edward affected the Hoadley cut-glass accent.

"Not like that, boy! Dear, dear. People of quality always move the soup spoon *away* from oneself, never towards oneself as in the case of the working clarrrsses." He watched the other guests and gathered that it was acceptable to tilt the bowl to obtain the last of the soup.

"No, no, no, Jack! Tilting the bowl towards you is indicative of lowly origins. A true gentleman will always tilt the bowl *away* from himself."

"All meals were dreaded," continued Edward. "Breakfast became an obstacle course of painful reprimands. He was berated for applying dabs of brown sauce over his grill instead of 'discreetly in one place at the side of one's plate, arrrfter the style of a cultured gentleman.' The eating of toast was fraught with perils. 'Cut it again, boy, like so, and for goodness sake use the correct knife. *That* one is for the butter!' He addressed the others around that table. 'I despair! It's like breakfasting with a peasant.' It was the same with English grammar. Split infinitives were a convenient target. Year after year this child would open up his heart, enthuse his enthusiasms, only to be savagely crushed over and over again by endless biting, cutting, comments from that sour, sadistic pedant. On one occasion he was pouring over a 'one inch' map, all excited about a forthcoming walking holiday in the Yorkshire Dales where, en route, they would encounter a curious rock feature.

'Here it is, Mr Hoadley, joost like you said, The Booter Toobs'.

'*How* many times must I remind you about sounding 'closed U's! It puts you firmly in the plebeian clarrss. Cushion, sugar and butcher are all closed U's, but, not the words - 'just' 'butter' or 'tub'. Repeat arrrfter me, Jack - batter tabs - batter tabs - batter tabs.'"

Edward explained how the sheer isolation of homosexuality could leave a working class youth open to emotional and mental abuse from a cruel man like Claud Hoadley.

"Just like the rest of us, the teenage Jack was vulnerable. He was trapped inside an alien world of heterosexual values, mores and customs. We've all been there. We know what it's like. He stood back and watched his mates get on with their lives - dates, girlfriends and eventually marriage. He looked to Hoadley for protection and guidance. Hoadley controlled Jack. He decided who Jack could meet and, more significantly, who he could *not* meet. Once, Jack disobeyed and had a disastrous love affair with a boy which reduced him to tears in front of his dearest friend - the friend he *trusted*, the friend he had consulted for comfort and emotional support ... "

Edward's voice cracked. He faltered on the edge of breaking down, composed himself and continued with determination and venom. "Hoadley showed Jack about as much compassion and understanding as you'd expect from a rattlesnake."

In the Upper Sixth, Jack Gormley expressed a desire to be become a teacher.

"We'll get nowhere if you are not prepared to be realistic, Jack," retorted Hoadley, concluding with his, 'I have spoken', thin lips pressed tightly together stance. "College is required for the profession of a schoolmaster and, I can assure you, Jack, that you fall *far* short of college standards. Give some consideration to an office job or, possibly, junior management in one of the better high street stores."

With encouragement from the headmaster, Jack did much better than shop work or even teacher training college. Eventually, he attended Durham University. Not a university which impressed Claud Hoadley. He commented to his disciples that standards were definitely below their pre-war level when a lowly boy of limited ability like Jack Gormley could find his way into such an academy. Full of misplaced hero worship, Jack was still working hard, desperately trying to make his friend and former master proud of him. In the second year he was set on becoming a writer.

"A writer!" cried the outraged Hoadley, spitting feathers. "Jack! Just listen to yourself; a writer, indeed! You can't spell. Composing a reasonable letter is a major undertaking. Your work is littered with grammatical inaccuracies."

This conversation and several others of a similar nature were related to one of Jack's sympathetic professors, who detected a malicious influence. He suggested a cautious approach to the advice of Mr Claud Hoadley and steered Jack into a different direction which would stretch his skills of debate, lucid argument and fluent expression. In 1932, he graduated and went to law school. In 1934, he took his Bar exams and was called to the Bar at Middle Temple. The following year, he was accepted into chambers in Nottingham and was launched on the road to a thriving practice as a barrister.

"I've never heard of a Nottingham barrister called Jack Gormley!" said a sceptical Alfred.

"Claud Hoadley has," replied a smiling and cryptic Edward. "You see, Alfred ... the trouble is ... in the name. Nottingham Road, with its long rows of terraced housing, was a fairly rough part of Belper in those days. Jack's father was a miner and Gormley was a common name. Hoadley brainwashed Jack constantly, reminding him of his low birth and so ... "

"Hang on!" interrupted Alfred in excitement. "Can it be that Jack changed his name to ... to ... "

"A name which reflected his new status, a posh sounding name which reflected his new found confidence ... "

"Martin Harcourt!"

"Exactly," said Edward in triumph. Jack Gormley had re-invented himself.

Chapter 24

"From Ancient Grudge Break to New Mutiny"

"It happened within a few seconds," said Edward, thoughtfully staring into the middle distance.

"Pardon?" said Alfred.

"The crash. The big collapse. The falling of the fallen idol. The moment when Martin Harcourt suddenly saw Claud Hoadley for what he was and realised that he was a fraud. Like the moment when that dog Toto pulled away the curtain and revealed the mighty Wizard of Oz, who turned out to be an ordinary man operating a theatrical front."

Edward had been a witness to this historic incident, which took place by candlelight one freezing Friday night in February, 1947, at the Friary Hotel bar. Non-stop blizzards and sub-zero temperatures had brought Britain to its economic knees and Claud Hoadley was about to lose one of his most devoted admirers.

Martin Harcourt had been at the Bar for twelve successful years. His reputation grew and briefs poured in. Judges spoke of his superb delivery. Every sentence was beautifully constructed. His vocabulary, his syntax, his approach in that persuasive, smooth, silver, silken tongue was without equal at the Nottingham Bar. Silken - that was the word seized upon by one supportive colleague.

"You're wasted here, Martin. You're an experienced advocate. They all ask for Mr Harcourt. Don't you think it's time you joined our small legal elite? Take Silk, my boy. Get down to London, earn some real money. Martin Harcourt KC. Try it on for size. How does it feel? How does it sound?"

It felt good. In the ear of Martin Harcourt it sounded very good indeed and, on that frozen Friday evening, he decided to consult his most trusted counsellor, who was holding a court of nodding heads. The Derby Camp had made a brave journey through snow and ice. They patiently listened to Martin's enthusiastic proposal to select two High Court Judges who would be prepared to act as sponsors to support his application for Silk. All fell silent in the flickering candlelight as they waited for their leader's response to this earnest appeal. He flicked off his immaculate sleeve, a tiny speck, and looked sadly at the boy before him. Indeed, the unsuspecting 37-year-old, with his boyish good looks, could easily pass for a boy in his mid-twenties and Jack Gormley would always be a working class boy in the envious eyes of the high and mighty Hoadley. A shadow of a condescending smile preceded a demeaning summing-up.

"Martin, dear Martin, you have enjoyed *more* than your fair share of good fortune since those far-off days when you first stood before me in my clarrrss-room. Of course, we're all delighted with your long run of luck. Haven't I always said, 'Jack always falls on his feet'." All heads nodded and Hoadley exchanged a sneering smirk with a recent recruit, a soft, pappy young queen called Hilary. "But *do* take heed, Martin. You are where you are because of ... how shall I put it ... serendipity? You have a knack of ... self-advertisement, a knack of oral presentation. You have skills, but they are the skills of a actor, not the skills of a lawyer. A series of flukes have put you into the company of your betters. Jack, forgive me, but I must call you Jack. People like you, Jack, people of your station do *not* become barristers. Be content with what you have achieved thus far. Be satisfied. Do not put your fortuity to the test. We, your friends, who speak the truth, genuinely fear that you will fail that test with disastrous results. For goodness sake, don't let them discover that Martin Harcourt is really ... well, really just Jack Gormley, the son of a collier."

The speaker concluded, pressed thin, anaemic lips together and stole eye contact with Hilary for a second time. The latter returned another reptilian smirk and uttered a simpering 'ha ha ha', a frequent motif which had already began to irritate Martin Harcourt who was, as usual, humiliated, crushed and defeated. But something in that dual 'put down', that observed exchange of smirks between those sneering snobs in that darkened cold bar produced, for the first time, a shaft of brilliant light illuminating Claud Hoadley and his disciples, a Damascene vision showing them up exactly as they were - pure poison.

After that heartfelt advice, Hoadley suggested that they adjourn early in view of the appalling conditions outside. Martin Harcourt was thoughtful. During that slippery, treacherous journey home in Edward's car, Martin fell silent and sullen. He reflected on 26 years of treachery, as he perceived, against himself. He reflected upon a fallen idol. He reviewed numerous past episodes of advice, lectures, comments, reprimands, embarrassments and saw them in a totally new light. In the warmth and safety of Edward's home, they talked and talked into the small hours of Saturday, February 15th - reviewing, assessing, trying to analyse the complex Hoadley / Harcourt relationship. The older man, who was free from the grip of emotional turmoil, attempted a neutrality and tried to show his friend that the tangled and dangerous world of homosexuality itself was a severe complication in this devilish process of apportioning blame. Edward never tried to excuse Hoadley, but urged his friend to forget the past and move on. He pointed to his success as a barrister and argued that, on the face of it, Hoadley had not damaged his career in any serious way.

Wise words, but Edward could not see into the heart of Martin Harcourt. Martin *was* damaged - seriously damaged. Martin was a brooder. Martin, the younger man, was open, trusting and able to forgive. Martin had a good memory - a long memory. He had a tendency to 'play back' the wrongs and humiliations he had suffered many years before. Martin, the older man, was beset with intrusive thoughts, ugly thoughts, thoughts of revenge. He became disposed to nurse a grudge, to conceive possible plans to bring Claud Hoadley low - and it would be important that a humbled Hoadley would know that his former pupil was responsible.

The larger part of this barrister was completely rational. The rational barrister sought closure, sought peace. He knew that revenge would not bring closure. A vicar friend had told him that only forgiveness could bring closure, but forgiveness was eclipsed by a miasma of hate which would have been equally at home in the dark heart of Becksitch Betty. Becksitch Betty! Martin wondered. A dim idea was conceived at that moment. No, he must stand back. He was able to stand back and observe. He could stand back and see the folly of the poison in his heart. He was aware that noxious emotions had driven the sadistic engine of Hoadley and that now he, Martin Harcourt, was being poisoned by that same hate. Even so, the years rolled by and the clever legal brain continued to search for a way, a scheme, a strategy in which he could wreak revenge upon the fallen idol, be able to enjoy the result and eventually dance upon his grave.

As Edward had suggested, Martin Harcourt did move on. He moved on into the following month and took part in an ancient ceremony at the House of Lords. Twelve years earlier he was 'called to the Bar'. He was now to be 'called *within* the Bar' by the Lord Chancellor. At the court of the Lord Chief Justice, he had to bow four times, one to the Bench, one bow to each side and one to the people sitting in the public gallery. Martin Harcourt KC took full advantage of his new elevated status, joined a thriving London practice, earned lots of money, met many exciting new people, enjoyed wild parties and ... and became rather homesick for Derbyshire and Nottinghamshire. He missed his former colleagues and some of his friends. He missed Edward.

On Thursday, November 6th of that same year, London was in the grip of a dense fog. As they used to say, a real 'pea-souper'. Five people died in three train crashes on that bleak, opaque day - but Martin, taking advantage of good hunting, had better luck. Strolling along the London Embankment, he discerned, out of the mist, near Cleopatra's Needle, the ghostly outline of a beautiful man who would transform his life. Both men had clocked up a number of failed relationships but, although they could never have known it at the time, the sheer energy and successful chemistry between these two individuals would enable them to celebrate their golden anniversary in 1997. Tommy Sperry had a number of qualifications to give this happy union an effective kick-start. For starters, he lived in Nottingham. Like Martin, he was 37, a well-paid high flyer, an upwardly mobile executive in a large organisation. They shared a strong sense of humour, a strong sense of generosity and a strong sense of outrage against a homophobic society, albeit that word 'homophobia' would not be coined for another four decades. And four decades on, Tommy and Martin would be legends in their own lifetime, legends of the Nottingham gay scene.

The spring of 1948 saw Tommy and Martin established in their new home in The Park, an exclusive residential area near the city centre. 'The Court' was stately indeed, stately from its ballroom in the basement, up the fine oak staircase to the very top of its Gothic tower. This mellowed, ivy-clad mansion was actually Victorian with an intriguing Jacobean influence. It made a stately statement to all visitors, who first admired the impressive entrance hall, a large welcoming area which gave on to a spacious, comfortable, dark-panelled drawing room with a splendid stone fireplace. Through large mullioned windows the guests of Tommy and Martin were able to delight in a mature, descending garden of various shrubs dominated by one massive copper beech to the north of the house. A swimming pool was installed in the magnificent tropical conservatory, which gave rise to invidious accounts circulating around the Derby Camp, accounts of lovely, naked young men cavorting around the palms and classical sculptures.

Tommy and Martin were different in temperament, but shared a wicked sense of mischief given expression, effectively and forthrightly, in a westerly direction by the razor-sharp tongue of the former. They also shared a strong sense of social responsibility. Mindful of the years of isolation and mental abuse he had suffered from the cruelties of Claud Hoadley, Martin Harcourt made a special effort to take special responsibility with regard to young men who found their way into The Court. From the very start, Tommy and Martin agreed that they should never operate as a predatory couple as, alas, was fairly common in the world of homosexuals. Boys invited to The Court were never pressured or manoeuvred into any unsolicited sexual situations. Any coalitions formed, were always coalitions of the willing. These two independent, professional gay men were all too aware of the problems of younger gay men either in the middle, or working-class, who were trapped, isolated, imprisoned inside a hostile heterosexual world. Unable to confide in their parents or friends, these youths were able to confide and *trust* Tommy and Martin, who had an extensive knowledge of the gay world, its dangers and its opportunities. Their kindness and reputation as surrogate parents grew over the years. By the time that Simeon Hogg reached Nottingham in 1965, hundreds of young gay men had received invaluable assistance from Tommy and Martin. Assistance was given in the form of emotional support, counselling and practical advice. Where appropriate, they used their considerable influence to give a helping hand to fledgling careers or fledgling relationships. It was always possible to visit The Court and talk out their difficulties with Tommy and Martin, who came to be, not just popular but for the rest of that century and into the next century, were regarded with great affection by a great many.

In those dark post-war days, Tommy and Martin analysed Claud Hoadley's long-standing power block in Derby. They reasoned that the Hoadley empire was built on his own innate snobbery and the need to deal with a hostile heterosexual majority. Hoadley had created a sect, an artificial elite, whose admission was principally determined on three main qualifications - conduct, obedience and accent. If they could stay out of the cottages, or at least not get caught; if they could do as they were told and sound posh - then they were eligible to become one of the nodding heads of the Derby Camp.

Tommy and Martin felt a need to respond to the Derby Camp. They felt a deep sense of social responsibility, a sense of social mission to re-shape the attitudes of society. In their own relationship, as time went on, they were able to set an excellent example to many heterosexuals and homosexuals whose partnerships fell at the first hurdle. It was noted that the majority of the Derby Camp were single men, largely because Claud Hoadley harboured and frequently spat out contempt for the sentiment of 'so-called love affairs'. On hearing that two boys were becoming fond of each other, his favourite ruse was to dab the side of his eye with the corner of his pristine handkerchief in an expression of mock sorrow. His followers would all fall into line, have a good laugh and condemn the foolish couple for engaging in unrealistic and soppy sentiment. In this way, Claud Hoadley destroyed many incipient relationships which might have prospered with the type of judicial encouragement often given by Tommy and Martin.

Tommy and Martin were realistic. They had to live in the real world with its dangers, its bigotry and prejudices. They had to deal with the reality of homophobia. However, they were determined to show the world that their social circle, their Nottingham Camp, their people were more secure, more confident and more comfortable with their homosexuality. They might not be able to change the world, but - at least within the confines of Nottingham - they would make an attempt by setting their own good example.

Chapter 25

Importuning

After time had been called, the Derby Camp trooped out of the Flying Horse and Alfred drifted back to his group in the Nottingham Camp. Prior to making his farewells, Edward suggested that he and Simeon might meet up again before the end of his holiday. Simeon was agreeable and gave him the address of Aunty Joyce in Horsley Woodhouse. He liked this smooth gentleman, with whom he felt entirely comfortable.

"I must get back to my friends," said Edward.

"I must find my toad," replied Simeon.

"Let's hope he hasn't fallen down the toilet!" joked Edward.

Would that it were as simple as that! Alas for Aubrey Pod, his long absence was explained by the fact that he had been arrested by the police for 'importuning', according to a member of staff who had just broken this upsetting news.

"Don't panic, Simeon," said Edward. "It's only a few minutes' walk from here. I may be able to help. Come on."

They arrived at the police station just at the moment when Aubrey Pod, arms up to shoulder level, shot out of the main entrance and was scuttling down the steps.

"So, Mr Toad escapes yet again!" said Edward, lightly, in his cultured voice. "Goodbye, my friend. I do hope you'll profit by this example." He offered his hand, a firm grip which was warm and comfortable.

"Who was that old queen?" said Aubrey, seconds later, pushing his face up close to Simeon.

"Old queen?" replied the boy. "Edward may be getting on, but is nothing like a 'queen'. A very nice gentleman. Cultured as well."

"I noticed he didn't want to meet *me* - or were you too ashamed to introduce me to him?"

"What am I supposed to ... hang about ... you've just been arrested! What the ... "

"Arrested but not charged." His face broke into an ugly, unpleasant gloat. "Arrested many times but never charged. I always manage to wriggle out of it."

As a high-pitched giggle escaped the crack below his nose, he exalted, with a half skip of his evil 'dance of delight' which signified triumph. Simeon formed the view that the police, defeated by his truculent denials and irritating, argumentative attitude, were, perhaps only too pleased to get shut of this odious toad.

"But you're a teacher for God's sake! Don't teachers get the sack for that sort of thing?"

"Only if it comes to court and gets into the papers."

"It's all very well for you. What about other folk? What if the police caught us today in that cave?"

"I should think it highly unlikely to see bobbies in helmets charging into that remote cave, with truncheons at the ready. Anyway, I always have a good excuse prepared."

"Excuse! How could you excuse what we were doing?"

"I'd say that I was doing a dear friend a good turn. I'd claim that I was looking for crabs," replied Aubrey, belligerently pushing his face up even closer. Simeon was puzzled. There may have been crabs in the rock pools but ... ? "How about a quick look at the Canning Circus cottage. It'll all be happening now. We're missing the action."

"You've got to be joking!"

"Best time to go. It's 'chucking-out time' in the pubs. Coppers will be too busy with yobs and 'punch-ups' to bother with the likes of us." Aubrey became excited and somewhat dramatic. "This is no time to buckle! Where's that fighting spirit, Simeon? The occasional arrest is an occupational hazard. The urinal still calls! I must answer." Outside the police station, on that corner, these 'tongue-in-cheek' histrionics became amplified. "I must not fail my public! They await me. The cottages *must* stay open in adversity and in all weathers." Imperceptibly, the toadal features, already rich in folds, gradually morphed into a consistency of blubber. Something of the bulldog took hold of Pod and the voice acquired dogged determination after the style of a familiar Churchillian lilt. "We are an army of sluts, fingers at the forefront, tongues at the ready. We will fornicate in the frost, fondle in the fog, rim in the rain, suck in the snow, wank in the wind ... we will *never* surrender!"

Looking back to 1965 from the perspective of 2005, Simeon Hogg realised that Aubrey Pod was an extraordinary entertainer, an extraordinary man who refused to be deterred by a calamity which would have been devastating to the average person. When the laughter had subsided, again he looked at the profile of his friend and saw him in a new light of respect and admiration. Against all the odds, against all the derision heaped upon him from both Derby and Nottingham, Aubrey Pod would win through and win cheerfully. He had spirit. He was an inspiration.

Chapter 26

The Bent Spire

The morning of Sunday, June 6th, was cool and all brilliant sunshine. Simeon, in front of number four Bog Hole, was giving his saddlebag one last check. Two changes of socks and underwear were intended to provide for up to a week away. Looking slightly bemused and slightly hurt, Aunty Joyce gently fussed and whined about general safety - 'mind them big lorries'. She seemed unable to understand why a trip outside of Horsley Woodhouse could not have a definite date of return and reluctantly accepted that her nephew would reappear 'sometime before the weekend'.

She was worried. It was not in Simeon's nature to be secretive and he was entirely candid with Aunty Joyce about all the new friends recently acquired. It had not been easy for the 'old' repressed spinster to deal with the culture shock of a teenager who, since the previous Tuesday, had been out, always out, meeting a bewildering assortment of quirky characters. On the Thursday morning, Joyce Hogg heard an interesting (if carefully edited) account about a mysterious man called Dolly, a man called Betty who dressed up as a woman and another man who looked like a toad. Over breakfast this morning, she had attempted to digest further data regarding a doctor called David, a super-snob called Mr Hoadley and a charming gentleman called Edward. Furthermore, she was unable to comprehend that visits to Bridlington, Derby and Nottingham could occur inside one single day. It seemed to her that Simeon had shoehorned more life inside four days than she had experienced in four decades.

A circuitous cycling trip to Chesterfield had been planned on the OS 'one inch' map to avoid all main roads. A right turn at the top western extremity of the village took him northbound on the straight Roman Road known as Ryknild Street. This led to a pleasant confusion of narrow, wriggly roads through Heage, past the windmill, down into Nether Heage, through Ridgeway and into the valley of the River Amber. Passing under the main Derby to Chesterfield railway line and over the picturesque Cromford Canal, he was forced to dismount and push his cycle underneath giant beech trees up the steep wooded Bullbridge Hill, which, in turn, was rewarded by arrival at the craggy village of Crich perched on an exposed ridge at the very top. At just under 1,000 feet, all Simeon's hard work was now over. He would climb higher still, but relatively gentle undulations, kinder gradients and magnificent views in all directions would ease his passage along the roof of Derbyshire. Heading north, along Shuckstone Lane, the lighthouse tower of Crich Stand with its famous view of five counties (and Horsley Woodhouse if you knew where to look) stood proudly to his left. To his right, looking north-east, the eye travelled along a distant ridge to other splendid landmarks. Barely discernible was a rocky spur supporting the impressive outline of a lofty castle. Some miles south, an equally large eminence dominated that long ridge. Both buildings were beyond the scope of his map and nobody was there to tell Simeon that he was observing Bolsover Castle and Hardwick Hall. As he raced down an incline, stunted, windswept, wind-battled and wind-bent beech trees began to obscure this vast easterly view. To the west, a series of distant hills appeared, the nearest crowned by Riber Castle. He pressed on north. High Lane became Lickpenny Lane and that changed into Holestone Gate Road, which eventually emerged onto one of the high tops of Derbyshire - Beeley Moor. From here, Simeon enjoyed a westerly panorama which overshot the Chatsworth Estate and the wide Derwent Valley. For quality, he had navigated a route which would lead him into Chesterfield from the west. Two right turns took him directly east, down a beautifully-wooded valley called Harewood Road, which follows the young and playful River Hipper all the way into the pretty village of Holymoorside.

Holymoorside was a disappointment; it had no tea shop. In three hours, Simeon had cycled about 25 miles. On average, he covered less than 20 miles to a pot of tea. Eagerly pushing eastwards, now running on empty, he was getting desperate as the famous crooked spire came into view, heralding the centre of Chesterfield. A short rest was taken to enjoy the sunshine, to take in that scene dominated by the image of an old, bent spire. Bent spire. This was one of those moments of relaxation when an idle reverie was unconsciously influenced by a structure, an object or a shape. He pondered the spire, which spoke to him as if in a dream. Unwittingly, he reviewed the twisted and bent characters he had met and speculated on the ones he had yet to meet. Vaguely, his thoughts touched on the crooked mouth of Becksitch Betty, the distended shape of Dolly, the misshapen features of Aubrey Pod and the warped impression he had received about the horror who sat for hours in public toilets - the appalling Jasper Wormall.

Rested, he re-mounted and raced into the centre of Chesterfield, where, on this quiet Sabbath day, all tea shops were closed, tight shut, as was often the case in mid-20th century Derbyshire. With resignation and a touch of sadness, Simeon followed the instructions of Dolly. He pushed his bicycle into Queen's Park, where a few strollers were enjoying the neat flower beds and early afternoon sunshine. After a casual inspection of a large pond under the shelter of willows, he selected a seat in the sun, but on the edge of shadow, giving a glowing green effect under a spreading horse chestnut tree. Bathed by the gentle warmth of sunshine and the receding soft sounds of happy kiddies feeding excited ducks, he passed into a short, shallow, peaceful sleep.

Minutes later, something woke him. A child's face was hovering. It was a simple face, almost a cartoon which could have been drawn by a child; three buttons, two for eyes and one for a nose. It was familiar for two reasons. A paperback in his saddlebag described a similar experience and, five years before, Simeon had seen this same child illuminated by a single shaft of sunlight in the deep dark ravine of Water-cum-Jolly Dale near Tideswell. As his focus and comprehension improved, the child became a boy and (as with his last meeting with this strange creature) the boy, with a cartoon head cocked on one side, became a man.

Nobody knew the age of Simon Tonks. He was one of the mysterious freaks of the Derbyshire homosexual underworld. Bitchy queens in their forties (who looked their age) had cottaged with him before the war. They swore blind that Simon Tonks must be at least 45. In 1965, he hunted for men with a new generation of teenage chickens, who assumed that he was one of their number - just another chicken, just another common slut ever searching for that next cock. Within living memory, Jasper Wormall had always looked old, bent and hideous. So it was that Simon Tonks, within living memory, had always looked young and pretty.

"Allo!" said Simon in a camp falsetto voice. "Am on me 'olidays."

Perhaps, thought Simeon, it was part of a clever technique to have the vocabulary and speech patterns of a child, together with quick, youthful, jerky movements. He sat down and, by and by, shuffled closer and closer. They had a brief chat of introduction, punctuated by inane comments and odd little interjections of Simon's silly little song.

" ... tickle my tummy and I'll suck your dummy ... "

It was a gentle comedy. It was an interval of simplicity giving the effect of innocence, the effect of two little boys meeting for the first time. Simon explained that he was staying with a friend who would very much like to meet Simeon ...

And then it happened. It happened to his leg. Suddenly, a camp little hand alighted upon the cyclist's bare thigh, just below his short shorts. Simeon looked down at the delicate, soft, feminine hand and then up, meeting the innocent, half-smiling gaze of the strange doll-like face with its curled up eyelashes. Entranced by those eyelashes, this working-class youth fully understood why other working-class lads (of similar inclination) made a dash for the closet and hid in that closet for the rest of their lives.

There was, some confusion, something surreal in the moments which followed. On the one hand, Simeon did not want to offend Peter Pan by removing his naughty hand. On the other hand, he was utterly repelled by (what felt like) the gentle touch of a little girl. There was also a third consideration. Something about this whole freak show put Simeon on the edge of breaking up into hysterical laughter. The silly song, the oscillating head cocked on one side and then the other, the child-like half smile - all made for hilarity and the impossibility of any sexual act to follow.

An uncomfortable wriggle produced a few more inches of separation, automatically freeing the thigh from that clever, long practised paw which, over many years, had given so much pleasure to so many. Simeon launched into what, he hoped, was a diplomatic assertion of his sexual preferences. Using local terminology, he explained that he was, in fact, 'useless'! He was neither 'butch nor bitch' and he did not want to be a 'time-waster'. Borrowing a term from the S&C Coffee Bar set, he confided to being one of the 'drones' of the gay world, not one of 'the workers' and, therefore, not much good. Fortunately, Peter Pan was quite happy with these disclaimers. He cheerfully suggested that Simeon Hogg, 'a nice young man', should be 'milked at least once a day' and would be just perfect to provide his friend, Guzzly Granddad, 'a nice old man', with his afternoon supply of vitamins. Accordingly, a scruffy chicken, wheeling his bike alongside a little camp queen, set off in search of a dirty old man.

In the centre of Chesterfield, Simeon was alarmed by sudden screams of derision erupting from three youths down the street, some way on the other side. He assumed that this yob attack was instigated by the odd gait and effeminate appearance of his unusual companion, Simon Tonks and, in sickening fear, his heart sank as the morons broke into a run, rapidly approaching. The hooligans were still in full cry when something sounded familiar, something in their voice, tone and use of language, lifted his spirits.

"Get lad out!" yelled the first one, who was limp-wristed, tall and lanky.

"Who ya picked oop, ya dirty slut?" demanded the second one, who was dark and attractive.

"We seen ya. Selfish bitch! Share an share alike. Give it 'ere," bawled the third, in a much deeper voice, lewdly grabbing at the cyclist's bottom. Of the rough trio, this third, masculine, well-built yob was the only one typical of Derbyshire working-class youth. He would have blended in at any local school. Consequently, this specimen, with his freckles and red hair, was exceedingly desirable, indeed, so desirable that Simeon would be prepared to abandon his usual status as drone and change to worker - hard worker at that. At this point, he recognised the last two as the infamous Monks and Muckles.

"Glad you turned oop," said Monks, salaciously licking his lips and rudely caressing the genitalia concealed within the cyclist's white shorts. "We couldn't touch ya at baths fa that bloody toad an t' snotty doctor."

"Stop that!" said Simon, slapping away the groping hand. "Folks is lookin'! An that's a special treat. Am tekin 'im back fa Granddad."

Against his will, the cyclist also desired Monks, who looked rather like Bobby Vee. But there, the similarity ended. Monks had beauty, but nothing of that pop star's warm smile, his charm or his sensitivity. No. It was in the eyes. Monks was hard. Monks was all sex and demanded instant gratification. Monks was capable of cruelty. Later that evening, Simeon was horrified to learn that, with his bare hands, Monks had extinguished the life of a hapless duck on the pond of Queen's Park. This happened the day before. The duck had been consumed for dinner.

The raucous exchange of insults, obscene and otherwise, continued for a few minutes. Simeon was relieved when the crude trio ran off and disappeared down a narrow side street, as fast as they had first appeared.

"Get lad out!" was the parting shot of the first one who, in repose, had something of an Errol Flynn look. He had delivered his favourite expletive three times. Indeed, he had said nothing else.

"Don't mind 'em," said Simon soothingly. "There's no 'arm in 'em."

"Who's the lanky one?"

"Sean Stokes. Is all right, is Sean. A good lad, looks after Granddad, keeps 'im nice an clean."

"He lives with the old man?"

"Thee all do. Nobody else 'll ave 'em."

Simon Tonks went on to explain how Guzzly Granddad had to leave Derby five years before, when the police were asking too many questions about his frequent visitors - teenage boys. Simeon was beginning to feel uneasy and unsafe. Partly suggested by the name of 'Monks', he was forming the impression of a Fagin character entertaining a harem of youths and conveyed his fears to Simon. Perhaps he should cycle on to Sheffield? Simon attempted to allay his anxieties.

"Nay lad, don't fret. Thee just kids. It's true, they'll do a bit a nickin' an a bit a rentin' - but what else *can* thee do? Thee give Granddad 'is juice and Granddad gives 'em a bit a spendin' money an somewhere ta live. Go ta Sheffield tomorra. Come an meet Granddad. 'e likes a bita fresh meat. Treat 'im nice an e'll let ya stay t' night. Is a grand owd chap really."

"How old?"

"Top side 80 - at least."

"Will there be any tea at Granddad's house?"

"I'll mek ya a big pot - after yav seen ta Granddad."

Simeon had no intention of staying the night or of 'seeing to' Guzzly Granddad - but tea was essential. He asked what the three yobs were up to and was told that they were 'doing the cottages', as was their custom most afternoons. Simon added that he disapproved of their 'mischief' in plaguing old queens who had sat for too long. Mischief took the form of 'bombing' old men who were in the habit of secluding themselves in a WC for long periods and the 'bombs' were bags of flour -

" ... chucked over t' top. Thee don't think. Thee'll be owd themselves one day."

Simeon had already heard an account of these cruelties from Aubrey Pod. Then, as now, he was filled with anger, moral indignation that members of oppressed minorities should inflict indignities upon their own kind. Then, as now, he had neither confidence nor competence to articulate his disapproval or his concerns. Who was in charge at Guzzly Granddad's house? Surely not the old man? Who was there to control these atrocious tearaways?

The conversation cantered on. Simeon guessed correctly that he was older than Monks and Muckles and a touch younger than Sean Stokes. Listening to Simon's continuing assessment of these amoral youths, he began to feel a pang of sadness and pity, wondering how these orphans had come to end up in such appalling circumstances.

"Oh, don't fret. Thee 'appy enough. Sean cooks an does, an keeps 'em all nice an clean. It's a nice 'ouse. Coppers keep away an Muckles 'll thump anybody as makes any trouble. 'e's called Muckles the Knuckles."

It was always a surprise for Simeon to discover that a fellow gay chicken was competent with his fists. In this instance, he expressed pleasure that Guzzly Granddad's boys enjoyed protection from one of their own.

"It's useful," agreed Simon, as they walked side by side, progressing into a dowdy residential area of terraced houses. "Chesterfield's dead rough, it is, not safe fa a little queen like me. A mean, last night, two big strappin' toughs grabbed me!"

"Oh dear. How awful!"

"It were that. One said, 'You look like a randy common tart.' Other one said, 'Wot's it gonna be then? Is it gonna be *this* ... '" Simon demonstrated by thrusting his fist up in front of Simeon's face. "' ... or *this?*'" He repeated this aggressive action, but this time, the clenched fist was clearly meant to represent a hard cock. "Ooo it were terrible! Them big brawny lads, all muscle, thee dragged me ta that lavatory next t' crooked spire an bent me over t' bog. Pushed me 'ead right in t' bowl thee did. Ooo thee banged me summat awful, one after t' other. Straight in, no manners, no ceremony - just brute force an ignorance an there's me, an innocent 'elpless little queen wi me ead in t' bog!"

They had stopped walking for a moment. Simon cocked his head and twinkled at Simeon.

"Nay lad, it's not funny. Thee were abusive as well, addin' insult to injury."

"What did they say?"

"One said, 'Ya as bent as that bloody spire, ya common cow.' Then other said, 'Come out! Yav 'ad long enough. It's my turn ta ram inta that scrubber.' Ooo a felt so *ashamed*."

"What a pity Muckles wasn't there to rescue you."

"'e'd ad joined in! No respect fa me, Monks and Muckles. Thee just as bad, treat me like a spunk-rag, thee do. But, a will say this, thee nice at t' end. Thee say, 'Eee ya 'av given us a good time, lass. Pull oop ya knickers, lass. A bet you feel such a slut!'"

At the conclusion of this heartrending and colourful account, they turned yet another corner into what could be described as the toilet of Chesterfield. This rather drab, terraced row was not unlike Bog Hole, decorated with various frowsy women, gossiping at doorways. Simon came to a halt in front of one dingy door which looked quite derelict.

"What about this?" said Simeon, concerned about parking up his bicycle.

"Tek it straight in. It'll not 'urt oat," replied Simon, opening and entering.

As he pushed his cycle through the dilapidated old door, he was horribly embarrassed by a high pitched shriek of laughter which shot out from two shabby women over the road.

"A nice tit-bit fa Guzzly Granddad!" shouted the first frump, nudging another, equally lowly neighbour, who was rudely sticking out her tongue directly at the cyclist. This was followed by a second, even more raucous, scream of laughter, still painfully audible behind the closed front door of the house of Guzzly Granddad.

Simeon was hurt. He desperately wanted to escape and was about to do so when something stopped him.

Chapter 27

Chickens in Chesterfield

It was a coarse, deep, guttural voice which, in dim light, seemed to come from a pile of human blubber pressing down into a mangy old sofa.

"Bring it over 'ere. Huh."

An instinct told Simeon that Guzzly Granddad was not referring to the bicycle which he leaned against tatty pre-war wallpaper. The old-fashioned pattern was almost impossible to discern in that musty room with closed curtains. Having said something about putting the kettle on, Simon Tonks had disappeared through a door, leaving the boy to respond to the demands and lust emanating from the pile of blubber. Obediently, in half light, he approached the unshaven mess who reposed in a grimy soup-stained shirt, largely covered with ancient baggy trousers hauled up to near nipple level by old braces.

The sight of a fresh chicken had touched off a conditioned, Pavlovian reflex, effecting a slimy toothless orifice surrounded by grey stubble. A salacious tongue stealthily, very stealthily, crept up from the blackness of the thick throat and, slowly, lasciviously, moved from side to side, making the lower lip viscous in an unspoken, lewd invitation. That tongue had a hypnotic effect, similar to the writhings of a cobra as it emerges from the deep darkness of its basket. Yet again, the guilty young man entered into a process of self-justification. He needed to justify his previous rejection of the much younger Tonks and the much more handsome Bond. In both instances, the process was easy. The first was the same as a girl, the second too sophisticated and Guzzly Granddad, a very butch Guzzly Granddad at that, was not one to brook rejection ... so he told himself ... as he yielded to the pleasures from a consummate master who had began to refine his exquisite techniques in the previous century.

Simeon was about to pour out a sixth cup from the large brown pot brewed by Simon Tonks when a disturbance of excited social chatter was heard in the front room. Monks, Muckles and Stokes had returned. Stokes greeted Granddad with a raucous -

"Did ya enjoy ya fresh cream, ya dotty owd sod? Get lad out!"

Other insults drifted into the back room. The deeper tones of Muckles commented on the need to buy Granddad a bib and the lighter tones of Monks made an unkind reference to the old man's false teeth. A low, self-pitying, gruff reply was inaudible. Animated chattering included two other voices, indicating that the trio had acquired guests and, seconds later, a total of five jolly people trooped into the back living room.

The first guest turned out to be one of Guzzly Granddad's resident chickens and, therefore, not really a guest at all. He was smaller than Simon Tonks and, if possible, more feminine. This tiny queen with pretty blond curls, looking no more than 12 years of age, was introduced as Tinker Bell, a nickname to complement the nickname of Simon Tonks. In spite of the 'little girl' appearance, Simeon found the slight form alluring and tempting, neatly-packaged in a short vest, revealing a few sexy inches of milky white tummy. Tinker Bell flashed sweet smiles. He was clearly enjoying the effect they had on the stranger in white shorts.

The second person caused Simeon consternation and anxiety. There was no mistaking the camp whine, twisted ugly face and mobile mouth of Becksitch Betty. However, Sean 'mashed' more tea and the merry assembly of seven crammed around the dining table, which had seen better days. Draining the second pot, Simeon began to relax and enjoy what was, in fact, excellent entertainment in good company. Inside a cheerful framework of general gossip and chit-chat, he received answers to several questions. He was assured that Guzzly Granddad was not at all offended by the customary welcoming barrage of offensive remarks. On the contrary, the old man enjoyed being surrounded by the fun and frolicking of his youthful harem. The four resident boys could stay as long as they remained boys and as long as they agreed to be 'serviced' on a regular basis. They were also expected to 'hunt' and return with the occasional chicken for the delectation of Guzzly Granddad.

"What about you, Simon? Does he expect to perform on you?" asked Simeon.

This question produced an explosion of screams and guffaws around the table, since it was an open secret that Simon was not a genuine chicken, far too camp and, consequently, of no interest to the old man. The question did reveal a very interesting (by the standards of the gay world) account of sexual deviation. Simon was sexually adept in many ways and, some years before, he had discovered that he could give Guzzly Granddad a great deal of pleasure without even touching him -

"Thee call it 'verbal abuse'," explained Simon.

The old man would, as usual, sit in his big old easy chair - but stark naked. Simon, fully clothed, would sit in front, observe and make a few critical observations -

"Ya too fat. Look at ya tits. Thee disgustin'. Look 'ow thee sag. Ad be ashamed to show 'em. Thee's ready fa t' knacker's yard, you, ya stinkin' fat owd bugger. Obese! That's wot ya are, obese. A bet ya bum's like a map o' moon. Ya ugly mug's like a map we all t' lines in it .. "

As the level of abuse increased in intensity, humiliation compounded upon humiliation, Guzzly Granddad derived more perverse pleasure and became more excited -

" ... such a vile, 'ideous lump a lard, toothless slobber chops ... "

At this advanced stage of Simon's outrageous set piece of carefully planned mortification, his laughing audience fell about in high hysterics and they begged for more. Becksitch Betty asked for the story of when Simon was arrested for cottaging, the time when he was caught in a WC cubicle engaged in an act of gross indecency with an even fatter man. Well-known to the police, this funny little queen was no stranger to the magistrates' court. Several of the present gathering were actually there in the public gallery, since it was common practice for his fans to attend and, in respectful silence, enjoy the comedy. On this occasion, the accused tried to explain to Their Worships that this particular charge was a mistake.

"I beg your pardon!" said the severe spinster.

"A mistake. A couldn't see 'im properly. A wouldn't 'ave let 'im in, 'e were *O - BESE*. A didn't know 'e was s' big until 'e were in with me. 'e could only just fit in ... "

"Hardly the point. You were engaged in an abominable act in a public place and ... "

"No."

"No?"

"No. No a-bom-ination was committed. Ya see, it's like this. A couldn't find it. A didn't touch it. 'is willie a mean. A looked. A admit that. A looked and looked and looked. Folds an folds o' flesh. 'Ooo, 'e were gross. A looked, kept liftin' 'em oop, but couldn't find it under all t' folds of blubber. A kept turnin' 'im round an round until 'e were dizzy. It were like bein' in with an elephant - ginormous. A couldn't even find 'is bum. So ya see, ya worship, am innocent ... arn't a?"

The irritated magistrate thought otherwise. She fined Simon £10 and told him to get out.

Each person round that table made contributions to this impromptu party. Simeon began to lose some of the initial hostility he had held for Monks and Muckles when they related various comical anecdotes about their adventures in the cottages of Derbyshire. He began to understand how they survived from day to day, scratching a living by stealing and selling sexual favours. Even so, their amoral philosophy was alarming -

"Why buy it if ya can lift it?"

Simeon quietly disapproved of some unkind reminiscences. Notwithstanding, the show went on and, it had to be admitted, was thoroughly enjoyable. They told funny stories; stories about the time they stole Dolly's fire engine-red underpants and made them into a flag, about the time Monks pissed on Mr Toad from a great height, about the time they smoked out Nobby the Gnome and about the time when Muckles offered to hold Jasper's teeth and did a quick fandango around the urinals, using them as castanets. Following this blast of laughter, an even more raucous blast was detonated by a reference to a snobbish youth known as 'Wingnut' in the Derby Turkish Baths.

" ... stuck up bitch, so a sez to 'er - 'bugger off, go an set fire to ya 'andbag, ya pissy ignorant cow."

From that simple description and brief reference to a fiery handbag, it became clear to Simeon that he had actually seen this superior Wingnut, a disciple of Hoadley, one of the nodding heads at The Friary. On that night, Simeon had been shocked to learn that there was a close connection between homosexuals and the Church of England. In particular, he discovered that there was a strong link between the Derby Camp and the Derby Cathedral. Discussing the group, David Bond had indicated a young chap with a long face and big ears who was the Cathedral's thurifer.

"What's a ... thurifer?"

"The queen who wafts about the smoking handbag," smiled David, with enthusiastic disrespect. "You should go to church. It's quite a show. He's an acolyte."

"Pardon?"

"He's the server, an altar boy, the one who ignites the incense, which gives out lots of white smoke and a rather pleasant scent. An important job. He's proud of it. He gets to mince around the Bishop. Better still, it keeps him close to our Claud, a good position. You're looking at future senior management material, a possible rival to HRH!"

Simeon's reminiscences of the sarcastic surgeon were interrupted by spitting hate. Becksitch Betty was in full flow, denouncing the pretentious high camp of Hoadley's Anglo-Catholic disciples.

"Ad like t' smack that toffee-nosed Wingnut right in 'is bloody gob 'ole, a would. 'ypocrites! All of 'em. Av 'eard about that place thee go to, that school, that college. A think thee call it a .. 'sem-in-ary'. Seminary! My arse! It's bloody rampant. Sodom an Gomorrah more like. Thee might read a bit 'o t' Bible, but thee'll come out wi a bloody sore bum, I'll tell thee. Thee stand need ta look at me like am a lump o' shit, that bloody snotty 'oadley an 'is lot. Bloody po-faced bastards." He calmed down and the next few seconds became darker, more menacing when he added quietly - "Well, thee might be gettin' a shock soon. Could be useful that. What a know about them 'seminaries' an what a know about 'oadley an 'is lot. Yes, could be useful ... "

Monks was about to launch into a Claud Hoadley yarn when Becksitch Betty, addressing Simeon, interrupted with -

"Strangers ta t' truth, these two liars. That snotty bastard wouldn't touch you lot wi a barge pole!"

The darkness lifted, followed by more laughter. It was one of those rare moments of social life, an impromptu party caused by a certain chemistry of certain rough individuals scratching a lowly existence. Yet, it was clear that these people had found an elusive quality, perhaps without being fully aware of it. It was a quality which often escaped Simeon Hogg in the course of his life. These rough people had found happiness.

Chapter 28

Pig In

Simeon noticed that Sean Stokes had become a surrogate mother to this odd family. He had kindly taken Granddad a cup of tea, cleared the table, washed all the pots and put them away neatly into a cupboard. A humble home it may have been, but, thanks to Sean, it was tidy and well-scrubbed. He offered Simeon an evening meal and a bed for the night. This was quickly followed by assurances that he would sleep in peace, have his own bed, a mattress on the floor, and be free from any unwanted molestation. On this last point, with an evil glint in his eye, Becksitch Betty warned that these terms included an obligatory private visit to Granddad after breakfast, before departure. Feeling comfortable in an atmosphere of warm camaraderie, the overnight guest was happy to agree.

Nobody offered to help, but out of that narrow crude back kitchen, Sean Stokes cooked and served up eight steaming roasts, followed by eight steaming puddings. He did all this work with enthusiasm and good cheer.

"Pig in!" he shouted, as the first course was laid before them. This was attended by the happy sound of clinking cutlery on plates and the exchange of playful insults in which Sean, for all his efforts, was referred to as 'a common cow'. Becksitch Betty called Simon a 'loose bitch' and Simon called Becksitch Betty 'an oogly owd 'ag.' Monks called Muckles a 'thick trollop' and Muckles called Monks a 'greedy slut' on the grounds that, in the Matlock cottage on the previous afternoon, he had attended to three chickens, one scrawny window cleaner with a nice bum, two rough road workers and, in desperation to 'get his rocks off', had approached his old enemy, Jasper, who was secluded in his usual cubicle on Saturday afternoons.

"You went with Jasper Wormall? Were ya that bad off?" said Becksitch Betty with a look of horror. Tinker Bell giggled.

"Well, what of it?" sneered Monks, his good looks temporarily marred by defiant sarcasm. "It's not s' bad when ya close ya eyes. 'e'd just finished 'is tea an cracker biscuits. 'e enjoyed a nice drink a spunk after 'is bita snap."

This last caused an outcry of hoots and chortles around the table.

"I thought you'd aggravated Jasper, driven him out of Chesterfield with ya tricks and torments?" asked Simeon.

"An owd crone like Jasper Wormall is never goin' ta refuse a youth like Monks. 'e'll forgive oat ta get 'is smackers round some fresh chicken meat," explained Becksitch Betty.

Simeon was curious about his fellow guest Simon and asked if he lived in Chesterfield. They all laughed when he replied -

"Nay, lad. A live near Bookston [Buxton] but a were born in a slum, oop a cobbled lane on Cow 'ill."

Cow Hill is a feature above Becksitch Lane, below a remnant of ancient woodland on the east side of the Derwent Valley in Belper. For several generations, the rough and ready Tonks family had lived in a poor cottage, one of several on that precipitous incline. Simeon mentioned Dolly's reference to a 'white witch', but was careful not to mention the 'black witch' sitting at the same table, who said -

"These two daft buggers started that," motioning to Monks and Muckles, who were giggling and fidgeting with the excitement of accreditation. "When thee see Simon in t' street, thee yell at 'im! Thee yell out fa all bloody Chesterfield ta 'ear - 'Burn the Witch!' - 'Burn the Witch!'"

"A do tarot readings," interrupted Simon, who took his psychic powers very seriously.

"Yeah, 'e'll tell ya t' future won't ya, Simon. 'e can talk ta folks that's dead, can't ya Simon. 'e brings me mam to me!" added Sean, warming to the subject of the paranormal.

"Bollocks!" exclaimed Monks. "It's all a load o' bollocks," insisted the youth, suddenly giving Tinker Bell a violent tickle, reducing him to a silly excitement of screams and wriggles.

Like a dry sponge, Simeon soaked it up - all of it. Many years later he would look back and realise the significance of his 1965 holiday. It seemed that he was viewing social scenes of a passing era, the last gasp of a rich, gay culture which had its roots in the previous century and the century before that.

They were now all rattling on about 'Whore's Wall'. He had already heard about the legendary old Whore's Wall from Aubrey Pod. It was just that, a wall, but a wall low enough for the whores, young roughs and the common queens of Chesterfield to sit upon. It was a community observation point. It was used to observe a very active, gas-lit, Victorian public lavatory near Harrisons Boot and Shoe Warehouse, eventually demolished in 1970. This was the old 1750 silk mill, once powered by the River Hipper. Simeon heard several anecdotes about the riotous fun, the screaming, the camaraderie, the cruel initiations and general 'piss taking' which were all part of the history of Whore's Wall -

"Look at that one! Wot's 'e goin' in there for? Bloody ancient - nearly bloody 40! 'e'll get nowt!"

The noisy fun and banter was still continuing after dinner when Simeon decided to wander into the kitchen and pick up a tea towel. It was just the two of them. Sean was pleased to have the company. He listened to Simeon's concerns about the attitude and unacceptable conduct of Monks and Muckles, especially with regard to old blokes in cottages. Sean agreed. He, too, disapproved. Flour bombs and rotten eggs were nasty. However, he told Simeon that not all old men tolerated these childish pranks.

"Toby Jug, ya know, 'im at Bookston, well, 'e give Monks a thick lip an a bloody nose! 'e did! Serves that wicked bastard right an all."

This was the second time Simeon had heard about the violent temper of the famous Toby Jug, who had sat in his usual cubicle for as long as anyone could remember. This assault on Monks occurred on the previous Easter Bank Holiday, when the evil couple decided to visit Buxton to do a cottage crawl. One of them had pushed under the partition wall an ignited sheet of newspaper with the intention of smoking out 'the Jug', to make use of his 'glory holes' and get the benefit of his clientele. The old fellow, as fat as he was, was also quite big and strong, reacting swiftly to this incendiary attack. Muckles was too quick and managed to escape into the Pavilion Gardens - but Monks ... Monks was seized by the furious Jug, was held fast against the urinal, still wet with stinking urine, and did there suffer, from the hard Jugular fist, two powerful blows to his mouth and nose. Monks and Muckles never visited Buxton again. Simeon listened to Sean's detailed account with malicious satisfaction.

Sean Stokes became serious and took the opportunity to reflect upon how he had come to be in his present situation; a long story, a sad story. At one point, he became tearful when speaking of the day his 'mam' died and, in those few poignant moments, the pot washing stopped and two boys embraced in a brief interlude of private compassion.

American city life never suited Simeon. He had a penchant for a wholesome Derbyshire lifestyle and, when possible, kept healthy habits by retiring early and rising (often with difficulty) after eight hours. Accordingly, he was surprised (but grateful) when all in Guzzly Granddad's residence were tucked up in bed by 11.00pm. As promised, he had a comfortable firm mattress on the front bedroom floor, under the window, opposite an old-fashioned brass double bed shared by the other two guests, Simon Tonks and Becksitch Betty. It was a hilarious sight. Simon's cartoon head was peeping out on the pillow, button eyes lightly closed above his button nose, above a pretty little mouth which seemed to wear an inane grin. Inches away, in stark contrast, Betty's horrible twisted mouth was the only visible part of an ugly face. The remainder was obscured by a Victorian sleeping cap. It could have been Scrooge. Regular breathing was the only common factor indicating sleep for both men. Simeon had carefully avoided the back bedroom, which he assumed accommodated the four other boys. Fully clothed, Guzzly Granddad dozed in his extra-large easy chair in the front room where, according to Sean, the front door which opened directly onto the street, was never locked. Among the low-life of Chesterfield, it was quietly understood that the famous toothless orifice was available all night long for any boy or man, waif or stray who was desperate enough to require nocturnal relief. After expressing anxiety about the safety of his bike, Sean had kindly moved it into the backyard.

It was shortly after midnight when Simeon was rudely woken by the percussion of heavy thumping upon bare floorboards. Two naked youths had burst into the bedroom, done a quick circle and run out again.

"What the bloody 'ell's goin' off!" shouted an outraged Becksitch Betty, turning on the bedside lamp. Before his angry words had hardly left a distorted mouth, the streakers were back, each proudly bouncing a fully-erect 'John Thomas'. The latter, attached to Muckles, displayed impressive dimensions.

"What about this then!" yelled Monks, leaping around the room, stopping only a second to flourish his bobbing member before the boggle-eyed occupants of the brass bed. After a dozy moment in which his eyes had an opportunity to focus, Simeon noted two very well-proportioned rumps, young and firm, rapidly retreating out of the door. He lusted a powerful lust for the rough and ready Muckles, who had briefly sported such a splendid body, yet, at the same time, was irritated by inconsiderate conduct. On the other hand, Simeon rather hoped for an encore which never came. The old queen groaned and muttered imprecations as he sank back between the sheets in a desperate effort to reclaim lost sleep, but this was not to be, no - not just yet. Giggles and guffaws, punctuated by the inane chatter of endless recycled anecdotes, beloved by those four youths, meandered out of that other room. Betty's heart sank when it all erupted into a raucous chorus of what sounded like an obscene rendering of *Old Man River.*

"Owd Man Jasper, that 'oomped back Jasper, 'e keeps on prattlin', 'is false teeth rattlin', 'is fish eyes leering, 'e keeps on peering through 'oles - those rude, naughty 'oles." And then much louder. "You and me, we suck and ... "

"SHUT OOP!!" shouted Mr Bestwick in desperation.

This had the desired effect. A great silence descended. After about ten minutes, the old queen and the little queen by his side had drifted back into slumber. Simeon remained awake, listening to the silence of the night, which was occasionally broken by childish giggles coming from the other bedroom. From time to time, the deeper resonance of an old man snoring wandered up the stairs. He pondered these intriguing sounds and the recent erotic incident of teens behaving like pre-teens. He wondered about the four boys in the next bedroom. Were they having sex together? Was he expected to join them? He lay awake for what seemed like a long time when, eventually, there was another sound; the sound of creaking steps. Someone was creeping down the stairs. Why? Did one of the lads need to use the outside loo ... or perhaps ... perhaps one of them, frustrated and horned-up, may have needed to use Guzzly Granddad. He wondered. Who? It was unlikely to be Tinker Bell. He did not think the old man would want an effeminate child. Sean? Again, unlikely - too camp, too silly, too outlandish, too familiar. Monks? Possible. Muckles? Probable. Guzzly Granddad would always welcome Muckles. Butch as a brick, lowly, vulgar and coarse. Yes, it *had* to be Muckles. That foul-mouthed lout, hot to trot, would rouse the ancient slumberer with indecent haste and ram it down his gullet with a total absence of any form of courtesy.

Many years later, Simeon Hogg would return to the thoughts of that night and realise that they said more about the dark depths of his own sexual psyche than it did about the morals of Muckles - if, indeed, it *was* Muckles 'tomcatting' at that time of night. Slender indications supported his theory. The gruff snoring ceased. Minutes later, he thought he heard a low, nasal whimper of surprised pleasure, such as he had heard at the conclusion of his own visit to the old man just hours before. The night walker returned with ascending creaks, which were slower and then ... silence. Simeon was frustrated. He took solace in the fact that, at least so far, he had been spared the soft, sissy touches of the two sleeping sluts in the next bed.

Simeon had great difficulty in getting back to sleep. His mind was racing. He was trying to make sense of his own reactions to the folks who inhabited this queer, fairytale world. He was reviewing the various new characters who had tumbled into his life in these last few days. He dreaded a further sexual assault from Becksitch Betty but, in truth, was looking forward to saying the required 'good bye' to the toothless old chap below. Some horrors he had yet to meet. Jasper Wormall? Why was Jasper always referred to as a 'crone' and Becksitch Betty always referred to a 'hag'? What was the difference between a crone and a hag? In the Flying Horse, he was referred to as an 'urchin'. What was an urchin?

Another disturbance! He was surprised to discover that, in fact, he had eventually fallen asleep - but now ... wakefulness ... something about tea?

"Tea! Go on, Simon. Make us some tea. We want tea. Bring us a pot o' tea." This raucous voice had broken the silence of the night and invaded the cold room, which was slowly filling with the murky grey of an early June dawn.

"Can ya 'ear, Simon? A said TEA. WE WANT TEA!"

"Yeah. An we want it *now*. Make tea," demanded the second, thicker, more husky voice of Muckles.

"TEA!" insisted Monks.

At this, the appalling figure of Becksitch Betty, in ancient night attire, rose up into thin air above his brass bed like a ghost from eternal slumber, his fearful features made even more grotesque by extreme anger.

"Go back ta sleep, ya selfish bastards!" he screamed. One hand was struggling to pull the sleeping cap further over his head, the other groping at his old pocket watch in an attempt to discern the time in poor light. "It's not four o' clock!" he spluttered in fury.

"Ask Sean," came a muffled, sleepy voice from down in the blankets. It was the voice of a hidden, recumbent Simon.

"NOBODY is going to make tea for ANYBODY."

"Shut it, ya foul filthy owd 'ag. Am talkin' ta Simon. WE WANT TEA. WE ... "

This demand was cut short by the enraged harridan who leapt out of bed in full battle cry. He charged into the second bedroom with clenched fists at the ready. Straining to hear fragments of this high drama, Simeon could just discern ominous oddments of the muttered, cross and crabbed threats from this dangerous drag queen who had suffered two interruptions to his rest. An abrupt silence followed, save for the slow, weary footsteps of the returning Betty, who looked drawn and even more haggard. The groans of old, complaining bed springs and groans from the aggravated old hag seemed to blend with mutual commiseration as he struggled between the blankets to make yet another attempt to find peace - to find sleep.

Chapter 29

Monks, Muckles, Mischief and Mayhem

A sleepy cyclist was stirred to consciousness by brilliant sunlight which flooded through that east facing bedroom window. It was some point between the hours of seven and eight. Clattering of milk bottles and cheery greetings down in the road announced the comforting feeling that all was well with the world on that Monday morning of June 7th. Subdued, sad voices from within told a different story.

"Don't ask. Me poor owd bones! A can 'ardly move," moaned a groggy Becksitch Betty to a solicitous Simon. "What must a look like? Go on. Say it: a bloody hoary owd 'ag."

"Well ... "

"Well what?" demanded the debilitated drag queen, who was still vain and always tried to make the best of himself. The self-criticism was delivered in the hope of a protest - a protest which never came.

"It's ya eyes, Betty."

"What's oop we me eyes?"

"Thee remind me o' them yellow 'oles in t' snow. Ya know, when yav 'ad a piss."

As the three dressed, Betty continued to grumble about his bad back and numerous other pains, all of which he laid firmly at the door of those -

"Ignorant common yobbos! Thee need a bloody good birchin'." Straining and grappling with his trousers, his voice softened to pathos. "Rate knackered I am, dead beat."

Half an hour later, they were all munching around the table. Sean Stokes had difficulty keeping up the supply of hot toast. Slice after slice and still more was demanded by hungry boys, led by Monks, thumping the table.

"Come on, ya slow skinny slag. Gerra a move on. More butter this time."

"An more tea. This pot's cold," shouted Muckles.

Sean was surprisingly indifferent to this self-centred, ungracious attack and mumbled something about taking Granddad's toast into the front room. After such an appalling night, it might have been supposed that there was a bad atmosphere in that gathering. This was not the case. The busy little mouth of Simon Tonks was glistening with sticky marmalade.

"Messy chops!" giggled Tinker Bell, who was happily chomping on his third slice. They began to be playful, to strike camp poses and make funny faces at each other.

"Sit thee sen down, Sean, 'av a rest and get thee own bloody toast," scowled Betty. "Am not stayin 'ere, no way, am buggerin' off after a drop o' tea," he added, addressing Simeon.

"Were ya goin'?" asked Monks.

"AM GOIN'!" he shouted over the table to the dark, smirking chicken. "That's all *you* need ta bloody know. Ya'll not see me again. An it's all your bloody fault." He pointed menacingly at Monks.

"Me? Ave not done oat at ya!"

"Both on ya. Ya selfish, ya don't think, ya don't care. There's *other* folks in this 'ouse, not just you two. Selfish bastards!"

There was a ferocity in the old hag's grating voice which galvanised full attention and abruptly stopped all chomping around that table. It ended the silly, playful poses of the two little queens. The responding attitude of Monks and Muckles caused Simeon to feel some sympathy for this older man, who should have received more consideration, more respect. The former took the reprimand with a look of resentment. The latter maintained an insolent, irritating smile throughout.

Simeon went upstairs to get his toothbrush, which had to be used at the kitchen sink, the only sink in the house. He returned upstairs, packed, checked his saddlebag and took a few minutes to study the one inch OS map. After the unpleasantness, the house was oddly still and quiet. It was time to say 'good bye' to Guzzly Granddad. Stealthily, he pushed open the door to the front room and silently entered the old man's private domain. Curtains, still closed, were keeping out the brightness and cheer of morning sunshine, keeping in the smell and musty atmosphere of a brothel. At the same instant, he was startled and embarrassed by the obscene sight and succulent sounds coming from the armchair where that ancient pile of blubber reposed. It could have been Muckles standing at a urinal and, indeed, the natural function involved was very similar. Muckles, with red hair and freckles, arrogant as ever, leaning backwards, pleased as Punch, sticking it out, giving it out. Hard faced Muckles with his rude tongue stuck out. Muckles was delighted to be suddenly on show. Muckles was complacent, was pleased to be observed by the rather sheepish and uncomfortable cyclist. He was relieving himself - using his Granddad to obtain relief. And relief came soon, signalled by arching of back, closing of eyes and a long, cavernous groan of pleasure rumbling from somewhere deep inside the old man. This young man, grinning from ear to ear, was clearly elated with his outrageous performance. Without as much as a glance at the old worker seated before him, on withdrawal, proudly, he bobbed and brandished his shiny, glistening weapon at the onlooker, wearing a smug smirk, uttering one word -

"Next."

Muckles left the room and left Simeon affected by a scene of powerful eroticism mixed with other emotions. With silent stealthy tongue, eager to continue, the old man in the gloom invited his visitor to approach. Guzzly Granddad took his time, made it a good one, guzzled well, extracting long, lingering moans, sighs and whimpers ... before the final extraction.

Helpful and thoughtful as ever, Sean had wheeled the bicycle through a dark, narrow entry, from the back-yard, on to the street where Simon Tonks and Becksitch Betty were waiting to walk into Chesterfield with Granddad's special guest. The cheerios to Monks, Muckles and Tinker Bell were cursory and barely acknowledged, but the parting with Sean Stokes was warm and tearful in a heartfelt embrace.

"Ya'll come back, won't ya?" he pleaded softly.

"I'll do that. Look after Guzzly Granddad."

"A will," said Sean, brightening, brushing away a tear. "'e's looked after *you* ant 'e!"

This bawdy quip completely lifted the gloom, producing hoots and screams of laughter from Simeon, Simon and Tinker Bell who had just appeared at the front door to join the farewell party. Sean was now back to his old, loud, cheerful self.

"Get lad out!" he howled, giving the cyclist a quick grope of parting.

A few slovenly slatterns had been observing this small, impromptu, ribald street party - thankfully without comment. Simeon was grateful that the two horrible, hurtful slags from the previous day were absent. However, they had hardly passed two doors - and then it happened.

"And don't ya bloody come back, ya 'orrible owd 'ag!"

This, an excruciating parting shot, was the bellowing voice of Monks. An appalling bawl; it shot the full length of that public street from the bedroom window of Guzzly Granddad's residence. The only person who appeared to be free from embarrassment was Simon, a mischievous twinkle in his 'doll-like' eye, a faint smile playing around pretty lips still showing traces of toast crumbs.

"Ooo, Betty! A say. Intit awful. It's Monks! 'e's shouting abuse."

"*Don't* turn round, Simon," urged the older man. "Don't look at 'im. Don't give 'im the satisfaction."

"Are ya listenin', ya camp owd bugga?" continued the street-long holler. "Becksitch bloody Betty, that one, she's ad more prick than a second 'and dart board, 'as that one. ARE YA LISTENIN'?"

As Simeon turned the corner, he heard the tail-end of an exchange between one of the common slatterns and the roaring Monks.

"Wot's oop, lad. As 'e oopset ya?"

"Shut it, slag." A slamming of sash window concluded this ugly scene.

In the aftermath of such unpleasantness, a great sadness now hung over the three. Nobody spoke. They rested on a public seat. It was secluded in a peaceful retreat in the centre of that busy old market town. Surrounded by ancient gravestones and pretty flowerbeds, they took comfort from these delightful precincts of Our Lady and All Saints, the largest parish church in Derbyshire. Moved by some small sympathy, Simeon had decided to delay his departure to Sheffield and pass the 20 minutes before Betty would catch the Belper bus back home. They looked around idly. Simeon's eyes moved up to trace the lines of that famous twist, the 14th century spire which had warped out of perpendicular. Vaguely, he was trailing the eight sides of ridges and channels of zigzagging lead plates - when Simon broke the silence.

"That spire's stood there fa many a year, antit, Betty? But you've not lasted long we Monks and Muckles 'av ya, Betty?"

This, uttered with a modicum of apparent pity, did not hide a sardonic tone of devilment from one who had relished the recent street drama.

"Oh, Simon, it's bloody awful. Am rate depressed, I am," whined the old queen. "An am not well, no, not well at all. Am shattered. I ache in all me poor owd bones. It's bin bloody awful. An 'im *screamin'* at me like that! Like a bloody fish wife. Showin' me oop like that. Well, 'e's not gettin' away we it. Oh no. I'll bloody tell thee. Am doin' summat," he added darkly.

En route to the bus station, they were walking across the Market Place, when, in a flash, it appeared that a running youth had struck the top of Betty's head. In that instant, an instant in which the haggard countenance distorted into shock, alarm and then panic, the old hag suddenly became ... a different hag! Astounded, acting on an impulse to lunge forward to protect the old queen, Simeon nearly dropped his bicycle. He was frozen by the sight of a profound change. The old queen, his hands clasped to his head in agony, was now more like an old man - and an old man shrieking and wailing - an old man who had promptly become a *bald* old man.

Everything fell into place when it could be seen that the original attacker, yelling, laughing and frolicking, had been joined by another youth leaping about in similar mode. In the blur of quick movement, a fraction of a second passed before they could be identified. Simeon had already noted two familiar bottoms, very alluring bottoms, bobbing around that market square with wonderful energy, a titillating display of liquid athleticism which is so typical of teenage boys. This was that dangerous duo, Monks and Muckles, playing ball, passing it to and fro but - it was *not* a ball. It was the wig of Becksitch Betty.

It was typical Monks - Muckles - mayhem. This childish act of revenge, ignored by most, was seen as hilarious by a few onlookers who clearly enjoyed the cruel entertainment. Betty, still using his hands as a hat, was standing, frozen to the spot, swaying in the pain of public humiliation. Simeon, never brave, in the urgency of this crisis, was moved to ask Simon to hold his bike. He approach the two louts who were having a great time making sport with the snatched property of Arthur Bestwick. Perhaps, vaguely, he believed that a polite request might shame them into doing the right thing. Muckles held the wig at this moment.

"Give it back. Come on. You've 'ad ya fun," he said calmly and persuasively to the well-built ruffian who stood his ground with an insolent sneer. As half-expected, the hair was then tossed over to Monks. Simeon went over to Monks, who became aggressive in his tone and body language. Once again, he noted how quickly exterior beauty can be warped by interior wickedness.

"Wot's it got ta do we you! Piss off."

Guessing that the disputed item was, yet again, about to take flight and, mindful that Monks was approximately his own size, Simeon decided to make a grab at the wig which was firmly clutched in the right hand of the smaller thief. This manoeuvre failed. For a few seconds the scene was like a basketball game in which Monks, taunting and swearing, bobbing and dodging on Chesterfield Market Place, attempted to pass the 'ball' to his malicious partner. Abruptly, Simeon was stung by a sharp pain across the side of his face. In a trice, stunned, he staggered to the side before recovering his balance and saw Betty's wig on the ground. With all his strength, Monks had wielded it as a whip in a split second before dashing away with Muckles. In front of that small public gathering, the two hooligans fled the scene in an obscene orgy of screaming vilifications to give an impression of triumph.

"Are ya all right?" asked Simon with genuine gentleness of concern, now free of his previous mischievous enjoyment.

With due respect, they looked away as the older man transformed himself back to Becksitch Betty by replacing and adjusting his hair-piece. He did not say another word. In silence, Simeon and Simon gave a small restrained wave to the Belper bus and watched it trundle out of sight.

"What will you do now?" asked the former in a hint of gloom. Clearly affected by this painful drama, Simon, in similar tone, let out a long sigh, with shaking head.

"Oh, a don't know. Do a bitta cottagin' I expect. Nowt else ta do is thee?" He looked at the cyclist and cocked his head on one side. "Did ya mean it, wot ya said ta Sean? Will ya come an see us agen?"

Simeon stroked the side of his face. It was still painful.

"A don't think so. No. Don't think a want ta come back ta Chesterfield."

"It's like a said. Thee don't think. Thee just kids really."

They walked together. Simeon wheeled his bike to the junction of Newbold Road and Sheffield Road.

"Well, cheerio then, Simon. It's bin nice knowin' ya."

Simon lit up in a sweet smile on his simple, unblemished face. It oscillated to one side and then to the other. Briefly, his little body writhed in pleasure. He showed off with a few funny poses before executing a half pirouette and scuttled back towards the centre of Chesterfield. Simeon mounted, turned, took one last look at the funny, sad little queen who was receding into the distance with his funny, sad little gait, en route to 'do' the public lavatories of Chesterfield. Simeon was strangely rooted to the spot, strangely compelled to watch the odd little fellow get smaller and smaller until he was out of sight. It was the same, strange compulsion which had made him watch Betty's bus until, it too, was out of sight. There was something so profoundly sad, so heartrending, so pathetic about that poor little figure disappearing into the distance. Simeon felt a sudden empathy with Simon. He missed him already. He desperately wanted to race his bicycle back into Chesterfield, the town with the bent spire, to find Simon, to be with him and to be with Sean. He missed them both. Momentarily, Simeon was terribly lonely and miserable. Why go to Sheffield? What was in Sheffield?

But it was a beautiful day. He had to be rational. He launched himself, cycling north, along the Sheffield Road.

Chapter 30

Sheffield

It was about a dozen miles to Sheffield, mostly downhill, taking about an hour. After living in the Detroit area, Simeon was keen to visit this English city of knives, forks, silver and steel, which held a special fascination. Would the industrial sprawl, so ugly in America, be just as depressing here on the eastern edge of the Peak District? He was delighted to find that this was not the case. True, there was plenty of pollution. Views were often blighted by the activities of smelting, melting and belching fire from numerous blast furnaces lit up like volcanoes. Unlike the unremitting flatness of Detroit, Sheffield was an old city, built on seven hills, divided by wooded valleys. Here was a city of beauty, a city with a soul. Victorian suburbs gave way to Georgian elegance when the cyclist dismounted and wandered into Paradise Square. The mid-day sunshine felt good on his bare arms and legs as he continued to wander around the city centre. In a process similar to osmosis, unconsciously, he was absorbing the solid, reassuring feel of bold architecture, the impressive strength of the Town Hall, when a voice interrupted this musing.

"It's Vulcan."

"Pardon?"

The man at his side was unremarkable in every way. He was just like Sid, the regular of the Derby Turkish Baths, an 'invisible man', Joe Average, a man who, with his indeterminate age and indeterminate looks, could disappear into the crowd at any moment and be gone forever. The reference to Vulcan was made when Simeon's eyes had travelled up the building, up the surmounting 193ft tower to an intriguing figure on the very top.

"Vulcan is the Roman god of fire and craftsmanship. You know, a sort of city symbol for Sheffield - metalwork. Where do you come from?" Briefly, Simeon explained. "America! Well now, I'll have you know that the bowie knife - the same one your great-granddad carried on the American frontier - was forged beside the Don. Oh, yes it was."

The boy, who was, in fact, very English, took a few seconds looking into the face of Mr Average, trying to make sense of his last statement.

"Pardon? What's a bowie knife? What's the Don?

"You don't know! And you being a Yank! It's a big steel hunting knife, single edged - about 15 inches long, with a hilt and crosspiece. Haven't you heard of the River Don?"

"Oh. It's Sheffield's river."

"One of five. There's the Loxley, Rivelin, Porter and Sheaf ... as in Sheffield - see. Now this River Sheaf, it worked the waterwheels which powered the tilt hammers at Abbydale. Ask yourself why this is a great city. Everything was at hand. See up there?" He pointed south west, up to the distant hills and moors of the south Pennines. "It's all up there. Trees for charcoal, iron ore underground and gritstone for the grinding wheels. It's all there."

Simeon looked back at Vulcan and again at the handsome Town Hall. Vaguely, he was beginning to get a sense of the wealth provided by centuries of enterprise, skill and sweat all embodied by that great, muscular man on top of that tower. The very name, Vulcan; it was an inspiration for this young man, who was once bullied at school to the point of considering suicide. Vulcan! God of Fire. He looked mighty, macho and fearless. Vulcan, god of blacksmiths; he was as butch as a brick, hard as gritstone, proudly surveying his domain, the gritty unpretentious city of Sheffield ... Mr Average? He was gone! He had disappeared into the crowd.

Lunch was simple, but delicious; beans on toast and a mug of tea for two shillings at a small, greasy cafe called 'The Golden Egg'. The old man behind the counter, staring at his only customer with a fixed grin, had a beaked nose and sharp chin which seemed to meet. He looked and sounded like an old witch. Simeon guessed that this old queen would probably know the location of all those dingy, Victorian, dirty nooks and crannies, the ones he had heard so much about, the ones hidden in old brick walls. Dolly had urged him to visit these active and popular gas-lit cottages which were sited in the various corners of old Sheffield. But a request for such information was fraught with danger. The old witch, having a scruffy chicken within his grasp, might lock the door and pounce. Or, the old witch might turn out to be not an old witch at all. He might be just an effeminate old man, an old man disgusted to hear such a question. The solitary diner might suffer the indignity of being swiftly ejected from a greasy cafe, leaving half a mug of hot tea going to waste! On the other hand, the old bloke, now looking more like Mr Punch, was still leering. Perhaps he might be talented like Guzzly Granddad? On the other hand, perhaps not. And, anyway, Simeon lacked the courage to creep around and haunt those lewd, shadowy locations all by himself. It might happen, but it would have to happen with an experienced guide such as Dolly, Simon Tonks or Aubrey Pod. He paid the old witch, who thanked him with sibilance, went to his bike, which was leaning on the cafe window, and studied the OS map to plan a quality route to Hathersage. He put back the map, checked that his saddlebag was securely fastened, mounted and briefly turned to see if the old witch was still leering. He was. Forty years later, the old witch was long dead and buried. Simeon discovered that he was a notorious old queen known as Ernie.

Leaving Sheffield was much more difficult than entering. He cycled up the main road, turned off on to a quiet minor road at Ecclesall and slowly pumped up the dead straight climb to Ringlinglow. The narrow, unfenced road continued to rise and peak between Hallam Moor and Burbage Moor, giving impressive views to the south-west over the Derwent Valley. It kinked and wound its way down, out of Yorkshire, into Derbyshire and into Hathersage.

That Monday night, Simeon stayed at the Hathersage Youth Hostel. Hathersage was interesting in itself, but nothing happened to him which could be described as interesting. Tuesday lunch-time saw him in the centre of Castleton, where he was importuned by another cafe owner, a reasonably good looking, fair-haired, but boring young man with no talent and no resemblance at all to Mr Punch. Simeon was beginning to appreciate the value of ugliness. He stayed the night at Castleton Youth Hostel. On the Wednesday night, he stayed at Buxton Hostel, an improvement because he had successfully located the infamous Toby Jug during that day. Toby Jug; aptly named, a dusty old antique, an image from the 18th century. Boy and man remained great friends during many transatlantic visits over the remaining 18 years of Toby's life, in that quaint old cottage, in the shadow of the Opera House.

In 2004, Simeon discovered a remarkable coincidence when he was researching personal details of the old man for his controversial book *Queens, Crones and Old Hags of Derbyshire*. The day of Toby's birth and the day of his death were both significant in the annals of homosexual history. In the middle of one bleak, Buxton winter, poor old Toby was found by a distressed and shocked toilet cleaner. His stiff body was stone cold. His jolly, Dickensian face, now bereft of once-rosy cheeks, had sightless eyes and a redundant mouth. It was still open! Even in death, he was still expecting, still sitting in his usual cubicle on that dazzling white morning of severe frost - Thursday, February 24th, 1983. Apart from his fat bulk, slumped, supported by the wall to the right, all was as usual. His bag of rags, his flask of tea, the crumpled grease-stained paper from half eaten sandwiches and his false teeth were reposing in their usual place in the pocket of his ancient shabby pre-war jacket. It was all there, but for the spark of life which had finally left the lewd old fellow - forever. It was a sad, bad day for his many hundreds of regular visitors, over the years, who had now suffered a grievous loss. Old Toby had devoted the bulk of his life to serving mankind, giving pleasure to others, to as many men as possible. Some residents of Buxton were puzzled to see the appearance of various wreaths with various inscriptions, some left outside that public lavatory and some left inside in front of cubicle number two, where Toby Jug had sat (perhaps sat for too long) during the previous 60 years.

If February 24th, 1983, was a bad day for Toby Jug, it was also a bad day for Peter Tatchell and a bad day for gay men in general. After weeks of smear campaigning on the subject of Peter's sexuality, he lost the Bermondsey by-election to the Liberal candidate Simon Hughes. By coincidence, Toby was born on Friday, November 30th, 1900 - another bad day for gay men. On that same day, Oscar Wilde died in poverty.

Back in 1965, the weather continued to be good throughout Thursday and the cycling continued to be magnificent as Simeon reached Hartington Hostel for that evening. He arrived back to a delighted Aunty Joyce at Bog Hole, Horsley Woodhouse, on the evening of Friday, June 11th.

Chapter 31

A Dancing Gnome

Early afternoon of Saturday, June 12th, we find Aubrey's ugly little tin box urgently tooting its way around the steep, narrow, twisty streets of Belper. The passenger sitting next to Mr Toad was just able to glimpse a splash of colour from rhododendrons adorning St Peter's Church yard. The whole scene was illuminated by a magnificent canopy of sun-enhanced, lime green light, filtering through many mature lime trees. When the car pulled up on Field Lane, Simeon escaped into the Champagne air of a clear spring day, with the toad close on his heels.

It was impossible to enter the Victorian Convent of St Lawrence. The imposing gateway was completely blocked by a dense audience, who were being entertained by an odd little man skipping about. Simeon recognised Nobby the Gnome immediately. Yes, definitely a gnome! Perhaps a touch larger than a dwarf, not quite so shrivelled as a very old man, but, yes, certainly a small old man of uncertain age. Nobby had a nice, simple face, reflecting a kindly nature which made him popular with children, popular with almost everybody - except Aubrey Pod. And, yes, there was an air, a suggestion of the supernatural about old Nobby under his funny little beaten-up cap, clad and shod in medieval attire. There was something timeless, something one hundred percent Derbyshire about this strange little man who belonged in the dales, in the woods, on the moors, alongside the canals, the rivers and would not be out of place in deep ravines or in the entrance of a cave.

Like the others, Simeon was absorbed by this strange spectacle. He was entranced by this funny little jig, performed by this funny little man. He was mesmerised by its hops, its spins and its whirls. It was magical in its effect and was entirely wholesome, in contrast to the spiteful prancing and capering of the toad, who, in *his* well-known, evil 'dance of delight', rejoiced in the misfortune of his enemies. Nobby's dance was free from anything like the effeminate pirouette of the outrageous Simon Tonks and totally free of any gestures Simeon had observed in that sickening, affected minuet he associated with the snooty Derby Camp. He decided that Nobby was nice.

The movement stopped, the delighted folk of Belper applauded and threw coins into Nobby's ancient battered cap as he bowed, thanked, quipped and laughed.

"That man has never done a day's work in his life!" complained the peeved toad. This heartfelt criticism was inspired by the trials and tribulations of a stressful teaching career, now in its 18th year. Each morning, Mr Pod had to drag himself out of bed and endure the tough regime of his strict, dictatorial headmaster and the tough regime of disruptive pupils, some of whom considered music (and Mr Toad) to be a joke. He was well aware that Nobby the Gnome woke up each morning in a different cottage, looked to the hole and simply waited for his early morning delivery of fresh semen.

"You what? I don't believe it!"

"It's true! He's nothing better than a sewer rat. He sleeps in public lavatories! There's pillows and blankets in that bag. It's a different cottage each night, so he's first in - in the morning - first in there to catch the cream, lives on it, bright and breezy. Oh, yes. Nobby's got it all worked out."

"The police ... "

"He's a tramp!" interrupted the toad with scorn. "What do the police care? Tramps get away with it. Nobby the Gnome gets more sex than anybody. I have to face those horrible girls who plague me all day, day in, day out and Nobby is having sex all day, every day - has been doing so, getting away with it, by all accounts since the First World War! There's me, stressed to a frazzle and there's him - man after man - all bloody - day - long. It makes ya sick!! Nobby should be *made* to work. Mr Wilson should *do* something about people like that bone-idle bugger. Listen here, Simeon and listen good; *don't* go back to America. Sign on for the National Assistance. Find a good cottage. Sit in it. Stay in it. Enjoy a stress-free life. You'll live to a ripe old age, like that idle bastard over there ... Are you listening to me?"

Simeon was listening and shaking with laughter. Aubrey Pod continued.

"Look at the prat now. Just look at 'im. Stashing away his pennies in that filthy old bag. That's it! That's all he's got. Everything's in that disgusting old sack. He carries it about on his back. He goes from cottage to cottage with that thing on 'is back. He can live off next to nothing 'cus folks *give* him things. There's always a crust for Nobby at any 'ouse if 'e does 'is daft, silly, stupid, little dance."

With further amusement, Simeon noted that, in such flame and fury, in the grip of strong emotion, Mr Pod's accent had a tendency to deteriorate, to regress to its original Derbyshire.

"Oh, yes!" he continued with vehement sarcasm. "No work for our Nobby. Oh, no. A nice easy life for Nobby - stupid little turd ... "

Aubrey Pod brought this tirade to an abrupt halt. His young friend's laughter had ceased. The smiling expression had turned to a look of sheer horror. The eyes of Simeon were fixated on two other eyes. They had met two hideous eyes. They were old, grey eyes, leering, eyes like the eyes of dead fish - cold, no warmth. These ghastly eyes were sunken into a face which was like something out of a nightmare. The boy was bayoneted to the spot. He was held in hypnotic fascination by penetrating, lascivious eyeballs, deeply set in a leathery, gnarled countenance which could have been part of the rough bark of an ancient oak. And, surely, this ancient man must be as old as any old oak? His large hooked-nose, complete with ugly warts and blackheads, was worthy of anything which could have been penned by the Brothers Grimm - and, indeed, it *was* grim. The mouth, which, at the present time, had teeth, seemed *not* to have teeth. It was a slash. It was a mouth which was more accustomed to being toothless.

Just as Simeon recognised Nobby, so now he knew that he was in the leering presence of the famous Belper Goblin - Jasper Wormall - no less. And, in an instant, he knew the reason why the revolting Becksitch Betty was called a hag and this freak of nature was referred to as - a crone.

"Do they really know?" he whispered to Aubrey, "those blokes who make use of those holes in those lavatories ... you know, Heanor, Ilkeston, Ripley and Matlock ... do they really know exactly who ... what is ... in the next penny house?"

"Some might, some don't care, some would sooner *not* know. It's experience, skill and technique which counts. Cottaging is not a beauty contest."

"Clearly not!" said Simeon, taking in the full impact of the creature before him.

"Oh, no," argued the toad, warming to his subject. "Imagine the horror of *my* customers if they could see what *I* looked like!" At this, to make the point, wearing a smug grin, the toad jutted out his ugly toadal countenance to within inches of the boy's face.

Toad and chicken went to a counter and obtained tea and home-made cakes, which were included in the admission fee. They were welcomed by an old, smiling nun with a thousand wrinkles. Kindly, she suggested that they enjoy their refreshments at one of the tables in the rose garden. Five minutes later, comfortably seated, they were taking pleasure from sunshine, the song of blackbirds, soaking up tranquillity in one of the most beautiful gardens in Belper. Alas, this tranquillity was soon to end.

"Oh, no!" said Aubrey. He had observed Nobby approaching across the lawn, negotiating rose bushes in a jaunty step, with the repulsive goblin scuttling close behind.

"Hello, little boy. And what have we here?" Nobby appeared to remove an acorn from Simeon's ear.

"Naughty little boy! You've been scrumping from the nuns' orchard haven't you!"

"You're joking," laughed Simeon.

"Yes you have. You've been stealing apples from these poor holy sisters. Disgraceful!"

"Shut up, Nobby," snapped Aubrey.

"What's this then?" replied the gnome, searching the boy, having a quick tickle, removing an apple from his pocket ... and then another ... and then another. He began to juggle the three apples which, inexplicably, were somehow joined by three oranges. The performance concluded when, in a cascade of giggles, Nobby lunged at the youth and inflicted a second tickle, in much the same way as Monks had suddenly attacked Tinker Bell.

"Behave yourself, Nobby!" said the irritated toad.

"You're quite a talented entertainer," complimented the delighted Simeon. "Isn't he?", directly addressing Jasper Wormall in an effort to reduce the undressing leer and force the bent old man into speech.

"Meh!" replied the goblin.

It was clearly an expletive - 'meh'. The first of many. This was an odd characteristic of Jasper's speech, a recurring motif which seemed to express contempt. Indeed, both goblin and toad seemed to be keen to diminish the cheery, funny gnome by making several deprecating comments until ... A look of delight suddenly transformed the grotesque features of Jasper Wormall. In a high, squeaky voice he said -

"Oh look! It's Mr 'oadley."

All eyes turned to the convent veranda. There, on that higher level, they beheld a bolt upright, smart figure, bright as a new pin. He was standing in snooty surveillance of the humble scene of common peasants before him. It was, no less, the much-respected leading homosexual of Derby - Claud Hoadley himself. Lord Claud, as ever disdaining the chatter of the common herd. Jasper jumped up, scuttled over to greet his honoured guest and proudly escorted him back to the table.

The contrast of the two mobile men walking across the neat grass made an impression on Simeon. The one, a man approaching 70, yet handsome, straight, suave, perfectly-groomed, and then the other - ancient, crooked, bent, humped and twisted.

"Was he born like that?" he whispered into the ear of Aubrey.

"He was certainly born like a gargoyle, but not with that hump. It's really a bend. Assuming he's 100 (nobody really knows), Jasper's probably spent the last 80 years bending down, trying to look under lavatory cubicle partitions ... well, you see, it causes the development of a hump," answered Aubrey Pod, with mischievous, twinkling eyes and waggling fingers.

An instinct told Simeon he should rise in the presence of this august gentleman, but Aubrey and Nobby showed no signs of extending the courtesy. With sickly grin, Jasper was bowing, prattling and fussing around the great man.

"So good of you to come 'ere. Such an honour, Mr 'oadley ... a think there's a ... Get oop!"

He snapped at Nobby, who jumped at this sharp command, bowed and gave the seat a quick wipe with a distinctly unclean brown rag. The guest (who had acknowledged nobody in that humble group) graciously deigned to be seated. Claud Hoadley had no intention of recognising the infamous toad or, for that matter, the scruffy chicken he had recently met. True, they *had* been introduced - but that was hardly the point, since their stations in life were so greatly dissimilar. And, after all, he had disapproved of David Bond, who, *without* permission, had brought a working class youth into the hallowed Friary Hotel. Of course, he knew of the appalling 'Nobby' by reputation and had always discouraged his subjects from discussing the lowly 'dancing gnome'. Once established in his chair, Mr Hoadley inclined his head very slightly to Mr Wormall, who was thrilled to be thus received

- and the goblin responded by bullying the one person who was (in his opinion) clearly an inferior. The sickly, obsequious grin disappeared and hard fish eyes were turned upon poor Nobby.

"Go and get Mr 'oadley some tea and cakes. Go on." Jasper gave him a push. "Tell them oo it's for, an they'll mek sure it's a fresh pot. An 'e'll 'av t' nicest cakes. Meh. An be quick about it. Meh."

As the gnome scampered away, Jasper launched into a well-prepared outline of the history of St Lawrence Convent, a litany of uninspired factual detail, delivered without imagination. It was a boring recital of dates, names of reverend mothers and sisters, past and present. Simeon was intrigued by this queer little deformity, his head nodding on each syllable, the Adam's apple bouncing up and down the scraggy old neck. Noting his friend's fascination, Aubrey leaned forward and whispered strange words into his ear -

"'His shrunk shank ... his voice, a childish treble.' That's from *As You Like It*, by Shakespeare."

Simeon was impressed. He had never been exposed to the beauty of Shakespeare. It seemed, so well, to sum up this shrunken, prattling, cackling crone. In his 2021 effort - *Hoadley: Portrait of a Pretentious Pedant* - Simeon made it clear to his readers that it was the despised *music* master who demonstrated a true grasp of the classics - not Claud Hoadley. During his long chat with Dolly a week before at The Corporation, the point was strongly advanced.

"Hoadley's position! What position? It's all bluff! That man is a complete artificial front. He's groomed himself to sound good. He's taken you in. He's taken them all in! Do you want to know more about English Literature? Do you want to have it explained properly in an easy and entertaining way? Well then, talk to your new friend, talk to the toad. He'll tell you all about Tennyson. He'll explain the Book of Daniel. Ask him."

Simeon did ask. Over the decades of strengthening friendship, Aubrey Pod encouraged and fed Simeon's growing appetite for romantic mysteries, folklore and occult associations in the wilds of gay Derbyshire. Drawing on his extensive knowledge of the history of music, Aubrey was quoted in Hogg's 2022 title *Nobby: True Tales of a Naughty Gnome.* The music master argued that Nobby and Mozart suffered from Tourette syndrome.

"I don't claim that they shared the same level of talent! There is, however, evidence that they shared similar symptoms of this strange disease. To start with, they were rude, vulgar, both of them sex-mad! They exhibited odd behaviour; suddenly spinning around, spontaneous dancing, leaping at people, uncontrollable chattering, silly laughter, going off at weird tangents, and they shared a mad compulsion for tickling teenagers."

Back in 1965, Nobby returned with a tray of best cakes and, especially for Mr Hoadley, the sisters had sent a full pot of fresh tea. All the other guests had to be content with one cup, poured from a large common pot. Nobby, cheerful as ever, was pleased to have been of good service.

"'Here you are, Mr Hoadley, the Reverend Mother's best teapot! All made especially for *you*. Now then!"

But Mr Hoadley was not looking at Nobby. Mr Hoadley never spoke Nobby's name. Mr Hoadley never spoke to Nobby at all. Mr Hoadley treated Nobby with supreme indifference, as befitted an invisible servant of the previous century. Simeon noticed how the valiant Nobby tried to rise above this Victorian arrogance. Buoyantly, he continued to make the best of such cruel snobbery.

"Now this is your hot water jug, Mr Hoadley." Just for a second, with smug satisfaction, a cool snooty eye rested on the gnome's shaky hand. "And here it is, here's your milk, Mr Hoadley, your sugar ... and here are your nice cakes - nicer than the ones we got, aren't they, young man?"

Simeon was quick to agree with the jolly fellow, to extend to him a little kindness in this, as he perceived, difficult moment. As the cup was put on the saucer - it fell over ...

"Be careful, Nobby!" barked the angry goblin, in a high, squeaky voice. "So sorry, Mr 'oadley," he said, pushing Nobby out of the way. Enthusiastically, Jasper placed the cup on the saucer with great care and poured out the hot tea. The sickly, obsequious smile returned. It spread across the hideous features, accompanied by bent, bowing solicitations and endless fuss around the Great Man.

After tea, Claud Hoadley expressed an interest in seeing the Convent Library. Eagerly, Jasper complied and the two very different men disappeared into the building. There were lots of books, religious and secular, on those quality oaken shelves, lovingly polished over many years by the sisters. They spoke of books - but not for long. They spoke of life. It was easy to steer the old man towards the more interesting subject of his small world, his friends and his 'visitors'. Hoadley trod very carefully. He flattered. He made reference to massage as a 'special skill' requiring an 'expert knowledge' of the human anatomy and expressed admiration for Mr Wormall's technical knowledge, long experience and ability. Jasper cringed, twisted and writhed in ecstasy under this cascade of compliments. Hoadley's questions were, on the surface, casual, diplomatic, innocent, but Hoadley's questions were also well-prepared and razor-sharp. There were a number of cross-reference questions to clarify important points from different angles. Some questions were put twice in a different way to make doubly sure of an important fact.

Different types of men were mooted, types from Derby and Nottingham. Many came to the humble cottage at Shire Oakes to seek 'relief'; labourers and professionals. Oh, yes - one was a doctor! Lawyers sometimes, the sort who wore wigs in court. They never *said* - but Jasper *knew*. Within his own social circle, names were mooted, such as a certain disreputable Arthur Bestwick. Folks were always keen to talk about Becksitch Betty. Jasper knew where he performed and how much he earned. He even knew all about the recent 'bust-up' between the drag artist and the manager of the Matlock Lido. Oh, yes, Jasper Wormall knew all about Becksitch Betty.

He spewed out petulant castigations of a certain smelly old man who harboured horrible boys in Chesterfield and, having named all these names, having revealed all these damaging details, Jasper Wormall claimed that he was the very essence of righteous rectitude.

"Oh, I see. But of course. You were very *wise*, Mr Wormall. Quite right. One has to be so very *careful*, doesn't one. Gossip! Nonsense! Perish the thought! My dear fellow, it is common knowledge that you are the *soul* of discretion."

Having crossed a certain line, Jasper would have told another interrogator to mind his own business but - for this goblin - it was a great day. He was in awe of Lord Claud and the lowly creature gladly revealed all. In such a majestic presence, he was obedient and pliable.

After half an hour, Claud Hoadley had all the information he needed to know. He could now form his plan.

The departure of Claud Hoadley and Jasper Wormall had left three people back in the garden - a difficult number. With his tricks, funny faces and silly stories, the gnome was amusing Simeon but irritating Aubrey. Eventually the music master stood up and announced the imminent departure of toad and chicken.

"That's enough of the convent. I'll take you to Newstead Abbey, Simeon."

"Oh! Very nice ... but ... shouldn't we say good-bye to the others?"

"Since my one-time colleague never even acknowledged my existence, I think, perhaps not."

"Well, OK." Simeon extended a hand to his charming new friend. "Cheerio then, Mr Nobby. You're a bundle of laughs and I've really enjoyed meeting you."

Nobby's hand, warm and friendly, made contact with the boy for a tad longer than normal. On withdrawal, he became aware of a coin in his palm, a shiny penny.

"Keep it for luck, don't be going spending it," said the gnome. The toad snorted.

"A new penny!" said an elated Simeon.

"Not new. It's freshly polished and as old as you, ya little monkey," replied Nobby, just before yet another lunge, yet more funny tickles and a few more silly skips.

"Isn't he a card!" said the giggly boy, turning to a grumpy Aubrey. Turning back ... the gnome had vanished!

"Amazing. How did he do that? Is he real?"

"You go to the public toilet in Cromford tonight, an you'll find out how real he is. He'll be there. You see. It's lorry drivers night," replied Aubrey, sagely, with an unpleasant chuckle.

The penny was dated 1950. Even as a teenager in late teens, Simeon was flattered to think that he had been assessed at 15. He was fully aware that, in the reclusive world of gay men, youth was all. It was the gold standard. Reflecting on this and looking at that same penny forty years on, he realised why that scruffy chicken on his bike, in provincial Derbyshire, had stirred up so much excitement, upset so many men and caused so much anxiety in an illegal homosexual world constantly under siege. Endemic jealousy and envy pervaded the two armed camps of Derby and Nottingham. For many years they had kept their powder dry. Little did they know that, in just seven days, their relatively safe world would be exploded by the spark of a scruffy chicken candidly giving information to the police about the disappearance of a vicious old queen.

Chapter 32

Corn in Egypt

Simeon made the best of the good weather during the following week. Nothing special happened, except for one day when he crossed the River Amber at Riversdale and climbed up a narrow road out of Ridgeway. At this point, heading south, Crich Lane became so steep he was forced to dismount and push his bicycle up the hill. Progress was slow, but most pleasant, ascending this quiet country lane. To his right were open fields, to his left, ancient woodland. He half expected to see Nobby the Gnome poke his head out of one particular old oak, which, being hollow, seemed to suggest a suitable home for such an a fairytale character.

And then, just a few trees up - there it was. It stopped him. It mesmerised him. It was not Jasper Wormall himself, but something which was entirely representative of that hideous old crone. Simeon was looking at a symbol, a representation of that ugly, deformed old man. It was a natural work of art. It depicted more about the hidden homosexual world of Derbyshire than any human artist could have achieved. He was admiring an old ash tree, pocked and rotting in places, very late emerging from a long hard winter, its leaves young, barely out of bud. Part of the tree was dead and haggard and part was still bravely clinging to life. The main trunk, gnarled and knotted, writhed and twisted skywards. Other limbs performed grotesque meanderings, insinuating a sense of the cruel deformity which had been inflicted upon that goblin from Belper. Equally symbolic of cruelty were the healthy coils of choking ivy. For many years, these thick curls had been slowly tangling, slowly strangling its host, the old ash tree, nearly to death - but not quite. Simeon meditated on the survival skills of the old man at Shire Oaks; bent and warped by a disapproving majority, yet, at a great age, still massaging under his ever-present companions, the cawing crows. It could have been a painting. Two slowly wrestling trees; there was much of warping and contortion, so, too, there was also much of beauty. Simeon wondered, in this natural formation, beauty and ugliness - the extreme ends of a continuum - had they finally met?

The clouds thickened over that old tree and, at last, the long spell of good weather broke. The following day was Saturday, June 19th. It was dull, cold and wet. In fact, it was a perfect day to visit his 'club' - the Derby

Turkish Baths. Others must have had similar thoughts, because several were there to keep Charlie and Fred busy as usual, thoroughly badgered and bad-tempered. On such a day the steam room felt good and the youth let the comforting heat penetrate into his cold bones. After a few seconds, through the thick mist, his eyes managed to discern the unmistakable facial outline and the revolting form of a naked Becksitch Betty (complete with wig) gently lolling his head against the white tiles in his favourite corner. Thank God he was dozing and social intercourse (or worse) was avoided.

Sexually, it was disposed to be a disappointing afternoon. The chemistry was all wrong for that sort of activity because too many people knew each other too well. It was very much an afternoon for regulars. As ever, Aubrey Pod made valiant efforts, running around, spinning around, as Dolly often commented, 'like an over-wound toy' - and getting nothing, because, effectively, at that stage, there no one to be had. He would not touch the Chesterfield gang with a bargepole. Sean Stokes, Simon Tonks and Monks stayed together most of the time as a social group, largely ignored by everybody else save for Simeon, who was pleased to note Sean's controlled demeanour in the hushed and sedate atmosphere of the Turkish Bath. They were chatting next to the cold plunge. Monks was sulky and Simon was cheerfully teasing Simeon.

"Oh, no! You'll never see Jasper *'ere*. 'e'd never get oat! They'd all panic and flee! Let's see ... " He placed a camp finger to his lips and cocked his cartoon head. "Saturday afternoon? Oh yes - Matlock cottage today, third one along."

"'ey oop, D' ya think 'e should 'ave plastic surgery, lass?" asked the lanky Sean, grinning from ear to ear.

"Bit late for that. But I *do* try to be kind to the old folk. I sent Jasper a packet of Polyfilla for 'is birthday and suggested that Guzzly Granddad grow a ponytail."

"What good is a pony-tail fa that owd bugga?" growled Monks.

"If it's tied dead tight at t' back, it pulls everything tight. All wrinkles gone! Eee - 'e'd look like a teenager - 'e would."

"No," responded a thoughtful Sean. "No - it wunt be right. A like Granddad's owd face. Best as 'e is: 'is face looks well lived in - dunt it?"

Simeon moved on. In the open fountain area he was smiled at by a little old man with quite a well-proportioned, compact body for a man of his years. He looked slightly familiar. A quick skip and jig identified him. It was a nude Nobby the Gnome! In hot pursuit of Muckles, he was too busy to talk.

This scruffy chicken was callow and impressionable. A rather distinguished, well-groomed, well-manicured man sitting next to Simeon made a major impression on him during that afternoon back in 1965, an impression which would never be forgotten. In the open areas, most bathers wore towels, as did chicken and gent, who sat together in silence, contemplating the central feature. Stealthy, Simeon had observed this rather desiccated toff with interest, on this and on a previous occasion. His slender body seemed to be as white as his very white face, which contrasted sharply with short, neat, raven black hair. Had it not been for David Bond, who called him 'the enemy', Simeon would not have known the name of this delicate gentleman. Like David, he seemed supremely indifferent to everybody, showing no interest at all. Had it not been for Edward, Simeon would have known nothing of this very precise stranger, a senior figure from the ranks of the Nottingham Camp, described as a 'social-climbing snob'. Here, at close quarters, was the one and only Clarence Soames, partner of Bob Phillips, who was, at that moment, hunting in some other corner of the Turkish Bath. The silence continued. Simeon was regarded with supreme insouciance, which became slightly irritating. Accordingly, he attempted conversation.

"I like your car."

After quite a long pause, the deathly-white face slowly turned to assess the young speaker. With legal precision, one sharp word was delivered in cut-glass quality -

"Indeed?"

"Oh yes. It's the new 1300 Vanden Plas isn't it? Neat, really neat. That expensive-looking conservative colour, lovely posh leather, nice wooden finish inside - all such good taste. I was admiring it when tying oop me bicycle to the lamp post."

"Bicycle. How quaint," came the concise reply, pregnant with derision.

"So well equipped for a small car," continued the boy with enthusiasm, trying to ignore the put-down, "switches and buttons everywhere ... and automatic transmission! Very few English cars have automatic transmission."

"We have everything .... except money."

This last line of five condescending words, carefully enunciated with subtle sarcasm, was offensive to Simeon. And yet, for the following 40 years, he remembered and admired those words as much as he had genuinely admired the 1300 Vanden Plas. Apart from the clear implication that Clarence was heading off a request for money, Simeon was enormously impressed with the way this gentleman had pronounced that one word - 'money'. It was drawn out to about ten times its normal length. It sounded like 'manaaaieryyy' - in stark contrast to Simeon's working class - 'm-oo-ny'. He must have heard aristocrats speaking on the BBC Home Service say 'money' thousands of times but, to hear it live, directly from the mouth of a *real* person (or perhaps an unreal person) was a striking experience indeed.

Unsure of how to respond to this memorable line, the scruffy chicken (and he certainly felt like a scruffy chicken during this exchange) was mute. At almost the same moment, a big, soft, pappy queen minced by, with a gait characterised by dainty steps, ridiculously too small for the size of the man. This immediately identified him as Hilary Raymond Hawley of the Derby Camp. Simeon noted that Hawley's slug-like skin had been a stranger to sunshine, but perhaps not quite as white or anaemic-looking as the thin, frail Clarence at his side. Idly, he wondered how Hawley's utterance of 'money' would sound. Would it achieve the same, impressive, dizzy heights as the affected utterance he had just heard from Clarence Soames? Soames and Hawley ignored each other.

People were moving about. Predation and activity hung in the air - yet it was so quiet! It was peaceful. Not a sound was to be heard but for the fountain and dripping water, with an echo which came from the cold plunge area. A muffled hiss of steam was drifting over from the steam room and an increase in volume announced the steam room door being opened. Out came David Bond, who nearly collided with little fat Dolly, who had just been enjoying refreshments in the dry hall of curtained cubicles and beds. Both men ignored each other. Both ignored Clarence, who stood up and walked into the first of the three hot rooms, but, to his relief, both said 'hello' to Simeon. He stayed put.

Simeon was comfortable, seated in this central area around the fountain, the hub of the Turkish bath, which gave on to all other areas, dry room, steam room, cold plunge, showers, massage table and the three hot rooms.

It was the best place to observe all the activity, all the comings and goings. A tall, handsome type came out of the steam room and used the shower. Simeon found the shower as interesting as the man. Set in its medieval Moorish alcove, it looked like a Victorian contraption; an ornate complication of plumbing - effectively a cage of pipes giving water jets vertical, horizontal and even a few at 45 degrees, together with one massive rose, producing a flow of Niagara proportions from above. It took some time for this well-endowed Adonis to open and eventually close all eight valves. This firm, thirty-something took two clean towels off the top of a pile and gave himself a vigorous rub down. He created the cheerful impression of noticing the sitting chicken for the first time.

"Hello there! You again. And, I'm pleased to see, toad-free!"

"He's probably getting a bit bored with me now," replied Simeon.

"Don't count on it. We call him 'the groping nuisance'. He never gives up. Speak of the devil!"

It was like a Tom and Jerry cartoon. By coincidence, the near-naked, grotesque body of Aubrey Pod, looking blotched, hot and bothered, shot out of the hot room in his usual urgent characteristic toadal gait. Arms in front, up to shoulder level, waggling fingers; he was chasing a rather desirable chicken into the area of the cold plunge. It was a hilarious sight, causing both observers to collapse into belly laughs. A splash was followed immediately by a greater splash, causing more laughter.

"Well, toads *are* amphibious. They can perform quite well under water, I'm told. A friend of yours?"

"That youth? No. He's one I've missed," said Simeon sadly.

"Try your luck later. My name's Bob, by the way."

Simeon had recognised Bob Phillips, partner of Clarence Soames, at once. Having exhausted the amusing subject of the frantic toad, once again the boy trotted out the details of his admiration of the Vanden Plas parked outside next to his bicycle. He received a much friendlier, more gracious response to his enthusiastic commendation than had been the case some ten minutes earlier in the frosty presence of the sardonic Soames. Interesting, thought Simeon; he judged both men to be of similar age, but the one who had sneered at his bicycle came across as much older.

"Is Becksitch Betty still in there?"

"Still steaming away," said Bob in his cheery, pleasant, unaffected voice.

"He's been in there a long time. Is he all right, do you think?"

"With any luck he'll be dead. Horrible old hag. I must say, he hasn't moved an inch in over half-an-hour, but then again, you can hardly see anything in that hot fog." His youthful features suddenly lit up in a mischievous smile. "I say! I was sitting next to something in there, *really* dishy - nearly made a play for it, nearly touched it. Thank God I didn't!"

"Why?"

"It was David Bond!" said Bob Phillips, laughing. "One of Hoadley's gang. Our sworn enemies, you know. We're Nottingham. We don't mix."

"So they tell me."

"You should meet Tommy and Martin. They'll be here today. Terrific guys. Legends in their own lifetime. Lots of fun."

"Really."

"And they throw big parties. They hire professional entertainers and extra staff. Loads of beautiful boys in the swimming pool".

"I'd like that."

"They're very kind ... do a lot of good."

The desirable chicken walked by, drying himself. In quick flashes, the moving towel revealed a recent erection, now in decline. Clearly, the moment had come and gone. In triumph, like a pale blob, Aubrey Pod skipped after him, pausing in front of Bob and Simeon to proclaim his conquest.

"There's corn in Egypt!" He addressed Simeon directly. "What! A young lad like you, still sitting there? As Dolly always tells me - 'You've to circulate to be noticed.'" He was totally elated and emphasised this with bending knees and flapping arms. "Must dash. My new friend will be wondering where I've got to. I'll order us tea and toast - and then, of course, he'll want afters ... "

He concluded this gloat with a giggle, a unpleasant grin, waggling fingers and a quick dash into the dry hall. Simeon and Bob enjoyed another mutual chuckle.

As Mr Toad said, it was time for tea.

Chapter 33

Legends of the Nottingham Scene

It was a grunt, a barely audible grunt. An unenthusiastic Charlie acknowledged Simeon's order for egg on toast and a pot of tea. The grumpy attendant took the view that there would be no tip from a boy who arrived on a bicycle. The cyclist walked down through the hall of curtains. To his left, the smaller curtained cubicles used for undressing and dressing, to his right, the larger curtained 'rooms', each consisting of two single beds, separated by a small table. One room was occupied by a nonchalant, recumbent chicken, being assaulted by constant prattle from an excited, gesticulating toad, going nineteen to the dozen.

" ... cus I like to entertain. This is my card. I've a nice little house on a hill with a nice view overlooking a nice river and you'll be very welcome ... "

Passing another room, very gently he moved a curtain to check if it was vacant. There was quick movement within; a tell-tale sign of two figures sitting on the same bed - instantly disentangling. One was young and attractive and the other, old and repulsive. After Monks had satisfied himself that the observer was the guest cyclist of two weeks back and therefore of no consequence, he continued in his illicit activity - an activity which horrified Simeon.

Many would suppose that the sight of a hunky, well-proportioned youth being serviced by an old man like Guzzly Granddad would horrify another youth looking on. The incident of Monday morning, June 7th, did not horrify Simeon. On the contrary, it turned him on to see Muckles in ecstasy. However, this current incident of June 19th in the Derby Turkish Baths was, to this youth, both sickening and shocking. The older man, probably in his late 40's, was much younger than Guzzly Granddad. Nethertheless, this soft, older man with the unctuous smile was bald. He had a curved nose and exuded an effect of oiliness. Simeon found his portly softness to be effeminate and repulsive. And this pale, portly man with his drooping breasts was, at this moment, being serviced by Monks!

But it was a different kind of service, in which genitalia were not involved. Man and boy were both well-covered by their towels. Simeon learned that this vicar (the gentleman's profession was disclosed ten minutes later) had paid Monks £10 for this employment. In 1965, £10 was half the average weekly pay for a working-man. Utterly appalled, Simeon would have refused to render this particular assistance to this particular man for the *full* average weekly wage. The show went on. The boy was rooted to the spot, ogling with loathing fascination, until Monks, working hard, slightly irritated, looked up and told him to - 'get lost'.

The voyeur moved on to find a vacant room. He had heard of the 'special services' rendered by Monks and Muckles and assumed this odious spectacle would come somewhere into that bizarre category of sexual favours. So what *had* Simeon been looking at which so disgusted him? Monks was *kissing* the reverend. Not just an ordinary kiss, but a long, lingering wet kiss in which both tongues eagerly sought every nook and cranny of the opposite mouth. When it came to kissing, Simeon was firmly in favour of the unwritten Detroit S&C Coffee Bar Code of Conduct - chicken shall kiss chicken only. There was something very personal and private about a French kiss. He could not comprehend that an attractive youth like Monks, even a duck murderer, could bear to smooch with an oily vicar at any price. Later, he was informed that the £10 bought more than just a long snog. In the vicarage that night, Monks gave the ecstatic ecclesiastic the full works, including a 'trip round the world'; a rather risky activity Simeon understood better by its American term - 'rimming'.

The egg on toast was delicious and Simeon managed to squeeze four cups out of that rather small pot for one. Reclining comfortably, still tuned into the faint slurping sounds coming from next door, he noticed two new arrivals disrobing in the cubicles opposite his bed. One was dark, with keen sharp eyes, and the other more mousy, with softer, more sensitive eyes. Both were tall, neither of them young, but both handsome, sporting a fine body, well-toned from a lifetime of regular exercise. Simeon's curtain 'door' was open a few inches. The newcomers looked in on him with smiling interest. Ready for the bath, complete with one towel covering the essentials, one draped over the shoulders, they entered and introduced themselves. From Edward's description, these gentlemen knew Simeon and Simeon knew them - but not by physical description alone.

Tommy and Martin, even near-naked, carried with them an aura of excitement, exhilaration, a power of personality. Immediately, Simeon could feel the energy, the authority, the leadership from these animated Kings of Nottingham - and 'kings' rather than 'queens' was entirely appropriate. On this side of the Atlantic, for once, he felt that he was in the presence of two real men who were totally free from any freakish peculiarity. After his experience with goblins, gnomes, toads, fairies, crones, hags and an assortment of affected snobs, here were two real blokes who were completely 'normal', in the best sense of that word. Tommy and Martin had brought with them into the Derby Turkish Baths - a breath of fresh air.

Their demeanour to this young man was exactly the same as their demeanour to all young men, indeed, to all people. They were sincere, friendly, generous and encouraging and, most important for a chicken - they were non-threatening in the sexual sense. There was no trace of the cronial leer or the toadal eagerness. For the first time on his holiday, Simeon did *not* feel like a scruffy chicken, nor was he embarrassed by his Derbyshire accent, his lack of sophistication, his working-class background, his lack of education or his modest means. Clarence Soames had subtly derided his bicycle, but Tommy Sperry, the highly-placed, highly-paid executive of a major multi-national company, took a genuine interest and asked intelligent questions about gearing and the thorny problem of punctures. In contrast to the total indifference of Claud Hoadley and his sneering second, Hilary Raymond Hawley, Martin Harcourt QC was very concerned to learn about Simeon's safety, to assess his progress in the risky subculture, in the illegal world of homosexuality. His interest and solicitude was caring, cautious and yet, at the same time, took full cognisance of the realities of gay life for a young lad with a healthy sex-drive. Neither censored nor disapproved when hearing the full details of the cycling holiday, now in its 19th day. They had been young themselves and took the view that a young homosexual was, by the very nature of the beast, disposed to be orgiastic and promiscuous. They were entertained and amused by Simeon's adventures. Advice, when it was given, was diplomatic and couched around the important issues of self-protection, common sense, vigilance, courtesy and consideration for others.

It was a great thing for Simeon to have the sympathetic ear of two intelligent, non-threatening adults, a great thing to openly chat, to be completely honest about his sexual desires.

A biting comment escaped Tommy when he noticed Hilary Raymond Hawley mince along, en route to one of the end rooms.

"Oh! How majestic. Her Royal Highness - no less."

"It's so odd!" added Simeon, "I can cope with the toad and Guzzly Granddad - but I couldn't *bear* the thought of *that* touching me. And yet, he's not exactly old or ugly, is he?"

"Easily explained," said Tommy, with smooth, dangerous sarcasm, "Hawley *is* handsome in an affected regal sort of way, but make no mistake, that thing is *all* woman - one large, squashy, squishy accumulation of female flesh. Notice the extra towel over the tits. Of course, a young lad like you will be repelled. What do you expect?"

The conversation became comical when Tommy warmed to his favourite subject - attacking the Derby Camp.

"A word of advice, Simeon. We all have our weaknesses. Make sure you know the weaknesses of your enemy. Now Hoadley, for example ... you've met him of course - the Grand Dame, the Martita Hunt of the Friary Hotel? Well, it's useful to know that he has a horror of women's tits and the bums of builders - the top crack that is, you know, when they're bending down ... Oh! On the subject of bums ... Anyway, I'll leave you two boys to chat."

Tommy Sperry had been severely distracted by a passer-by. He walked down the aisle, but was slowed in his progress by eager exuberance from Charlie, who was delighted, now being assured of a large tip at the end of the afternoon.

"Mr Sperry! Good to see you again, sir."

As Tommy disappeared through the door into the wet bath area, Charlie's warm praise was avidly pressed upon his more taciturn and indolent colleague, Fred - who, at this point in the afternoon, was almost asleep.

"Lovely gentlemen, Mr Sperry and Mr Harcourt. *Real* gentlemen they are, always a treat to serve them. Yes, always a treat."

Back in Simeon's bed cubicle, Martin Harcourt became thoughtful and a touch pensive.

"I'm sorry, Simeon. I really am."

"Pardon?"

"I should have done more. I *could* have done more."

"I'm ... sorry. I'm not with you ... "

"Forgive me. I'm speaking generally. Not just to you, but to all homosexual boys. We - the professionals - we could have made a better world for you. Damn it all, it *is* the 20th century ... let me try to explain. Many barristers go into politics. *I* should have gone into politics when I was a young man. I could have made a difference. It's too late now. I'm nearer to 60 than 50 ... "

Downcast, he contemplated the dirty old carpet, which was also more than half a century in age. Martin looked up with sad eyes and met the eyes of Simeon, who was puzzled and disappointed with this sudden dip into the dumps.

"You see, my friend, it's up to people like me to make things better for people like you. I've failed."

"Nonsense! What about those massive wild parties I keep hearing about? They must cost a fortune. And then, all the help and advice you give ... you bring people together."

Martin Harcourt smiled.

"It could be said, indeed *is* said frequently in the Derby Camp, that our social gatherings in Nottingham are for our own benefit. We're human. It's true, we've had a good life. Simeon, let me put it to you this way - *somebody* has to stand up and make a start. If life for homosexuals is ever going to improve, then somebody has to be brave. I've been a coward. If everybody behaves like me, nothing will ever change. Nothing much *has* changed." He spoke in a whisper, "Look around you at these sad people. For example, the odious youth you were telling me about behind that curtain."

Martin explained to Simeon that Monks and Muckles were, amongst other things, prostitutes known as 'rent boys'. The older man with Monks, behind the curtain, was a regular client, a local vicar, married with children who were themselves older than Monks.

"That man, one of millions, should never have been married. He's living a lie, possibly tormented by religious conscience, terrified of being discovered, no doubt under constant threat from those young criminals who extract the occasional bonus for their continued silence. And this is the world you have just discovered; the world we have left you. You'll have to deal with hate, bigotry, discrimination and ignorance on a massive scale - and I have allowed that to happen."

Again, Martin was acutely disheartened. Again, he looked down at the floor.

"Well ... " Simeon was struggling to find the right words. "What exactly ... *could* you do. You can't change the world. How can you change people. There isn't anything you *can* do - is there?"

The mood changed at that moment. Martin Harcourt had recovered all the confidence of the famous barrister. It seemed that the well-known Nottingham QC had just become several inches taller. The boy was now in the witness box. He was fixed with that firm, intimidating Harcourt look - just before the assault of an incisive question. The towel draped around his neck was hitched in the manner of a silken gown, in the time honoured style of the barrister-at-law.

"Where were you on the afternoon of Wednesday, August 28th, in 1963?"

"I can't remember!" replied a startled Simeon. "I can tell you this, three months later on November 21st, the day before the assassination of Kennedy, I was just stepping off the Queen Elizabeth."

"Ah. In that case, are we to assume that you were not in Washington DC?"

"No! I mean, yes - I wasn't there."

"Do you claim that you were nowhere near the reflecting pools of the Lincoln Memorial?" The towel was pulled and hitched up a little closer.

"I was probably looking at my fish in the garden pond at Horsley Woodhouse."

"May we then, therefore, conclude that you were *not* one of the crowd of 200,000 people who listened to the inspiring words of Dr Martin Luther King on that day?"

Simeon was stunned into silence, wondering where all this was leading. The barrister dissolved. He melted back into the gentle man with a conscience. He spoke softly and slowly.

"You see, Simeon. Dr King was brave. *He* stood up for his people. His people suffer ignorance, bigotry and prejudice just as we do. He spoke of justice and equality. That's what *we* can do. We *can* stand up and be counted." He inched closer and lowered his voice. "It's like this, my friend. I don't want to sound pompous or too dramatic, but I, too, 'have a dream'. I have a dream that, one day, homosexuals can be completely open about their sexuality. I have a dream that, one day, homosexuals will be able to enjoy those few precious moments of ecstasy with each other *without* the constant fear of being banged up in prison for it. I have a dream ... "

Suddenly - a hag halted the speech. The alarming sight of an ugly face with a twisted mouth was peering through the curtain gap. The odious proportions of the grim face of Becksitch Betty seemed to require attention.

"Excuse me, Simeon."

The two men moved down the corridor, deep in a private conversation which lasted less than three minutes. When he returned, Martin seemed introspective and concerned but, due to custom and common courtesy, the boy asked no questions. The man resumed his seat on the bed. For a moment, he stared at the curtain gap where the face had been. He then recalled himself, looked at the boy and the serious features softened into a smile.

"Where was I?"

"You were dreaming," said Simeon, smiling back.

"So I was." He suddenly became energetic. "Let us be more practical. Let us attack this from another angle. Let us speak of words."

"Words?"

"Terms. You gave me the idea. You were telling me about the cultural differences between homosexuals in Detroit and homosexuals in Derbyshire."

"Was I?"

"Indeed you were. I've been with Tommy for 18 years. We are known as 'an affair'. Sounds a bit prissy doesn't it? What was your word?"

"An American would say 'my lover'."

"Mmm. Better. I refer to Tommy as 'my friend'. It's safer. All of us, homosexual and heterosexual, we need a new word, an all-inclusive-word which acknowledges the fact of same sex couples."

"There's another word you don't seem have here. If you have casual sex with a guy in Detroit, he's referred to as a 'trick'."

"But the best advance," replied Martin with enthusiasm, "is the American term 'gay' - an inspired word. 'Homosexual'! It sounds like a disease. Its constant use keeps reinforcing that particular prejudice in the heterosexual mind. Most gay people around here use the word 'queer' to describe themselves! And men who are not 'queer' are termed as 'normal'!! Beat that!"

"I'm not too keen on the word 'straight' - as used by the S&C boys in Uptown Detroit. That suggests that I'm bent!"

"You'll never be that," laughed Martin, "Only crones are bent. It comes down to this, Simeon. We, the homosexual community, are impaled on a whole lexicon of terms which continue to degrade, to demean, continue to reinforce our feelings of inferiority with reference to the heterosexual majority. It has to change. It *must* change."

"How?"

"I wish to God that I'd spent the last thirty years trying to deal with that problem, trying to do something worth-while, rather than prosecuting and defending. It's all to do with the call of the cash-box and, I suppose ... trying to rub Hoadley's face in it ... "

"Pardon?"

"Nothing. Damn it, I *will* answer your question. To start with - role models."

"What?"

"Role models are people you can look up to, people you admire, people you would like to be like. Someone you can identify with, who will help you to feel good about yourself. So who is *your* chosen homosexual role model, Simeon? Mmm, speak up ... Jasper Wormall? Aubrey Pod? Nobby the Gnome? Simon Tonks? Guzzly Granddad?"

"How about David Bond?"

"Not bad."

"Martin Harcourt QC."

"Improving - but I've made my point. How often are we represented positively in films? There are plenty of effeminate spies, effete traitors and cowards. Pod's a good example of a poltroon. What do the public see? They see that sad, ugly, camp thing in *A Taste of Honey* and they see 'queer' - and thousands of young guys like you rush off to hide, to take refuge for the rest of their lives behind the shield of an unhappy marriage."

Simeon remembered the gentle and kind Geoffrey, who was played by Murray Melvin.

"Gay Detroiters even have a term for repressed homosexuals. They're known as 'closet cases'."

"And, look at what it does to us ... ," carried on Martin. "We are a pathetic bunch! The Derby and Nottingham scene is infested with a culture of pretentiousness and affectation. It's as though we've come to detest each other, to despise each other ... "

"So ... ," ventured Simeon.

"So, back to your question of 'how'. It will be a long haul. A lot of hard work, and we'll need a good leader - like Dr King."

Martin Harcourt QC sprang up, paced up and down the short space of that tiny 'room' a few times and came to a halt in front of the homosexual boy whose future had ignited this current agitation. He sat down and fixed the boy with a determined look.

"OK. I'll tell you how. I intend to dream on. I *do* have a dream. Money. Public money. Tax-payers' money will be needed from the very public who have put us in this precarious situation in the first place." He leaned forward. "Remember this, Simeon - human unhappiness has effects far beyond the individual himself. It reaches out to touch the lives of everyone. It is in the interest of the state to help all homosexuals. Accordingly, we'll need money. We need money to employ a team of professionals in every town and every city in Britain. We need to build up a homosexual community for men *and* women - a whole lot better than the bitchy mess we have at the present time. We need trained counsellors to help and to give chaps like you (and girls) the free advice you need. We need diplomats, people in government who are competent in public relations to improve the homosexual image. We need experts from the world of advertising - image makers who can change perceptions. We need professionals who are accessible, who will encourage, advise and warn. We need an alternative to stinking toilets, dangerous parks and seedy pubs. We need a friendly, comfortable place where old, young and even the freaks of Derbyshire like your toad, your goblin and that gnome, can all drop in and have confidential chats - a sort of support service. We must forge links, meet the needs of the *whole* homosexual community, stop ignoring the women, pull together ... I suppose - I'm talking politics ... it *can* be done. We must, at least try ..."

Chapter 34

A Conjuring Trick

Charlie Birkin, the attendant of the Derby Turkish Baths, wanted to go home. It was well past 8.00pm. Normally, he and Fred were cleared up and away by 6.30pm. He was wishing that he had not called in the police in the first place. The grumpy, bald rotundity and the gaunt, dozy Fred were sunk deep into their armchairs at the head of the hall of curtains, facing Detective Sergeant John Winter. The latter was reading a note which had just been passed to him.

"Well, this *could* become quite serious."

"Why? What is it? asked Charlie.

"We've established that Mr Bestwick hasn't returned home."

Fred grunted. Charlie sighed. They had been through the sequence of events of that afternoon several times. Winter had asked questions and more questions for the purpose of cross-reference. He made copious notes, corrections and clarifications. The two attendants had examined every room in the Derby Turkish Baths for a possible hiding place, several times since 6.05pm. The kiosk lady had volunteered to remain at her post to see that no one left the building by the front door. It was the only exit and entrance to the building. There was no other way out. Winter had satisfied himself that no one could have escaped from this specialised suite of rooms, some with small, high windows and most with no windows at all. He had carefully inspected the hall of curtains, the central area, the shower and massage area. He took his time. He scrutinised the steam room, the cold plunge, the adjacent passageway with its various alcoves and the small 'sun room-cum-storage room'. Winter inspected the cul-de-sac of the three dry rooms - the warm dry room, the hot dry room and the very hot dry room at the very end.

Common sense told them that a human being could not just vanish into thin air. It was impossible - yet the impossible seemed to have happened on that afternoon of June 19th, when the untouched clothes of Arthur Bestwick were found in one of the small, curtained, changing cubicles. Everyone else had left. It was just after 6.00pm. His jacket, trousers, braces, underpants, vest and shirt were still hanging on the brass peg above his shoes and socks.

Nobby the Gnome, keen to get his money's worth, was the last man to leave the Derby Turkish Baths at 6.05pm. That had been established by three independent witnesses, in fact, three women who were adamant that they had seen all 17 bathers leave. Hilda Fox, of the kiosk, had been in the service of the Derby Turkish Baths for 53 years, even longer than Charlie and Fred, who were, themselves, both past retirement age. Over those many years, Mrs Fox in her little box took a keen interest in the gentlemen who paid over their five shillings for admission. Over those years, she had become curious about certain gentlemen, those who were so unlike the macho Mr Fox and other men in her world, a world of heterosexual working-class culture. When making small talk, Hilda Fox got to know her regulars, the ones who were excessively charming and polite, those who used big words, those who lisped, those who spoke posh, those who were odd, those who were like women and walked funny. Mrs Fox's job was the most exciting part of her uneventful life. In that job, for the most part, she did very little. Accordingly, in her tiny world, in her little box, she had ample leisure time to hone powers of observation, to consider, to wonder about her regulars. She knew all their names because she had to write the name on the back of each five shilling ticket. Armed with this formidable knowledge and the skills of surveillance, Fox of the box was able to reel off all the names of all those regulars, in their correct order, as they left the Derby Turkish Bath on that afternoon.

She told Detective Sergeant John Winter that all 17 bathers had left the building during the last 40 minutes of the session. She considered them to be all regulars except for two who left first, about a minute apart, at approximately 5.20pm. The first was -

" ... a swarthy, unfriendly youth of about 16. Gave his name as Blount. The second, a well built stranger, just as abrupt, a Mr Marshall. He'd be 22, or so. Now then ... next would be Mr Croft, the nice vicar. He comes about once a month. He marched out just before half past. Five minutes later, a whole batch of them left. Mr Sperry and Mr Harcourt, very courteous, never leave without a friendly word and a smile - 'Cheerio, Mrs Fox' - ever so nice. Then them ignorant buggers! Sign in as Monks and Muckles. Not their real names, I shouldn't think. Not likely. That stuck-up Hawley ignored me, always does. Too good for the likes of us. Miss Dainty Steps!" She wriggled her shoulders to effect a brief impression. "Thinks he's *it,* he does, swanking in his posh black overcoat.

Dr Bond speaks now and again - when he thinks he will. Now then, it would be about twenty minutes to five when that spotty youth left. What's his name ... like a pig ...

"Hogg?" suggested Winter, examining his hand which was full of tickets.

"That's right, Hogg. Not exactly a regular, been about three or four times. He left with those two noisy characters, Tonks and Stokes. A barrel o' laughs, they are, a right scream. Mr Stokes always calls me 'lass' - 'are ya all right, lass' - ooo, he *is* funny! Now then ... at about ten to ... oh yes, it was Mr Phillips and Mr Soames. They speak. They're polite ... but, well ... shall we say ... a bit reserved, especially Mr Soames."

"That only leaves Mr Pod and Nobby," said Winter.

"No. You've forgotten Mr Smith. The tubby bloke. Now he's a *lovely* little man, ever so nice, nicely spoken. *Then* we got Mr Pod. Hum," she added with contempt, "If you ask me, Mr Pod is only interested in Mr Pod. An *odious* man!"

"So Nobby the Gnome left at just gone six. How does he sign himself?"

"Just 'Nobby'," laughed Mrs Fox. Always does a turn, gives us a bit of his little dance."

"Who is 'us'?" asked the policeman.

"May does the kitchen, you know, food for our customers. Beryl the cleaner comes in at about 4.00pm. They both watched all the gentlemen leave. They're not overly busy," sniffed Hilda Fox.

"And you're *certain* that Mr Bestwick never left this building?"

"Fetch me a Bible. I'll swear on it! Mr Bestwick might be a bit odd, a bit common, but he's a *real* gentleman. *Never* passes me without a kind word. Asks how I am and enquires about my sister, who's a cripple. Ask Beryl and May. They've seen him perform. May said *his* Old Mother Riley was as good as Arthur Lucan's - now then!"

Charlie, Fred, May and Beryl could not be so positive about the order of exit, times or names, but they were all positive about identification. Those diverse, individual personalities were clearly imprinted upon the minds of all five observers. Below the name on each ticket Winter had added the approximate time of departure according to Mrs Fox.

The attendants were keen to stress to Detective Sergeant John Winter that Mr Bestwick's clothes had not been touched. Winter found the ensemble to be on the drab side, well-worn and old-fashioned.

"Could do with a dry-clean. Good quality. Pre-war I expect. How old was this chap?"

"Never thought about it," said Charlie, stroking his chin. "Been coming here ... ooo, what d'ya reckon, Fred?"

"Well ... we didn't see 'im *before* t' war," answered Fred, reluctantly, in his slow speech."

"Soon after, though. He was warming himself in my steam room in that terrible winter. Yes, been coming regular, at least twice a week, these twenty years."

"How old was he?" asked Winter.

"Oh ... Well past 60. As old as us?" Charlie directed this question to his colleague.

"Younger! Much younger. Am certain," said Fred, "A was once talkin' about t' General Strike, 'ad n't a clue, said 'e was just a kid."

"Not short of money," said Winter, examining the contents of a wallet. It contained one of the new ten pound notes, two one pound notes and two ten shilling notes.

"That's daft," said Charlie, "We always advise our bathers to check their valuables with Mrs Fox. There's been a fair bit of thieving lately. We've an idea, but can't accuse anybody." He and Fred were both thinking of Monks and Muckles.

"This has seen better days."

Winter was commenting on a yellowing pocket watch on the end of a short fob chain. He tapped it a few times in an effort of thought. At this stage, he had interviewed the two attendants, the three ladies and considered that all useful information available had been extracted and written down. John Winter was experienced. He judged that there were two possible solutions to this mystery. Arthur Bestwick might have performed some sort of tasteless disappearing trick, after the style of Agatha Christie's example in 1926. Winter, a Christie fan, had always believed that it was a publicity stunt. If this unlikely solution was, indeed, the case, Bestwick the entertainer, would eventually reappear. The other possibility was more sinister. Bestwick, a man of modest means had left behind nearly £14 including loose change - a lot of money. That did not make any sense at all ...

This Detective Sergeant had been on the Derbyshire force for over 20 years and had seen many sides of life. He recognised a few names on those tickets which were associated with the murky and secretive world of queers, a line of enquiry he found distinctively uncomfortable. He and his boss, Detective Inspector Derek Russell, had come across Simon Tonks in connection with two previous serious cases. The odd little fellow was often in sexual trouble and well-known to the Derbyshire police. Indeed, on one occasion, Simon was accused of indecency in this very establishment. For a period, he was banned from the Derby Turkish Baths. Aubrey Pod was a familiar name ... as was Martin Harcourt. He had no doubt at all that 'Smith' was, in fact, the notorious Adolphus Coggan, the short, plump, podgy bloke better known as the famous Dolly of Derbyshire. He provided guided tours around homosexual pubs and sexually-active lavatories.

Winter considered ... but, in truth, he did not know *what* to think. He looked at the two attendants. Charlie and Fred looked back at Detective Sergeant John Winter with faces expressing something between a blank and puzzlement.

"I'll take these." He picked up the tickets and put Bestwick's clothes into a bag. "Can't make much more progress tonight," he said quietly. "If Bestwick turns up he'll have some explaining to do. If not ... you two will be here on Monday?"

"We'll all be back on Monday - every Monday," sighed Charlie.

"Nothing more to do here," replied the detective. "You can all go home now."

Chapter 35

Police!

This one word, dreaded by all professional gay men - police. If attacked by queer-bashers - and they take care *not* to make an official complaint - professional men have a chance of survival. The black eye and the thick lip will eventually heal, but in 1965, a career in education, the law, politics, medicine, the church or any number of well paid and respected positions would not survive the publicity of a homosexual scandal. The mysterious disappearance of Arthur Bestwick (better known as Becksitch Betty) was a time bomb which would, in due course, rock the whole homosexual populace in Derbyshire and Nottinghamshire.

Detective Sergeant John Winter and Detective Inspector Derek Russell visited the Derby Turkish Baths early on the Monday morning of the longest day, June 21st. For clarification, Russell asked the staff similar questions Winter had asked on the previous Saturday and a few more. He established that Mr Bestwick was a man of average height, approximately five foot nine inches. The same could be said of Mr Phillips, Mr Soames, Mr Croft, Mr Hogg and Dr Bond, as he was incorrectly titled by the staff. Mr Harcourt, Mr Sperry, Mr Hawley, Mr Muckles and Mr Stokes were rather taller than average height. There was general agreement that Mr Monks was a touch smaller and Mr Pod, Mr 'Smith', Mr Tonks and Nobby were certainly on the short side.

"Did Bestwick seem ... the same as usual?" inquired Russell.

"Doesn't say much to us," sniffed Charlie, taking another swig of his morning tea.

"That's not what I asked."

"Well ... yes, I suppose he was just as he usually is."

Russell picked up latent hostility, born of the fact that Becksitch Betty was a confirmed non-tipper and had little use for Charlie or Fred.

"Did he look the same as usual?"

"If you mean, 'was it *really* Mr Bestwick' - no doubt at all."

"There's plenty that saw 'im and know 'im," added Fred.

"Quite. I wasn't getting at that. Let me be more direct. Bathers always present their ticket before they conceal themselves and strip in one of these cubicles - correct?" Both attendants nodded assent. "Good. Did Bestwick have anything at all with him?"

"What d'you mean?" said a puzzled Charlie.

"Was he holding anything? Perhaps he'd been doing a bit of shopping."

"Oh, no. Not that I noticed," replied Charlie, looking to his colleague for confirmation.

Russell formed the impression that the attendants had hardly noticed the missing bather and further questions would be useless. Earlier, he had established from Mrs Fox that Becksitch Betty was in his usual pleasant demeanour, wearing his usual old suit. No, she noticed no bag or packet, but then, she might not, considering her limited view point from the oaken kiosk.

The examination was now aimed at establishing contact with the other bathers. This presented little difficulty. Detective Inspector Derek Russell knew Tonks and Coggan of old. Many in the Derbyshire police force would fall about laughing when recycling anecdotes about the notorious Mr Toad. Through these characters, he could easily find Monks, Muckles and possibly Hogg, since the latter had been seen with them. Nobby could be found in any local public toilet. A vicar called Croft - if he *was* a vicar and his name *was* Croft - could soon be uncovered. An eminent consultant surgeon was no problem at all and there was only one QC in Nottingham. Russell was thinking of a valuable contact, an old friend with long-standing, specialised knowledge of the local homosexual community. Specialised help was called for in this rather tricky case. In due course, all the other bathers would be located. His instinct told him that the two strangers, the two non-regulars would be of little help.

Coming from Belper himself, Russell knew something of Becksitch Betty. He knew that Bestwick could be an unpleasant man. He was aware that, for some years, that drag queen had been the source of a great deal of stress within the secretive and nervous homosexual brotherhood. There had been gossip, suggestions of threats, of blackmail. In the car, en route to Belper, Russell immediately dismissed Winter's theory of the publicity stunt.

"It won't do, John. If anything, Arthur Bestwick was winding down his entertaining. He's been doing less and less over the last five years. No. The solution to this dark business lies somewhere in that motley collection of odd bods."

"Best to start with the lads, boss. You know, before the word gets around. Get to them quick. Give them a shake-down. We'll get more out of the boys than most of the men," said Winter.

"My money would go on that newcomer, Hogg. Yes. I think a surprise visit to Mr Pod is indicated. Any ideas, John?"

"He'll not be overly chuffed if we turn up at the Herbert Strutt School."

"No. I meant Becksitch Betty. How did he manage his vanishing trick?"

"It's a perfect challenge for Poirot. Not so good for John Winter. Are we certain that he really did leave that place?"

"Oh, I think so, John. No dead bodies in the Derby Turkish Baths. No nasty smells, we made sure of that. He got out somehow. Most people do what we did, John - they *walk* out of a building."

"Is that what the 'how tall' questions were all about?"

"That - and the 'did he have a bag' questions. He didn't walk out naked, did he? I think the ladies would have noticed and mentioned it. So, he was wearing clothes and he *must* have walked out. If you make yourself look different (and just remember that Betty made his living by looking different) you must be the same height or taller. Very difficult to make yourself shorter, unless, of course, you're bent double with a fake hump, disguised as Jasper Wormall - and we know that Jasper was not there, don't we?"

"Is that thing still alive!!"

"Absolutely! The Belper Goblin is indestructible, still very busy, still massaging under the crows by all accounts - and I'll wager he knows something about this business - no joke."

"And yet our witnesses," continued Detective Sergeant John Winter, ignoring Russell's flight of fancy, "the three women who were a bit bored, three women who had nothing better to do than *be* a witness; they're certain that they correctly identified all 17 bathers leave that building. Makes it so damned awkward!"

"Indeed, John. Indeed. Most awkward."

They pulled up at the foot of Becksitch Lane.

"Detective Sergeant Field is round the back, sir," said the constable who was guarding the front door.

"That's right, sir," said Field, "had a good look round last Saturday evening. No problem getting in - key under one of the plant pots. Never learn, do they? It certainly looks as though he expected to be back for his evening meal. Look."

They looked. Somehow, this was a sad sight. In spite of himself, Russell felt a pang of pity for this (generally) unpopular man, who had spent most of his life on his own. The table was laid out with one place setting of humble cutlery from the last century. There were a few tomatoes, pickled onions and a few drooping flowers which had, by now, given up any hope of seeing their owner. The kettle, ready on the hob, was full and ready for a light. An old gas stove incorporated a simple grill. Underneath this was an elliptical, oven-proof plate, ready prepared with two slices of bread, covered with small pieces of cut cheese. This tiny kitchen was neat and clean.

"I came back to finish off on Sunday afternoon," continued Field, "and found signs of a break-in! Made a bit of a mess, but they didn't find what they were looking for."

"How do you know?" asked Winter.

"Because I've got it here. Removed it with several other items on Saturday."

It, was an opened envelope addressed, in type, to Mr A Bestwick. A postmark clearly indicated Nottingham, June 2nd. The typewritten letter within was brief and unsigned - 'Come to <u>back</u> of shop Tuesday 7.30pm. Side entry to left. Will pay extra if they stay the night.' Attached to the letter were three £5 notes.

"So who do we know in Nottingham who keeps a shop?" mused Russell, more to himself than to his colleagues.

"They?" asked Winter.

"Boys ... by the sound of it," murmured Russell. He continued to stare at the letter and the money with unfocused eyes. "So, to add to his sins, perhaps Becksitch Betty has been pimping."

"And this," said Field, handing Russell a plastic pack of 'Sqezy' the 'wash-up wizard'. "Give the bottom a pull - it comes loose."

Russell did so and a tight bundle of bank-notes fell into his hand.

"Three hundred and forty eight pounds, sir," said Field, suppressing his feeling of pride and pleasure in discovering such a clever hiding place. "Not bad for a drag artist!"

"Not bad at all," said the Detective Inspector. "I shouldn't think our Arthur saw very much of the tax man. I doubt this place is worth three hundred quid. Rented, I expect?" Field nodded. "Anything else?"

"Just this." Field handed over another opened envelope with a Nottingham postmark indicating June 7th. It looked as though a drunken spider with inky feet had walked over the small sheet of paper. The barely legible scrawl said - 'Two under twelve if possible. Will be talking to friendly horse at Upperwood Farm at 2.30 on June 10th.'

"No advance payment this time?" asked Winter.

"Just as I found it, John, with the other envelope, up there behind the right hand vase." Field indicated two matching vases on the mantelpiece above the fireplace. "Good God, letters like that ... " he shook his head, "they're dynamite! He didn't try very hard to hide them."

"No," said Russell, thoughtfully. "Everything here indicates that Arthur Bestwick expected to return home on Saturday evening after his session in the Turkish Baths. Folks who deliberately vanish usually take their loot with them; they need it. What do you reckon, John?" Winter took the note and delivered his opinion in seconds.

"Dangerous stuff. I'd say it was deliberately written badly to disguise the hand."

"I know Upperwood," said Russell slowly. "It's right up on top, near the Heights of Abraham; a pretty little community on the west side of Matlock Bath. I've walked there with the kids quite often. There *is* a friendly horse up there, at a farm, near ... near to the woods."

Immediately, the other two men understood his line of thought. Russell looked at his watch.

"A quick conference, gentlemen," he waved a hand at the chairs. They sat at the table and Russell leaned forward. "Now then - who broke in? What was he after? Did the burglar know that Becksitch Betty was worth a few hundred pounds in cash? Or did the burglar have a guilty secret? Was he desperate to remove the evidence of that secret? Field?"

"More likely to be somebody who wanted to get his letter back - don't know which one, but I'd back the typing job with the fifteen quid."

"Which points to somebody who *knew* that Betty was not at home," added Winter.

"Somebody at the baths?" said Field.

"Probably - but not essentially," said Russell. "Incidentally, Field, can we be sure it was just the one break-in?"

"From the looks of it, almost certainly just the one, sir. Can't be one hundred percent sure."

"Neighbours?"

"I've talked to them both sides. Didn't hear anything. Didn't like him. There's a single woman, next door down, with loads of dirty kids. She was positively crowing. 'Good riddance to bad rubbish', she said. There's been a feud raging for some time. She complained of some minor vandalism in the garden. Much the same next door up. Seem a nice couple, sharing with the old grandmother. *She* hopes he's gone for good. No love lost there. They all referred to him as Becksitch Betty or just Betty; never Mr Bestwick or anything as friendly as Arthur. Not much respect for his 'celebrity status'. Dressing up as an old woman ... they thought it right peculiar, not normal for a proper bloke. They spat it out in their own colourful way."

"Yes. Belper folk would see drag as repulsive and degenerate," said Russell.

"Of course," continued Field, "they all knew the score. He was variously referred to as 'a Nancy', 'a queer', 'a pervert' - but no talk about visiting boys but for one recent exception. It seems that Bestwick had just one regular visitor, a little fat bloke in a green Morris 1000. Both sides say that he brought a young fellow to this address about a fortnight back."

"That squares with the evidence of the two attendants," said Winter.

"Young Hogg," said Russell, "When we find him ... "

"There was something else," continued Field. "Bestwick was a bit more friendly with the old lady three doors up. She said he's always nipping off to Blackpool for a few days if ... " he consulted his notes, "Dolly Clacket could fit him in." All three men smiled. "She wasn't alarmed. She said 'go to Blackpool. That's were you'll find Arthur.'"

"Oh yes," said Winter, with sarcasm, "he's in Blackpool all right! He leaves his clothes and £13 at the baths, dinner all ready in the grill, table set, fresh flowers, life savings nearby, incriminating letters - not to mention ... "

"*Is* he in Blackpool? Did you check?" interrupted Russell.

"I did." retorted the Detective Sergeant Field, with a smug smile. "Mrs Clacket hasn't seen him in weeks."

A few moments of silence hung over the conference of three. It was broken by the senior man.

"Returning to your previous point, John, it will be difficult, but useful, if it can be proved that any of Bestwick's fellow bathers *knew* that he wasn't going to be going home last Saturday evening.

"Problem is," said Winter, "we didn't exactly caution the baths staff, did we? To keep quiet about it, I mean."

"That's because I *wanted* them to gossip - in the hope that somebody might come forward and tell us they'd seen Becksitch Betty somewhere, or whatever. That's probably still our best bet - publicity. I'll ring the *Derby Telegraph* later. You'd better brief the *Belper News*, Field."

Another silence descended. Eventually, Russell took a deep breath, leaned back and looked at both subordinates.

"Well, gentlemen. Can either one of you make any sense at all of all this? Because I'll be damned if I can!"

Chapter 36

Burned Alive!

Detective Sergeant John Winter, never keen on exercise, was slightly out of breath and slightly irritated. Detective Inspector Derek Russell had insisted that they walk the short distance from the foot of Becksitch Lane to the local Grammar School. Understandably, Aubrey Pod was alarmed to be interrupted in the middle of a class and relieved by another member of staff. The long-suffering headmaster looked at the two officers, shook his head and, in a tired voice, suggested that a quiet room be made available for the interview.

Aubrey had nerved himself for yet another ordeal with the police. He jutted out his toadal countenance with confidence.

"Yes?"

"Becksitch Betty," said Russell simply, leaning back, folding his arms, waiting for the result.

This was a relief. Pod was ready-steeled to deal with the much more dangerous subject of his interest in the rough chicken on the previous Saturday. Pod knew how to deal with Becksitch Betty.

"Never see him, never speak to him, won't have anything at all to do with that sort of person. Next question?"

Pod estimated that he had left the Derby Turkish Baths a little before 6.00pm, just after Dolly. He noticed Nobby the Gnome getting dressed and assumed Nobby would be the last person to leave. No, he did not speak to Nobby, had no interest in Nobby, did not like Nobby. No, he could tell them nothing about Dolly. Nobody knew anything about Dolly. Pod was in full-sail of full denial: no, no, no. No, he had no idea when Becksitch Betty left. Becksitch Betty spent most of his time in the steam room -

"Nobody spoke to him, but then again, nobody ever does. A nasty piece of work, if you ask me! Next question?"

"Simeon Hogg," said Russell.

Pod was bowled a googly. He did not see it coming. This *was* dangerous. Homosexual activity was forbidden - full stop. Homosexual activity with teenage boys was the forbidden fruit of the highest order. Pod was experienced. He knew something of the police. They *might,* just might look the other way when a leering old crone was massaging a mature man in an isolated cottage. On the other hand, it was common knowledge that they would move heaven and earth to 'protect' teenage boys from predatory toads - regardless of how much the teenage boy might protest his enjoyment of said experience. But, this was a tough toad and Pod was a realist. In those few seconds available to him after the Detective Inspector had uttered the name of a youth, Pod assumed that several witnesses had very likely reported his association with young Simeon in the Derby Turkish Baths and other locations. Pod needed to sound credible. He must tell the truth - but not the whole truth. Defiantly, he pushed his face out over the table.

"Yes. My friend from America. What about him?"

"Rather a youthful friend for a man of your years, don't you think, Mr Pod?" said Russell in a slightly snide tone.

"I haven't given much thought to his age. My friends are not selected on the basis of age. What would he be? Early 20's? Is he in any trouble?"

Russell said that Hogg could be an important witness. Perhaps Mr Pod knew where he was staying? Without hesitation, in all apparent innocence, the Bog Hole address of Aunty Joyce was given. Russell then proceeded to give a full account of the extraordinary disappearance of Arthur Bestwick, including his abandoned clothes and the thirteen pounds. Aubrey Pod came over as genuinely amazed. Russell pressed on.

"You say that you saw very little of this character. That's as may be, but you were on the spot. You were there the whole of last Saturday afternoon and may have noticed something unusual ... some small clue?"

Aubrey Pod considered.

"Not really," he mumbled, pulling at his chin in an effort of thought. "I can't believe it! Completely gone - no trace at all? Have you checked all the public loos?"

"Not yet. But we have checked hospitals."

"Loss of memory? I expect you're ahead of me there. It doesn't bear thinking about, a naked Becksitch Betty wondering around Derby, asking folk who he is! Have you ever seen him naked - the most revolting ... "

"Let's keep this serious, Mr Pod. We haven't all day," warned Russell.

"Quite, quite. Let me think. Becksitch Betty had plenty of enemies, mixed with a right bad lot he did. He never tipped Charlie and Fred. They *loathed* him, you know! Oh yes, quite nasty to him they were and ... Did you say he left his money?"

"I did."

"I that case it *is* serious! Meanest man in Derbyshire. That old queen's as tight as a gnat's foreskin. He'd skin a flea for its fur ... Hang on!" Mr Toad suddenly reclaimed his usual zeal. He became animated as a gloating smile spread across his amphibian face. "I *know* where he is! It's come to me in a flash. I'll tell you *exactly* where Becksitch Betty is located."

"Please do," said Russell, slightly irritated by the poking finger on the word 'exactly'. "We'll be much obliged."

"He's in the furnace at the back of the Derby Turkish Baths. What's left of him, that is. He's been cremated. Probably been burned alive!"

"You what?" exclaimed an incredulous Detective Sergeant John Winter. "What the ... "

"Let him finish, John. I want to hear more. Carry on, Mr Pod."

"You shall hear it all!" cried the triumph toad. "It's the only solution which fits. It fits all the facts and it fits perfectly. Now listen to me ... "

Aubrey Pod spent the next ten minutes gesticulating through a fascinating narrative involving the general gossip about the evil deeds of Becksitch Betty. Careful to avoid naming names, he spoke of leading respected figures, leading professionals in Derby and Nottingham who had been recently threatened in various ways, some of whom were present at the baths on that Saturday afternoon. Aubrey took the view that a conspiracy had come together to remove Arthur Bestwick in the same way as -

"... a surgeon might remove a malignant growth! Now then! Of course, Charlie and Fred will be in on it - probably well-paid to play their part and keep their mouths shut. If you press me, I could give you the names of those most likely. Money's no problem for wealthy gentlemen. *My* complete innocence can be guaranteed by the fact that *I* am totally ignored by that toffee-nosed elite. They would never allow *me* to be part of their murderous plan. Oh, no. *I'm* not good enough. I ... "

"Can we have some details, Mr Pod?" said Winter, "We're all agog, desperate to get to the last page."

"It *is* rather like a whodunit, isn't it?" smiled Aubrey. "They're all in it together. That was the solution to an Agatha Christie novel. I'm proposing a limited conspiracy, about four of them plus the attendants, I'd say. Can't be sure of the details but the generalities are not difficult. At the end of the afternoon, bathers, including Becksitch Betty, are resting, sometimes sleeping on those beds. Somebody with medical knowledge creeps up, gives him an injection to induce unconsciousness. After all the bathers have left, he's bundled into the furnace, the same one which heats the baths - voila!"

"According to you, Charlie and Fred are in this gang, but, do tell us, how did they get the body past the watchful women up front?" inquired Winter, with a distinct sardonic tone.

"Simple. They push out a load of dirty towels after each session. The boiler house is also the laundry. The unconscious Betty is buried, hidden under a pile of dirty towels."

"Why didn't they burn his clothes?" persisted Winter.

"So you'd think exactly what you probably *have* thought."

"What have we thought?"

"You thought that Becksitch Betty has engineered some sort of mysterious escape."

For a few moments the two policemen stared at the clever Mr Toad.

"Thank you, Mr Pod. Most interesting. We'll look into it," said Russell, without a trace of the mocking attitude of his colleague.

"It may be too late," responded Aubrey in a dry tone.

"Too late?"

"The boiler man would have cleared out the Saturday ashes this morning before re-firing. Your forensic team will need those ashes, assuming, that is, Saturday's ashes are still around."

Aubrey sat back in stoic comfort. The officers returned his supreme smugness with distinct *dis*comfort. Russell changed tack.

"In the meantime, you'll appreciate that we're investigating a missing person; according to you, a dead person. Just routine, you understand, but we'd like to have a look around your house." Aubrey's face fell. "Of course," continued the detective, "if you insist on a search warrant ... "

"Nonsense! I've nothing to hide. Search away. Mavis is there now. She's my housekeeper. She'll let you in."

Walking up the steep jitty between Derby Road and the top of Becksitch Lane, Russell was remonstrating as much with himself as with Winter.

"We should have thought that one through. No excuse. That man is intelligent. He's nothing like as stupid as he acts, or as stupid as he looks. He's not the Mr Toad of the famous book. We've got to look at that boiler house - as soon as possible. Remember what Holmes said, John ... "

"Yes, boss. When you've eliminated the impossible ... "

Whilst Russell was asking Mavis about any interesting visitors she had noticed at the residence of Mr Pod, Winter, having had a quick look around the bedroom, was now examining the study, which had the old-fashioned smell of his grandmother's home. It was never intended to be a thorough search. At worse, he expected to see magazines of muscle-men, since Pod was careful of himself. The Pod library included no such publication. Most of the books were on the subject of music, as befitted a man who had the reputation of being one of the finest musicians in Derbyshire. A framed poem, *Two Loves*, by Lord Alfred Douglas, mounted over the bureau, caught Winter's attention. He skimmed through a few lines.

Sweet youth,
Tell me why, sad and sighing, dost thou rove
These pleasant realms? I pray thee tell me sooth,
What is thy name? He said, 'My name is Love ...
I am the Love that dare not speak its name.'

It was an old bureau of good quality and unlocked. Winter was intrigued. He perused the interior, which consisted of pigeonholes, small drawers and a few innocent letters which were scattered around. As a child, he had enjoyed the challenge of discovering the secrets of his grandmother's escritoire. Accordingly, he pulled out all the tiny drawers and let his fingers explore the top, bottom and sides of each recess in turn. Success was achieved when he touched a spring in the bottom of the recess in the centre drawer. The bottom section clicked and slid back to reveal a secret shallow well beneath.

John Winter, expecting a long-lost Victorian document of immense value, was slightly disappointed to withdraw a fresh-looking, standard, business-size envelope which had been opened. The top left proclaimed - The Studio, PO Box 511, Bronx Station, New York, NY 10008. On the top right was a metered postmark - New York, May 18th '65, US Postage Air Mail - .18. Carefully, with fingertips, Winter removed a single sheet, the American equivalent of A4.

Even to Detective Sergeant John Winter, an officer of some years experience, it was shocking. It was some sort of promotional material inviting the client to purchase a set of photographs of a frolicking naked boy. There were several miniature insets of 'Tim'. He was advertised as an 11-year-old with -

" ... enormous midnight blue eyes, cornsilk hair, skin with the texture and glow of apricots, slim legs, small freckled nose and a berry-stained mouth."

Ten minutes later, outside the house, Detective Inspector Derek Russell was holding this same sheet, carefully, with his fingertips. He studied it in serious silence and remained silent for a few moments after the examination.

"I expect Pod thought his secret compartment would never be discovered," said Winter.

"Secret drawers in writing bureaux are fairly well-known. Not so very secret, really." Russell's voice drifted into abstraction and a further silence.

"He's overplayed his hand this time! Our Mr Toad is in big trouble now," said Winter with relish.

"Is he?" replied the senior detective, giving his junior a sharp look. "Did you look at the envelope, John?"

"Well, yes, I expect ... Oh Lord!"

Detective Sergeant John Winter had looked at the envelope. He had looked at the top left and the top right and had assumed that it have been addressed to Mr Aubrey Pod. He could now see that it was addressed to another person. It was addressed to Martin Harcourt, The Court, Cavendish Crescent, The Park, Nottingham, England.

Chapter 37

Screams in Darley Park

Shortly after lunch, a large, black Austin Westminster drew up outside number four, Bog Hole, in Horsley Woodhouse. Several interested neighbours sat out, enjoying a rare sunny interlude between showers. They were all members of the Hogg family, all looking on with keen interest, all displaying various shades of emotion; curiosity, incredulity, dismay, excitement and ghoulish anticipation. Upon a firm official knock, Aunty Joyce gingerly opened the door and peeped round. Her features, generally sad at the best of times, were further distorted by the sight of two darkly-attired strange men asking after her nephew. Gradually, very gradually, the weak, sunken mouth recovered some of its original form when the charm and impeccable courtesy of Detective Inspector Derek Russell began to reassure and soothe. Derek was an attractive man. He had something of the appearance and easy suavity of Cary Grant, which worked its magic on women of 'a certain age' - even on the timid Aunty Joyce.

"Well ... if ya put it like that ... well ... ya'd better come in then."

"Thank you, Miss Hogg."

Miss Hogg, (tickled and thrilled to be so addressed) explained to the gentlemen callers that her nephew was usually out somewhere, she never knew where, anywhere - and today they were fortunate to find him at home -

" ... cus ya see, 'is oopstairs, 'is got some letters ta write. There's two men!" she shouted up the stairs.

Simeon Hogg took in the situation at a glance. In an effort to spare Joyce any further alarm, he concealed his apprehension with polite surprise and indicated his willingness to assist the police in any way he could. Russell asked to see the young man's passport.

"Just routine, you understand."

If Miss Hogg had no objection, the senior man also suggested that the front room would be most suitable for the interview. With fawning thanks and an unmistakable dismissal, he closed the door, making it clear that the conference was private between two men and one boy. They sat down in furniture as old as the century, faded by time alone. In this 'best room', reserved for high days and holidays, the leather sofa and two armchairs were effectively new, having hardly been touched by the human body.

The passport was good news for Aubrey Pod. Simeon was confirmed to be 19 years of age. A few years younger; that could have been problematic for Pod. And it would do no favours for some of the other members of the gay fraternity. Russell gave the youth a sharp look and made an oblique remark which made him feel uncomfortable.

"Well, well. Who would have thought. You're still a teenager - just. I expect it's an advantage, looking much younger."

As the passport was handed back, Simeon recalled a recent comment in the S&C Coffee Bar. A newcomer described him as 'an old chicken'. The interview proceeded. He was puzzled by the question about a man in New York who may have wanted to photograph him. He did not mention the guy in Detroit with the Polaroid camera.

Even before an explanation for the visit was given, Simeon had worked out his strategy. He took the view that he had nothing to hide. If asked, he would give a full account of his holiday to date. It had been an interesting holiday and he had met many interesting people. Enthusiastically, he intended to give full details, names, places and events. In fact, everything except the sexual details, which were private and, in his case, illegal.

Russell came to the point. A certain Arthur Bestwick had gone missing. Did Simeon know anything about Arthur Bestwick? Yes. The two detectives were treated to an exuberant and voluble account of Simeon's holiday so far. He started with the first visit to the Derby Turkish Baths on June 2nd which ended with the meeting of Dolly, Arthur Bestwick (who everybody called Becksitch Betty) and lastly Aubrey Pod (who everybody called Mr Toad). He found them all very funny. On June 3rd he bought a bike and paid his second visit to the Derby Turkish Baths on June 4th. He told them all about meeting David Bond, Claud Hoadley and the snobs of the Friary Hotel. He told them about Bridlington on the Saturday, the Corporation Hotel and the Flying Horse. Obeying some instinct (he was not quite sure why) he made no mention of Edward. Simeon gave an in-depth report on his Chesterfield adventures of the Sunday and Monday of June 6th - 7th and his second meeting with Becksitch Betty. He expressed disapproval of the two louts, Monks and Muckles. In spite of careful editing, it was quite obvious to the two policemen that attacks on old men in toilets had lewd connotations. He found Guzzly Granddad rough, but enjoyed meeting Tonks and Stokes. He quickly zipped through Castleton, Buxton and Hartington without mention of Toby Jug. The Belper Convent event of June 12th, together with the horror of meeting Jasper Wormall, triggered loud laughter from Simeon's small audience.

This working-class youth was not very articulate. He struggled to express his meaning, but the officers listened sympathetically when he compared the 'Belper Goblin' with the contortions of the impressive old ash tree, the one which was choked with ivy. In this way, he conveyed his love for the colour and variety of the Derbyshire countryside and its curious fairytale inhabitants.

"Take Nobby the Gnome, for example. You couldn't possibly have a Nobby the Gnome in Detroit. He's be dragged away by the police at the first dance! And that brings me to Bill and Ben the Burton Baby Shop Men."

"Do they dance?" asked Winter.

Not that he knew of. This was an odd discovery which occurred during his tour around south Derbyshire, June 14th to the 18th. Bill and Ben were two eccentric old queens who kept a baby shop in the town centre of Burton-on-Trent. Eccentric, to be sure. Ben was bald, fat and hardly said a word. Bill was thin, may have been bald, but never seen without his woolly hat - even indoors. Bill was chatty, amusing, very camp, especially when knitting small items for the shop. He gave Simeon a pressing invitation to stay in Burton for a few days, a few days which turned out to be very pleasant for various reasons, not least that he was allowed to take Bonzo (the large St Bernard who looked just like Ben) for long walks alongside the River Trent. Of course, Simeon was careful not to mention the sexual element of this 'kind invitation'. In brief - Bill was a useless nuisance and Ben was the 'Guzzly Granddad' of Burton - an experienced gentleman of great talent.

Simeon was asked about the Saturday of June 19th. He was able to give the police a complete list of the people who were at the Derby Turkish Baths. He named them all except the vicar, the coarse chicken (the prey of Pod) and the young man who tempted Tommy. Simeon had a lot to say about Tommy and Martin. Without using the word 'gay' or even 'homosexual', he heaped praise upon them with passion; how Tommy was so amusing and bitchy, how they were so generous, helpful, respectful, sincere and superior citizens of the first order.

This candid (if somewhat expurgated) contribution from Simeon Hogg was extremely helpful to the police. He and Miss Hogg were thanked. Russell and Winter drove away under the severe scrutiny of other curious Hoggs, still sitting out on that street, enjoying another brief patch of blue sky over Bog Hole.

Fast-forward two weeks to the Tuesday morning of July 6th and we find Derby under a persistent band of rain; yet another spell of unsettled weather. It also found Detective Sergeant John Winter sitting opposite Detective Inspector Derek Russell, who was reading a commissioned report containing information on a number of characters in this dark mystery - for dark mystery it still was. Claud Hoadley. Hoadley was known to the police by virtue of his prestige, a leading, respected member of the community. He was also known by virtue of his unspoken, but de facto position as the First Homosexual of Derbyshire. Russell was obeying a gut instinct, a hunch that Hoadley was either somehow connected with this curious business or, at least, could furnish some intelligence, could throw light upon darkness. The report, which became known as the Brentnall Report, was furnished by a reliable private detective of that name, often used by Russell. Brentnall (on the gay scene known as Sid) was in a good position to sleuth in the homosexual underworld, himself, being homosexual.

The Brentnall Report confirmed the recent threatening behaviour of Arthur Bestwick to Claud Hoadley over a perceived slight. It also confirmed Hoadley's attempt to build up a dossier of information on Bestwick. This started with his interrogation of Jasper Wormall on June 12th.

"I'm a regular visitor to Jasper's cottage," wrote Brentnall in his easy, chatty style. "He's useful, a nice enough bloke, a simple sort, an encyclopaedia of facts and dates. It seems Hoadley turned on the charm and made a good catch. Hoadley is an extraordinary man. He can command great love and loyalty. At the same time, he has a evil ability to demean and undermine confidence. He can destroy a person. He's clever, very clever, subtle, rarely gets caught out. However, he slipped up with Tanner. Not a good idea hiring Tanner (the Derby private investigator) for that type of job. Tanner is experienced, a reasonably competent sleuth, but he writes down too much and his office records are not nearly as secure as he thinks they are. Hoadley consulted him in his Derby office at 9.30am on June 16th. Wanted Tanner to get, if possible, compromising written information about Becksitch Betty's largely undeclared income from entertaining. Tanner was also asked to sniff out any gossip on him 'running' rent boys or hiring thugs for violence. Jasper Wormall confirmed these rumours. Hoadley needed to be in a position to trot out details which would alarm Bestwick, to claim he had evidence, statements, photographs, letters which would stand up in court. Mainly, he wanted to be able to threaten Arthur Bestwick, to scare him, if possible, to move to some other part of the country. It's been an expensive job for Hoadley. He's paid through the nose. Did he get his money's-worth?

"No. The tax man knows all about Arthur Bestwick, has descended on him many times. Records of interviews with the Inland Revenue go back to 1936. Betty is a slippery customer, but has always got away with it. He was never really a big success or a big earner. Procuring boys? As much as I can get to know, same thing; small scale, local stuff.

"You'll not be surprised to learn that some types will tell me things they won't tell you. Fred, the Derby Turkish Baths attendant, said that, as far as he could see, on June 19th, Becksitch Betty spent most of his time in the steam room and spoke to nobody - except just one person one time. He had a quick word with that Nottingham barrister at about 4.30pm. 'They both looked very stern' - nothing more known.

"Here's my BIG story. (Thank God for my mole in the *Derby Evening Telegraph* - but, then again - we help each other) Hope it's useful. Last Wednesday, June 30th, *The Telegraph* received a phone call at about 3.00pm. A woman's voice, it's thought.

'Quick! Get ya sen ta Darley Towers at Darley Park, that big 'ouse just off Darley Grove. There's 'orrible screamin' - like a stuck pig!'

"Before it could be suggested that the police should be informed, she rang off. A reporter was dispatched only to be received by a puzzled Miss Minchin, who assured him that all was well. 'Yes, Mr Hoadley was within, taking a bath. Yes, as usual, he was in excellent health.' Ten minutes later, Claud Hoadley greeted his visitor.

'Good heavens! We're not usually honoured by gentlemen of the Press. *Do* tell me all about this rather *alarming* telephone call?'

"After being impressed by the refined vowels of Hoadley's impeccable diction (he seemed reasonably composed) the *Telegraph* man regarded the matter as a hoax and returned to Northcliffe House. Miss Minchin, a pungent Miss, guards her master well. She's too shrewd for my games. On the other hand, (having discovered that she had a mother) I reasoned that her old mother might be more pliable, so I decided to sniff around and pump - with great success!

"I don't know about the screams of a dying pig, but, at just after three on that afternoon, Miss Minchin paid a surprise visit to Darley Towers. A surprise visit, because it was her day off. She found her lord and master whimpering and cowering under the kitchen table! He was naked, except for a dog collar. The collar was attached to a lead, which was firmly hammered on to the underside of a massive Victorian kitchen table. The collar and lead had been fixed in such a way as to be immovable from his person. With a great struggle, he'd managed to move the table a few feet in a failed effort to reach a knife, when the horrific embarrassment occurred - the appearance of Miss Minchin. Naturally, she was appalled, distressed and, according to *Mrs* Minchin, swallowed his story. He claimed he was attacked by two burglars. They robbed him of his dignity because they were disappointed with the small sum of money found in his wallet. After reducing Hoadley to the pitiful condition of an ill-treated dog, the two youths helped themselves to a rough lunch, making a thorough mess of Miss Minchin's pristine kitchen. They sat at the table, near their victim, shouting obscene abuse, giving him the occasional kick and throwing scraps of food at him. All this was confirmed by the total mess of morsels scattered under the table. Unusually, the strong and severe Miss Minchin broke down in front of her Mum, recalling the stink of urine in Hoadley's hair, on his body and pools of same on the kitchen floor.

"First names which spring to mind - Monks and Muckles; one of their 'special services'?

"It begs several questions. Claud Hoadley was not expecting Miss Minchin to turn up on her day off. Therefore, it was an ideal day to engage Monks and Muckles (or a different firm) for this form of S&M sport. If that was the case, why did they not release him afterwards and clean up the place? Why did they go to such extremes? Why did they destroy the trust of a regular and lucrative client who would have continued to pay well for fantasy sex? It's a fascinating possibility, but I can't see Claud Hoadley risking such an activity - assuming, that is, he's actually into S&M. For many years, he has never been caught out doing anything sexual. Hence the general belief that he's celibate these days.

"For what it's worth, here's my theory. Hoadley's ordeal has all the fingerprints of somebody's revenge on it. Assuming he's still alive (which I believe to be unlikely - he's upset too many people) it *could* have been planned by Becksitch Betty. The lads were *probably* Monks and Muckles. The phone call to the *Derby Evening Telegraph* fits in with a desire to shame and debase Hoadley. Miss Minchin saved the day. She arrived minutes before the reporter and found the front door wide open. He would have seen it all, but, of course, it's very doubtful that the *Telegraph* would print anything more than a simple break-in - if that.

"As requested, I checked out Monks and Muckles. Nasty pair - very nasty. A real mystery those two. Couldn't get any gen on their backgrounds. No records, nothing. Tonks and Stokes haven't a clue where they came from and, believe me, anything told to Tonks is as good as putting it in the *Derbyshire Times*! Suspect 'Monks and Muckles' are professional names. Age, another mystery, but I'd class them as bona fide chickens by the way they act. They've been with the old man about four years. It's quite possible that Monks and Muckles genuinely don't know how old they are, don't know where they came from, genuinely can't remember. If you press me, my best guess - Monks would be 15 and Muckles 16. Not nice boys at all. A terror in toilets, seem to enjoy hurting old men. During the few days of my Chesterfield investigations, Monks stamped on Nobby's hand and Muckles stamped on the poor man's foot. Other frequent tricks: blowing pepper through peep-holes in the lavatory wall into the eye of a peeping victim and bombing them with bags of flour.

"They seem to be fairly independent. They do their own pimping around Chesterfield, Buxton, Bakewell, Heanor, Ilkeston and Ripley. They may have some 'professional' help for Derby, Nottingham, Sheffield and Manchester, where they operate on occasions. Guzzly Granddad's real name is Toby Piggs. He's lived at that address in Chesterfield for five years. He was in Derby before that. Regarding any financial arrangement, I was unable to connect Monks and Muckles with Piggs or Bestwick. However, according to Simon Tonks, an unpleasant incident took place in the middle of Chesterfield on Monday, June 7th."

Here Brentnall described the wig drama which occurred on Chesterfield Market Place.

"One last thing. You'll probably know that Hoadley meets his disciples and holds court in the Friary Hotel each Friday evening. For this commission, I've hid myself in a corner and conscientiously attended the two Fridays of June 25th and July 2nd in the hope of hearing something useful. During the latter, Hoadley said next to nothing, for reasons explained above. During the former, he was quite perky and keen to hear all about the exciting news. Hilary Hawley (between giggles) said something about - 'the wicked witch has finally gone.' Several others made their own half-serious jocular contributions. One suggested that Becksitch Betty was hypnotised to dress in another bather's clothes and leave as another person. Interesting, but no attempt to explain how it was that nobody missed their clothes and everybody else managed to walk out fully dressed. It was all very festive and silly until that quiet psychological moment when all admiring eyes turned to their great leader, Hoadley, for *his* pearl of wisdom. It was cryptic: interesting. I hope you find it helpful. He said -

"*'Mors janua vitae.'*"

The Brentnall Report concluded with an extract of dates, times, hours spent, expenses incurred and his professional fee.

Chapter 38

"Mors Janua Vitae"

"*Mors janua vitae*?" mused Winter. "What does that mean when it's at home?"

"Latin, John. Hoadley's never happier than when he's said something which nobody else can understand. Roughly, I think it translates to something like 'Death, the gateway to life.'"

"So the toffee-nosed schoolmaster thinks that Becksitch Betty is really dead!"

"Well ... I'm not so sure."

"None of us are bloody sure," snapped Winter.

On the whole, it had been a disappointing fortnight for Russell and Winter. On the previous day, they had made an early Monday morning trip to Chesterfield; a surprise visit to Guzzly Granddad and his harem of resident young lads. The two officers gave a gentle knock and heard a faint grunt from within. They entered to find the old man established in his darkened front room, seated in his usual armchair, leaning forward, teeth out, all ready in anticipation of breakfast. Guzzly Granddad was as disappointed as the police. Monks, Muckles and Tinker Bell had gone, had not been seen since the previous Wednesday. Sean Stokes said they had taken 'their things' with them. Where had they moved to? Stokes claimed he had no idea.

"It's made me rate depressed," Sean whined in his effeminate drawl. "There's only me left 'ere now. Simon's gone back to work at Cressbrook. T' owd man dunt say much, only slavers an slobbers all day - dotty owd sod. Ya what? Ya can look fa me. Yal not find oat 'ere."

A brief search uncovered an interesting (possibly sinister) discovery in one of the bedrooms - a cheap suitcase inscribed with the name of Mr Arthur Bestwick. It contained general overnight items, including a wig and false teeth. Stokes appeared to be staggered. He insisted that Becksitch Betty never had a suitcase during his occasional visits to Granddad. He took his 'bits and pieces' with him in a paper carrier bag when he stormed out of the house on June 7th. He had never been back. Stokes admitted that, at first hearing, he was amused to learn that Becksitch Betty left the Derby Turkish Baths without his clothes and money.

"We all killed us sens laughin', thought it were a joke! Gobsmacked when folk started talkin' about bloody murder. Mind ya, there's many as ad like ta strangle that nasty owd bugga."

Simon Tonks was back in harness as a servant at Cressbrook Hall. A brief chat revealed precious little. He suggested that he hold a seance in the old cast-iron urinal at Bridge Foot in Belper. It might establish if Betty had 'passed over to t' other side' or not.

"'er spirit 'd still be 'angin' about. It were 'er favourite cottage, ya know. Yes, she stood in there fa hours an hours she did - greedy bitch. An thee talk about me!"

The report on the ashes from the Derby Turkish Baths furnace came back to Russell as -

"Inconclusive! Can't be sure. Can't even be sure they've examined the right ashes! Pod may be right. Betty might be fertiliser, scattered around Claud Hoadley's garden."

"Hoadley's garden," growled Winter. "Anyway, how the hell can a retired schoolmaster live in a place as grand as Darley Towers and have a full-time housekeeper? Shouldn't we check into that?"

"I've checked it. To start with, his previous Belper house on Green Lane was a substantial property. You've got to remember that Claud has been lording it over the homosexual population of Derby over the last 35 years. In that time, a number of his doting followers have died and left him money. He's probably better off than his arch enemies, Sperry and Harcourt."

"Did you ever find out about those strange words? The ones we saw on their flag at The Court? You know, the flag with their personal coat of arms. It was fluttering over that sumptuous garden. They hoist it up when guests are present. That was Latin wasn't it?"

"According to Sperry, it dates back some years to a time when he was very ill. There were some nasty comments and unkind gloating."

"You're joking!" said Winter, appalled by such cruelty.

"Not at all. I've learned a lot about those two in these last few weeks. Tommy has an acid tongue. He goes for the jugular, can be quite vicious."

"So what does their motto, insignia, or whatever you call it on a flag; what did it mean? Bums are best? Or, bum chums for ever?"

"Hardly. Tommy Sperry told me that it translates as 'In poor health - mischief. In improving health - malice!"

"Bloody hell! Aren't these queers bitchy!" said Winter.

"Indubitably," replied Russell with a smile. "Didn't turn a hair did he? Harcourt, when we confronted him with that letter."

"He's a clever bloke," agreed Winter. "And, let's face it, he *did* have a point. 'Dear Sir, Please send me some child porn. I am Martin Harcourt QC!'"

"They deleted the QC on the address."

"Didn't seem to bother about where it was found either. He told the 'Super' any number of people could have planted it in the bureau of a fool."

"Incidentally, 'The Studio' in New York seems to have disappeared. No surprise there," added Russell, who became pensive. "Yet it was genuine. It *was* posted and it *was* in the postal system."

"So damned frustrating!" said Winter. "What are we to make of it? *Was* it posted through Harcourt's letter box? If so, and *if* he's as innocent as he claims, why didn't he hand it to us straight away?"

"He's a homosexual, John. Ask yourself. Is it likely?"

"Is that common knowledge, boss?"

"It is to a few of us. Perhaps we should concern ourselves with the 'fool', as Harcourt called him. We know that Aubrey Pod feels ostracised, blackballed, hates Harcourt, hates the lot of them in Nottingham for that matter. Now these photographs of little Tim; are they Pod's pension?"

"Pod hates them all in Derby as well. Blackmail? Could be. I've gone over it, but ... Well ... just doesn't seem to fit with Pod."

"I thought that, John. Pod might want to give Harcourt a bloody nose, but I don't think he's all that interested in money. Anyway, he'd never take on a prominent barrister and ... How in hell's name did Pod obtain such a letter?"

"He was severely rattled when we tackled him," laughed Winter. "Went up like a firework! I thought he'd never calm down."

"To get such a damning piece of evidence, if evidence it is, Pod would need to be in league with one of those young men who romp around the swimming pool during the big parties at The Court. I can't see Martin Harcourt QC leaving such an item in any place where it could be nicked. I can't see Harcourt having such an item in the house at all."

"No use asking about prints, I suppose?" asked Winter.

"That's a laugh! You may as well try to dust young Hogg to determine who's interfered with *him*. No chance. Everybody's touched the Harcourt letter, useless dabs and smudges all over it. Same with the typewritten job and just the same with the 'Upperwood, friendly horse scrawl.' However ... "

"Yes, boss?"

"Well ... we *might* find out more about those letters. You've to tread very carefully when dealing with a senior barrister. I've sent them to an old friend of mine, a VIP, in fact. It'll be a treat for you, John. We're going to see him in the morning."

Chapter 39

Mr Big

It was shortly before 11.00am on Wednesday, July 7th. Driving into the private area of The Park in Nottingham, John Winter thought they were going to pay a second visit to Sperry and Harcourt, but the car drove past their impressive residence and came to rest in front of a similar house further along - equally impressive. Approaching the door, Russell asked his subordinate for co-operation.

"This is all off the record, John. It's a personal favour to me. We may get some useful information on the Bestwick case and I'd appreciate your discretion with regard to the origin of that information."

Winter gave an absent nod. He was in awe of the size and splendour of the portico, the large black door and highly-polished brasses. They were admitted by a very correct butler, who led them into a richly-panelled reception room.

"Please take a seat, gentlemen. Sir Edward will be with you shortly."

After a few minutes, they rose at the sight of a tall, white-haired, strikingly handsome man. With military bearing he strode into the room, wearing a warm smile of welcome. Winter was introduced, greetings and pleasantries exchanged before they were graciously invited to be seated.

"This is good of you, Edward. I don't mind admitting that I'm completely out of my depth with this business. I take it that you've had a chance to read the relevant papers?"

"I have ... and must warn you. You may have overestimated the effectiveness of the machinery I can bring to bear on this sort of thing, Derek."

"Any help will be welcome. Just talk to us. Just ramble on. What are your general impressions?"

"I can certainly ramble," smiled Sir Edward. "Officially, of course, my department has no interest in this ... unpleasant female impersonator ... who may or may not be dead. From a personal point of view, as it touches on a few friends, I *am* interested and can hardly be described as impartial. Martin is entirely correct in the arguments he's put forward. Despite appearances, there's no credible link between him and that sordid publication. Two of my men have been looking into it. I have their report, a copy's been sent to the Lord Chancellor and you'll get your copy in the morning."

"Thank you, Edward I wonder ... "

"Forgive me, but may I ramble on a little about Tommy Sperry and Martin Harcourt?"

"Please do."

"It's just that ... it might be rather difficult for you gentlemen to be able to fully appreciate their importance to the world in which I live. You'll have heard the whispers, the scandal regarding the bacchanalian orgies under the palms in their beautiful conservatory, which, come to think of it, houses quite a good marble statue of Bacchus. I'm not going to tell you it's all lies. I'm not going to say that they are both the very essence of moral rectitude. But, I will tell you this; revelries in The Court are not the reason why Tommy and Martin are know as legends in their own lifetime. No. They'll be remembered for the *good* they've done and for the good example they've set. Since the war, Tommy and Martin have successfully forged a family for the Nottingham homosexual community. A family under a regime which encourages tolerance and inclusivity. I use the word 'family' deliberately, because it is the heterosexual family mentality which has been most hostile to unmarried men who live alone and fail to mate in the 'normal' way. I hate to sound so dramatic but, it is my belief that these men have been at the cutting edge of a social revolution. They've tackled some of the undesirable quirks which arise out of heterosexual pressures on homosexual thinking. When they come across it, they prick the bubble of pomposity. Young men are reprimanded if they show disrespect to older men and older men are persuaded to show consideration for the young, to be aware of their vulnerability and special difficulties. Effectively, Tommy and Martin are an unpaid support service for anyone who seeks their help ... and ...

"And something very special happens when Tommy and Martin come together. I don't understand it. I don't know how they do it. Some sort of magic occurs, magic which gives people a good time - and you don't have to be homosexual to enjoy that magical experience."

Derek Russell nodded his head. He himself had felt that power of personality when he and Winter were first received at The Court. Tommy and Martin were electric. The entertainment was electric. They bounced off each other. It was a privilege, like having a private show in an exotic setting so near to the centre of Nottingham.

"Such parties!" continued Edward. "Delicious food, beautifully presented. The artistic skill, planning, preparation and the sheer hard work involved in creating these events compels our admiration. You'd be surprised at the number of young heterosexuals who try to get an invitation to a Tommy and Martin event. It's a great way to meet people, everybody so friendly, everybody wanting to speak to everybody else but not enough time to get around to everybody."

"Sounds like a lot of bodies," said Winter - who regretted this sarcasm the moment it left his lips.

"I wonder if it is possible for a man like you to understand the importance of Tommy and Martin to the people of my world?" responded Edward, with a measured coolness. "They share a common anger over the daily injustices inflicted on our people. They are trail-blazers, reformers. They are making Nottingham a better place for the young men of the future."

"I do apologise, Edward," responded Derek, giving Winter a sharp glance. "Please try to understand, there seems to be criminal activity afoot in this murky business, criminal activity beyond the apparent dematerialization of one drag queen. We seem to have a possible murder and a possible conspiracy involving child prostitution. You, Edward, have a formidable reputation and formidable resources not available to mere mortals such as ourselves. So, I ask you bluntly: is Arthur Bestwick alive or dead?"

The handsome gentleman with the white hair considered. He interlocked his fingers and relaxed a little more into his easy-chair.

"Probably dead - but we can't be sure. Perhaps, Derek, you've asked the wrong question. Perhaps we should be asking how and *why* did Becksitch Betty abruptly depart in such a mysterious manner?"

At this juncture, Edward passed Russell a paper with all the names of the men who were at the Derby Turkish Baths on the afternoon of June 19th. They were listed in order of their time of departure, based on the available evidence -

5.20 - Blount and Marshall
5.25 - Croft

5.30 - Sperry, Harcourt, Monks, Muckles, Hawley and Bond
5.40 - Hogg, Tonks and Stokes
5.50 - Phillips and Soames
5.52 - Smith
5.53 - Pod
6.05 - Nobby

"Does anything strike you about the shape of this list?" asked Edward.

"Shape?" asked Russell.

"The 5.30 line is the longest. According to your observant ladies, all six men came out at almost the same time. In fact, a little group creating a soupcon of confusion, a moment when the picture is less clear for your witnesses. Yes, they identify the individuals, but for a few seconds, their identification necessarily becomes somewhat unfocused by a picture of mingling men. Also, one of your onlookers, Mrs Fox, is distracted for a moment by the exchange of pleasantries with Tommy and Martin."

"So, you're saying that ... "

"You said it yourself, in your report, Derek. Somehow, Becksitch Betty *walked* out, as did the others. Half past five, that was the best moment. I don't think he was pushed out under a load of towels and later cremated on the premises, but, I am inclined to the view that he has been killed - and had no suspicion that he *would* be killed."

"Are we back to the conspiracy theory, sir? The kind of thing suggested by Pod?" asked Winter.

"Like you, Detective Sergeant, I'm groping in the dark. As you've already checked - so have my agents. They've checked on all these people. Dolly, or 'Smith' as he calls himself, we all know about Adolphus Coggan, the gardener at Cressbrook Hall who does precious little gardening. For the last ten years he's been offering 'special' tours around the more interesting pubs of Manchester to paying guests."

"Not to mention his excursions into the weird and the wacky of deepest, darkest Derbyshire," laughed Winter.

"His freak show!" said Edward, grinning mischievously. "I'd dearly love to jump into that old Morris 1000 and view some of the old fossils on Dolly's Tour of Old Queens."

"Any progress on the Nobby character?" asked Russell.

"If Nobby ever did have a family name, it's as lost to him as it is to us. Everybody on that list is exactly who they say they are, with two exceptions."

"Monks and Muckles?" said Winter.

"Even my department can't do any better than Brentnall with that puzzle. No records at all. I'm inclined to agree with him. Those boys will not know how old they are or where they came from. From an early age, they've been trained, well-trained to do their job. We'll probably never know for sure, but there's a sinister chance that they were deliberately bred for the sex market, hence the total absence of official records."

On hearing this, Derek Russell, a father himself, felt a wave of horror and pity for those feral boys who seemed to be running wild around Derbyshire, preyed on by older men. Edward was also thinking about victims, but the victims of *his* mind's eye were not Monks and Muckles. Edward's victims were people like himself and his friends. Like the Derby Camp, the Nottingham Camp diligently strove to avoid any social contact with Monks and Muckles and their type. These beautiful, desirable youths had been around, out and about for several years. No. Edward was not thinking about abused boys, he was thinking about abused men. He was thinking of a doomed rabbit, transfixed, frozen to the spot by the stare of an approaching, writhing snake. In the same way, Monks and Muckles, a dual resistless evil, held *their* victims in the grasp of lust and desire.

"Guzzly Granddad ... "

"Unlikely, Derek. It doesn't fit. Toby Piggs has provided them with a home for four years, made use of them, but he's the wrong type to be managing them. He's simply not up to the job, lacks the necessary discipline, lacks the necessary intelligence. He's too old to be a pimp."

"That would seem to leave Becksitch Betty?" said Russell.

"In my view, he's too close and, again, lacks the organisational ability - too short on the intelligence. No, we need to look for somebody who is well removed from Chesterfield, somebody who will find it convenient to put Becksitch Betty up front, in the frame for pimping, somebody who gives them their instructions, issues their assignments - remotely. It will be important for that person to be completely safe if, as they say, 'the balloon goes up'."

"A sort of Mr Big!" mused Winter.

"A touch dramatic, perhaps, but, yes, if you like," agreed Edward.

"But those two letters, it can't get much clearer! They suggest that Bestwick is definitely overseeing sex with young lads," said Russell.

"And Brentnall thinks he's involved with the sex trade. We've always found Brentnall to be reliable," added Winter.

"You're both right," replied the distinguished figure, with his eyes closed. "The letters are important and, no doubt, your mole has sniffed out the current lavatory gossip, but, gentlemen, we must stand back and try to see the larger picture. It is possible that those letters were planted by ... shall we say - Mr Big. If Monks and Muckles or the like are being controlled by him, the customers are hardly likely to be making arrangements or requests in writing. Think about it, gentlemen - *in writing,* times and places; payment up front? Is that credible? From what we know of them, these hooligans give a damn good service and that service is expensive. It's feasible to suppose that the customer is usually a professional man. More often than not, he is a respectable married man with children. He'll need to be a high earner who can pay the price. We're speaking of criminal activities which are punishable by very long prison sentences. It is much more plausible that all arrangements / negotiations involving the sale of boys will be by word of mouth."

"So you think ... you think that Betty's been set up?" asked Winter.

"Very likely. My department has checked both letters. The scrawl could have been done by any fool and how many thousands of businessmen in Nottingham have a shop with an entry on the left?"

So spoke Edward, who, at that moment, was thinking of Bob Philips and Clarence Soames. For some time there were whispers around the Flying Horse that Bob and Clarence had been enjoying the delights of Monks and Muckles. It was joked by the bitchy brigade that Bob was sore. He had been worked hard by the M&M 'Round the World' special and Clarence had been exhausted after one session in which he had been 'emptied' four times. They ran a successful antique business which had an entry on the left. They also owned a typewriter.

Within the inner circles of the Nottingham elite, the spidery hand of Tommy, in letters and on invitations, had attracted some jocular comment over the years. There were similarities, it was true, but ... but Edward could not be sure.

Within the space of the same few seconds, John Winter was entertaining his own secret thoughts. Mr Big? What better person that this mysterious 'Edward'. Audaciously discussing the idea with the police? Yes. Why not? He would feel safe enough. Who the devil *was* this mysterious Sir Edward, who had acquitted himself so well as to merit a knighthood from the Queen? Russell would never divulge. Did the boss even know? MI5? MI6?

Detective Inspector Derek Russell was mindful that Edward had to be very careful in what he said to the regular police. Was he hinting? Was Edward subtly steering him towards a man of some considerable intelligence and considerable influence? Hoadley, perhaps? Was Claud Hoadley, that famous monument of affectation and artificiality, the centre of all this - the mastermind? The 'dog lead' incident could have been deliberately staged by Hoadley to divert any suspicion away from him. And, after all, Edward himself was a part of the homosexual underworld. He was in a position to know about these things.

"I rather warm to your assertion, Derek," continued Edward, "where you say that Arthur Bestwick walked out of the Derby Turkish Baths of his own free will. It seems to me that he was probably following a carefully prepared plan hatched by X. A plan which persuaded or tempted him to walk out in some sort of disguise, leaving his own clothes and money behind."

"Tempted?" said Russell.

"Tempted by some sort of reward."

"What reward?" asked Winter.

"Normally we'd be looking at financial gain, but we must consider the type of vicious man we're dealing with. I'd put my money on some kind of act of revenge. It may have been put to him that he should act out his own murder with the idea of framing an enemy. In the homosexual world, it's very easy to get professional men into serious trouble. For instance, Becksitch Betty would rejoice to see the fall and disgrace of Tommy and Martin."

"I thought you said that they were 'inclusive'? inquired Winter with an air of scoring a point.

"The Nottingham Camp would never include a character who has made threats, tried blackmail, associated with low life, hoodlums, rent boys and the like."

Russell also picked up on Winter's point about inclusivity. The Detective Inspector admired the idealism of Sperry and Harcourt, but could never see Aubrey Pod lounging his soft, naked body of hideous aspect under the palms, around the exotic swimming pool at The Court ... and ... yes! The excluded toad, that bitter, twisted toad was *another* person who would gloat, gladly gloat at the destruction of Tommy and Martin.

"I'm drawing your attention to the group of six," continued Edward, "the six who came out of the Derby Turkish Bath at 5.30. With co-operation from one or some of those men, it is just possible that Bestwick could have eluded the eagle-eyed women."

But care was taken here *not* to draw Russell's attention too close to his old friend Martin. On first hearing of the disappearance of Becksitch Betty, Edward feared that it might, somehow, be part of an elaborate plan designed by Martin Harcourt to wreak his hateful vengeance on Claud Hoadley. He had hoped that the ancient grudge was, at long last, subsiding. But was it? Edward was deeply disturbed by the reference in Brentnall's report to a brief meeting between Martin and Bestwick at the baths. In all the years he had known him, Martin had conscientiously avoided social contact with the detestable Becksitch Betty. Notwithstanding, it had to be acknowledged - given sufficient financial incentive - that evil old queen would be an ideal accomplice to assist the barrister in the ruination of the high-and-mighty Hoadley. Martin Harcourt QC had the necessary connections, had the imagination, had means and expertise to execute an operation which could, effectively, delete the person of Arthur Bestwick and establish a new person, a new identity, in a different country. A body might, or might not be found. Just the same, employing manufactured evidence and possibly the professional services of Monks and Muckles, Hoadley could be made to suffer the agonies of public degradation and possible criminal prosecution. He would never recover from such an ordeal. He would die a broken man. So ran the worst fears of a concerned friend. In addition, Edward was not satisfied with Martin's casual and confident explanation of that short conference in the Derby Turkish Baths.

"Oh, God, yes! It was just like the sudden appearance of Marley's ghost. Made my flesh creep. Wanted legal advice about his recent arrest at the Chester Green public loo."

"And?"

"And I was sharp. In no uncertain terms, I informed him that he should not approach a barrister on the subject and certainly not *this* barrister; told him to get a solicitor. I'll be damned if I'm going to be dishing out professional advice in the Derby Turkish Baths."

Becksitch Betty was an old hand at cottaging, reasoned Edward. He had been arrested several times and would be familiar with the routine. Legal defence was a nonsense. Betty had always found it faster, easier and cheaper to plead guilty, pay the fine, get it over with. And why address a fellow bather who had always been so aloof and frosty?

"So, correct me if I'm wrong," said Russell. "Arthur Bestwick had been invited, tempted, encouraged (whatever) to go along with some sort of disappearing scheme? And you're suggesting that, possibly, a 'Mr Big', or Mr Big and one other, or several others used this as an opportunity to get shut of Becksitch Betty once and for all?"

"You asked for help, Derek. I wish I could be more definite. I'm afraid that my next theory is even more vague, but, within my bitchy environment, it deserves consideration. Becksitch Betty may not have been the target at all! His removal may be a happy by-product of the *real* crime - the destruction of an old enemy."

"Oh!" said Russell. "The mind boggles at the possibility. I can see the headline in the *Nottingham Evening Post* - ROTTING BODY DISCOVERED - Under Flagstones of Flying Horse Courtyard. Nottingham police found dyed hairs on the body, matching the same colour as on the vain head of the eminent barrister Martin Harcourt QC."

"Improbable, but not impossible," smiled Sir Edward.

Chapter 40

All Boys, All Butch, All Beautiful

Simeon had a great time during the last few weeks of his English holiday, the sort of great time which can only be truly experienced as a teenager, but Simeon's days as a teenager were numbered. In fact, it came as a shock to discover that, on July 8th, he had just four teenage days left.

On that Thursday morning, a smooth little fat man knocked at number 4, Bog Hole in Horsley Woodhouse. Aunty Joyce liked Dolly, but then again, so did everybody else. As the little car zoomed down the M1, en route to London, Simeon was bathed in the soothing sounds of curvaceous vowels which were as plump and plush as the rotundity next to him.

"It's a puzzle isn't it? Of course, the police won't have much success. You need *inside* information," purred Dolly, smiling, head-half turned to the fascinated scruffy chicken at his side.

"Out with it, where *is* Betty?"

"Somewhere comfortable," replied Dolly, glancing down at the boy's bare legs in his short shorts. "She'll see to that. The key to this conundrum, Simeon, lies in the *character* of Becksitch Betty. You've had the solution to this mystery all along. You just haven't seen it yet, have you?"

"What should I have seen?"

"You saw those wild boys grab Betty's wig. He was mortified, disgraced in the middle of Chesterfield. He was very upset - well?"

"Well what?"

"Ask yourself, do you think Becksitch Betty is going to let Monks and Muckles get away with it?"

"How does that explain the disappearance of Betty? Have the police visited you as well?"

"The police have interviewed all of us, but they're looking at it the wrong way. They think Betty's been murdered. They're wondering where his body's been dumped. They've assumed that Monks and Muckles have got the wind up, cleared off somewhere."

"Where?"

"London's the best place to hide," said Dolly with a maddening smile, his sibilance trailing to a whisper.

"Are you taking me to see them?"

"Certainly not. They're not safe - and, anyway, I don't think they're there - because ... because you see, Simeon - I think Monks and Muckles are dead."

Pressed with further questions, Dolly outlined his theory based on Betty's reputation for malicious retribution. Dolly reasoned that Betty would have pretended to forgive his assailants. He would then ask for their help to play some sort of practical joke, in fact, the Derby Turkish Baths stunt. At some later stage, now as a 'non-person', he would have taken his revenge. He killed them or he had them killed by somebody else.

"Has Betty murdered Tinker Bell as well?"

"Oh, no. That little fairy isn't in the same league as M&M Inc. I told Detective Inspector Russell exactly where to look for Tinker Bell. He's back with granny in a small mining village called Clowne, but he won't know where Betty or Monks and Muckles are."

Simeon found this conversation disturbing. What sort of people had he been getting mixed up with? He steered the subject back to more wholesome associations and encouraged Dolly to talk about the funny folks of Derbyshire, the types which had made him laugh - Peter Pan, Nobby the Gnome, Mr Toad and the Belper Goblin. Dolly expressed sadness that he had fallen out with the latter.

"Of all my ugly old queens, Jasper was the oldest and ugliest of all. I billed him as 'The Crone Under the Crows'. He never failed to fascinate my clients. Poor Jasper. Have you heard the latest about Boy Scout's underwear?"

"What?"

"Another of Simon's tricks, I expect. Jasper received a parcel through the post which contained a quantity of unwashed underpants. He was outraged! Took them to the police station, ranted and raved at the duty sergeant. It seems that somebody put an advert into one of those new 'contact magazines' - 'Required to assist masturbation; unwashed or soiled Boy Scout's underpants. Send to J Wormall, Old Crows Cottage, Shire Oakes, Belper, Derbyshire'."

"Sounds more like a Monks and Muckles trick," said Simeon.

"It might be, if they could read or write," replied Dolly

Without being ruffled in the slightest by horrendous city traffic, Dolly gave Simeon the 'grand tour' of the capital's queer pubs, its odd clubs, specialised coffee bars and, of course, Dolly's speciality - its most ornate and active public lavatories. They stayed the night at the Imperial Baths in Russell Square. The next day they went to enjoy the delights of Kew Gardens and were delighted to discover, among the exotic ferns, a new chicken whose name was Bruno. Bruno, butch and slim, had a strong aversion to fat old queens. He was horrified to learn that young, innocent Simeon, a mere country bumpkin, had been dragged around so many public loos, searching for sex.

Bruno was as young and beautiful as the tropical flowers he was admiring. Well, he *looked* young, claimed to be a teenager, a genuine chicken and he was certainly beautiful. This German-speaking Swiss boy, visiting London to improve his English, was very keen to make the acquaintance of a fellow chicken but, he was utterly repulsed by the older fat man.

"Vy do you let such a creature come near to you?" he asserted in masterful mode when Dolly was out of earshot. "Is disgusting! Ze cream cakes - too many. And such scent! He smells like ze woman. Ze chubby cheeks, he is, what you say - obese? He is like ze balloon. Zat car, so dull, so small, so old, so poor. My daddy, in ze Switzerland, he commands ze new gleaming LeBaron! Yes, it is very impressive. All ze low poor people who must walk on ze side-walk, yes, zay stop and luke at it. So proud, me and daddy in ze new LeBaron."

Simeon was in awe. He had always admired Chrysler's top-of-the-range model, the enormous Imperial LeBaron with its unusual rocket launcher tail lights. It had to be admitted that Dolly's Morris would easily fit into its back trunk / boot. Simeon imagined 'daddy', with hands lightly resting on the large, translucent, elliptical power steering wheel, commanding the great car to obey his orders along steep, winding roads through the Swiss mountains. Even so, Bruno was glad of Dolly's faithful old Morris to convey his sexy body back to his exclusive service flat in Mayfair. The alternative would be - ze tube, or ze bus or ze taxi.

"Now don't worry about me," insisted Dolly outside the rather posh-looking residence. He and Simeon stood a little apart from Bruno who was in his doorway. "I expected this. Can't keep you to myself forever. This is as it should be. You need to meet people more of your own age. I've seen his type before - *very* choosy. He doesn't want *me* in there and you may as well get the benefit of some of 'daddy's' money. Do you have the means to get back to Derbyshire?"

Simeon did, but felt very guilty about abandoning a friend he rather liked. They waved goodbye. Bruno managed an unsmiling nod of acknowledgement - nothing more. The scruffy chicken watched Dolly's little green car recede and disappear around the corner. Standing on the kerb, suddenly he felt a moment of panic. Simeon wanted to run after Dolly's little car, to be with funny, chubby, friendly, soothing Dolly, rather than be left with this arrogant young stranger from an alien land. Suddenly, he was alone in a big city, dreadfully alone. It was the same feeling as when he watched Simon Tonks walking away from him in Chesterfield - a painful parting from someone who was intrinsically sympathetic and comfortable to be with.

The name Bruno would suggest something soft and cuddly. He was the opposite. He was a martinet, Teutonic, stern and authoritative. Like his expensive, highly-polished chrome furniture, this desirable, chic young man was ultra-modern. He had sharp edges and was as hard as his glass tabletops. However, all those hard mirrors, all that cold white leather, all that thick cream carpet was very impressive to a scruffy chicken who had become accustomed to the dowdy standards of Aunty Joyce in Horsley Woodhouse. Bruno picked up a white telephone and barked out his instructions regarding food. He put the phone down and pointed at the entrance to another room. He spoke *at* his guest rather than *to* him.

"Vee eat in 20 minutes. To ze bedroom."

Those 20 minutes were not a problem, since they involved little conversation. The fact is, these two boys had very little in common and conversation was difficult during that excellent meal which was served up by a waiter of impeccable dress and perfect manners. Bruno was not interested in tours offered by Simeon's fat friend. Nor was he interested in the recent drama of the disappearance of a drag queen. The idea of a man, an effeminate man, an old provincial man, dressing up as a silly old woman was utterly repellent to this connoisseur of handsome young males. No, he had never heard of Old Mother Riley and would be obliged if the whole sordid subject could be dropped at once.

Simeon was consumed with curiosity over an odd incident which had taken place upon the imperial sized bed. At the time, although quite alarmed, he did not feel able to question the sudden appearance of nail scissors and the snipping of a tiny lock of his pubic hair. More relaxed after cheese and biscuits, he asked his question. Bruno went over to his glass and chrome bookcase and retrieved a large photograph album.

"You may luke," he said.

There were no photographs. Each page of thick card displayed, neat, evenly spaced, small locks of human hair. Bruno carefully examined his guest's reaction to this bizarre collection of trophies, but Simeon, quite sickened, tried to mask his response to such a nauseating hobby. He turned three full pages, each exhibiting five rows of five columns - 25 specimens per page. Each boy's name was carefully printed by his lock, together with his age and the date of the conquest. The earliest date was December, 1961. Simeon could find no age below 14 or any above 19. The last lock of the fourth incomplete page was dated just a few days before, July 6th, 1965 - Calvin, 18-years-old.

"He was an American soldier," he said haughtily. "I prefer ze Americans. Zay are so very butch, so clean, circumcised and, yes, goot sex. Zay go wild! And luke, luke at ze age. You see? Do you see? Luke, zay are *all* teenagers! Yes! Zay were *all* desirable, all boys, all butch, all beautiful. No fat Dolly will ever darken *my* bed!"

"Dolly's never touched me," said Simeon, defensively in sulky tones.

"Zat is *goot*," said Bruno, nodding his head in satisfaction. "Teenagers only. Trim, slim, teenagers. Twenty is too old. If zay are 20, zay are not invited here. Zay are not permitted to touch ze Bruno. Zay do not get into *mein Buch*. It is an honour to be in ze *Buch* of ze Bruno!"

At this last, his voice held a hard ring of authority. He sounded like a Nazi and may have detected Simeon's repugnance to this loathsome book, this tasteless parade of past triumphs. To be on the safe side, during the next few days in London, Simeon was careful to avoid any mention of the toads, goblins, gnomes, fairies, pantomime dames or any of the fascinating aberrations he had so enjoyed in Derbyshire. Even so, from time to time, he suppressed a mischievous urge to arrange a blind date between his new Swiss friend and Jasper Wormall, the famous Belper Goblin. Years later, Simeon often recalled Bruno's rants over that long glass tabletop. Notwithstanding the polemics, it was a gorgeous face which was partly obscured behind the spiky glass flowers in the cut glass vase. He wondered about the age of Bruno. Yes, he certainly *looked* young enough to be a teenager, he was certainly immature enough and *behaved* like a teenager, but - over ze 20? Perhaps, or perhaps not.

Simeon remembered his final night with Bruno. Conversation was not a problem. It was Sunday - late. They were puffing and panting, bouncing and bounding on that bed of imperial proportions. It was a few seconds before midnight on July 11th.

"Yes. Yes. Do not stop! Not now," he begged, his voice weakening, trailing away. "Soon I spend. Soon it comes, my fine young stallion, serve me well, my rough peasant ... very sooooon ... "

As articulation failed Bruno, Simeon could hear the chimes of a modern, longcase clock drifting in from the living-room. Those tones meant nothing to the pampered Swiss youth on his soft sheets, still savouring the dying spasms of his orgasm, but they meant everything to the hardworking scruffy chicken who had just lost his chickenhood. As the last note faded away into the ether, Simeon Hogg, the teenager, was a teenager no more. He shared the same birthday as Julius Caesar - July 12th. Simeon was 20. He looked down on Bruno, replete yet empty, a face perfectly relaxed after ecstasy. Exhausted Bruno, he was drained, breathy with fast beating heart. The birthday boy wondered. Should Simeon make an announcement? Should he ask for congratulations, suggest a round of Happy Birthday?

Perhaps not. It was rather late to risk being ordered out, SS style, to be evicted, to be booted out onto the streets of London. No, he was too comfortable. Within the next few minutes, those peaceful, quality minutes which usually follow mutual orgasm, they embraced and dissolved into a delicious unconsciousness between soft, expensive sheets.

Chapter 41

Bouncing Chickens

London had been an adventure, great fun, but Simeon was glad to be back on the Tuesday evening of July 13th to the relative tranquillity of Derbyshire and Aunty Joyce. That tranquillity was shattered the following morning. In the working class tradition of Bog Hole, aunt and nephew were seated outside the front door, enjoying the sunshine, when an old slattern shuffled along at a speed of well under two miles per hour. She had all the time in the world. She stopped and gossiped to Aunty Nelly for about ten minutes before making a slow progress to Aunty Joyce, who spoke first in her usual, slow, sad, whining style.

"Are ya all right, Fanny. Wot ya doin' 'ere?"

"Ave coom wi this. Thee gen it me at t' post office. Asked me ta gee it ta 'im." So spoke Fanny, indicating with her dirty thumb, the seated Simeon, who did not feel obliged to rise.

This item, a 1965, 'snail mail' telegram addressed to Simeon Hogg, filled Joyce with great alarm. No telegram had ever arrived at her house before. She was fully aware that an expensive missive of that order usually carried urgent news of life-threatening disaster or death. Indeed, it was doubtful if any telegram had ever arrived at any house in Bog Hole.

"Thank you, Fanny," said Simeon, accepting the telegram from the reluctant slattern, who clearly felt that such an important communication should be handed to a responsible guardian - not to her underage charge. Furthermore, Fanny scowled down at the boy, affronted at the use of her Christian name by a mere slip of a lad.

Unaware of Fanny's emotions, Joyce's grey, sunken face, was a picture of pain, misery and dread. She studied her nephew's expression as he tore open the envelope and absorbed the contents within.

"Oh!"

"What is it?" she wailed.

"I've been summoned!"

"What!"

"Nay, lad!" exclaimed Fanny. Several other relatives were now craning to eavesdrop on this rising drama concerning the telegram.

"No no, not 'summonsed' as in summoned to a court of law, in fact, summoned to a different court, *The* Court, the residence of Tommy and Martin."

Three hours later, a scruffy chicken, after his long cycle ride, was in a very different environment. He was relaxing into the luxury of an upholstered, wickerwork armchair. Nearby was a raised pond, made interesting by the movement of brightly coloured fish and the soothing sound of a small fountain. To his left and right was a tropical garden. Coleus varieties sporting showy leaves of red, yellow and white, formed a border to a garden of ferns which, itself, was another border to large, exotic palms - all underneath an impressive Paxtonesque conservatory, so beloved of the Victorians. In front of Simeon was the expanse of the famous swimming pool he had heard so much about, glistening and shimmering in the afternoon sun. His wickerwork armchair was one of a suite of four - all occupied. Two of the occupants were fighting to be heard.

"Well who cares how or why it happened?" said Tommy, warming to his theme. "Good bloody riddance, I say!"

"Yes, but ... " attempted Martin.

"Never mind any 'buts'," parried Tommy. "I don't know why we can't all breathe a massive sigh of relief. We should throw a party, celebrate ... "

"Russell said ... " tried Martin.

"Oh bugger the police! What do the police know about it anyway? The wicked old witch is dead - we hope. That's the main thing. Should have happened years ago - *evil* old cow - serves her bloody right. Hope the bitch rots in hell ... what's happened to that tea? Where's Butch?

Simeon was amused. Edward was amused at Simeon's amusement.

"Look at the way she upset poor old Harry," continued Tommy. "He was never the same. Drove him to an early grave, she did. *Nasty* bitch ... "

Tommy was interrupted by two things - the shaking belly-laugh which escaped Simeon and the appearance of Butch pushing along a trolley of tea and cakes. As the two guests craned their necks to get the benefit of the sexy, retreating black bottom, Tommy poured the tea and they all tucked into home-made refreshments. The conversation resumed. At times, it was serious, thoughtful, analytical - and, at other times, flippant, entertaining, tongue-in-cheek. Simeon was flattered. He felt privileged to be included in this select circle, to be, effectively, in receipt of the full body of information available to Edward and the police. They were examining the possible identity of 'Mr Big'.

"Of course, it's no use, no use at all," said Edward rather gloomily, playing with the crumbs on his plate. "We'll probably never know who he is."

"Well ... I think Aubrey Pod is Mr Big. Really!" said Martin in reaction to half-sceptical, half-amused faces. "He does have a reputation, you know, in that particular department."

"Yes. I've heard about it," drawled Tommy in his relaxed, smooth, dangerous tones. "I suppose it compensates for a total lack of brains *and* beauty."

"Then again," said Martin, in an effort to keep the comedy going, "They *do* say that old Jasper Wormall ... "

He was halted by a sucking in of breath, an exhaling of an 'oooww' and the bulging, ogling eyes of Simeon, who was leaning forward in his armchair, having just spotted the most extraordinary sight in the garden outside. Beyond the glass panes of the conservatory, he could hardly believe this arresting spectacle. Bouncing chickens! Beautiful chickens were being thrown up into the air by an unseen agency. Two grinning youths were bouncing up and down. Simeon was riveted by this sight of two bounding bums. These two shapely bottoms, nicely wrapped up inside tight blue jeans, were bobbing up behind the shrubs - and then down and then up and down, up, down ...

"Ralph and Ricky!" laughed Edward. "Your fellow guests, enjoying the trampoline. You'll meet them later.

"Oh, yes, please!" pleaded Simeon with feeling.

It was a good conclusion to his English holiday, that last week in Nottingham with Tommy, Martin, the bouncing chickens and the occasional visit from near-neighbour, Edward.

At noon on Monday, July 19th, 1965, the extraordinary seven week vacation came to an end when Simeon, standing on the stern of the Empress of Canada, was waving goodbye to Tommy and Martin, who had kindly conveyed him to Liverpool.

It had been a once-in-a-lifetime experience. It had been packed with adventure, full of incident, full of fun, full of characters, a barrel of laughs, a mind-blowing education for a scruffy chicken.

Chapter 42

Blackpool's North Pier

It was what he had come to expect from Blackpool; his favourite weather - sunny, but cool and windy. Derbyshire had been too hot and humid during the recent heatwave and these invigorating westerly breezes blowing off the Irish Sea were a healthy change of climate. Everything about Blackpool was reassuring, predictable, nice and old. It was favourite weather, favourite view, looking south east at the famous old tower from his seat on the famous old pier. Simeon was taking the advice of his old friend Aubrey Pod who always said -

"Go on to the North Pier and take deep breaths. Do you good. It's the finest air in the world."

He was resting and sunning with the old folks on a continuous wooden bench. Their backs were supported by ornate iron castings fashioned two centuries before. Simeon was no chicken, but he did not exactly feel like one of the old folks. A part of him still felt like the scruffy chicken he had been forty years before. His dress was similar, casual with rucksack, boots, close-fitting white shorts, track suit top under a dark green Helly Hansen jacket, topped by a dark green woolly hat. A lot to wear for mid-July, but he was well-protected from the sharp, salty wind. And that brilliant sun, it did feel rather good on his legs. Those around him, old-fashioned folks in their seventies, eighties and nineties, Aunty Joyces and Uncle Wilfreds - they made him feel young, on this day in 2005, the day of the 'big six', a significant birthday. It made him think about Bruno. Ze Bruno; what would he look like now? Of all the dozens of people he had met four decades before, only a handful had remained friends over the years. Mr Toad, now in his 70's, more of a character than ever, continued to delight, continued to inspire, continued be a barrel of laughs.

At the end of his English holiday in the July of 1965, Simeon Hogg returned to Detroit to consider his future. In that September he obtained a place at Eastern Michigan University. Hardly an academy which would impress Claud Hoadley, but, three years later, he graduated and was appointed to the post of history master at Dwight D Eisenhower High School, located on the south side of Lincoln Gardens. This was the same school he had visited with Ben and Ricky on the day President Kennedy was slain.

As a writer in his sixties and seventies, Simeon was ambitious. The author aimed for fame and fortune. The teacher was more modest. Quite simply, he wanted to concentrate on the basics, master his craft and be competent in the classroom. Management had never interested Simeon. Accordingly, he remained an ordinary member of staff, one of the foot soldiers defending traditional standards, teaching history in the same school, in the same classroom, for the following 34 years until one wonderful day in 2003. It was April 17th. A opportunity to retire early offered itself. He grabbed it.

He grabbed it because the world had changed - not always for the better. In some quarters, common courtesy and good manners were increasingly seen as freakish behaviour. The one-time chicken of 1965 now avoided the other chickens of 2005. Simeon felt safe and comfortable sitting with these old folks from a previous generation. His chickenhood has seen the first green shoots of progressive education, which eventually grew into a monstrous vine which would strangle everything he held dear - deference, respect for authority and consideration for older people. The retired schoolmaster felt that British comprehensive education had plumbed new depths when, just a few days before, he viewed a Channel 4 programme, on Thursday, July 7th; a bad day for education and a terrible day for London. In the *Dispatches* series, this one was called *Undercover Teachers*. Alex Dolan was surprised and shocked by the appalling anti-social behaviour she experienced in 16 state secondary schools over a period of six months of secret filming. Simeon Hogg was familiar with some of these horrors, affronts to common decency. He had witnessed them during his last few years under a new 'enlightened' liberal regime at Eisenhower High School. Outrageous indiscipline included disruptive pupils wandering about the classroom, hitting each other, sucking lollipops, putting on lipstick, playing with mobile phones, using threatening and obscene language to staff who might attempt to assert any kind of authority. Most depressing of all for Simeon was the familiar staffroom culture of denial which tried to pretend that 'all was well'. Yes, the world had changed since 1965.

After his retirement, the one-time scruffy chicken returned to his native England and started to research and write about his former friends and acquaintances, the goblins, gnomes, fairies, toads and other curious characters of Derbyshire. That was what had brought him to Blackpool today. Like Coney Island, Blackpool could be garish, cheap, tacky and tatty. Unlike that American equivalent, this glittering and cheerful resort of the North West held his affection. It had a past - Simeon's past. As a child, Duck and Mrs Duck had brought him here to sample the thrills and spills of the Pleasure Beach, walked his little legs along the promenade full of shrieks of joy, jammed with the working-class at play, jammed with amusements, ghost trains, shooting galleries, dancing girls, palmists, vulgar postcards and the salty smell of jellied eels. Simeon had returned to Blackpool to find out more about a man who was closely identified with that rough-and-ready seaside town, a man who could be just as crude, rude, tasteless and tawdry - Becksitch Betty.

Becksitch Betty had been famous. Everybody knew him. They could quote him and enthuse about his impressions of Old Mother Riley and Norman Evans doing his 'Over the Garden Wall'. Old fans would praise his Gracie Fields singing voice, his Carmen Miranda dancing, but the older homosexuals, the old queens who knew him personally - they held darker memories which included threats, blackmail and rent boys. Even those old timers could not give Simeon any definite information about Arthur Bestwick, his real name. Forty years before, he had, apparently, disappeared into thin air. The row of old cottages at the foot of Becksitch Lane had been demolished in the early 1970's - gone forever. About a fortnight after Bestwick's strange exit, his sidekicks, the notorious Monks and Muckles, also vanished. Like their mistress, they were never seen or heard of ever again. Here in 2005, the collective memory of gay communities in Derby and Nottingham vaguely assumed that all three must be long-dead.

The few days' visit to Blackpool had not been much help either. In an effort to dig out information on Betty's old landlady, Simeon had marched up and down the long Albert Road, knocking on numerous doors, asking for any memories of Dolly Clacket. His well practised spiel was getting monotonous -

"I'm trying to trace an old Albert Road landlady by the name of Dolly Clacket. Have you ... No? Oh, dear. Are any of your neighbours likely to be of any help? If they're elderly they may ... I see. Well, thank you anyway."

How odd! Each time he spoke the name 'Dolly Clacket', it still rang a faint bell of familiarity, just as it had done forty years before when Becksitch Betty first forced the name out of his horrible, twisting, mobile mouth in that tiny cottage in Belper. Who *was* 'Dolly Clacket'? Where had he heard that name before? No matter. Each shaking head made him more despondent - until ...

"Dolly Clacket," said a woman, slowly and carefully, who would certainly never see 50 again. "Dolly Clacket," she repeated. "Joost a minute, I'll get me mam. MAM." She yelled into the interior ARE YA THERE, ARR MAM?"

'Arr Mam' appeared. This wiry old soul shuffled to the door and gave Simeon the following useful information. Mrs Clacket had been the landlady of -

"Now what was it? It's over there, on t' other side. Name? Well it's Sunny Side *now* ... it was ... wait a minute ... before that ... it was Scunthorpe 'ouse ... an ... something crab ... 'ang on ... That's it! Dolly kept The Crab Pot! When? Now then ... it'd be 1959 ... well, she'd already gone when 'Arry died. That'd be 1985. Yes, she'd gone then."

Simeon learned that Dolly kept herself to herself. She was not popular, nor was she a conscientious businesswoman. She refused more guests than she took in. She took frequent breaks even in the high season! Arr Mam vaguely remembered that it had something to do with an ailing aunt in Morecambe. No, Arr Mam had never heard of an Arthur Bestwick or of anyone known as Becksitch Betty.

"Were they married to each other?"

The owner at Sunny Side was no help at all. Detective Inspector Derek Russell had, yet again, been a great help. Two years before, Simeon had asked the long-retired Detective Inspector for assistance in finding an old school-friend who had gone missing on a cycling trip back in 1960. Russell, now 90 years of age, had responded positively to the request for information on the 1965 case of Arthur Bestwick. Several typewritten sheets giving comprehensive details were dispatched some two weeks before and had now been eagerly studied. Together with the data Simeon had recalled from the 'Nottingham Conference' of July 14th, 1965, he had considered himself to be well equipped to solve the puzzle of four decades back.

Had considered, but now, even in this lovely Blackpool sunshine, his spirits were drooping. Perhaps there was too much bumf, too much confusion, too many questions still unanswered. Conundrums continued to bewilder him, all made worse, much worse, by the deceit and deviousness of homosexual secrecy and the protective culture of misinformation. A crime *might* have been committed. That crime might be the murder of an old drag queen. In his account, Russell had hinted that the murder of Bestwick might not be the primary crime. The Becksitch Betty misdeed might have been a clever attempt to get somebody else into trouble. Russell clearly indicated that the 'somebody else' was most likely to be Claud Hoadley, a man who had been respected but, also, intensely hated in some quarters. If Hoadley was the principal victim, his assailant failed, *if* the intention was that Hoadley should be charged with murder. If, on the other hand, the intention was to cause Hoadley pain and humiliation from being questioned by the police, the plan succeeded. But, surely the old pedant was never a serious suspect? Hoadley's embarrassment from the 'kitchen table incident' could have been achieved quite independently of Bestwick's sudden departure.

It was no good. Simeon could make no sense of it, no sense at all. Perhaps he was 'looking at it the wrong way', as was often said in an Agatha Christie mystery. He shared Russell's scepticism regarding the Derby Turkish Baths 'cremation theory' which was advanced by Aubrey Pod. No, Simeon's opinion was at one with the Detective Inspector. Arthur Bestwick had agreed to the stunt, a stunt which had been planned by someone more intelligent. In fact, the mysterious Mr Big. He would need to be better placed socially and have a comprehensive knowledge and understanding of the gay scene. To manage rent boys he would need to be unobtrusive, articulate and ... mobile ...

Mobile! Surely not! Could *Dolly* be Mr Big? Frequent excursions to Manchester, Sheffield, Leeds, London ... And Dolly was so sure that Monks and Muckles had been done away with ... His mind was racing. He must keep in touch with the credible, the plausible. He had read too many whodunits and was groping for the 'least likely'; may as well suspect silly, simple Simon Tonks. And yet, there again ...

Chapter 43

The Old Folks

Silly thoughts. He had given it his best shot. True, he had solved the mystery of the lost lad, two years before, only by a fluke, an accident, a lucky chance. He was unlikely to get so lucky a second time. Becksitch Betty was probably up there somewhere (or down there) having the last laugh. He had taken his secret to the grave - assuming he *was* in his grave. How old would he be now? Ninety? More?

Simeon told himself that he was on holiday. He should just try to enjoy the moment. He should relax in the sun, watch the sea, the white horses, enjoy the sea breeze, close his eyes and enjoy the crashing and sloshing of waves against the massive, 19th century supporting stanchions far below him. And above, the nostalgic cries of plaintive seagulls merged with the nostalgic voice of Aubrey Pod - 'take deep breaths!' Old-fashioned folks, quaint folks like Aubrey continued to shuffle about on Blackpool's North Pier. Some limped. Some hobbled. Some toddled. Some had sticks and some managed without. Some were solitary and some were still with 'the missis'. Occasionally they faltered, recognised a familiar face and passed the time of day with pleasantries. Old folk were nice to have around. Better than yobs, old folks were safe - more than that, they were an inspiration.

Simeon was looking at his future, his *near* future; like the old chap coming towards him now. He was using a walking frame; slowly, very slowly making a painful progress down the length of that venerable pier. Clearly, he had every intention of reaching the very end before making the long journey back - quite an achievement for this old-timer who was determined he would never give up. Obviously a regular, a local character, he was greeted by several cheery 'Hello's' and 'Are ya all right, youth?' and 'That's it, keep goin', lad' and 'Ya'll be breakin' t' speed limit, you!' This old man, slightly stooped under his grubby sunhat, struggled to lift a yellow haggard face, crooked, sunken and stained with age. He struggled to force his face into a sickly smile for those who had bothered to acknowledged him. And then - an extraordinary thing happened

"Didn't you go to the hospital, Arthur? The lump's still there."

This question and comment came from the man who operated an impressive, two-tier carousel near the end of the pier. At this range, Simeon could discern, just above the cheek of the old man's face, an angry red lump or carbuncle. Such a nasty swelling would normally be disfiguring, but, so it seemed to Simeon, not in this case - and not on this face. This man was ancient, Jurassic, wizened beyond any hope of repair. He could have been the model for H Rider Haggard's monstrous character Gagoole! This protuberance was just one more blemish upon a hideous landscape of discoloration and complete disfigurement. The old fossil replied in an unexpectedly effeminate whine.

"Well ... t' doctor said, 'We can cut it out, if ya want, Arthur, *but* it's in *deep*, an it'll leave an 'ole - a bloody deep 'ole! T' doctor said. So a thought ta me sen ... now Arthur, wot do ya want? Wot's it ta be - loomp or t' 'ole? An a thought ta me sen - I'll keep t' loomp."

It was the mouth - positive identification. The only mouth Simeon had ever seen which moved around the face; a mobile mouth, the same mobile mouth, the same grotesque twisting orifice, dragging out words, which had mesmerised him forty years back when that face was just as ugly as it was now. It was all still there; a vile display of kinks and warps accumulated over a lifetime of hate and resentment.

The carousel man walked off to attend to his ride. Simeon jumped up, went over and asked him about the old bloke with the walking frame.

"Arthur Huggins? Been here for years! Everybody knows Arthur. Grand old chap. Oh yes, lives over there in that hotel." He pointed in the direction of the North Promenade. "Park House Hotel. All right for some isn't it? Quite posh, very nice. Been there donkey's years, a suite on the front, filthy rich, plenty a moolah for our Arthur ... excuse me."

Customers interrupted as several seagulls screamed overhead. The old hag, having resumed his laboured and painful journey to the pier's end, had made only a modest headway. A few brisk strides and Simeon was at his side.

"Mr Bestwick? *Is* it Mr Bestwick?"

He seemed not to hear. The lugubrious motion of wizened arthritic claws gripping the walking frame continued without interruption. Just for an instant, did the grip tighten? Did the knuckles become whiter with greater grip? Simeon was not sure. He moved in front of the ancient plodder and stalled his slow progress. That foul face slowly looked up to inspect the impediment. What did those, sad, rheumy eyes say? Did they seem to say - 'Have pity!' 'For God's sake just go away.' 'Leave me in peace.' Or did they say - 'Who are you?' 'Who is Mr Bestwick?' Simeon repeated his question.

"Nay, lad. Yav made a mistake," said the hobbler, softly, in a lower register, a dangerous register which seemed to imply a threat.

"I don't think so."

"Me name's 'ooggins, Arthur 'ooggins."

Simeon apologised for the error and asked politely if Mr Huggins could spare a few minutes for a chat.

"You see, I'm trying to locate a man I once knew in Derbyshire many years ago. He was fond of Blackpool and used to holiday here. As a resident ... well, you've knocked about, seen a few things, I think you may be able to help me."

For several long seconds, the suspicious rheumy eyes steadily held the eyes of the younger man. Mr Huggins lowered them to midriff, white shorts and bronze legs. He seemed to make up his mind and moved slowly over to the side of the pier. Simeon held him, steadied him, and gently lowered the frail body to repose on the continuous bench.

"Eee it's *grand* ta 've a young un ta do for ya, it is."

"Not as young as you might think!"

"Nay, lad. You're a chicken, you are. It's grand ta 'ave a nice chicken next ta ya," said the camp old queen, laying a brownish, yellow claw upon the 'chicken's' leg.

Simeon decided to play a game. Mendacity might be a way forward. He made it clear that he was merely curious. He wanted to know what had become of an entertainer he had once met in 1965. Any information obtained Simeon would keep to himself. Indeed, all of the other people who might have known Arthur Bestwick were now long dead. He vanished one day at the Derby Turkish Baths and Simeon would like to know what happened to Mr Bestwick.

Once again, Arthur Huggins, now with a twinkle in his rheumy eyes held the sincere gaze of the younger man. That twinkle seemed to say - 'So that's how it's going to be - is it?'

"Well, lad, I'll tell ya, a *did* know that chap, Arthur Bestwick."

"Why did he disappear?"

"*Why*! A thought it'd be *'ow*.

"If you'd be so kind, we can come to that later. Why?"

The old man became thoughtful. He seemed to go off at a tangent and drew Simeon's attention to the appalling events of just a few days before, the tragedy of July 7th which claimed 54 lives.

"Arthur were a bit like them youths in London, ya know, nig-nogs wi rooksacks."

"How? What on earth did Arthur Bestwick have in common with faceless fanatics?"

"Arthur ... Arthur ... 'e were full a 'ate," croaked the old man, his voice nearly breaking. "Arthur were a 'suicide bomber', 'e made 'is own bomb, timed it right - an then 'e let it off."

The analogy was fascinating. In his own thick accent, this old queen continued to tell his story in the third person. He was speaking of someone who had 'blown himself up' - had utterly destroyed himself and them re-emerged in a different form as a different person. It made Simeon think of David Bond's pond, his dragonfly larva which crawled out, underwent metamorphosis and flew off as something else. The hateful Becksitch Betty had carefully planned his attack upon that Derby - Nottingham homosexual community which had despised him, had belittled him. His 'bomb' was perfect for the assault on that fragile brotherhood. It consisted of the disappearing act and a trail of misleading evidence designed to hurt as many people as possible, as much as possible. As he pressed on, his narrative became more enthusiastic, unburdening his long suppressed story. Eventually, the third person was dropped and, at last, Simeon Hogg was talking directly to Becksitch Betty.

"Sperry! 'arcourt! 'oadley! Snotty bastards! Thee think a were bloody thick. Joost cus a talk common. Arr showed 'em, a did!"

He spat out the names and dived into the evil details of destruction. Simeon watched the twisting and intertwining of that vicious mouth as it explained how parts of the 'bomb' worked and how parts did not work. Becksitch

Betty had gone to some trouble in forging the spidery hand of Tommy Sperry - 'Two under twelve if possible' - but that letter completely failed to implicate Tommy as a paedophile. He had gone to even more trouble getting inside the home of Bob and Clarence in Nottingham, the flat located above the antique shop. 'Come to back of shop. Will pay extra if they stay the night.' - was typed by the old queen on Clarence's own typewriter. If the police had checked ... But, again, thanks to Edward, the police did *not* check.

With his plans all carefully laid, Becksitch Betty simply waited for a wet Saturday. He knew that all the regulars would be at the Derby Turkish Baths on any rainy Saturday. He was confident that his clever conjuring trick, on that day, would cause every single person in those baths to be interviewed by the police and, worse, *investigated* by the police. True or not, it was always said that files were kept upon all suspected homosexuals who came to the attention of the authorities. In 1965, gay men lived in fear and dread that employers, colleagues, relatives or straight friends might discover their true sexual orientation. Becksitch Betty took great pleasure in the certain knowledge that some of the bathers would be terribly upset by those interviews and enquiries. Some would suffer dreadfully. Hilary Raymond Hawley in particular. He never returned to the Derby Turkish Bath. David Bond, the respected surgeon, was quite shaken and did not return until late 1967.

Betty chose his moment to speak to Martin Harcourt. He reasoned that a convenient witness, a chicken, (Simeon) would be questioned, 'shaken down' by the investigating officer - and, eventually, would blab. Bestwick reasoned that the slightest suspicion of any connection between himself and Martin Harcourt QC would have a good chance of destroying his career. The very fact of Harcourt being exposed as a regular at the Derby Turkish Baths, itself, would be very damaging. As it happened, Harcourt was protected by a powerful friend. The barrister was somewhat embarrassed, but not damaged.

"What about that child pornography addressed to Martin? We all knew he'd have nothing to do with anything like that. He swore blind that it never arrived at The Court. How was it possible? How did you get it officially postmarked?"

The old queen responded with an unpleasant, soft chuckle.

"There's a lot possible wi me. Postmen were never paid much money. A knew one in Nottingham, ya know. 'is name were Tony. A knew all them places in America, dirty pictures an stuff. A wrote, signed it Martin 'arcourt - an a told Tony ta keep an eye open ... an a thought ... now Arthur, where's best place fa this little bomb? A could always get into 'ouses, ya know. No problem. Then a thought o' that bloody daft toad, just up t' lane. A thought, yes, I'll ave that bastard - ignorin' me in King Street. A knew t' police 'd search 'is 'ouse - an search it well. Always come down 'ard on cottage queers, ya know, when summats gone off, police do, specially oat ta do wi little boys. A thought it were good really, that letter an pictures o' t' little lad. Dropped both on 'em in t' shit, dint it?"

Simeon ignored that nasty gloat and pursued the answer to another mystery.

It doesn't add up, you know? *Somebody* made you leave in a hurry? Cash was found in your pocket in the Turkish Baths and well over £300 was discovered hidden in your kitchen. All told, it wasn't far short of £400 - a huge amount of money forty years ago ... well ... let's see ... it would have the buying power of about ... £10,000 today! Who was it? Monks and Muckles? Did they threaten you? Did *they* force you to leave?"

Becksitch Betty threw back his head and let out a raucous laugh which ended in a phlegmy coughing fit. Moments later, he recovered his composure and looked directly at his questioner with a sickly smile.

"Monks and Muckles! Monks and Muckles made me a bloody fortune! Eee, thee were good lads ta me. It were me that named 'em, ya know." He started to chuckle again. "Aye, loovely lookin' little lads wi a twinkle o' mischief - just wot punters like. Two willin' rogues, playful, keen ta learn naughty tricks an pranks." He nudged his elbow into Simeon's side, moved his head closer and whispered "Thee could be rude - *very* rude. Thee got naughty fingers! Many a bloke were glad o' them little fingers ... Anyway, a took one look at em, an a said - 'Monks and Muckles!' Thee were rate tickled thee were. Now wot would thee be ... 'bout six an eight. *They* didn't know. Stonch didn't know either."

"Stonch?"

"'im that sold 'em to me. 'e'll be dead now."

"Sold!"

"That's it, lad - a bought 'em. That's 'ow a made me money. Four 'undred quid!! You - don't - know - nowt, do ya? Four 'undred quid!" he spat out the words with a gob of phlegm on to the wooden boards. "A were worth *thousands* - tens o' thousands! A could buy this bloody pier!"

"OK, take it easy. Dolly thought you'd killed Monks and Muckles - did you?"

"Did a 'ell as like! Ya don't kill t' goose that lays golden eggs, do ya? Nay, lad, sold em back ta Stonch, dint a. Four 'undred quid were nowt ta me. 'ave ya any idea wot punters 'll pay fa a bita fun wi rude little lads? Thee chucked *bundles* o' fivers at me, thee did. Rich blokes, posh blokes from London; thee queued oop ta play wi me little urchins. Them as got good jobs, thee like a bita rough."

Simeon had to tread carefully with his questions and watch the tone of his attitude. If he betrayed moral outrage, if his curiosity developed into an interrogation, the old queen might clam up and the precious flow of information could be lost for ever. He steered the conversation towards problematic teenagers and the stress they caused parents and teachers. Becksitch Betty agreed eagerly and revealed that Monks and Muckles, in mid teens, were getting too difficult to handle. He reminded Simeon about his sleepless night in Chesterfield and the incident of the wig. That particular humiliation brought forward his plan of retirement, a plan which would facilitate the equivalent of a terrorist outrage on the gay populace.

Chapter 44

7 / 7

During the previous five days, '7/7' was frequently uttered on television, radio and in all the newspapers; a phrase on everybody's lips. It referred to the terrorist outrage committed in London on July 7th, 2005 - an appalling event which had shaken the country. It was the British equivalent of '9/11' - a reference to the September 11th attack on New York's Twin Towers, four years before. Becksitch Betty had spoken of 'bombing' the gay community and this phrase, '7/7', continued to pop into Simeon's head.

He asked the old man if he was aware that his house had been broken into and ransacked sometime during that Saturday night of June 19th, 1965, after his disappearance.

"It weren't Satdy night, it were early Soondy mornin'. Course a bloody knew. Ooo d' ya think did it? It were *me* that did it!"

"You burgled your own home! Why?"

"To tie a bloody noose round the necks - an to pull it bloody tight. Wot d' ya think!"

"Yes ... I'm beginning to see. It was an attempt to implicate Tommy, Bob and Clarence, wasn't it? It would look as though they were trying to retrieve those incriminating letters, which had already been removed by the police on the Saturday evening - hence the frenzied ransack."

"A wanted to get back on 'em all. If it looked like ad be comin' back, dinner all ready, it'd look like they'd done away wi me - *murdered* me. It might 'ang t' bastards. A knew ad stirred oop a 'ornet's nest. Bobbies were talkin' to all on 'em, Derby lot as well. Thee'd all be shit scared."

"You certainly did a good job."

"Not good enough. 'oadley got off light. It were *me* that rang 't *Telegraph*, but thee dint print oat. Pity. A should 'ave told Monks and Muckles to beat 'im oop, knock 'is bloody teeth out, put 'im in t' bloody 'ospital! Still ... thee gen 'im wot for, dint thee? Thee tied 'im oop like a dog, kicked 'im a bit - pissed on 'im."

Again, Simeon was transfixed by this vicious jaw. As it deformed from side to side, spitting out, ranting rancour, he felt the need to change tack.

"Tell me more about this 'deadly duo'. You sold them back to ... who was it?"

"Stonch. 'e could deal wi 'em better than me. Thee were gettin' less an less profitable. Thee started to do foreigners."

'Foreigners'. If an employee did a 'foreigner', he was breaking a rule of his contract, cheating on his boss. If a plumber (employed by a company) repaired a leak out of his normal hours and accepted payment into 'his back pocket' - this was called a foreigner. Simeon recognised this Derbyshire word from his childhood and immediately understood that Monks and Muckles were becoming independent, not 'declaring' income from assignments they had negotiated themselves.

"The attack on Claud Hoadley took place on June 30th. I presume that was their last job for you? Sean Stokes said they left Chesterfield for good on that same day. Was that the day you handed them over to this ... Stonch? Who was he? Where would he have taken them?

"That's fa me to know an fa you to wonder." So spoke the old queen in a soft, sinister purr. Simeon had gone too far. "Ya seem to be well informed on days an dates forty bloody years ago?"

"Forgive me. I didn't mean to pry ... it's just that you ... well, all this is quite fascinating. You must remember that 1965 was a very significant year for me. Please answer this, or not, as you please. You were wealthy, OK, understood. You could buy the most beautiful boys available - so why on earth did you make such an effort to, shall we say, 'put the make' on - Aubrey Pod! *Aubrey Pod*! I ask you! Of all people - the ugly toad! Do you remember that afternoon at his home when he'd been buying new clothes to improve his image?"

Becksitch Betty recovered his good humour. He started to laugh. He remembered it well and told Simeon that some boys would not 'touch him with a barge pole' - at any price! He also explained that Aubrey's ugliness had the effect of being a perverse kind of 'turn-on' and, it was a fact of human nature; we often want something which we cannot have.

"e'd ave nowt to do wi me. 'im! - wi a face like back o' a Trent bus! A seen 'im at them baths. A saw wot 'e'd got. Yes. It were BIG! A like 'em big." He gave Simeon another nudge. "It were a whopper!" he whispered, "Takes summat to fill me. A thought to me sen, ya could do somethin' fa me. Me shutters opened oop three inches when a saw it."

Simeon nearly fell off the bench, doubled up with hysterics, listening to this repulsive whining old hag, with his ugly red lump, recalling his long-past lust for - of all people - Mr Toad. He laughed now, just as much, just as hard as he had laughed back on that notable Wednesday of July 2nd, nearly half a century before. Some part of Becksitch Betty was likeable. Was it possible to see him in a sympathetic light? Terrorists justified their actions - and so did Bestwick. All this talk of buying and selling boys like slaves and yet ... In old age, Arthur Bestwick could be as entertaining, as charming and as popular as he was with the ladies of the Derby Turkish Baths; those same ladies who had, so carefully, watched and identified all 17 bathers who left on that day.

"Are you going to tell me how you did it, Arthur?"

"Did wot?"

"Got out of the Derby Turkish Baths. It was thought that your best opportunity to slip out was at about half past five when a little knot of bathers left. That put the focus on Sperry, Harcourt, Hawley, Bond and especially those feral lads - Monks and Muckles. Did they help you? Was it Monks and Muckles?

"No, it wasn't Monks an bloody Muckles! Yav got Monks and Muckles on t' brain, you."

"Come on, tell us. How did you do it? How was it possible? Those women were watching *all* the time!"

"A know thee were." He said it softly, with a sigh. "Yav not given it enough thought, av ya? A told ya, dint a. Am an actor! A do impressions. Ave ya seen me perform?"

"Sadly no. I'd love to have seen your Old Mother Riley."

"Ya should av seen me do 'ilary Raymond 'awley, shunt ya?"

"Hilary ... but he went out at the same time!

"Not quite t' same time," said the old hag in soothing, sardonic sweetness. "Easy-peasy wont it? Simple as oat, to mince out like that snotty camp prat wi a big long black coat like 'is. Just a few seconds after 'e'd left. Ya see, yav got to *know* an audience. Magicians know an audience. Thee see A leavin'. Thee distracted, thee lookin' at other folks, thee lookin' at C, D, E an F talkin', movin' about - whatever. Thee look again. Thee look at a big soft queen - A. Thee see 'im leavin' - *still* leavin'. Thee don't realise wot thee've *really* seen. Thee've seen *B* leave. That were *me* - B, doin' me dainty steps, wi me big coat, wi a bita paddin'. It were all in a paper carrier bag when a came in. A flushed t' bag down t' bog. Two sets o' clothes. Nowt to it, lad. An you, ya daft lookin' bugger! Ya've bin forty bloody years puzzling' ... "

In triumph, he shook with more wheezing, phlegmy laughter which concluded with another assault on the old pier.

"So, exit Arthur Bestwick - enter Arthur Huggins!

"If ya like," he replied, softly, in the light tone of a child concealing a secret.

Simeon related his adventures on the Albert Road, looking for anyone who might recall Dolly Clacket. Again, a soft sarcastic chuckle seemed to ooze out of that horrible mouth. Arthur conceded that the obtained data was correct. Dolly Clacket took over The Crab Pot in 1959, sold up and retired in 1985.

"Why is the name Dolly Clacket so familiar to me? When you first said 'Dolly Clacket' to me and Dolly back in 1965 - apart from finding the name funny - I felt sure that I'd heard it somewhere before."

"'appen ya did. 'appen it's cus she dunt exist."

Simeon looked directly into the face of Becksitch Betty.

"Think about it, lad. Dint ya listen t' wireless or watch telly? Dint ya like 'ancock or Steptoe an Son?"

And there it was, in an instant. Of course - *Dolly Clacket* - the humorous creation of Ray Galton and Alan Simpson. Simeon had always loved their work. He had all the tapes of all the Hancocks and all the Steptoes and had played them over and over again. Dolly Clacket was a frequent reference to any rough, common woman. She might be Hancock's girlfriend, or his landlady, or she might be a local slut - same with the Steptoes. Dolly Clacket was never seen, but the very name conjured up the exact female image Galton and Simpson wanted you to imagine. And now, Simeon was thinking ...

"That's right, lad," said Becksitch Betty without blinking, tilting his head slightly, reading his thoughts - "A *told* ya a was an actor. An a bloody good actor as well. Meet Dolly Clacket!"

It all became so clear. Simeon was no Poirot, but Poirot would have tumbled to the clues; keeping herself to herself, taking in very few guests and frequent absences to attend a fictitious invalid aunt in Morecambe. Set these clues next to the behaviour of Becksitch Betty: winding down his entertaining, keeping a safe distance from his boys in Chesterfield - but all the time organising lucrative deals with the customers, wealthy punters. Arthur Bestwick started to plan his retirement in 1959 by buying a boarding house in the Albert Road. At that address, he donned his Clacket drag and became Dolly for the next 26 years until it was safe to sell up, re-invent himself and re-locate at the Park House Hotel as the popular, charming rascal - Arthur Huggins. It was 'Mrs Clacket' who (at the request of Detective Sergeant Field) told the Blackpool police on the Sunday afternoon of July 20th that she had not seen Mr Bestwick in weeks. Mrs Clacket had only just returned from Morecambe but, in reality, Arthur Bestwick had spent the morning travelling by train from Belper.

And there it was. Both men sat side by side in brilliant sunshine on the continuous bench near the end of Blackpool's North Pier: the old chicken and the old queen. They sat in silence because there was no more to say.

"'elp me oop," asked the old man.

Simeon obliged. In silence, he guided wizened, yellow, arthritic claws onto the walking frame and set him in the direction of the pier's end. The old hag could now complete the first half of his daily journey before he would undertake the long trek back. Some instinct of common courtesy nagged at Simeon. He should utter a few words of farewell ... good-bye, best wishes, cheerio, take it easy ... but the words failed him.

With mixed feelings, Simeon sat down and watched the decaying frail figure of Arthur Huggins recede. Slowly, very slowly, he made his painful progress towards the end of that venerable old pier; just another old man, one of many, one of the old folks.

Old folks continued to walk by the one-time scruffy chicken, plaintive seagulls continued to cry and scream above him. Big waves with white horses continued to crash, to slosh against the stanchions beneath him ... and the sun felt good on his bare legs.

ACKNOWLEDGEMENTS

Yet again, I am grateful to Lesley Robinson the artist of Shipley Park. Her imaginative design and skilful painting has given the front cover its eye-catching, unique appearance.

Judy Rose, formally Judy Cullimore, Crown Court Reporter of *The Nottingham Evening Post*, has kindly spent a great deal of time and trouble proof-reading this book. Thank you, Judy. Your work here, encouragement and general support over the years has been greatly appreciated.

A big 'thank you' to Matthew Parris of *The Times* for encouragement and allowing his good name to appear in front of my work. That famous and much-respected name will make a huge difference to the success of this book.

About the Author

Narvel Annable's first book *Miss Calder's Children* (1997) described his early post-war schooldays in Belper, a quaint Derbyshire mill town. A few copies of this book are still available at Shipley Park. His second book *Heanor Schooldays* (1998) was also autobiographic, covering his unhappiness in a grim, gas-lit, Dickensian, Church of England junior school from 1955 to 1958. Adolescence and the move to William Howitt Secondary Modern School, "A culture of kindness", in September, 1958, was a dramatic improvement, graphically retold in the second half of the social history.

In 1963 he emigrated to the United States and arrived in Detroit on the day before the assassination of President Kennedy. The next seven years saw him in a variety of jobs which included labourer, lathe-hand, bank messenger and camera salesman. In 1975 he graduated from Eastern Michigan University (magna cum laude) and taught history for a year at St Bridget High School in Detroit.

In 1976 he returned to Derbyshire to help organise and launch 'Heritage Education Year 1977' at Sudbury Hall. From 1978 to 1995 he taught history at a large comprehensive school which gradually became more progressive. Mr Annable criticises these changes in some detail in his first two books. Seizing retirement at the earliest opportunity, he started to write historical and educational articles for the local Press and has been interviewed several times on BBC Radio Derby and BBC Radio Nottingham. *Death on the Derwent* - A Murder Mystery set in Belper 1949, his third book and first novel, was published in 1999. His fourth book, *A Judge Too Far* - A Biography of His Honour Judge Keith Matthewman QC of the Nottingham Crown Court, was published in 2001.

Inspired by *Heanor Schooldays*, Mr Annable's second 'whodunit' novel and fifth book *Lost Lad* A Mystery set in Derbyshire in 1960 (ISBN 0 9530419 6 4) was published in 2003. His sixth book *Scruffy Chicken* A Derbyshire Mystery set in 1965 (ISBN 0 9530419 4 8) was published in 2006. At the present time he is working on his seventh book *Secret Summer* A Derbyshire Mystery set in 1966.

LOST LAD

In the glorious summer of 1960, six pals from William Howitt Secondary Modern School in the hilltop mining town of Heanor, decide to cycle up into the high Derbyshire hills. They have a great time. Everything goes well - until they cycle out of the village of Litton, along a narrow country lane and speedily descend the 550ft steep drop into a deep, wooded ravine which is called Water-cum-Jolly-Dale. Six boys were happily racing down the hill, but only five reach the bottom!

In the following hours, the boys make a thorough search for their friend - in vain. Eventually the police are called in and make a careful professional search - in vain. Where is the lost lad?

Forty-three years pass and one of the original pals who has spent most of his adult life in the United States returns to England to re-open the search. An odyssey develops which takes many twists and turns around the lives of different men, some of whom can hardly recognise each other four decades on. An investigation which turns lives upside-down. A quest which eventually comes to a dramatic and stunning conclusion when we finally learn the devastating truth about - the 'Lost Lad'.

This is an autobiographic, sometimes comic, sometimes erotic psychological thriller; a 'rollercoaster of emotions' from the depths of despair to the heights of happiness. Along the way, Narvel Annable skilfully blending fact and fiction, reveals a secret history and vividly recreates the gritty realities of his youth on both sides of the Atlantic. A local story of long-lost friendship and a Derbyshire travelogue which combines elements of folklore, legend and quirky, crooked old men who inhabit the murky depths of a sleazy underworld. It is all set against the magnificent moody backdrop of a 'howling wilderness', spectacular ravines and lush green valleys. This entertaining and ingenious whodunit will take you through the recesses, nooks and crannies of a life, which, for many years, lay hidden behind the mask of a stern and respectable schoolmaster.

"Intriguing. We are made to wait nearly half a century before Narvel finally reveals to us the secret of his devilishly clever conjuring trick. *Lost Lad* is an entertaining, interesting and well constructed novel. It'll be a real eye opener to the folk of Derbyshire.

"I've never featured in a mystery thriller before. I've enjoyed every minute of it."

John Holmes, BBC Radio Nottingham.

"Written by a guy who so obviously loves this county of ours, the novel's Derbyshire backdrop is spectacular. It is a blend of fact with fiction and is packed with characters and events which many of you may find familiar.

"*Lost Lad* is a fantastic read. We at the Cash Project have no hesitation in recommending it to you."

Gary Woodhouse, *The Bent Spire*, Chesterfield. Easter 2005

"*Lost Lad* is written with conviction. In its way, it works quite well, and canters along at a reasonable pace. It's just that, the world unlidded for us here strikes an innocent like me as loathsomely tacky. But that at least underscores Narvel Annable's competence in bringing the more revolting characters so horribly to life! All in all, it is an odd book, and, for all I know, epoch-making for its genre."

Maxwell Craven, *Derby Evening Telegraph*, 13.02.04

"Here's a thriller for the fireside. Narvel Annable's easy style, coupled with local knowledge, makes this an entertaining read and will have the reader determined to find out what happened to the lost lad."

Judith Halliday, *Derbyshire Today*, December 2003

"Annable's prose is generally excellent - evocative without being torturous. It is sharp and witty. His characters are well observed and the story - on the whole - unfolds well. Narvel Annable is undoubtedly a talented author."

Mark Michalowski, *SHOUT!* March 2004

"The narrative seamlessly blends fact and fantasy, vividly recreating scenes from a tough and sometimes sleazy youth. The story follows the fates of six friends and the investigation which lays bare their fears and weaknesses, building to a dramatic final twist."

Ian Soutar ***Sheffield Telegraph*** **10.09.04**

"An interesting tale in which truth and fiction are cleverly blurred."

Derbyshire Life and Countryside **December 2003**

"Some very strange 'goings on'. Narvel Annable weaves his narrative, carefully travelling from the Derbyshire Dales to the urban landscapes of America, and back, through a minefield of intrigue and mystery before the story reaches the final conclusion."

Keith How, ***Peak Advertiser*** **03.11.03**

"It offers a unique insight into the former history teacher's life. The story takes us back to a Dickensian style school which almost drove Mr Annable to suicide. A word of warning: some of the action is not for the fainthearted and is more suitable for adults than children."

James Mitchinson, ***Worksop Guardian*** **17.10.03**

"Compulsive reading for those who have grown up in Derbyshire, but also for anyone who enjoys a good mystery."

Emily Davies, ***Ilkeston Advertiser*** **30.10.03**

"*Lost Lad* reveals Narvel's lifelong passion for cycling along leafy lanes and his appreciation of natural beauty. The spirit and atmosphere of the novel is cleverly captured by the Shipley Park artist Lesley Robinson."

Pauline Oldrini, ***Belper News*** **and the** ***Ripley and Heanor News*** **30.10.03**

"An entertaining and gritty mystery of a missing cyclist."

Jonathan Dodds, Buxton ***Advertiser*** **19.12.03**

Lost Lad can be ordered from bookshops or directly from the author by sending a cheque for £9.95 to - 44 Dovedale Crescent, Belper, Derbyshire DE56 1HJ.

A Judge Too Far

A Biography of His Honour Judge Keith Matthewman QC
of the Nottingham Crown Court

ISBN 0 9530419 9 9

A tough judge with a tough reputation, he is more concerned for the victim than the criminal; a judge whose sentences are often reduced by the Court of Appeal, but a judge who is regularly applauded for his outspoken radical views by the Press and the public.

Narvel Annable explores the fascinating story of his former teacher who has spanned the social divide from a Yorkshire coal mining background to being listed in *Who's Who* and *Debrett's People of Today* and is now described as legendary in the local Press. This is an extraordinary lifetime in which praise is matched with criticism, as we follow the twists and turns of the last six decades to see Keith Matthewman, the student, the Scout, the memorable and creative schoolmaster, the enthusiastic left-wing politician, the film maker, the articulate barrister and the stern judge who -

" ... had to deal with the raw end of life, the mad, bad and desperate - a parade of failed humanity ... rapes, incest, violence, dangerous driving, arson .."

Judge Matthewman went on to become a broadcaster, a controversial television personality, strident critic of the Criminal Justice System and latterly the President of the Friends of the Galleries of Justice Museum in Nottingham.

In 1992 he featured in Central TV's award-winning documentary *Caution - Our Hands Are Tied* and a year later he was the first British judge to have a regular slot on *Crime Stalker.*

Readers will also find, imaginatively interwoven in this life-span, an enjoyable and informative history, brought to life by photographs, documents and newspaper extracts which will re-kindle local memories.

This book takes you through the years of the Second World War in Chilwell, the 1950's in Long Eaton Grammar School and then on to University College London. The 1960's will see shop-keeping at Aldercar, school-teaching and politics in Heanor, leading on to Rolls Royce in Derby and ending up with many examples from the riveting daily drama of lives in crisis in the Nottingham law courts. This work of 271 pages is supported by forewords from -

The Rt. Hon. Geoffrey Hoon MP the Secretary of State for Defence and
Lord Bach of Lutterworth.

"I found it an entertaining read. If I am looking for an outspoken judge in future, I shall certainly know whom to contact."

Joshua Rozenberg, Legal Editor, *The Daily Telegraph* 02.05.02

" ... a career which is interesting in itself, but is also a glowing example of the strengths of our social and education system as it was before it was finally dumbed down in the name of equality of opportunity.

"In general, this book is enjoyable, instructive and refreshing. Narvel Annable has researched well and interviewed widely. For my money, Judge Matthewman ought now to be Lord Chief Justice rather than a retired Crown Court Judge."

Maxwell Craven, *The Derby Evening Telegraph* 18.01.02

"Personal tales add to the character of the story ... a must read for former pupils of the Long Eaton Grammar School. This intriguing and amusing biography is thoroughly enjoyable."

Karen Payne, *The Long Eaton Advertiser* 20.12.01

"Narvel has painstakingly researched the full background of Keith's life. Controversial and imaginative."

Pauline Oldrini, *The Belper News* 12.12.01 and the *Ripley and Heanor News* 13.12.01

"An extraordinary life and an informative social history."

***Derbyshire Life and Countryside Magazine*, February 2002**

"Congratulations to Narvel Annable ... so many interesting stories in this biography about (as he is dubbed by the Press) 'the hanging judge'."

John Holmes, BBC Radio Derby 06.12.01

"Narvel's made a very good job of this book."

Brian Tansley, BBC Radio Nottingham 07.12.01

"Eagerly anticipated and twice read to date! I was full of admiration for the way in which Narvel Annable has successfully translated such obviously painstaking research into such a fascinating insight into the life and times of a colourful character.

"I feel very proud to be associated with this publication which brought memories flooding back and felt quite a few pangs of nostalgia."

Judy Cullimore, former Crown Court Reporter of the *Nottingham Evening Post* 19.03.02

"A fascinating story with photographs, documents and newspaper extracts which stir local memories. As many criminals have found to their cost, Judge Keith Matthewman is indeed a tough judge with a tough reputation."

Mike Astill, *Nottinghamshire Today*, April 2002

"A pity that it had to end - I had to make myself put it down during the read in order to give time to reflect and consider what had just been read to see how it fitted into the 'big picture' of Mr Annable's subject - a man with such outstanding and distinguished features and qualities. A big 'thank you' to Narvel Annable for giving readers the opportunity to have his biography to read and enjoy. I particularly appreciated his unique style which demonstrated that biography is not linear but a complex mesh of happenings and features. It was simply superb. I am left in wonder as to the author's skills to compile, collate and style such a portrait and insight of, and about, such a wonderful person."

Philip Judge, Lambley, Nottingham 28.12.01

"An excellent book providing fascinating social and historical insights."

Nick Seaton, The Campaign for Real Education 30.12.02

"Mr Annable, an author with unusual disciplined powers of concentration and single mindedness, has done enough meticulous painstaking research to have earned two doctorates in this work which is interesting and highly educational. I am envious of his creative drive. The few create; the many enjoy."

Alex Hart, Highland Park, Michigan USA 04.04.02

A Judge Too Far can be obtained from bookshops or directly from the author by sending a cheque for £11.95 to -

44 Dovedale Crescent, Belper, Derbyshire DE56 1HJ.

Death on the Derwent

A Murder Mystery set in Belper 1949

ISBN 0 9530419 2 1

Join the formidable schoolmistress Miss Florence Calder and her small, cantankerous, hunchbacked sister Miss Madge, as they detect and attempt to unmask a clever murderer in the leafy, ivy-clad, quaint and quieter Belper of 1949.

This entertaining blend of fact and fiction, set against the skilfully described background of spectacular Derbyshire scenery, is both an intriguing 'whodunit' and also a local history. Atmospheric narrative will take you around the nooks and crannies of the old mill town, in both bright sunshine and also in menacing thick fog.

It is complete with a body in a boat, psychic phenomena in the candle-lit haunted halls of the rambling old Bridge House School, a seance, a conjuring trick and all ending in a surprise.

Some hilarious, colourful and quirky characters spanning the social divide from the past poverty of Cowhill, to the opulence of Bridge Hill, combine with suspense and dramatic tension to produce a thoroughly enjoyable thriller. 204 pages.

"So who has done it? Well Narvel has, but he'll keep you guessing right up to the final breath."

John Holmes, BBC Radio Derby.

"A remarkable murder mystery novel ... gives a new twist to the whodunit genre ... a skilful mixture of fact and fiction ... strong historical interest ... complications and twists, red herrings and false trails. Mr Annable has got himself a real-life, ready-made character in Miss Florence Calder. This could be - should be - the start of a series of Miss Calder novels."

Geoff Hammerton, *The Derby Evening Telegraph* 17.12.99

"Peopled with distinctive characters ... meritorious for the descriptive detail. A well-produced book. Worth reading a second time or more to fully appreciate the construction of this ingenious novel."

Margaret Beardsley, *The Belper News* 23.02.00

"Great characters!" **Bob Attewell, *The Belper Express* 13.01.00**

"I loved the rich and qualitative language, the machinations, twists and turns of the plot. I was empathetic with the characters as they desperately tried to unravel the mystery Mr Annable has so brilliantly created."

Terry Ladlow, 'Terivision Productions', Wetwang, Driffield, East Yorkshire 22.03.00

"Simon Tonks is the village fool who ends up as a servant to the Calders, Claud Hoadley is the pompous Belper man-turned-snob who teaches elocution so that the townspeople can 'better themselves' and Aubrey Pod is a pushy 'Mr Toad' character always full of himself."

Paul Imrie, 'Talk of the Town', *The Derby Evening Telegraph* 23.11.99

"Interesting and amusing." **Marla Addison, *Peak Times* 10.12.99**

Death on the Derwent can be obtained from **Derbyshire County Library** and used copies are available on the internet.

Heanor Schooldays
A Social History

ISBN 0 9530419 1 3

This book deals with the last hundred years but majors on the author's personal experience of the 1950's and 1960's in which he recreates the optimistic social atmosphere of teenagers enjoying the popular culture of the day. You will also gain insights into the gritty, unpretentious, honest character of Heanor folk.

It is a graphic, colourful and emotional journey from the depths of despair to the heights of happiness. Along the way, Narvel Annable honours the memory of teachers, headmasters and headmistresses who have shaped the lives of countless Heanorians. Disquiet is expressed, as discredited modern teaching methods are contrasted to the successful tried and trusted methods of past years.

Forty-five photographs and fifteen documents will rekindle memories. The work is supported by a foreword from His Honour Judge Keith Matthewman QC and contains first-hand accounts from many contributors, including the one-time local lad, The Rt. Hon. Kenneth Clarke QC, MP, the former Chancellor of the Exchequer from 1993 to 1997. 205 pages.

"I was enthralled. A cracking collection of tales."

John Holmes, BBC Radio Derby.

Vivid and detailed memories of a 1950's childhood. Sensitively written, Narvel explores the vagaries of the educational system which helped to develop his character and prepare him for adulthood. This is an important snapshot of social history, and the author brings it to life with recollections of strict discipline, bullying and extreme forms of punishment. A rollercoaster of emotions."

Pauline Oldrini, the *Ripley and Heanor News* and the *Belper News* 05.11.98

"Mr Annable mixes anecdote with comment to provide an important record of changes made in education as seen from the sides of both pupil and teacher."

Geoff Hammerton, The *Derby Evening Telegraph* 04.12.98

"This autobiographic book charts a gritty history and weaves a graphic tapestry of Derbyshire school life 40 years ago. It is littered with colourful characters, interesting facts and first-hand accounts."

David Mark, The *Nottingham Evening Post* 27.10.98

***Heanor Schooldays* was on the 1998 list of 'Recommended Publications' by the Campaign for Real Education at 18 Westlands Grove, Stockton Lane, York YO3 0EF.**

"Narvel Annable has managed to do what most authors never could; that is, to make a book about his schooldays a thoroughly enjoyable read.

In his unique style he gives us a history of people and institutions. He gives us his views on education, past and present, and we are treated to a fascinating glimpse of a school-life in the fifties and sixties, complete with all its sorrows and joys. You do not have to remember those days to enjoy this book: you do not have to be an educationalist to enjoy this book: but if you are in either group, or both, you will enjoy it all the more - and so will your children."

His Honour Judge Keith Matthewman QC, November 1998

"Thoroughly enjoyable and a privilege to read. He writes in such an enthusiastic way and keeps one enthralled to the very end of the book. Indeed, I wish it would have not ended!"

David Tye, Oban Divers Caravan Park, Laggan, Glenshellach, Argyle, Scotland PA34 4QJ 12.05.02

***Heanor Schooldays* can be obtained from bookshops or directly from the author by sending a cheque for £8.95 to -**

44 Dovedale Crescent, Belper, Derbyshire DE56 1HJ.

CASH

No, not cash as in money. This is CASH of 4 Rose Hill, Chesterfield, Derbyshire S40 1LW. Phone number - 01 246 559431. Community Action on Sexual Health. cash.project@btopenworld.com

In *Scruffy Chicken* you may have empathised with the disappointment and frustration expressed by Martin Harcourt QC. He was lamenting on the lack of professional support for the gay community in the dark homophobic years of the mid-1960's in Derbyshire and Nottinghamshire. Martin had a dream. He dreamed of a social support service for lesbians, gay men and bisexuals. He outlined the advantages of a comfortable 'drop-in' place, where people could socialise and receive friendly advice from trained counsellors in a pleasant, non-threatening environment.

Forty years on, Martin's dream has now come true. If you would like to know more about it, ring the above number and talk to Elly, Gary, Joy or Richard in Chesterfield.

Most towns and cities in Britain now have a support centre for the gay community.

Eulogy spoken at the funeral of Derek Goostrey on Monday, March 7th, 2005

It is a privilege to have composed this tribute to Derek Goostrey, who was better known to readers of *Lost Lad* as Danny Forrester. I would like to thank Kali and Ross for asking me to read it in front of the largest congregation Heanor Church has seen in 20 years.

On Monday, July 16th in 1945, the first ever atomic bomb was exploded by the Americans in New Mexico. The flash, which was seen 250 miles away, cast a shadow over the lives of us all.

On that same day, nearer to home, at number one Preston Street, Broken Cross in Macclesfield, a less flashy event took place; the birth of Derek and his twin brother Barry Goostrey - half an hour apart. Less flashy, perhaps, but it certainly had an impact on my life and, I suspect, greatly improved the lives of many people here today. A few years later, the Goostrey family moved to 32 Nelson Street in Heanor. In *Heanor Schooldays*, I wrote -

"If you seek the source of the magic which made the days of Howitt Secondary Modern School so special, I suggest you go to 32 Nelson Street. That Spartan dwelling, the modest home of Derek and Barry, was diffused throughout with a quality of consideration, camaraderie, caring and kindness. A cheerful atmosphere was presided over by mum, Nora and stepfather, Christopher Dodsley. They had almost nothing, but they were prepared to share what little they had."

I give thanks today for the friendship they shared, the happiness they gave, at a time when I needed it most. For almost the half century which followed, Derek, that surviving brother, a character of buoyant and uplifting personality, right up to the end, could still work his magic on me. The Goostrey charm defied analysis, that same charm inspired me to write two books about them forty years later.

Derek Goostrey was, quite simply, the best example of all the finest qualities of Heanorian youth, as we were during that wonderful period of 1958 to 1960. He was open, honest, sincere, good-natured, easy-going and totally free from any of the artificial affectation which has so often infested the world in which I live - and we did live in different worlds. Perhaps he is now reunited with his twin brother Barry who, tragically, died young in 1964. Barry inspired the original 'lost lad' in my book. I invested our collective grief into shaping his character - Brian Forrester. *Heanor Schooldays,* an earlier effort, was actually dedicated to Barry Goostrey - 'One of our mates who was taken early'.

As school pals, Derek and I were close. As adults, we were separated for many years by the Atlantic Ocean. In those years, he married Karen and leaves behind one much-loved daughter Kali, who gave him two beautiful granddaughters, Gaia and Kristie. He also leaves behind many special friends such as Julie, who tells me that she'll always treasure some fantastic memories. His best friend was Mick Hancock.

Friendship! Derek had friends in abundance. It won't be the same in the Derby County Supporters bus when it makes its next journey to Pride Park, will it? There'll be a yawning gap there which won't easily be filled. And, of course, we've all heard wild accounts of much rejoicing and great jollity in the public houses of Heanor. He often told me about the fun he had with his mates, his adventures, the quiz nights and the competitions. Perhaps this is not quite the time or place to relate such riotous details.

Derek was well supported by his employer, Robert Pretties, and will be greatly missed by colleagues at work. He was a principal personality at our William Howitt Secondary Modern School annual reunion each October. The organiser, Kathy Syson, and many former pupils, too numerous to mention, will certainly feel his absence when we next meet.

Ten years ago, Derek and I were reunited. A reunion which gave birth to this extract from *Lost Lad*. It's a fictitious BBC Radio Derby interview in which Derek makes an appearance as Danny Forrester. [Here I read a short extract from page 216 in *Lost Lad*]

In recent years, as adults, Derek's cheerful support and loyalty never once wavered. He enthusiastically encouraged my work by attending every launch, every talk and buying all five titles, all of them signed - 'Dobba'. When together, we regressed. We enjoyed being trapped in a time warp somewhere in the summer of 1960 at Howitt School, always in role of two mischievous fifteen-year-olds, always recycling funny stories about grumpy old Mrs Buxcey

Yesterday, Derek Goostrey, one of Heanor's most popular, one of Heanor's best, made our lives a little richer. Today, Heanor is a little poorer. Good night, dear friend ... a bit of young Dobba died with you on February 23rd ... he'll miss you.

Look out for Narvel Annable's next whodunit novel -

Secret Summer

A Mystery set in Derbyshire 1966

Why secret? Because when you are young, when you are in love and if you are gay in 1966 - it must be secret. You must love in secret, lust in secret, hunt in secret, meet in secret and play in secret. The alternative would be unthinkable. And in 1966 - if things go wrong, horribly wrong, dangerously wrong, criminally wrong - you can't tell your heterosexual friends, you can't tell your parents and you certainly can't tell the police!

Real friends, true friends must be kept apart from parents, family and regular friends. Nineteen hundred and sixty six was the summer of secret love for Simeon Hogg. See Simeon in love; a rollercoaster, a frantic mixture of agony and ecstasy spanning the Atlantic Ocean, with no support save for that which was available from the secretive and frequently unreliable world of gay men who were riddled with all their own personal problems, repressions and hang-ups. Here is a world which could be very miserable indeed, a world which existed long before the advent of CASH in Chesterfield and Derbyshire Friend in Derby.

Meet the old quirky characters and a few new ones in this heartrending tale of young love in which, yet again, Narvel Annable reaches down into the joys and sorrows of his past and produces an autobiographic account of laughs, adventure, secret passion and pain. All the usual ingredients are here for another cracking good whodunit; a missing person, suspected murder, threats, extortion - all set against a backdrop of beautiful Derbyshire hills and the unforgiving criminal underworld of Detroit.